RENOVICTION

RENOVICTION

The True Cost of Gentrification

By: Myles Bradley

Dedicated to Tommy,
and the beach of Escuminac
where one can find their peace.

Based On a True Story

Renoviction: *The illegal eviction of a rental tenant on the grounds that renovations are planned.*

Rent Seeking: *Is a concept in economics that states: When an individual or entity seeks to increase their own wealth without creating any benefits or wealth to society.*

Chapter 1

"'Do unto others as they would do to you'—isn't that how they said to live your life?" Well, that's how I was living, and they came and messed with me anyway. I was a calm, easygoing guy, but if I had been awake when they slid that letter under my door, I would have chased them down the stairs with a bat and broken their legs. Being cowards and weasels, they knew that, so it's why they delivered it under the cover of night. Lately, there had been a flurry of letters from Denise, the building's owner, about repairs or people coming and going. But this one wasn't from Denise; it was from someone or 'something' I didn't recognize; it was from 'One-Four-Seven-Zero-Zero-Seven Limited Liability Company,' and it wasn't about repairs or visitors. It was an eviction letter. I was being thrown out, not for anything I had done; they were throwing me out because I had cheap, affordable rent.

I had been living at Three-Ninety-One Empire Avenue for about two years. I had been bouncing around aimlessly from shitty building to shitty building ever since a car accident changed my life. The accident took place fifteen years ago on a beautiful sunny morning. I almost died and was airlifted out, but my beautiful son of eight years old wasn't; he lost his life that day. After that, I was never the same, and rightfully so. I was left with PTSD and something they call 'survivor guilt.' They said I was lucky to have survived, but they couldn't have been more wrong. After something like that, it's hard to care—about yourself or anything else. I didn't care about possessions; I didn't care about making money; I didn't care about impressing anyone, and I hardly cared about myself. I only wanted one thing in this world, and in my mind, everything else was just noise and clutter. That's the thing about PTSD, you are never really happy, and it's why I didn't care about living well or even having a secure, consistent home.

I had moved so many times that I had a stack of driver's licenses that looked like a deck of cards. I was never kicked out or evicted from where I was; sometimes, I would get bored and pack my stuff up and leave; other times, I would realize I had moved into a shitty building and left when I couldn't take it anymore. Being a minimalist, I had given up many of my useless possessions so I could usually pack up my car and go. After the accident, I never felt anywhere was 'home'; I always felt lost and wandering through life, which worried my family and friends; they felt the constant moving and changes in my life weren't healthy or 'normal,' and they were right.

Before moving into this building, I had been crashing on my cousin's sofa for a couple of months after I had hastily left the apartment I was living in. I had been living in a building I called 'The Palace,' which, in reality, it wasn't; it was actually a shithole. It was a thirty-story high rise on Danforth Avenue, a street that ran from one end of the city to the other, and the further you got away from the downtown core, the shittier it became. And I was far, far away from the core. I didn't know anything about the building, and when I checked it out, it seemed all right on the surface. The first clue it was going to be a shithole when I moved in was the 'immigration and welfare office' that was around the corner, which was unbeknownst to me at the time of moving in. Once I moved in, I learned that the building was the welcome wagon to new people from all over the world coming to the country. Now, I'm not a racist or a classist, but these people had different living and hygienic standards than we did. Not only was it the United Nations of Toronto, but it was also the first stop for people just out of jail, halfway houses, and psychiatric wards; it was quite the eclectic mix.

After being in 'The Palace' for a couple of months, I discovered that the building had bedbugs, and that was my breaking point. I always saw people in the laundry room putting their clothes into plastic bags and tying them up when finished. I had no clue that this was a sign of bedbugs. I just thought they were too cheap to buy a laundry basket, but apparently, you do this to keep the bugs out of your clothes; who knew? Not me.

I discovered the bugs one morning after working fourteen hours a day for seven days straight on a night shoot. I got home at seven in the morning and saw them in my bed before I lain down and I was horrified. I was so freaked out I grabbed a blanket and pillow from the closet and crashed on the bathroom floor. I figured it would be safe—it wasn't. I was so exhausted I slept through most of the day, and when I woke up, I opened my eyes to see a bedbug crawl out from under the seal of the bathtub. Once again, I was horrified. I realized that they were everywhere in the building, and I started drinking heavily; I had beer after beer, and by the time nightfall came, I was hammered. Everywhere I looked, there were bedbugs, and I was losing my mind. I started freaking out and began throwing anything that could have bedbugs off of my seventeenth-floor balcony; blankets, clothes, pillows, anything that could have bugs on it, went over the railing, including the bed.

The following day, with my head pounding and hungover, I walked out of the building lobby. I was trying to keep my head down to shield myself from the sun when I noticed a bunch of people standing around, looking up at the front of the building. I stopped, gazed up, and started laughing. All the blankets, pillows, hats, and everything I had thrown off the balcony were stuck up in the branches of the trees, including the bed. I went to grab a coffee and decided that I was going to move out. The next day, after the 'yard sale in the sky,' I packed up my car and crashed at my cousins until the opportunity of moving to Three-Ninety-One Empire Avenue came up.

I was referred to Empire Avenue by Andrew, a friend of mine from work. Andrew was a fellow actor I met while working on various TV and movie sets. We were union actors stuck playing background parts being Extra's, being a 'stand-in,' or the dreaded job of being a photo double, which was doubling for the actor, doing the shit that they didn't want to do. Andrew was like me; making the rent could be tough. Affordable housing was a necessity in our line of work, and trying to find it in Toronto was getting harder and harder as real estate prices were soaring at a ridiculous rate. Andrew came to me one day saying there was a vacancy in his building and that he could arrange a meeting with the owner. When he told me what the rent was, I jumped at the opportunity. It was about twenty-five percent less than market value, but he was hesitant and nervous to refer me, and he explained why; it was a rundown, three-story 'walk-up' located in 'Christieville.'

'Christieville' was a neighborhood near the water in the city's east end. It was one of the city's original industrial areas and was home to the original 'Christie Cookie' Factory, hence the name 'Christieville.' The neighborhood had been struggling to get through gentrification for the last ten years, but there was a problem: the people who lived there didn't want it gentrified and weren't leaving. A lot of the people in the area inherited their houses from their blue-collar, working-class parents who were by no means wealthy but who lived in a time when it was reasonable that if you worked a full-time job, you would be able to afford a house.

And that's all they had: their house. The people living here didn't earn a lot of money, and many of them weren't even employed, so staying put and living rent/mortgage-free for the rest of their lives was in their best interest. This ruined the developer's plans of gentrification, as not many people were willing to sell, leaving the neighborhood with a diverse population of rich and poor.

The streets were a mix of 'latte moms,' day drinkers, drug addicts, homeless people, upscale urbanites, hipsters, artists, and unemployed locals. The main street in the neighborhood was Queen Street. Stores were occupied by trendy new cupcake/coffee shops, rundown machine repair shops that were humming and buzzing back in the booming days when things were actually made and fixed locally; there were old tailor/shoe/sewing stores; stores that were sitting vacant; trendy bars that just opened; and rundown bars that had been in the neighborhood for decades. There were a lot of 'revolving door' shops, too; these were stores that had tenants for a few months, but they couldn't survive in the neighborhood, so they just closed their doors and walked away. These stores would sit empty until the next pet grooming, cupcake, or stationery store would move in and close just as fast, and the cycle would continue.

The neighborhood was a constant battle of old vs new. The 'latte moms' would have their eight-dollar mochaccino lattes in one hand, cell phone in the other, all the while trying to steer their 'Bjorn Baby' stroller down the sidewalk, which they thought they owned. It was always fun watching them trying to navigate their way around the day drinkers and people sitting on the sidewalk just passing the time. On any given day, you'd see arguments and fights between the new dwellers who thought they were better because they paid a couple of million dollars for their new house or condo and those who thought they were better because they had lived there all their lives.

The neighborhood included a homeless shelter where the odd corpse would be taken out on a stretcher due to an overdose; there were food banks; and even a 'safe injection site.' The funny thing was, the safe injection site was right across the street from a new condo building that cost a minimum of one million dollars to move in, and right beside that was the homeless shelter. Imagine that. You pay a million bucks to look out your front window to see people shooting up in the park, and when you look out the other window, you see the homeless shelter, and all the while, all you can hear is sirens.

The funny thing is, the people who moved in would complain and set up protests to remove or 'relocate' the shelter and injection sites, even though they knew they were already there when they moved in. I always laughed and thought what selfish ignorance, when I heard them say, "Well, of course, shelters and injection sites are needed, just not in my neighborhood."

Andrew had set up a meeting for me with the owner, and the way he described her and the building, it sounded exactly what I was looking for. It was owned by a lady named Denise, who had owned the building for almost forty years. This showed me she would understand what being a 'landlord' means: responsible for people's lives and homes. I was glad the building wasn't owned by a business, speculator, developer, or some REIT, a Real Estate Investment Trust. These were all entities just trying to make money off people's homes, with no idea what it means to be a landlord. These investment-type owners only consider one thing, and one thing only, and that was profits. These types of owners are far removed from the building and the tenants that live in them. Daily tasks are contracted out to a 'building maintenance' company that isn't even on-site, so these third parties' daily contact and commitment are minimal. The workers around the building don't care about the building, so everything is done half-assed if it's done at all, and again, everything comes down to the bottom line. These real estate investors put profits over people, which shouldn't be the only priority when dealing with people's homes. Now, I'm not a communist; I believe in Capitalism and that everyone has the right to make a profit, but when dealing with renting out homes to people, there should be different considerations and a different set of rules.

When I met Denise, it was a twenty-minute meeting/interview; it was a one- on-one conversation between two people just trying to get to know each other. It wasn't about submitting credit checks, bank accounts, paychecks, or letters of employment; she wanted to know about my history, and she wanted to hear it from me and not try to read it on a piece of paper. She knew Andrew was a good person, and she went on his word since he referred me. During our meeting, I'm sure that if she thought I was lying or got a bad feeling from me, she would have immediately ended the conversation and said, "Thank you, I will let you know."

She was a 'hands-on' owner, a professional landlord who had been doing this for decades, and she wanted to know 'who' and 'what' type of person would be living in her building. At the beginning of our conversation, I had to ask her why the rent was so cheap. First, she admitted that the building was old and there hadn't been many renovations over the years, and what she said next surprised me and made me respect Denise a bit. She said she also liked to keep the rent a little cheaper to help artists, writers, musicians, young families, and people on fixed incomes save a little money and not struggle so much with the day-to-day expenses of life. She also explained that over thirty years ago, when the industrial companies were shutting down in the neighborhood, she saw that people had nowhere to go, so she converted the basement into a 'rooming house' type of situation where four units share a kitchen and a bathroom.

During our conversation, she asked if I had any concerns about moving into the building. The first thing I had to ask about was about the guys in the basement. Did I need to worry about them? She reassured me that they were just old-time 'Christieville' residents who had lived down there for about twenty years. She never had a problem with any of them and said that most of them lived off their disability payments and drank most of it; I wouldn't even notice them. She also explained that there wasn't a lot of turnover in the building. The most recent tenants were my friend Andrew and his friend Bree, who had been here for six years; all the other tenants had been here anywhere from ten to thirty years, and even one tenant had been here for forty years.

Finally, I asked her about the future of the building, which was my main concern. Property values had skyrocketed in Toronto in the last five years, and unreasonably so. Housing prices were in a bubble, and anyone who said they weren't, was either delusional, a real estate agent, or a mortgage broker. There were even plans for a subway station to be built around the corner from the building next year that have sent prices even higher in this neighborhood, making me think the temptation for Denise to sell was strong.

She told me she wasn't going anywhere and reassured me that she planned on owning the building for another forty years if she could, and I believed her. This put me at ease that I would be safe from any greedy companies or slumlords for at least a few years, and I might actually live in a building I could call home.

After hearing Denise say she wasn't selling for a while, I told her I would take it. Andrew had told me that she was old-school and would want first and last month's rent in cash. I pulled out the money, and Denise smiled. She pulled out her beaten-up, generic receipt book that she got at the local convenience store and asked me what my last name was. I spelled it out for her, Brent Bingham, and she wrote me a receipt and said the place was mine. She welcomed me to the building and said I could move in anytime since the unit was empty. When we finished, I got my stuff, drove three carloads of possessions to the apartment, and slept on the floor that night.

I had been here in the building for almost two years, my longest stay anywhere in a long time. I was getting better with life here; it was a good building, and I was starting to care about the future. I even recently ordered a new sofa that was going to work great in the apartment, and when I read the eviction letter, it looked as if I was going to have to call and cancel the damn thing. What was worse than that was that I would have to tell my friends and family that I would once again have to move and find a place to live. I could hear the worry in my Mom's voice already, "Oh, Brent, what now?"

I looked at the letter one more time, and I was fuming; it was short, only a couple of lines in length, and no one even personally signed it; it read:

"Please be aware that Three-Ninety-One Empire Avenue has been purchased by 'One-Four-Seven-Zero-Zero-Seven LLC.' We are terminating your lease agreement as of today. You have sixty days to exit the unit."

That was it; sent by Brownstone Management on behalf of 'One-Four-Seven- Zero-Zero-Seven LLC.' I had no idea who these companies were, nor had I ever heard of them before this; my new sofa hadn't even arrived yet, and all I could think was, 'I never should have ordered that damn thing.'

The day after I received the eviction letter was interesting. I spoke to more people from the building that one day than I had during my entire time of living here. I was woken up by someone knocking on my door, and it was Robert from across the hall. Robert seemed like an interesting guy, but I knew nothing about him because, like myself, he kept to himself. We would always say 'hello' in passing, but we'd never say more than a few words to each other. It wasn't that we didn't like each other; we were just two guys who kept our heads down and minded our own business. He kept the door to his apartment open a lot of the time, which I thought was weird, but I figured, whatever, and I never said anything about it.

I opened the door, and he was waving the letter angrily in the air. It looked like he had more than two words to say.

As soon as the door opened, he asked me, "Did you receive this? Did you get one of these?"

I told him to step in, and I grabbed my copy, "Yeah, I received it; I had no idea that Denise had sold the building. Did she say anything to you?"

"No, not a damn thing." He started to turn red and looked off in another direction as he ranted. "I've lived here for over twenty years, and she doesn't even have the respect to tell me? To tell us? Some people have been here for thirty years; Tommy has been here for forty! She didn't even have the respect to say anything? We've made her rich, and she doesn't have the decency to tell us?"

Robert was getting mad. His face was getting redder and redder, and he was starting to get that white stuff in the corners of his mouth. He walked by me as if I wasn't even there and began to pace by the kitchen.

He continued to rant as he paced, "And who is this new owner? Not only didn't they introduce themselves to us, but they didn't even have the guts to tell us to our faces that they are going to evict us. And who the hell is Brownstone Management? Do we have to deal with these people now? There isn't even a name on the letter. 'One-Four- Seven-Zero-Zero-Seven LLC, who the hell is that? Does that company own us now? I'm calling Denise today; I'll let you know what she says."

That's all he said as he flew by me out of the apartment. I didn't try to stop or answer him; he was on a rant and needed to vent. I was learning that he was wound a little tighter than I thought and wasn't as easygoing either.

When I moved into the building, Andrew gave me a rundown of some of the people he knew. He said he probably hadn't seen half of the people in the building, and he wasn't too optimistic about the ones he did know. He complained about most of them but didn't have anything bad to say about Robert. Andrew thought he was kind of weird and said he was very quiet, and it was for that reason he felt Robert was one of the 'good ones.' According to Andrew, there weren't many 'good ones,' and he downright despised a couple of people; one was Danny, and the other was Roman. Danny was one of the 'Christieville Drinkers' in the basement and was Denise's handyman. She would give him cash and beers to do minor repairs around the building, and the quality of work reflected what she paid for it. Andrew couldn't stand Danny because of his smoking and stumbling around drunk, and he said the same thing about Roman. Roman didn't work; he lived right next to Andrew and was always home smoking, which Andrew said made his apartment and the whole second-floor smell like a rundown bingo hall, and it did.

Andrew couldn't stand either of these guys, but Benjamin was the guy he was most weary and scared of. Benjamin was a thirty-something-year-old, overweight, angry, rage-filled 'Ginger' who Andrew said was certifiably insane and from what I knew of Benjamin, he was right. I had seen Benjamin yelling at garbage trucks that were loud, yelling at construction crews working near the building, and I even saw him yelling at squirrels in the park one day. He was always going off on Denise about repairs and issues in the building, and every argument they had ended with Benjamin calling Denise a 'slumlord' and storming off. He was always putting up his own 'notices of infractions' around the building that he felt Denise was committing as a landlord; the notices were so constant most of us ignored them whenever he put them up.

I looked at the letter and read it one more time before I left to get coffee; I crumpled it up, threw it towards my desk, and headed out. As I left, I bumped into Benjamin in the stairwell, and he was as angry as ever. Denise had snuck into the building during the night and put up notices announcing a meeting on Saturday morning to inform us of some changes with the building. What she didn't mention in the notice was anything about new ownership.

When I saw Benjamin, he was using a black marker to deface all of Denise's notices, accusing her of being a greedy, heartless slumlord. I tried speaking with him, but he was in fine form; he even scared me a little. He was like Robert; he got redder and redder as he spoke, but the difference was that this guy had rage to go along with his anger.

He was irrational, and I couldn't speak to him; as I watched him, he abruptly left and proceeded up the stairs to deface the next letter Denise had put up. As I headed down the stairs, all I could do was laugh. He had written on every notice, and his words got nastier and nastier as he progressed through the building. As I walked out, I stopped on the stoop to look at the sun for a minute, and I thought, 'It's going to be an interesting meeting on Saturday; Denise, better look out.'

I went to our local coffee shop, Beanzies, to grab a coffee. Beanzies was great and was right beside us on the corner. It was an odd building that stuck out, so you could see two blocks either way, giving you a great view of most of the neighborhood. Sitting in the front window seat of 'Beanzies' was better than watching TV. The most entertaining thing I ever saw while sitting there was a naked homeless guy on a stolen bike trying to joust an oncoming streetcar with a mop; it was unforgettable.

When I walked in, I was greeted by Sally's usual smile. Sally was a singer and slung coffee during the day. She would let me hang out for hours and would keep refilling my cup for free because, as a fellow artist/creative type, she understood being poor. We always talked honestly about life, the industry, upcoming gigs, or the lack thereof. She was good people; she was direct to the point and always had a good zinger or comeback line.

She saw me coming and had my coffee ready; when I got to the counter, she passed it over and asked, "What's going on? Working as usual, I see."

I chuckled and said, "Yeah, and apparently, I'm getting evicted too."

Sally wasn't sure what to say. She looked at me and said, "I see Denise finally came to her senses." She laughed, looked at me quizzically, and added, "You're kidding, right? You're the quietest guy I know; what did you do?"

A couple of customers started coming in, so I told Sally I would explain later and took my coffee to go. I started walking around the neighborhood and thought, 'I'm going to miss this place.' Even though Benjamin said this was illegal and was adamant that Denise wouldn't get away with it, I didn't agree with him. I wouldn't say it to his face as I knew it would just set him off, so I wasn't going to argue with him, but I know money always wins. I didn't know anything about tenants' rights or rental laws, but I knew whoever has the money wins, and his statement that 'Denise wasn't going to get away with this' was idiotic. It was her building, and she could do whatever she wanted to do with it; no one could stop her from selling it, not even a lunatic like Benji.

When I returned to the building, I bumped into a couple of tenants by the mailboxes. It was Cindy, a tiny Chinese lady who couldn't speak much English, and Melissa, who lived in the building with her two kids. I didn't want to interrupt them, but as I passed, they pulled me into the conversation, and we talked for a few minutes.

Cindy asked if I had received the letter; I looked down and nodded slowly, the same type of reply someone would give upon hearing the passing of a friend or relative. Melissa was upset and almost in tears; she was talking about how hard it was already to pay rent and how it wasn't fair to the kids that they would have to move and maybe even change schools. I felt so bad for her and the kids. We spoke briefly, but I didn't have much to add, so I kept going upstairs.

As I walked away, our situation hit me harder. I was a single guy, and getting thrown out wouldn't affect me much except for my wallet, but Melissa, with kids, it would mess those kids up. Which made me realize this was bigger and shittier than I thought.

I continued up the stairs and bumped into Reggie. Reggie lived on my floor; he weighed about three hundred pounds and had a hell of a time going up and down the stairs. I think he worked nights because I hardly ever saw him; I saw the pizza delivery guy more than I saw Reggie. He was halfway up the stairs taking his mid- stairwell 'rest,' as I passed him, I said 'hi,' and he asked about the letter immediately.

Reggie seemed like a nice guy, but it was hard to talk to him while watching him gasping for life from just walking up two flights of stairs; I honestly thought he was going to die any second. We spoke for a couple of minutes, and I did most of the talking so he could catch his breath. I told him to rest easy because Benjamin was on top of it, and he'll figure it out for us. Reggie started laughing, which made me feel bad since he had trouble breathing at the same time. I left him wheezing in the stairwell and headed up to my apartment.

It's funny, before the letter, no one spoke to each other in the building; everyone kept to themselves; everyone was too busy, wrapped up, or swamped with the day-to-day bullshit of their lives, so we just passed by each other in the halls or stairway. But now it seemed like we were all friends and had something in common: a common enemy. It made me realize something sad: in this day and age, people need a catalyst; we need a reason to talk to our neighbors; we can't stop and say hi to converse with a fellow human unless it directly affects our world. It was a sad wake-up call for me.

No one had a clue that the building had been sold. With the recent influx of visitors to the building and the onslaught of letters from Denise, everyone knew something was up, but people were thinking big renovations were going to happen; no one thought or even imagined that the building would have been sold. The one complaint everyone had was that Denise didn't have the respect to say anything to anyone. Most tenants were offended because they thought they were owed something or deserved to be told, not me. From my experiences and what I learned in life, no one owes you anything, people owe you no explanations, and people only care about themselves.

The week leading up to the meeting was mostly uneventful; there were more conversations in the building, and people seemed to linger around longer and talk a little in the hallways. Even though it was a shitty situation, it was nice, it was bringing the tenants together, and it gave people a reason to talk to each other. When people passed each other on the stairs or saw each other at the mailboxes, there was now a little 'chit chat' of, 'Have you heard anything new?' or 'Has there been any more letters?' People started talking to each other; they were relating stories of people they knew who had gone through similar situations; they'd discuss Denise, the new owner, and what they thought our outcome would be, but whatever they thought would happen was all speculation.

The only noteworthy thing that happened was Benjamin started putting up his own notices. He was calling for a tenants' meeting to take place on Saturday immediately after Denise's meeting, and in pure Benjamin fashion, his meeting notice was more entertaining. He listed the topics to be discussed and used the word 'nefarious' numerous times. The first topic was Denise's 'nefarious' action of selling the building; next, it was the 'nefarious' actions of the new owner for evicting us; then, it was the 'nefarious' actions of the city for letting this happen. He mentioned setting up a 'Building Tenants Association,' and lastly, he wrote, 'We need a plan of attack against those trying to take our homes.' He had put pictures of the 'raised fist of communism' and even 'Che Guevara' on the notice, and in my mind, I could see him wearing a beret getting redder and redder as he was writing it.

I was amused at his choice of words, but there was nothing 'nefarious' about it on Denise's end; it was just business. It may be nefarious of the new owners to try to kick us out, but not on Denise's end; it's her building; she can do what she wants with it. Even the new owner, it's their building, it's their investment, and they should be able to do what they want with it. But, when you buy a building with tenants, you become a landlord, and you're now held accountable to different rules, laws, and regulations because you are dealing with people's lives; you can't buy a building, kick out the tenants and try to flip in new renters for a profit. I wouldn't call Denise's actions nefarious, but the new owner's actions definitely were.

Chapter 2

Even though I was getting pushed around and pissed off, I wasn't in the mood for a fight—let alone leading one. I was willing to follow along, be part of the fight—but I sure as hell wasn't leading it. I already had the fight and piss taken out of me over the years through some of the different systems. As a young man, I had been beaten down and crushed by the family court system when I was trying to be a nice guy and doing the right thing. Then a few years back, I was raked over the coals in the bankruptcy court system when my ex-employer screwed me over. So, I wasn't in the mood to fight another system; I had no more fight in me. For me, it was easier to walk away instead of fighting. Even though I was pissed off and disgusted with the letter I received, I figured it was just my luck and I probably deserved it.

Benjamin was the guy for this fight—passionate, informed, and best of all, pissed off. I was positive this guy wouldn't back down and wouldn't be pushed around. I felt a little bad for Denise; the meeting on Saturday was going to be explosive. Everyone in the building agreed—this was a shitty move, and Denise owed us. Some even thought she owed them cash for staying so long. This was when the reality of renting their entire lives was going to hit them hard, but most of them felt, at the very minimum, they should have been told. Her action of not informing the tenants showed me she didn't care about us; we were just paychecks to her, but the other tenants didn't see that. They sadly thought that the people making money off them actually cared about them; it was a pretty naive way to think.

When Saturday came, I was surprised at the turnout. Everyone in the building came out. There were a couple of people I didn't recognize, and even Tommy, the eighty-something-year-old shut-in, showed up. There was hardly any space by the mailboxes, so everyone gathered on the stairs that wound up three floors. It was enclosed so they couldn't see; all they could do was hear, but that didn't stop anyone from attending. I got there early so I could have eyes on Denise and Benjamin. There was no way I was going to miss this show. Denise hadn't arrived yet, but Benjamin was front and center, starting to get everyone riled up. I was sitting on the first set of stairs, drinking my coffee, and listening to everyone else talking amongst themselves.

Everyone was upset, and I even heard a couple of people say that they thought we would be able to stay in the building; people are clueless.

When Denise showed up, Benjamin went into full gear and announced her entry with extreme mockery, "Ladies and Gentlemen, your enemy and mine, slumlord of the year, Denise!"

When Denise was inside, she immediately brushed Benjamin off and put him in his place. It was as if she didn't care and finally knew she didn't have to listen to this guy anymore. She barked, "Benjamin, this is my meeting, not yours. Listen to what I have to say; then, you'll have your chance to speak. In the meantime, be quiet and just listen, young man."

I thought Benjamin was going to lose it, but he was very polite. "OK, Denise, have your say, but be ready for what I have to say when you are done."

Even though they obviously didn't like each other, there was a tad of respect between them; it was entertaining to watch. Denise started by apologizing and saying that she was sorry she didn't tell us about the sale of the building. She claimed the new owner wasn't supposed to say anything for another two weeks and that she was very upset about it.

She tried explaining, "When I discussed the sale with the real estate agent, I told him my concerns were about you, the tenants. I wanted to make sure the tenants would be allowed to stay, and I wanted to know what would happen with you. The real estate agent assured me that it would still be a rental building, and everyone could stay if they wanted to; everything was supposed to be OK."

Right away, Benjamin shoved the letter in her face and asked, "Well, what the hell is this, Denise? Is this OK? They're trying to throw us out in the first week of ownership."

She looked down at her feet, "I know, Benji. Just settle down. I will talk to the real estate agent and clear things up."

Denise sounded sincere, and it seemed she was honestly confused with what was going on, but my guess was that she was naïve and had been lied to; I'm guessing the new owner told the real estate agent to say anything to appease her through the sale process.

Benjamin immediately asked her, "What do you mean you'll talk to the real estate agent? What about the owner?"

That's when Benjamin realized she had never even talked to the owner, "Who's the owner, Denise? Have you ever talked to the owner, Denise?"

The next thing she said shocked us all, and I don't think anyone was expecting it, "Well, no, I never actually talked to them; I just talked to the real estate agent."

You could hear the hesitancy and weakness in her voice; this was when she realized that she had no control over what would happen with the building and the tenants.

Benjamin's voice lost its anger as if he knew we were in trouble. Sadly, he said to her, "You have no idea who you sold the building to, do you, Denise?"

Her silence was the answer.

Robert piped in; he was calm, and in a part 'matter of fact' and part mocking tone, he asked Denise, "Can you provide me with the name of the real estate agent, Denise? Can you tell me what company or who signed the check? I'm sure you received a big fat check, right Denise? I'm sure you've been paid already." He was very business-like until he got to the 'big fat check' part; that's when his voice became very mocking.

Denise's answer summed it up, "No. I can't tell you anything; all terms of the sale are confidential. But don't worry, I'll talk to the agent and get this straightened out.

Her statement was like putting gas on a fire for Benjamin; he lost it and started to go off on her, "You greedy, greedy woman. You sold to the highest bidder, didn't you, Denise? You always said you were concerned with your tenants and the community if and when you ever sold; you said you'd never let the building go to someone who didn't care about the tenants and the neighborhood. Remember saying that, Denise? You're so full of shit; you were only concerned about the money. Are they a developer, Denise? Speculators? Are they going to tear down the building? Are they going to fix it up and Renovict our asses out of the building, Denise?"

I thought, 'Renovict? What the hell is that?'

Benjamin kept going, "Is it a person, Denise? Is it a business? You have no idea who you sold to do you Denise? Are they even from Canada? Did you sell to Chinese or Indian people, Denise?"

I know why he said that, Denise was, how should I say? Denise was racist, and Benjamin knew this would press her buttons.

He calmed down, and in a tone of disappointment, he said, "Just get out of here, Denise. Take your millions and get lost. You don't own this building anymore, and you don't have any friends here. Just leave."

Benjamin threw her out of the building, and the tenants applauded. Denise slinked out of the building. She might have millions, but I'm sure this isn't how she expected to leave the building she owned and loved for over forty years.

As soon as Denise left, everyone started talking amongst themselves; Benjamin said to give him a second while he organized some handouts.

I took the opportunity and asked him, "Benjamin, can I ask you a question?"

He didn't look up, and as he rifled through his papers, he said, "Well, if you wait a minute, I'll probably answer it when I speak."

He was a controlling kind of guy, and he just loved the attention, but I asked anyway. "Well, while you are getting ready, do you mind telling me what is this 'Renovict' thing that you mentioned?"

A couple of people agreed and asked, "Yeah, what the hell is that?"

He kept his head down and said, "That, I can answer. Renovict, or Renoviction, is the shady and slimy process that landlords are using to get people with low rents out of their apartments in order to rent them out to new tenants at higher rates. They use the excuse of renovating the unit or the building to evict people; hence, the term 'Renoviction', it's the tool of landlords and owners used to evict people for profits.

"Thanks, Benjamin." I was still unsure, so I had to ask him, "So it's legal or illegal? I'm confused."

Benjamin was fired up, "It's bloody illegal. The problem is the grey areas in the rules and laws, and when you accompany those with weak fines and punishments, they get away with it."

He was ready to start his meeting. He began to pass out a package of about twenty pages to everyone. He began, "First off, thank you for all coming. I think we have a full turnout. Next, take that eviction letter they gave us and throw it out. It's illegal and isn't worth the paper it's written on."

Benjamin had everything in the handout: newspaper articles, housing and rental laws, and the Landlord and Tenant Board of Ontario rules. There was a form for us to sign, authorizing the tenants to create and register a 'Tenants Association' for the building with the city. I glanced at the form and noticed it said Benjamin would be the 'President', which I had no problem with at all.

I flipped through the package as he spoke; I was amazed there were so many articles about people getting illegally evicted, all in the name of 'Renoviction'; it was an epidemic, I had no idea. I didn't follow the news or pay attention to current events or politics, and now it was biting me in the ass. Before this, I didn't care what was happening in my city or what was happening to the marginalized people who couldn't afford to protect themselves. I was like the rest of the population, only caring and worrying about myself, but now, I was one of the marginalized. I was just like everyone else, unless it hits people in their wallets, we close our eyes and look the other way; we only open our eyes and pay attention when something affects our world or our wallet.

Benjamin continued, saying, "This letter from the new owner means nothing and everything to us. What I mean by that is that the letter means nothing because they can't just write a letter and throw us out; there are rules and regulations against doing something like this. But it means everything to us because it shows us their true intentions, it shows us they want us out, and it looks like they don't care how they do it. This letter intends to scare you out of the building if you didn't know the laws; well, we do, so we aren't leaving."

There was a bit of clapping when he said that, and he continued, "Next, they'll start to try to buy us out; they'll make us some crappy little offers to entice us to move, but don't fall for it folks. What they offer us will be nowhere near what it'll cost us to move out in the long run."

I was impressed with Benjamin; although he might be a bit crazy, he was sincere.

Someone I couldn't see spoke up from around the corner and asked, "You mean they'll pay us to leave?"

As soon as I heard that question, I knew we were doomed. As soon as they start offering people money, they'll take it. There will be no camaraderie, no sticking together, and no 'we're all in this together' bullshit; as soon as the money comes out, it's every man for themselves.

The voice continued, "What do you think it would be? Ten? Twenty?"

This got Benjamin fuming, and I could feel his frustration.

Holding back, he said, "It won't be anywhere near that amount, and they won't do it for everyone; they'll offer a couple of people buyouts to break us because they know our best defense is a united front. They'll try to divide us. Just like society, if we're divided, we fall."

I thought to myself, 'Oh shit, we're doomed.'

Benjamin continued, "They want to separate us. The public won't pay attention to a couple of people being kicked out, but an entire building being evicted? People will notice that, and they know this. A whole building of people being evicted will get the attention of the community, the media, and, hopefully, politicians. It's the only way we stand a chance."

You could hear Benjamin's passion as he tried to make everyone understand what was happening and he opened the floor to questions.

I could tell some people understood, and some didn't have a clue. Brian, one of the oldest and longest tenants in the building, spoke, and everyone was quiet and quite surprised that he was talking: "Denise will take care of us; she always has. I trust her; she's never let me down before."

The poor guy thought Denise cared about him and would take care of the tenants. The other comments were even less encouraging; most people were asking about buyouts and wondering how much money they could make from being thrown out of their homes. I could only shake my head and look down; I knew we were done in the long run. But as disappointed as I was, Benjamin was pissed, and the only reason he held back was because it was Brian saying it. I could see his face get redder and redder, and I thought there was going to be smoke coming from the fiery, freckled ginger.

He breathed in deeply, took a couple of seconds, and as the red started to fade, he explained the economics of a buyout; he calmly said, "People listen. Anything they offer us won't go very far if we have to move."

Someone chirped from the stairwell, "Yeah, but a few thousand dollars could go a long way."

Benjamin lost it, and it looked like his head would explode. He started to lecture us, and it was in an angry, mocking tone, "Don't you people understand, this is their game plan. They offer a few bucks to some of us, weaken our numbers, and then they start to get rid of us one by one. Don't just think about the money going into your pocket; you have to do the math and think of the money you'll be paying out in the long run. If they give you four, even five thousand dollars, how long will that last? That's nothing in the long run. Folks, how long have you all lived in the building?"

He yelled up the stairs to Brian and joked, "Brian, how long have you been here? I think you were at the ribbon-cutting ceremony when they opened the building, weren't you?"

Everyone chuckled.

Brian said, "Tommy has the record; I'm a freshman of thirty years."

"Well, Brian, I can't even guess what your rent is now, but if you were gone, they could easily get twenty-five hundred to three thousand a month for your unit."

Brian replied, "Twenty-five hundred what? For my place?"

Benjamin calmly explained, "If you want to find something in this neighborhood, you won't. You'll have to move and pay at least three to four times more than you are now. You have to consider everything; think about how much money they will make from these apartments. The way prices have been rising, they could easily get that, so kicking us out will make them at least five to ten thousand dollars or more a year per unit, and that's just the beginning."

Even after Benjamin's passionate and logical buyout explanation, all people wanted to talk about was a buyout. I could see Benjamin's frustration and bewilderment on his face. He was angry and dismayed that that's all people wanted to discuss. I understood his frustration. How do you stand up and fight for people who are too ignorant, naïve, or stupid to know that they need fighting for? These people didn't think they were in trouble, and their comments proved it.

I tried to bring Benjamin back to reality, so I asked him some questions about the time frame of this 'Renoviction' and the procedures involved. I just blurted out, "So how long is this process of them trying to evict us going to take? What do we do?"

He thanked me for asking some good questions and replied, "This process will end up going through the Landlord and Tenant Board, and our 'case' will eventually be heard by an adjudicator who will decide and make a ruling. But there isn't a timeframe for how long this will take. With the ineffectiveness of the Tenant Board and depending on how much paperwork goes back and forth, this could take six months to a year until we have a conclusion. As for a lawyer, yes, we need someone to help us. Everyone can go their separate ways and hire their own lawyer or paralegal, or we can get a lawyer or paralegal as a group and fight this together as 'one,' which is our best defense. On that note, we might be able to hire a 'legal aid' community lawyer; since this is a low-income housing issue, we might get lucky, and the city might pay for it."

It seemed like Benjamin knew his stuff, so I kept asking questions, "Will the owner have lawyers representing them?"

"Damn straight they will, and the lawyers they have are probably experts in this kind of stuff," Benjamin said this in a defeatist kind of tone, almost like he knew what we were going to be up against.

Benjamin proceeded to wrap up the meeting. He said the first thing we needed to do was to form a tenant association for the building. This would give us some recognition from the Landlord and Tenant Board and show them we are a united group. Next, he said we had to schedule regular tenant meetings to discuss and review the situation as it progresses. He asked if we could have the papers signed and placed under his door as soon as possible so he could get the ball rolling. A few of us filled them out and handed them to him immediately.

Someone yelled out, "What about the letter we got?"

Benjamin replied, "Like I said, just ignore it."

He reassured us that it didn't mean anything because it was illegal, and we should keep living like nothing happened and wait for their next move. The crowd started to disperse slowly. Some lingered to talk to each other a little, and some just went back to their apartments. I headed upstairs and decided it was time to start reading up about 'Renoviction' and learning about the Toronto rental and real estate market.

Chapter 3

Benjamin opened my eyes to this 'Renoviction' thing, and it got me worried. I had to start learning what the hell was going on with the rental market in Toronto. After the meeting, I went straight to my computer. First thing I typed in? 'Renoviction.' I couldn't believe what came up; it was horror story after horror story of people getting thrown out of their apartments, all in the name of 'Renoviction.' Property values had been skyrocketing in Toronto, which was fortunate for renters whose rent hadn't caught up to current market prices but was unfortunate for the landlords. But now, the landlords were trying to get their piece of the action.

I started searching the web, and there was no lack of stories. I learned that the 'Renoviction' phenomenon began in Vancouver a couple of years back and has now spread to every city across North America. It seemed like landlords out west had developed tactics—a whole damn playbook—on how to evict people 'legally.' The first trick they pulled? Claiming they needed the unit for 'personal family use.' As a landlord, you are allowed to evict someone for no reason if you want to use the unit for your personal family use. So, what did the landlords do? They started evicting people using this loophole, but after a while, it was hard for landlords to say and prove that an entire building with multiple units was needed for their personal family use, not to say that they didn't try. There were cases of landlords evicting people and putting their dog or cat's name as the person moving in on the eviction notice, saying the unit was now for them. When people started to figure it out, they began to crack down on that loophole, so landlords started looking for other ways to evict people, and then they found the renovation trick.

It was spreading so fast that it was now being called an epidemic and becoming a plague. It was so common that 'Renoviction' was becoming a recognized word in society. I couldn't believe some of the stories I was reading. I had no idea this kind of stuff was happening in my city and it was ruining lives. People were being thrown out onto the street; it was unfortunate, but it was just another case of the rich taking advantage of the poor. From what I read, the laws and fines were antiquated and ineffective, and the building companies, developers, and speculators knew this and took full advantage of it. The rental market had become like the 'Wild West.'

I read stories about doctors, dentists, and even veterinarians getting in on the rental/landlord game. People no longer bought rental units to own and become landlords as a vocation and to acquire an income to live. Now, people were getting into it purely for speculation, the dream of 'passive income', and greed. Property rental was now a very prosperous, almost risk-free proposition where people were guaranteed to make money by evicting the people with affordable rent, throwing them out, doing some 'lipstick' renovations, and then re-renting the units to new tenants who would pay two to three times the original price. It's why everyone and their brother wanted to get in on the real estate/rental game.

The stories I came across were mostly the same: landlords withholding repairs as long as they could to make the tenant uncomfortable, turning the heat down to the lowest legally accepted temperature, and reducing the cleaning and maintenance to the very least they could get away with. But landlords were starting to get creative on how to get people out of their units. One gentleman, who had lived in his apartment for twenty years, had his fridge break down, and when the landlord replaced it, they replaced it with a fridge that didn't fit in the spot where the old one had been. So now, this poor guy had his fridge in the middle of his kitchen; they intended to make this guy's apartment so uncomfortable that he couldn't stand to live there anymore and would move out. The guy went to the landlord-tenant board to complain, but the board ruled in favor of the landlord because, though landlords are legally obliged to provide a fridge, there was nothing in the rules saying where it had to be placed in the unit.

A couple of other stories I read were of a landlord who painted all the common areas and hallways black; one landlord installed lighting in the common areas that was so bright it was almost blinding; and another landlord installed a PA system through the building and pumped in AM radio stations that weren't quite in tune and mostly static. Another story I read was about a landlord who was caught paying someone to vandalize and paint graffiti all over the building. The tenants were able to prove the landlord was behind it, but the landlord didn't pay any fines or suffer any consequences because it was their property, and they claimed the graffiti was art.

Every story was worse than the last, but they all showed how despicable these people were and the lengths they'd go to get people out of their units. There were stories accusing landlords of 'planting' cockroaches, mice, and even crickets in their buildings to try to force people out; I'm assuming the crickets were for the noise factor to drive people crazy. The cricket and fridge stories were the more creative things I had read, but some of the stories were right out of the movies like landlords sending in 'eviction crews' to get people out. These 'eviction crews'—thugs, addicts, and goons sent to harass and scare tenants. One would think these tactics were only in the movies, but they were real.

Another repercussion I learned about this 'Renoviction' epidemic is the destruction of neighborhoods that once made this city great. Areas of the city that had character and a distinct feeling once deemed cool were disappearing. Neighborhoods once populated by artists, musicians, and interesting characters, along with cool independent stores run by the owners themselves (a true rarity in today's economy), were now being populated with a new class of people moving in. With them, they brought the Starbucks, Pinkberry's, A&W's, numerous vegan bakeries, and coffee shops. It's funny; my neighborhood Christieville, was trying to gentrify, but nothing was getting better. The only thing that was happening was that the rents and property values were skyrocketing. The artists, authors, actors, singers, and creative types that once lived in and made the neighborhood cool were slowly being pushed and priced out. What the people moving in didn't realize was that everything and everyone that made the neighborhood cool was disappearing.

I was shocked, it was disgusting what was going on and the way landlords were behaving. Evictions had skyrocketed in Toronto lately; the total number of evictions this year had already outpaced last year's numbers four to one and there was no end in sight. It seemed that the Landlord and Tenant Board was on the landlords' side and not the tenants, almost always ruling in favor of the owners. Tenants were outmatched, outgunned, and outlawyered when they got to the Tenant Board. The owners had lawyers or paralegals acting on their behalf who could quote every rule, regulation, and law in the 'Landlord Tenant Act.' If the tenant couldn't refute, disprove the claims, or quote the rules, the adjudicators would always side with the lawyers because they knew the laws and loopholes. It was a 'David and Goliath' battle at the Landlord and Tenant Board, and Goliath was always winning.

While searching for 'Renoviction' online, I came across a poll ranking Toronto as the 'Best' city to live in; whoever voted in that poll needed to read what I was reading. Toronto was turning into an expensive shithole, but at least the poll said it was the best city. Something struck me as odd as I researched everything; no prominent publications ever talked about this problem. All the stories I read were in local newspapers or the 'subway' handout papers; not one major publication was talking about this. It struck me as odd, and I wasn't sure what that meant.

I returned to the Landlord and Tenant Board's website to read up on what they do. I learned that they are an independent judiciary board that solves disputes between landlords and tenants. The board is made up of a dozen arbitrators/adjudicators appointed by the Government, which means that most of them are there for a reason; these people are there as political favors to the city's rich and elite. If someone at the top of one of these mega commercial rental companies or REITs wanted someone in as an arbitrator, all they had to do was go through the political channels, grease the wheels with payoffs and bribes, and voila, their person is appointed. This would come in handy if they wanted any 'shifts' or 'changes' in the Tenant Board's rulings and if they wanted to clear out low-income renters from the very properties their 'backers' owned; it was a very slimy system. After reading every page on their website, I realized that though it seemed the rules were set up in favor of the renter, the deeper I looked and read, the more I realized there were a lot of grey areas and loopholes that landlords could exploit and abuse.

As I was sitting at the computer, I heard a letter being slipped under my door and voices in the hallway. Thinking it was another letter from the new owner, I ran to the door. I picked it up and opened the door, and I was surprised to see Denise talking with Robert, I could tell he was irritated. He wasn't as red as he was when he was speaking with me, but he was getting there. He was lecturing her about not telling anyone that she sold the building; she apologized and said that it was in the terms of the sale that she wasn't allowed to say a thing.

In a sympathetic tone, he said, "That's ridiculous, Denise. This was your building. You could have dictated the terms. You let them push you around, or you just sold us out. It's one of the two, and at this point, I don't care which it is."

Denise couldn't look him in the eye and stared down at the ground. "I know Robert. I was just doing what the real estate agent told me to do. I didn't want to upset anyone or jeopardize anything."

Robert looked at her with pity. "Well, Denise, a lot of people thought it was very insulting; you could have handled it better. You have scared and alienated most of your tenants, the people you considered friends."

From listening to them, I got the impression that Denise wasn't too business savvy. She looked ashamed, and her face told me she was feeling played and taken advantage of by whoever bought the building. She was way out of her league. She had just been steamrolled in the sale process, and now there was going to be a new kind of landlord taking over.

Robert hadn't opened his letter yet, but I was reading mine as they talked. I chuckled, interrupted them, and asked her, "Denise, what the hell is this?"

She was nervous and couldn't hide it; she said, "Well, I wanted to offer you folks a little something for your troubles and try to make the process easier for all of you."

Robert asked me what the letter was without opening his. I laughed, and looking directly at Denise, I replied to Robert, "It looks like a bribe. She wants to give us five hundred dollars to move out, and oh, it's conditional. We have to be out by the end of the month to get it."

Robert went beet red, actually 'fire engine' red, as he stared at Denise. After about thirty seconds of awkward silence, he finally spoke, and with that white stuff in the corners of his lips, he asked, "Do you want to explain this, Denise?"

"Well, the new owner thought it might be better if we offered the tenants something extra to make it easier for them." Denise still couldn't lift her eyes from the floor.

Robert shook his head and rubbed his face as he said, "Oh, Denise, you're either greedy as hell or even dumber than I thought. You're doing the dirty work for them, and you don't even realize it. Five hundred dollars doesn't help anyone; it's a band-aid fix for the hemorrhaging you are about to cause us."

I looked at her, shaking my head. "Denise, I'm not moving, and I want to remind you that when I moved in, I asked you what your plans were; you looked me straight in the eye and said you weren't selling for another forty years. Do you remember that, Denise? This is exactly why I asked you that, Denise. You're just another liar."

As I said that, we could hear someone running up the stairs, and it sounded like a herd of elephants coming at us. I looked at Robert and said, "Benjamin."

We looked down the stairway and we saw the big ginger come barreling around the corner. He was so mad he was redder than Robert. It's a good thing we were there, as I had to step in front of Denise, and Robert stepped in to block Benjamin. If we hadn't, he would have barreled right over her.

He was loud and angry, "What the hell is this, Denise? Are you trying to bribe us out of here? Did the new owner offer you some sort of bonus to clear the building out?"

I hadn't even thought of that aspect, but it made sense. If the new owner could get the building with empty units, they are free and clear to rent them out at higher prices to new people immediately. It never dawned on me that the new owner would pay Denise to clear out the units; it never even crossed my mind. Now it was clear to me this eviction shit is going to get slimier and slimier the more I learn and the more I have to live through it.

Benjamin was pissed off, "How could you do this, Denise? You are helping the new owner and not the people you have known for years, decades even. The people that put money in your pocket, year after year, making you rich, and now you are selling them out for an extra few thousand dollars? What are you getting for the building, Denise? Three, four million? And now you're trying to get these tenants, your tenants of decades, out of the building for an additional couple thousand dollars? You are horrible, Denise; you should be ashamed of yourself."

The three of us stood there shaking our heads and looking at Denise with disgust. When she finally looked up from the floor, she could see it and just uttered, "I'm sorry."

We didn't want to hear anything more from her. Robert politely asked her to leave, but Benjamin wasn't so forgiving; he said, "Get the hell out of here, Denise. You make me sick."

Once again, Denise slunk away, no one wishing her well or telling her to take care of herself. As I watched her go, I thought to myself that Denise is what's is wrong with the real estate market in Toronto: no one is looking out for the tenant, the neighborhood, or the community, and everyone is just looking for the bucks. I almost felt sorry for her, but then I didn't; if she wanted to sell out, it was her right, but she wouldn't have any respect from the people she affected. You can't serve two masters; you either want money or you want to help people.

Later, we learned that she sold the building for four million two hundred thousand dollars. All that money and she still wanted a little more to clear out the building; it was disgusting and disheartening to know that she would screw all of her tenants for an extra few thousand dollars.

I asked them, "Is this for real? Is Denise really asking us to move for a five- hundred-dollar payment? She's sold the building already. Are you serious about the new owner paying her to empty the units?"

Benjamin answered, "Yeah, Brent, and this is just the beginning. Now that Denise did this, we know we're in trouble, and we'll need to fight like hell if we want to keep living here."

"Holy shit." My response was reflex; I couldn't believe it; what a shitty move it was on Denise's part; I was starting to get mad and felt like I was being bullied.

"No one is going to accept a five-hundred-dollar payout, are they?" I looked at both of them when I was asking.

Benjamin shook his head. "I don't know Brent. I don't think anyone will take this, but you never know. I'll write a notice informing everyone of what Denise's true intent is with this letter."

And off he went, head down, on a mission.

Robert looked at me and said, "I'm glad he's on our side."

The following day, Benjamin slid the notice he had written under my door. I smiled and chuckled as I read it; he didn't hold back any punches. It wasn't long, only a few lines, in huge bold text, and of course, it was typed all in caps; it read: 'TENANTS OF THREE-NINETY-ONE EMPIRE AVENUE - DO NOT FALL FOR DENISE'S OFFER OF FIVE-HUNDRED-DOLLARS TO MOVE OUT. WE ARE NOT FOR SALE. THIS IS A TACTIC FOR THE NEW OWNER TO GET US ALL OUT. SHE IS WORKING WITH HIM. SHE IS A GREEDY, MONEY- GRUBBING SLUMLORD AND IS NOT YOUR FRIEND. WE ARE ONLY A $ SIGN TO HER. COME TO THE TENANTS' MEETING THIS SATURDAY AT 10 A.M., AND WE'LL DISCUSS HOW WE FIGHT THEIR GREED.

I shook my head and thought, 'What a waste of time.' I put the letter down and headed out for a coffee; I laughed as I shut my door and turned to leave. There was a notice in the hallway, and as I walked down the stairs, his notice was plastered all over the walls. By the time I got outside, I must have seen at least twenty notices on my way out; I had laughed and thought, 'Well, at least this is going to get interesting.'

The next few days were uneventful, and I didn't see anyone around the building. I was working thirteen to fourteen hours a day on an American political propaganda show, which didn't give me much time to research my housing predicament. But surprisingly, the show gave me an idea of what to start researching next. There was a scene that involved a lobbyist working for the 'Balloon Council of America'; in the scene, he was paying off a politician on behalf of the balloon industry. Listening to the dialogue, I wondered, 'What the hell does the balloon industry need a lobbyist for?'

I started to read the sides, and apparently, balloons were getting banned all over the United States because an endangered turtle swallowed and choked to death on a balloon that had floated hundreds of miles. This outraged the environmentalists, leading to a national crusade against balloons, which hurt balloon sales, so what do the balloon manufacturers do? They hire a lobbyist to go to Washington to pay off the politicians and get them to start preaching about the goodness of balloons, their usefulness, and how much happiness balloons bring the American people. But more importantly, the lobbyist would pay the politicians to vote against any bans on their beloved product, 'Fuck the turtles.'

Watching them shoot the scene made me wonder, do these landlords have a lobby group? Is there some association or group that these guys belong to? It was kind of curious that they all seemed to be following the same playbook for evicting people, maybe they were all in on it, and there's a more significant reason why the laws are screwing the people. I never learned too much from my job, but today it was surprisingly educational.

On Thursday, I got home at about three a.m., and when I walked in, I noticed something different in the building. All of Benjamin's notices were down and only one was up at the mailboxes. This one was from the Brownstone Management Company on behalf of the owner, One-Four-Seven-Zero-Zero-Seven LLC. Ironically, it was a notice about putting up notices in the building, and it stated: 'Please be aware, the common areas are not to be used as a message board. If you wish to post something, there is a message board in the laundry room. Posting notices or letters on the walls is considered vandalism and defacement of private property. Also, the hallways and stairwells are communal areas, and due to fire regulations, no 'loitering' or 'gathering' is allowed.' And it was signed by Brownstone Management.

These people were terrible. So far, no names have been on these letters; we're dealing with cowards who probably say things like, 'It's just business,' and hide behind their company's name. This was a low tactic. They're actually trying to block our right to gather, trying to stop us from having a tenants meeting in our own building. It looks like Benjamin was right, these guys are going to try anything to get us out.

I woke up around noon on Friday and decided to go out for coffee. As soon as I opened the door to my apartment, I started laughing. Benjamin reposted his notice, and he put it up everywhere. I must have passed fifty of them on the way out of the building, and he had yanked down the letter from the management company that was at the mailboxes. Benjamin was quite the character.

When I arrived home with my coffee, I sat at the computer and started to dig into the housing market. I knew the easy places to look, newspapers and network news, but where would I look to learn the truth about what was going on? I decided I would start with the company signing the letters and trying to throw me out, Brownstone Management. Let's see what these guys are all about.

I typed their name in Google, and a ton of links came up; most of the links were for other buildings they had under their management, which was a lot. All the other links were reviews, and there were a lot of those, so I started with them. Every review I read was terrible; link after link were complaints, and I couldn't find a good review about them. Most reviews were about how people couldn't get repairs done in a timely manner, if they were done at all; many were about dirty and rundown conditions, and many were about people getting thrown out or evicted. It seemed like this was their thing, and by the number of complaints online, it looked like they were very good at what they do. Review after review was about them trying to evict people all over the city. There were different reasons for the evictions, but most were 'Renovictions'.

After reading about a dozen reviews, I visited the Brownstone Management website. It was a good-looking website, making them look like a building management company that cared about the people in their buildings. There were pictures of smiling families, people riding bikes, kids playing in a playground, and in the front of one of the buildings, there was even a fountain; they projected some real 'feel good' moments. You'd never know they were a slumlord management company until you read the services they provide to their customers, who, in essence, are the landlords and owners.

There was a page called 'Maximizing Your Per Unit Rental Income'; this is where the truth of how shitty these guys actually were was hiding. This page outlined how landlords can use their proven 'system' to attract new renters that would pay top market rate for their units.

This page was where they laid out the steps for performing 'Renovictions'; I couldn't believe my eyes. They explained the laws regarding evicting people, and they laid out how their 'renovation process' was able to 'assist' the existing renter out of the unit; they shamelessly use the word 'assist,' which in reality means evict. These scumbags weren't even trying to hide what they were doing.

I looked around their website and went to the 'about us' page, and I saw that they belonged to a couple of Associations. One, in particular, caught my eye, 'The Alliance of Commercial Housing Rentals.' Hmm, I wondered what those guys were all about; they sounded like 'The Balloon Council of America' bullshit, and it didn't sit right with me; they would definitely be who I looked at next.

I went to their website, and it wasn't so elaborate; there were only a couple of pages to the whole thing. I learned from my past experience of sourcing clients in a law office for collection services that when you come across a website that is only a couple of pages with limited information, the company usually doesn't want the general public to know about them or what they do, and this site looked exactly like that. It was plain; there weren't any pictures or graphics, and it was just a couple of pages with only two or three lines of text on each.

They didn't elaborate or explain in detail anything they did; they used words like 'enacting cultural change,' 'shaping and assisting governmental procedures,' 'increasing our stakeholder's presence,' whatever the fuck that meant, and 'developing sustainable rental housing.' None of these phrases instilled confidence or hope that this 'Alliance' did anything good for society. I went to the 'Contact Us' page, and there was only one contact on it. I sat there in disbelief when I saw the name of the President of the 'Alliance,' Kerwin Cummings. Kerwin was an old childhood friend of mine; I couldn't believe it.

I first met Kerwin as a kid at the ballpark where I grew up; his father and mine were friends, and both were very respected men in the community. We knew each other as kids but got to know each other in high school on the baseball team. He couldn't play, was awkward as hell, and could hardly see; he had to wear two-inch-thick glasses that didn't appear to do too much. Instead of playing, he was the equipment manager, scorekeeper, and statistician; it was his way of fitting in and getting on the team. Though he didn't play any sport, he worked for every team in high school, including the soccer team, hockey, football, baseball, and even the rugby team; he was the manager for all of them.

He was a good guy in high school and quite popular since he managed all the teams. No one had a bad thing to say about the guy, and rightfully so; he was a decent kid. Kerwin came from money, went to the best schools, and apparently made some pretty good contacts along the way. I had followed his career from afar when I first saw him on TV with the politician scumbags of the Progressive Conservative Party of Canada. During their 'Common Sense Revolution' of the early 2000s, they slashed and burned all the public services they could get their hands on. They privatized every government service so they could 'line' their own pockets and make the budget look good, all in the name of greed and in the hopes of getting re-elected.

He learned early from his time as the statistician and scorekeeper on the teams in high school that he had the power to improve your stats and make you look better by 'scoring' you a base hit here or a stolen base there. It got to the point that he let you know he would gladly do it for you in exchange for a chicken burger or French fries and a Coke in the cafeteria at lunch.

Apparently, this behavior continued into his time in politics; he knew that access to politicians had power, and he could benefit financially from it, so after his days in politics, he branched out on his own and became a lobbyist. Instead of selling out and cheating for burgers and fries, he's now selling out society and his fellow man for cash. After politics, he began working as a Lobbyist for such 'reputable' industries as the automobile insurance industry, the predatory payday loan industry, and now, commercial landlords. And even though he was a nice guy in high school and wears suits and ties now, this guy is a real 'enemy of the people.'

After a week of working long hours every day, I was looking forward to the tenant meeting on Saturday. I hadn't seen anyone all week except for Robert, which had only been for a few minutes when I came home one night at three in the morning. His door was open as usual, and since he was up, he came out when he heard me.

"Oh, hey Robert, I hope I wasn't too loud coming in," even though I was just in the hallway.

It seemed he was going through a bout of insomnia, and it looked like his nerves were getting the better of him, "Not at all, Brent; I haven't been sleeping too well since the letter, and I've been busy reading and researching."

I agreed with him: "Yeah, it's nerve-racking. I've been digging and reading as much as I can as well."

He laughed and asked, "You keep some crazy hours Brent, what line of work are you in? Are you in the bar industry?"

I always hated telling people what I did. Trying to be an actor was a tough haul, and when you get stuck in the rut of being a stand-in or an 'extra,' it's always shitty to try to explain exactly what I did for a living. Even though it was a union job and good money when you worked, it had become dull and mind-numbing. Yes, there were fun moments, but T.V./Film is a highly hierarchal industry, and 'extras' were at the bottom.

When asked what I did for a living, I usually said, 'I work in T.V./Film.' but I was tired and pissed off, so I said, "I'm an actor, but apparently, I'm a career extra, stuck in the background world right now."

"Oh, that sounds fun; it must be exciting." It was the exact answer I hated hearing from people; it wasn't much fun, and there wasn't much excitement.

"Well, not really. It's good money, and it isn't nine to five, so yeah, it's not bad." I tried to change the subject as soon as I could. "I've been doing a little reading and investigating into this 'Renoviction' thing, and the more I read, the more worried I get about our situation."

Robert tried being slightly more optimistic: "I agree, but there have been people who have fought and won this sort of thing. I've reached out to an old lawyer friend who said he would do some digging into this. He's going to do a business search and do some investigating. I want to find out about this new owner. I want to know who they are and what they are all about."

"That's cool, Robert. Let me know what you find out. It's good to know your enemy. Have a good night, I'll see you at the meeting." That was the only contact I had with anyone in the building for the week, and I had no idea what was happening.

Myles Bradley

Chapter 4

When Saturday came, I was exhausted. I had worked seventy-six hours that week. I got home at 4 a.m. didn't fall asleep until 5:30 and woke up at 10. No coffee, no time. Just threw on sweatpants, a hoodie, and headed downstairs. I had gotten to the meeting just as it was starting; I was stuck at the top of the stairs and couldn't see Benjamin; I could only hear him. I heard him start the meeting, but then, all of a sudden, he stopped. I couldn't hear much; I could only hear two voices, one of which was Benjamin's. I couldn't make out what was being said at first, but then I could hear Benjamin getting louder and louder.

I asked the people around me what was happening, and someone said, "I think we are getting thrown out of the building."

"Thrown out? Who's throwing us out? What's going on?" No one near me knew what was happening, and I was starting to get a little pissed off.

I heard Benjamin announce, "OK, everyone, we're going outside; we're getting thrown out of our own building."

Everyone started heading down the stairs; no one knew what was happening; we were just heading out the door. When we got outside, Benjamin was arguing with a casually dressed man in khaki pants and a button-down shirt. He had a lanyard around his neck with some I.D. attached to it, and he was holding a clipboard. When I got close, I could read, 'City of Toronto BYLAW OFFICER.'

As I got closer, I could hear Benjamin berating the guy, saying he's just a 'lackey' doing the owner's dirty work, picking on the little guy, and that he's just an enforcer for the 'man.' The breaking point for the city worker was when Benjamin compared him to a Nazi; at that point, the guy just turned and walked away. That's when I realized that though Benjamin was passionate, he could also be a detriment if he didn't keep his anger in check.

When the guy left, I asked Benjamin what was going on and why we were outside.

He started to say, or more correctly, he began to yell, "Everyone, your attention, please. That was a bylaw officer from the City of Toronto; our new owner called the city, trying to shut down our tenant meeting. They called the city and said there was a fire hazard in the building; they said we were the hazard! This is what we are up against, they don't want us organizing; they don't want us talking and uniting because they know that if we do, it only makes us stronger. This is a violation of our rights; they want us out of our homes; this shows us that they are going to play dirty, and they are going to try to use anything at their disposal to stop us." Benjamin was fuming, and rightfully so.

I couldn't believe they called the city bylaw officer on us; I didn't think they would stoop so low or go to such extents to try to stop us from organizing. I was shocked.

Benjamin asked everyone to gather around. He sounded like a genuine 'revolutionary' trying to rally and motivate everyone. He started saying things like, "Come on, everyone get closer. The closer we are, the stronger we are. Come on, everyone, get as close as you can. The closer we get, the harder it is for them to break us."

This was starting to go to his head a little now.

When everyone was close enough, he started strong. "I'm not leaving this building, and no one should; if we stay united and act together as a building, we will have a better chance than if we try to fight on our own."

He looked around at everyone, and heads were nodding with him.

He continued, "Now I have some bad news; we have lost a few people already: Cindy, Roman, and all the guys from the basement. It seems that five hundred dollars was more money than they have all ever seen, so they took it. Roman said he was moving anyway. Cindy thought it was a good deal, and the guys in the basement, well, who knows, they're already gone."

There was some talk from the group, and then Brian spoke up; "I took the deal, too. Denise came and offered it to me. She said it would be best for me, so I took it. Like I said, Denise has never done me wrong, so I'm not worried."

The whole group was in disbelief. There were a lot of bad words said about Denise because everyone knew Brian didn't have a clue about what was going on. We couldn't believe how low Denise had sunk.

Right away, Benjamin started questioning him, and he was angry: "Where are you going to move to, Brian? You know you have to be out by the end of the month, you have been in the building for thirty years, Brian. Are you ready to pay rent that's probably at least ten times more than you're paying now, Brian?"

Brian kept saying, "Well, Denise said it would be best for me, so I took it."

His reply was sad and scary. It was sad that this guy didn't have a clue what was going on, and it was scary that Denise and this new owner wouldn't think twice about conning someone out of the building as naïve and pathetic as Brian.

Benjamin said, "Brian…I'll deal with you afterward."

Everyone shook their heads, and you could feel the anger grow in the group.

There were thirteen of us left in the building; we were a ragtag bunch, and Benjamin was definitely our leader. In my mind, Robert would be second in command; he seemed to know what was happening and always had a lot of papers and files with him. He would point and pound his fists in the air when he was discussing this issue. After those two, the most vocal in the meeting were my neighbors Krystle and Nolan; though Krystle was the vocal one, Nolan just went along with her. He seemed like a cool guy, but you could tell who was in charge, and it seemed like she was up for a fight.

Benjamin was on the front steps of the building with everyone crowded around him. It was quite the sight, and it turned the heads of people walking by, and a couple of them even stopped to watch and listen; Benjamin loved it. He started by telling us that he will be getting the meeting space in the library for future meetings, which is free of cost; he also said that he has been in touch with our City Councillor, and our Member of Parliament, both of which said they were very interested in our story and situation.

Benjamin smiled as he said, "Where politicians go, the press will follow. This will be great press for the politicians. Affordable housing issues, evictions, and evil landlords—they'll love to support that, they'll get their face on TV, and hopefully they can draw attention to our problem."

It looked like Benjamin would push this as far as he could; he knew how to play the game, involve the press, and get all eyes on the city's affordable housing issue. He said he would contact ACORN, a community activism group that can help get more attention on the situation. He also said he was in contact with reporters from 'various outlets' that were very interested in this subject. Most importantly, Benjamin stated he had found some legal help through legal aid, a 'free' lawyer who works for the city. They take on residential issues at the Landlord and Tenant Board for low-income and affordable housing issues, especially instances like this. They will fight matters like this, trying to save and help protect 'affordable housing' from disappearing in the city.

Everyone nodded and agreed that was the best option. Benjamin then handed out all the information and encouraged us to sign up with the lawyer as soon as possible.

He finished by saying, "We will fight this as a united front. We will stand together, and we will stand strong."

There were a couple of 'cheers,' and everyone was clapping; Benjamin had his fist up over his head, and, if I'm not mistaken, I think I even heard him say 'Libertas!' at one point.

After the meeting, a couple of us stayed and hung around. It was me, Andrew, Benjamin, Robert, Krystle, Nolan, and Sarah, the squirrely girl from the first floor with four cats. Sarah was thirty-something years old; she had a revolving door of idiot boyfriends and was always playing catchup when the adults were speaking; she was a genuine annoyance.

Reggie, 'the three hundred pounder', had stuck around also, I thought he stayed around to talk, but he was only still there because getting back up those stairs was a real pain in the ass for him, and he needed a break.

Bob and 'Bo' also hung around, which wasn't unusual, as Bob was usually outside drinking and smoking. Bo was a one-hundred-and-fifty-pound boxer terrier that was in charge of Bob. Bob could hardly hang on to him, and when Bo wanted to go somewhere, Bob was going too. Andrew hated Bob and Bo; Andrew had a little teacup schnauzer, appropriately named 'Teacup,' who was nervous as hell, constantly shaking and barking. The poor dog was so scared of everything that it was even scared of cracks in the sidewalk, and of course, 'Bo' and 'Teacup' didn't get along.

Benjamin and Robert were talking; Robert said he was getting the business search done on the new owner and that 'his guy' would find out who owns and is behind this 'One-Four-Seven-Zero-Zero-Seven L.L.C..' He added, "Well, at least lawyers are good for something after all."

I started to like Robert. He really had disdain for the whole system and authority. When I mentioned politicians to him before, he would shake his head and rub his thumb and fingers together like he was rubbing money. Robert seemed to get it.

Robert said that when we get the business information, we'll know who exactly is responsible so we can identify a person. He was starting to get that white stuff in the corner of his mouth again as he explained, "We are going to expose the people behind this and put a face on our enemy."

I asked Benjamin about Brian's fate. He told me not to worry about it and said he'd get Denise to correct and reverse it. Benjamin reminded us to get to the community lawyer and sign with him as soon as possible so we can all be ready for the next letter. It was a grim reminder that the bullshit in our lives was going to go up tenfold, and the only thing we could do was get ready, ready for the next letter and ready for some dirty trickery. Benjamin told us to be prepared for letters about shutdowns, tests to the building, visitors coming to the building, entry to our units, and, most likely, another letter of eviction.

After the meeting, I had to meet Eric, a friend from work, for breakfast. Eric was cool and down to earth because all he wanted to do was make movies. We met while working background on various sets as 'extras,' and after getting to know each other, we started to work on some short movies and projects together. The good thing about Eric was that whenever we got together, we were always able to laugh, we shared the same sense of humor, and we saw the world in the same way, that it was mostly fucked up.

When I arrived at the restaurant, Eric was already there. I walked up to him from behind, jumped in the booth, and started complaining about what was happening with my building. Eric started to smile as I was ranting, and once I calmed down, he grinned away at me.

I said, "You're getting a kick out of this, aren't you? You enjoy seeing Bingham all worked up, don't you?

I looked at his twisted look of satisfaction and the joy of him seeing the pain in my eyes. I said, "Why do you just keep smiling? Why don't you record it? Record it so you have my pain at your disposal anytime."

I was starting to smile and laugh with Eric.

But he just sat there smiling. When I finished, he looked at me and said, "Don't worry, I am filming it. Man, this is a documentary waiting to be made. Seriously, this is a Michael Moore film. You were so passionate and angry; it was 'angry Bingham,' and it's good to see 'angry Bingham' come out. It's nice to see a little passion and fire from you for a change. You sounded so pissed off about this whole thing, yet you seem to have the realization in your eyes that you are fucked, and that you already know that you are going to have to move out sooner or later, don't you?"

I just shook my head and agreed, "Yup. I think it's just a matter of time."

"But…" Eric continued, "This is one hell of a story; it's a real social issue right now; it's happening everywhere. I'm serious; this is a documentary. Your eviction is going to happen one way or another, right? Whether you like it or not, so why not film the whole damn thing? It's like you said, either you or the 'bad guy' will win, so who will it be? I'd pay to see that."

He was getting excited about it now.

I laughed it off at first, but he persisted, "No, I'm serious. Let me film you and the people in the building going through this, and we'll make a documentary, shit, we just played out the storyline 'either you or bad guy is going to win,' and we already have a title, 'Renoviction,' this thing writes itself."

I thought about it for a moment and said, "So, you want to film me and document to the world the fact that I'm poor; that I'm being thrown out of my home; that my professional life sucks; that I can't afford my own legal counsel; and that I can't afford to own a home? You want to show everyone that I'm single, have no prospects, and that I don't have anywhere to go?"

He chuckled back and, in a matter-of-fact tone, said, "Yeah, would you mind?"

I grinned back and said, "What the hell. Apparently, I don't have anything else going on."

"Yeah?" Eric was shocked that I agreed, and he started planning right away.

We talked a little and decided we would do this; we were going to make 'Renoviction' together. Just talking to him, I started to get a little excited; I started feeling like I wanted to fight back. I knew I was 'right' in this fight, and I knew this eviction was for pure greed. Even though I was forced into this 'Renoviction' fight and had to deal with it, doing this project motivated me to get more involved; it turned the tables on my motivation. After talking with him, I found myself wanting to stand up for myself and for a group that couldn't stand up for themselves; we were the good guys.

Eric loved it, and he was getting excited. He scribbled some stuff down and said, "OK, keep me posted. I might stay at your place for a couple of days for this. I want to meet the neighbors, see the building, and see what we'll be shooting. We have to get you set up with a camera and lighting so you can film your sleepless nights and hopefully catch you crying thinking about being homeless. We'll record your anxiety throughout this; we'll film the meetings, the planning, and whatever might happen from start to finish. Let's see what happens to Bingham through this process. Let's see if there is any justice in this world and he ends up with a roof over his head or he ends up on the street giving hand jobs for food stamps."

I laughed and jokingly cried at the same time while replying, "Thanks man, real encouraging."

As we got up to leave, I noticed Eric grabbing another camera he had put up on the railing in the plants. I didn't even see that one, and that's when I knew we would get some good footage. It was reassuring to see Eric get pissed off with my situation.

As I explained it to him, he couldn't believe that I could ultimately be kicked out of my place through this process, and it be legal; the more I explained it, the madder he got, and the more he kept saying, "this is going to be some good shit, this is going to be some good shit..."

By the end of breakfast, we were both pumped and excited. I told him I wanted to give these guys a fight, and now we could do something we've both wanted to do for a long time: make a movie. I looked at him and said, "Don't worry. I won't disappoint you; I'll always keep you entertained, that I promise."

He smiled, laughed, and said, "Oh, I know you will, Bingham. I don't have any doubts about that."

Eric said he would devise an outline and think of where this thing could go.

I reminded him, "Hey man, this story goes where it goes; there are only two outcomes in this story: either I get to stay, or I have to go."

Even though I had to go through this eviction process, I was getting excited; if something good might come of it, that's all the better. And if I can actually get a documentary made about this, it might wake people up to what was going on.

I went back home, and I was pumped. I wanted to learn as much as I could, and I wanted to fight. I had been living in a haze for the last few years, and I finally had something that motivated me. I had just been going through the motions of life for the last couple of years, and nothing got me excited or my blood boiling. If I came across a situation of someone taking advantage of others,

I would just walk away and say, 'Yeah, that sucks, but that's not my fight.' Even at work, sometimes producers would bend the rules in their favor that would screw the actors if we were performing a stunt or getting upgraded with lines. We knew we should be getting paid extra, and when the other actors would want to fight, I would just say, yeah, well, good luck with that. I didn't think anything was worth fighting for anymore.

And that's a sad position to be in, not caring about anything; it's a horrible and crushing way for a strong, passionate person to live. You begin to fade away, you start to disappear into the background, and that's exactly what my life had literally become; I was a 'background performer' working as an 'extra.' I didn't care about anything; I would shrug my shoulders and say, 'It is what it is.'

But I hated that phrase, I was saying it way too often, and it was starting to piss me off. In my mind, whoever came up with that phrase was a loser who didn't care about anything. I hated it, but I was saying it like it was my mantra; it dawned on me that this was one of the reasons I wasn't happy with myself.

But the threat of getting evicted and making a movie about it gave me something more to care about; this was about injustice, and I started to see that it was bigger than evictions. 'Renoviction' was affecting senior citizens, young people, single families, the vulnerable, the disabled and the poor. The trickle-down effect from these 'Renovictions' was far-reaching, and over time, it affected social programs, hospitals, shelters, and the welfare system. People on fixed incomes, whose doctors and support systems were in the community, will be displaced and will need the system to help them find all those resources wherever they go. This affected vulnerable people who couldn't stand up for themselves and affected the community and all of society.

The sad part is that the city is partially responsible for it; they support this one owner when evicting an entire building of tenants. All the 'bylaw' people, all the 'inspectors,' and all the 'city resources' are at the owners' disposal to harass and evict us, and we're paying for it; it's our taxes that help him earn his profit. But what truly pissed me off was that people were being bullied and taken advantage of because of this bullshit, and I didn't like to be bullied. I decided it was time I stood up; I was ready.

Chapter 5

It had been a couple of weeks since our *tenant meeting on the street,* and things had been pretty quiet. There was nothing from the new owners or Benjamin. At eight in the morning, Eric called me, and it sounded like he had already had four espresso shots. He said we had to meet immediately and told me to put on a pot of coffee because he'd be at my place in ten minutes. I thought, 'What the hell is he thinking now?' Even though I was a little annoyed he was coming over at eight in the morning, it felt good to have Eric in my corner. I knew he wanted me to succeed and didn't want to see anything bad happen to me, but I also knew he was probably more interested in the Documentary than the outcome of my situation. Nonetheless, it felt good to know he was in my corner; it gave me motivation.

I had known Eric for about five years. I remember when we met—we were doing background on some cop show. He was playing a uniformed cop, and I was a detective. He stood out to me because he was five feet five inches tall and white, while all the other uniformed cops were at least six feet two inches tall, muscular, and Black. He had a great sense of humor about it; he joked that 'one of these things isn't like the others,' and since that day, we have been friends. He was a musician/aspiring filmmaker who didn't go to school for either, but was damn talented at both. He showed me a few shorts that he had made, and they were fantastic. One was a drama love story on a train, one was about a weird hoarder guy, and the other was a 'Terminator Fan Film' with over two million YouTube views.

After running into each other on different sets, we got to know each other and started working together on a couple of shorts. He was behind the camera, and I was in front of it. It was fun stuff. The only problem was his overenthusiasm. He could never stick to a script or a shooting schedule. Whenever we were shooting, he would always get 'new' ideas and want to add scenes or dialogue, but no one else on set knew what we were doing.

But his desire to make a documentary about my predicament was encouraging, and I knew he would put his heart into it. After all, it's a documentary; he couldn't write or add stuff because it was a doc-it was real life, so I assumed only reality would direct this project.

When he got to my place, I buzzed him in, and he was up the stairs, knocking at my door in just a few seconds with a bunch o f equipment bags.

I opened the door, he walked by me and asked, "Where's the coffee?"

I laughed and said, "Buddy, you just called and were here in a flash; how much caffeine have you had already?"

He said, "Not enough, Bingham. Let's go; we've got a lot to do."

I chuckled and said, "OK, so what's going on? Have you been thinking about the Documentary?"

He sat at my desk and pulled a bunch of papers out of his bag. There were paragraphs upon paragraphs and a lot of scribbling; there was writing in the margins, bullet points, numbered points, red, blue, and black ink notes, and little pictures drawn like he was already storyboarding.

I said, "Wow, you have been thinking about the documentary."

"Damn right," he said.

He sat down, and I got coffee for us. He spread out the pages of notes on the desk. Through all the scribbles, bullet points, and arrows, I could see he had broken the story into acts; I was impressed, "Wow, you've been busy."

Eric was focused and excited, "Yeah, I've been busy. The more I thought about this, the more excited I got, and the more excited I got, the more I wrote, and the more I wrote, the more excited I got. Whatever happens, this is a story that has to be told. It's a great story; it's the classic 'rich taking advantage of the poor,' 'good vs. evil,' the good and bad side of gentrification, morals, or the lack thereof; this is real people's lives being affected, it's got everything."

Smirking, I said, "I'm glad my hardship can bring you such joy."

Reassuringly, he said, "Come on, Bingham, lighten up; this will be great, but remember, you must open up. We want to see the human and emotional side to this; I want you to put all your feelings out there and express what you are going through every step of the process. I'm going to be around a lot, and I'm going to keep a camera here at all times; if you can't sleep and are nervous or anxious, I want to see it. I'm going to be around you so much that you'll get sick of me."

It started to sink in that I had to put myself, my life, and my feelings in front of the camera. I began to worry about it and felt a little sick, as the reality started to sink in, I became nervous and got butterflies.

He sat me at the desk and set up the camera and a ring light on a tripod; he said anytime I talk to someone on the phone, anytime I want to vent and vent to myself in the middle of the night, sit at the desk, and hit record.

We started to go over his outline and notes; everything looked good. He charted how he saw everything progressing, talking about how we would need to include statistics using charts, graphs, and visuals to keep people entertained and informed.

As we were talking, I saw a note that said, 'daydream' sequence, and I thought, 'oh shit, he's strayed from the script already.'

I asked him, "What's with the daydream thing? This is a documentary, right? There aren't any flashbacks in documentaries, are there? I thought this would be real life, you know, real events as they happened. I mean, aren't all documentaries actual events? Doesn't the story direct itself?"

He replied smiling, "Yeah, normally, but this one is going to have both reality and some cutaways to what Bingham would really like to be doing. Nothing big, just a couple of scripted, pre-filmed moments, you know, things that Bingham would like to see happen."

Begrudgingly, I had to ask him, "OK, explain one of them."

He started to grin; I knew that grin; he was up to something.

He leaned back, raised his hands in exclamation, and said, "Imagine, if you will."

Oh shit, I knew I was in trouble with those words.

He continued, "OK, one of them is a moment of no return; it's the finale; you end up getting so frustrated and tired of the system that you wish you could just blow up the building or kill the owner and end the whole situation. I'm not sure yet, something big, something illegal, and something that gets a lot of attention; we'll figure it out as we go."

We both laughed; I smiled, shook my head, and said, "Well, you're the director; I'll leave that to you; I'll just worry about trying not to get thrown out."

We drank coffee and talked for over an hour. We discussed potential events, meetings, and confrontations that might take place. Eric was getting passionate about it and had thought it out thoroughly.

I stopped smiling, looked at him, and said, "Oh yeah, there's a new enemy in the mix."

Eric looked at me, smiled, and said, "Looking at the expression on your face, this is going to be good. Put on some more coffee, and we'll talk about that."

I poured more coffee, and as Eric was sipping, he leaned in and excitedly said, "OK, tell me about the new 'villain'." So far, we have the new building owner and the building management company doing the owners' dirty work; who else is there? City Inspectors? Politicians? Yeah, I could see the politicians being dirty as shit. Is it the Landlord and Tenant Board? I'm sure they're slimy as shit, as well; please tell."

I sipped my coffee and explained the 'Alliance of Commercial Housing Rentals' and my old friend Kerwin Cummings. Eric's face lit up as I told the story, and he smiled ear to ear.

After my rant, Eric kept asking, "And you're friends with this guy? You're friends with this guy?" He laughed and said, "I told you, Bingham, this story writes itself. This will be awesome, but promise me something; promise me you don't call this guy until we figure out how we will play this. Do you think he'd be able to help you, or will he just ignore you? He is the lobbyist, after all, so we know he is definitely on the owner's side, but how do you think he'll be with you? Wow, this is great. What a plot twist! Come on, what are the odds you know one of the people at the top who is directly involved with this? You were born for this role, Bingham; everything is getting you more involved in this; the universe is telling you that this is your fight, this is your fight, Bingham!"

Eric was on a tear and pretty excited about our new antagonist. He couldn't contain himself. He was so excited that I also started getting excited about the fight. When I finished telling him about the new plot twist, Eric was practically drooling.

As we sat and had even more coffee, Eric started to go over some logistics for the Documentary. He pulled out some forms and said they were for the other tenants and anyone else who would appear on camera.

He didn't give me a chance to say anything and continued, "I have been reading a lot and talking to a few people at work about documentaries, and they sent me some good info. There are a ton of websites about doc's detailing what to and what not to do, some really good stuff. There's a bunch of paperwork to get ready, and the first thing we have to do is get everyone in the building on board for it; we need everyone to sign a release before they talk to us on camera; that will be your job. And when you are at work, talk to as many people as you can; you never know who will want to help or who will have some knowledge about making these things."

I nodded and agreed, "I get it. And I agree, the more eyes we have on this situation, the better. But I'm not sure how releases are going to go over with some of the people in this building; I don't think the younger people will have a problem, but I think there might be some pushback with a couple of the old timers, but I'll do my best."

Just as we were going over the paperwork, we heard someone knocking. It was so loud that we thought it was my door, but it was Robert's.

I went to see what was up, but Eric said, "Hold on, let me grab the camera and record just in case."

Eric stood back as I opened the door, and I saw Benjamin knocking on Roberts's door.

I said, "Hey Benjamin, it was so loud, I thought you were knocking on my door; sorry, I won't bug you guys."

He was holding a stack of papers and said, "No, you should stay; you need to hear this as well."

As he said that, Robert opened his door. I looked back at Eric, who was recording and he gave me a little thumbs-up.

Benjamin started by saying, "I wanted to give you some of the information and contact details I've come across and what I've been working on."

He gave Robert the stack of papers and passed me a printout. It had names, phone numbers, and notes about each contact person. I was impressed; Benjamin had done some real work so far.

"Thank you, Benjamin. It looks like you have done a lot of work. This looks great." You could tell Robert was impressed.

Benjamin continued, "There's more guys, and you aren't going to be thanking me after this."

Robert and I looked at each other, not expecting what was coming next.

Benjamin's head dropped, and his eyes went to the carpet, "I'm leaving, I'm moving. My girlfriend got a job in Montreal, and I've decided to go with her."

As he spoke, the energy got sucked out of all of us. I could tell Benjamin was upset.

He continued, "The timing is just coincidental, and it's kind of lucky for us since we got some money from the new owner. This came out of nowhere, but it's what's best for us."

We agreed and couldn't argue with that; everyone needs to look out for themselves, and it was our bad luck that he was leaving. We needed Benjamin, but he had to do what was best for Benjamin.

He wasn't his usual high-energy self, and he seemed defeated as he explained, "My girlfriend just got the news of moving to Montreal about a week ago, and the owner offered me another buyout to leave the building."

As he spoke, his energy and anger started to return. "You know I was ready to fight, and I feel bad that I'm bailing on you guys, but unfortunately, it's what I have to do. I've given you all the notes with the names and phone numbers of people I have spoken with."

I could tell he didn't want to stop fighting. I could tell he was really into it, almost like he got off on it.

He continued, "Hey Brent, I came to Robert because I've spoken with him the most, and he seemed most dedicated to the fight. You asked good questions, and you seem to be pretty concerned. I think you and Robert would be good to take the lead."

I thanked him and thought, 'Yup, everyone is in it for themselves. They may say we're all in this together, but when it comes down to it, people only look out for themselves. 'We're all in this together?' My ass, we are. The one guy I thought would go the distance, the one guy I thought I would see chained to the building as the wrecking ball swung, and the one guy I thought would be our 'rock' bailed as soon as it worked out for him.

Robert made a good point, "I never got a buyout option after the tenants meeting," he said, looking over at me.

I shook my head, "Nope. I didn't get anything."

He continued, "So, if we didn't receive an offer, it looks like you were the only one to receive one, and good for you for getting one, but it looks like they singled you out. It looks like they went after the leader; they went after the strong one."

Robert looked at me and pursed his lips as he said, "These guys don't mess around."

I looked at Benjamin and asked him straight up, "How much did they offer you, Benjamin?"

He answered precisely what was wrong with the world today, "I can't tell you; I signed an NDA. I can't tell you a thing. I can't even talk about this situation or anything about the building ever again."

An NDA is a 'Non-Disclosure Agreement.' It's signed for confidentiality, sometimes to protect trade secrets or to protect companies' operating procedures, but most often they are used to silence people when something terrible has taken place. The victim or whistleblower will accept a 'payoff' and sign an NDA to keep their silence. It's the epitome of 'looking out for yourself'; NDAs only serve two parties: the guilty (the payor) and the victim (the payee). It's why companies still poison and why rapists keep raping, the most notable people to sign NDAs that come to mind are Harvey Weinstein and any actress that has starred in one of his movies, and most recently, the Diddy party attendees. They are never signed in the public's best interest.

But Robert and I were very curious. We both wondered if they offered Benjamin more than they offered us because he was the leader.

I asked again, "Come on, Benjamin, between us, what did they offer you?"

He wouldn't answer, but you could tell he was dying to tell us and trying to think of a way he could tell us without 'telling us.'

After a few seconds, he winked and said, "OK, guys, I'm going to go; you can ask me how much they offered me, and when you are right, I'm just going to walk away."

You didn't need to be the F.B.I. to figure out what he was doing; he wanted to tell us so badly, but being such a stickler for the rules, he wouldn't.

Robert started by asking, "Two thousand?"

Benjamin just stood there with his arms crossed.

I asked, "Three, four?" Benjamin just rolled his eyes.

I said, "Five thousand?"

That's when Benjamin smiled, waved goodbye, and started walking down the stairs.

I said, "Thanks, Benjamin, and don't worry, we won't tell anybody."

He looked back up and gave us the thumbs-up sign. I never spoke to or saw Benjamin ever again.

I looked at Eric back in the apartment, "Did you get all that?"

He nodded and smiled.

I said to Eric in a mocking tone, "Shit, Benjamin, you should've looked around before you broke your NDA, verbally or not. We all have to do what's best for ourselves, right?"

Robert went back into his apartment and motioned for us to come in.

We went in, and I said, "I wasn't expecting that. I thought Benjamin would be the last one to go, not the first. What the hell are we going to do now? Who's going to pick up the slack for Benjamin?"

We were both feeling a little defeated.

Robert looked at Eric, asked who he was and why he was filming.

The cat was out of the bag, so I guess now was the best time to tell Robert about the documentary. I introduced Eric to Robert. I said he's a friend from work who's an aspiring filmmaker and wants to help us with our predicament.

I continued to explain to Robert, "When I was 'venting' and explaining our situation to him, his first response was that this was a Michael Moore film just waiting to be made. We talked and agreed that this Documentary could help us and that it might actually be watched."

I explained to him what we had in mind, "he'll be following me through this process from beginning to end, and it'll simply be called 'Renoviction.'"

Robert's reply surprised me. He was such a private guy that I didn't think he would be into it, but he loved it. He agreed that this is a movie people need to see to make them aware of what is happening in their cities and to highlight how affordable housing is disappearing. When I mentioned the release form to sign, he didn't have a problem with it, which made me think that people might be interested in this movie after all.

Eric was still standing back, filming me and Robert as we discussed what we had to do now that Benjamin was gone. We looked over the package Benjamin gave us and saw that he's already done a lot of work. He had already booked the meeting space at the library once a month for our tenant meetings; he had been in touch with our local politicians; and he's been in touch with reporters and had notes from all of the conversations; he had the community lawyers name who was taking our case and had a checklist with everyone's name in the building on it.

I was disappointed with Benjamin's exit and explained to Robert, "Robert, I don't mind taking on more responsibility. I kind of have to with the documentary, but I don't want to lead the charge for these people. I'll fight for what I believe is right, but I don't want to be responsible for other people's lives, and I don't want to tell the other tenants what to do. I'll do what I feel needs to be done, but I'm not going to ask these people to follow or even listen to me. I've been thrown under the bus too many times, and I know how deep loyalty truly runs. Short of that, I'll be a good little foot soldier and do everything to help our cause, but don't ask me to lead."

He agreed and said, "OK, Brent, I understand. I'll be the ringleader of this ragtag bunch. I don't mind the fight, and I've known these people longer than you. I might not be as loud and angry as Benjamin, but I can take the lead."

I laughed and said, "Don't worry, Robert, I don't think anyone can be as loud and angry as Benjamin. So, what do you want me to do?"

Right away, he said, "Start with Acorn. Can you reach out to them? Let them know what's happening and find out how to get them involved. We still have a couple of weeks until the tenants' meeting, so we have some time. Also, go see the community lawyer and get signed up as soon as possible, and don't forget to take Michael Moore with you wherever you go."

He winked and smiled at Eric, who gave him a chuckle and a wave from behind the camera.

We left Robert's apartment, Eric headed home, and I went to the computer immediately. I googled 'Acorn Community Group Toronto,' and I wasn't impressed when I found their website. There wasn't much to it; it was only two pages. It contained a brief description and a couple of pictures, and it only had one person listed on the website: Jordan Rickman, President of Acorn Canada, and no other employees were listed. The pictures were of a community event with most of the people wearing red 'Acorn Canada' shirts, and Jordan wasn't pictured in any of them.

I began reading a few articles and was getting mixed emotions about them. I learned that when a neighborhood had issues with developers, crime, or businesses polluting, Acorn would suddenly appear, mobilize the community, have some protests or rallies, and make their presence known at city hall. But as quickly as they began to protest an issue, they were gone just as quickly. It seems their most recent conquest was protesting and fighting against 'The Loan Shop,' a predatory payday loan lender that was proliferating poor neighborhoods and charging exorbitant interest rates that were taking advantage of the poor and unbankable population. Now, they were bringing attention to the affordable housing crisis and illegal evictions.

After reading about them, I had concerns and doubts that they would be able to help. I Googled their office address, and when I saw it, I wasn't impressed. It was above an abandoned store on the Danforth, the same street 'the palace' was on. The picture from Google Earth didn't even show a sign on the building that indicated they were there, but according to their website, it was their current address.

I called Eric to see if he was available to go down and check them out.

He was ecstatic. "You mean hunt someone down in their office? Hell yeah. I'll try to get someone for 'sound' with a big boom mic. Text me the address, and I'll meet you there half an hour before. Let me start planning. I'll see you tomorrow."

Eric was jazzed up about this.

Chapter 6

The following day, I met Eric at a parking lot near the Acorn office. He wired me up for sound and apologized for not getting a sound guy. When we got to their office, neither of us was impressed. They were located above a store that looked like it had been empty for years, and there were no signs indicating anyone was even there. The mailbox was full and hadn't been cleared out, and the only thing that proved that Acorn was here was all the mail addressed to them. Seeing that, I assumed they were gone, and thought the door would be locked, but surprisingly, it was open.

I opened the door and yelled up the stairs, "Hello? Hello?" There was no reply. I started up the stairs and kept yelling, but there was no answer. As I got to the top of the stairs, I heard a couple of voices behind a closed door at the end of the hallway.

I decided I would nose around until someone came out. The building was old and rundown. The floors squeaked with every step, the railing was wobbly, and the walls looked like they hadn't been painted since the place was built. Protest posters covered the walls. It looked exactly like a place that an activist group would occupy. The rent was probably cheap and didn't require any maintenance; the office was a mess and poorly organized. Picket signs, placards, and posters were strewn about everywhere with no sense of organization, and there were stacks of phone books everywhere.

Eric couldn't help himself and said, "Phone books? Who the hell needs phone books? And where the hell do you even get phone books these days?"

The picket signs were everywhere—in every room, on top of, behind, and leaning against every piece of furniture. All of them were protesting 'The Loan Shop,' evidence of their last crusade. I flipped through a stack of the signs and said to Eric, "Well, what do you know? Look at this." I pulled a sign out and faced him.

He read it out loud, "The Loan Shop Kerwin Cummings Must Be Stopped."

He moved the camera to catch all of the sign and said, "damn, this guy gets around."

As we walked around the office, Eric followed a few feet behind. I pushed open some doors and peeked in; it was most of the same: messy rooms with old wooden tables, rundown chairs, filing cabinets that looked like they were from the sixties, and carpets that were even older. But one room I looked in seemed oddly out of place; it didn't look like any of the other rooms; it looked modern; the furniture was chrome and silver; it had nice swivel ergonomic office chairs, and whiteboards were all over the walls.

But what I noticed the most was the phones on the tables. There must have been at least a dozen of them; it looked like your regular 'boiler room' setup. As I glanced in, I noticed that all the writing on the whiteboards was regarding membership targets, donation goals, and closing percentages.

And there it was.

These guys are in the business of selling memberships and asking for donations using social causes and people's fights and plights as their product.

I shook my head and asked Eric, "Are there any honest people out there just trying to help? Well, at least we know what they're all about, so let's see if we can use any of this to our advantage."

Just as I closed the 'boiler room' door, a casually dressed, professional-looking guy came out of the office with the voices and asked, "Can I help you?"

He was smiling and walking towards me, but as he looked past my shoulder and saw Eric with the camera and light, his demeanor immediately changed, and his tone wasn't so friendly. "Excuse me, why are you filming? Can you shut that off, please?"

I wanted to get some of this on film, and I figured he wouldn't mind the camera rolling. I put on my happiest face and said, "Hi, I'm Brent Bingham, and I'm being 'Renovicted.'

He stepped between me and the door and closed it; he said, "I'm Jordan Rickman, President of Acorn." He looked at the camera and asked, "I'm sorry, but can you please ask your friend to turn off the camera?"

Eric kept it going.

I explained to him, "Jordan, I'm getting 'Renovicted,' and we're making a documentary about it; I'm hoping Acorn can help me and my building and hopefully be a part of it."

"I appreciate that, and I'm sure it won't be a problem, but up here for now, would you mind if we talk off-camera." I could tell from his tone he was pretty adamant about it.

I looked at Eric, told him to shut it down, and apologized to Jordan. "I'm sorry, Jordan. I didn't mean to get off on the wrong foot with you."

He assured me it wouldn't be a problem, and he took us into the room he came from. Sitting at the table was a young guy no older than thirty years old, and if I hadn't seen him indoors, I would have taken him for homeless. He was unshaven, his hair matted and oily, and he wore tattered clothes. It looked like he hadn't showered for about a week.

He stood and said, "Hi, I'm Kyle, the Community Outreach Organizer."

This didn't impress or give me any sense of confidence in these guys at all. I sat down and said, "Well, guys, I'm getting evicted, or more specifically, I'm being 'Renovicted.' I had no idea what that meant a month ago, but apparently, it's a thing."

Jordan explained, "Yes, it's the plight of the Toronto rental market, and it's the reason affordable housing is disappearing at record rates. Landlords, developers, and speculators know how to do this without repercussions. They have realized that even if they get caught evicting people illegally, the fines and penalties are so minimal that it's just another line on the balance sheet, an inconsequential line at that. Illegally evicting people has become just another cost of doing business."

I wanted to see how these guys explained themselves, so I asked, "How can you help me? What are you guys, and what can you do in my case?"

He cleared his throat, and with a salesman's smile, he said, "Well, Brent, thanks for asking that."

Oh god, he was answering like a politician, and I had a feeling his next words would be exactly what it would say in a pamphlet.

I was right. He regurgitated their mission statement: "We are a community- based activism group that gives a voice to its membership that otherwise wouldn't have one against issues that affect their community."

I thought, yup, right out of a pamphlet.

"Membership? So, I have to be a member for you to stand up for me?"

There it was, the money-making aspect of their grift. Yes, I understand everybody has to eat, and nobody does anything for free, but to make money off this kind of thing? I guess a grifter's hustle never stops.

He explained the membership as a good thing, "Well, yes and no, Brent. We fight for the community, but it is our membership that drives the issues, and as a member, when you have a problem, we all have that problem. And right now, evictions and 'Renovictions' are a huge problem for our membership and the community."

I agreed with him, "Yeah, apparently, they are."

I thought I'd change the subject a little; I looked around the room at the signs and asked, "So, what's with all the signs protesting 'The Loan Shop'?"

Jordan leaned back and sighed, "They're predatory lenders who you mostly see in poorer neighborhoods; a few years ago, they were lobbying the government for legislation to be able to change the fee structures, terms, advertising rules, and a lot of other changes that would hurt the consumer. They lobbied, they won, and corrupt legislation was passed. It's why you are seeing an onslaught of changes in that industry. Now, you see advertising everywhere and locations on every corner in lower-income neighborhoods. With the changes, they can now charge usury interest rates and service fees, making it almost impossible for people to get out from under their original loans. It's quite disgusting; the laws and regulations they were able to enact crushed the consumer. They must have greased the politicians extremely well because what happened was a travesty. What they did guaranteed that if you couldn't pay a loan back in full on time, you'd never get out from under it; you'd constantly be paying off the interest and inflated service fees, never actually reducing the principal. The practice of payday loans is even worse than credit card rates."

I shook my head in disgust. "You know, it's funny. When I was faced with this 'Renoviction,' I started investigating and researching the housing market, specifically the rental industry, and I came across 'The Alliance of Commercial Housing Rentals.' Are you aware of these guys?"

Jordan chuckled, "Oh, we're aware."

I was glad he knew them; it showed me they were in touch with what was really affecting the rental market.

I continued, "When I went through the Alliance's website, I came across their President, and lo and behold, he's a friend of mine from high school."

Jordan leaned forward in his chair, removed his glasses, and said in disbelief, "You went to school with Kerwin Cummings? That could be of some interest to us."

"I'm sure it could be," I said, grinning back. "The last time I ran into him was at a funeral for one of our friends' mother a few years back. I was impressed with him because, over the years, I would see him in the news with Premiers and even with the Prime Minister. While we were milling about, I asked him about being in politics, and he explained that he wasn't a politician; he just used to work for them, and now he was a lobbyist. Now, I know what that means, and I asked him who he lobbied for, and his reply disappointed me; he said after politics, he first worked with the Automobile Insurance Industry and that he was now with 'The Loan Shop,' and this was almost ten years ago."

The boys from Acorn were hanging on every word, and I continued, "I didn't mince words with him. I told him he should be using his powers for good. At this point, I had lost all respect for him and said, come on, Kerwin, you should be using your smart brain to help society, not screw it."

Jordan was enthralled with what I was saying, and this is where I started to go off on a tangent, "Now that I looked back at his employment history, it all makes sense. He lobbied for the insurance industry; now, Canadians are getting ripped off by paying some of the highest insurance rates in North America. Then he went to 'The Loan Shop,' the predatory lending industry of 'payday loans,' an industry that completely takes advantage and rips off the vulnerable and unbankable. And now he's with Commercial Landlords? An industry that is causing an affordable housing crisis, and he has his hands in this, too? This guy is a real 'piece of work.' Here's a guy who has used his previous connections in politics to facilitate money-changing hands for legislation being changed, all against the best interest of society and just for the benefit of a few rich pricks and some politicians. This guy is truly an enemy of the people. Our political system has been hijacked, and this guy and people like him are largely responsible; people can't pay their bills, they are paycheck to paycheck, and are getting thrown out of their homes because of asshole lobbyists like this and greedy, self-serving politicians with their hands out, it's horrible."

Jordan agreed with me and was very intrigued. He saw that I was passionate, knew I was pissed off, and knew I could get to Kerwin; what he didn't know yet, was that I was ready to fight tooth and nail to expose this morally corrupt ex-friend lobbyist. I asked Jordan how we proceed and what we need to do to get started.

"First," he said, "let's get you signed up as a member; then we'll get you in touch with a group facing this issue that have already started to organize. Then we'll get people into your neighborhood and start a 'door knocking' campaign; we'll blanket your neighborhood with members to knock on doors and make your neighbors aware that you are being evicted by a new landlord just for the sake of profit. We'll get local city Councillors and politicians, we'll talk to the Press, and then we'll have a rally at your building. We can do a few things, but they don't happen fast, and we need people to get involved and start organizing. Can we count on you?"

Before I answered, I asked, "Well, all those things are good, but what does all that actually accomplish?"

"Brent, the best we can do is raise awareness and hopefully get such a groundswell that politicians will start to change the laws and the system."

I looked down and said, "I don't see much faith in that, but I'm up for a good fight; I just really want to find out who is doing this to me and expose them as the greedy pricks they are. I want to make their family, their wives, their kids, their friends, and everyone they know aware that this is how they make their living, evicting poor people out onto the street, just so they can make a buck."

I pulled out my credit card and said, "Make me a member; I'm in."

Jordan explained that there was a large contingent of Acorn members going through this all over the city; he told me of a meeting coming up on the weekend and that, as a member, I am more than welcome to attend. He asked if I could help get others from the building to sign up and said once the building was 'signed up,' they'll make Three-Ninety-One Empire Avenue one of their causes.

I was curious about the documentary; I asked him if 'Acorn' would like to be a part of it, and his answer surprised me; he flat out said no. He said that he didn't want any official of 'Acorn' to take part or appear on camera; he wouldn't even agree to an on-camera interview to discuss the affordable housing crisis that was taking place. I found this very odd as I wondered why they wouldn't want any exposure for their cause. He gave me a stack of sign-up forms, and we were on our way.

When we got back to the car, Eric put the camera down and removed my wire. After he did that, he unzipped his jacket and started smiling. I saw that he had a hidden camera inside his jacket.

I asked him, "Were you rolling the whole time?"

He laughed and said, "Smile, you've been punked!'

Chapter 7

It was our first tenant meeting at the library and our first meeting without Benjamin. I wondered how people would react and if anyone would want to take the reins and lead the group. I hadn't spoken to Robert at all, but he emailed me a few times letting me know his progress; he was very detail-oriented in his emails or his 'correspondences' as he would call them. I was learning that he really liked to write his correspondences, they were always very detailed, and very elaborate. It wouldn't be unheard of to get emails that were a few pages long from him; Robert really liked writing emails, which I'm sure will be good for us.

He wrote, 'Brent, if we don't have a chance to talk before the meeting, I would like to get you up to speed with events and actions that have taken place at the building.' He started by saying, 'It's time to start complaining and reporting every infraction we come across in the building.' He said he had already had to chase a couple of surveyors out who didn't have any ID or paperwork to be in the building.'

He detailed all the phone calls and all the emails he had sent and received, and he wrote his opinions of all the assistants, personal aides, and everyone he spoke to from each office. He had comments like, 'sounds pompous on the phone' or 'disrespectful tone'; he even scored them based on whether they would be on our side or not. I didn't reply to him with as much detail; all I had to tell him was that I was able to meet with 'Acorn' and that they were interested.

I felt bad; I was unsure what to write back to him. He wrote pages surmising everything, and I only wrote a few lines in reply. It was one of the reasons why I wanted to avoid getting too involved with the group; I wasn't looking to meet any new friends or get in on any email chains.

It was an hour before the meeting when Robert knocked on my door. I was ready and also a little surprised—I had expected him a lot earlier. He came in, and after a little small talk, he asked if we could review what had taken place. He was curious to hear what Acorn had to say.

"Yes, of course," I motioned to the desk, and we sat in our usual chairs. He started pulling out some notes and forms he had gathered, and I pulled out the forms 'Acorn' had given me to sign people up.

"Robert, this is why I wish Benjamin didn't leave; this is his kind of thing, not mine. I'm not the emailing type." I looked at Robert's binder and said, "But it looks like you have the 'memos' and emails pretty well organized."

Robert smirked and said, "Don't worry about documenting anything. If you send it to me, there's a copy."

I was relieved; there was no way I'd be the guy to coordinate all the emails or paperwork. He had already talked to a couple of reporters willing to hear our story and left messages with a few others. The last thing he said was that he spoke to Krystle and Nolan, who were willing to get more involved and are coordinating with the community lawyer.

I guess it was my turn to 'report' now, "that's good news about Nolan and Krystle. I finally met with 'Acorn,' and it was interesting. I met Jordan Rickman, who is President, and his 'Community Organizer,' Kyle. From what I gather, 'Acorn Canada' is just the two of them. They said they already have groups organizing for 'Renoviction' and that they'll coordinate with us to help bring more attention to our problem when the building signs up."

I continued to explain how Acorn operates and how we get them involved; I said, "In order for them to listen to you and for you to have a voice with them, you have to be a member. They gave me information sheets and sign-up forms for the people in the building, which cost ten dollars a month. When you are a member, you can attend monthly meetings and get other 'Community Helpers' to help organize and rally in your neighborhood. I don't know, but maybe we can get a T-shirt from them too. They can't make it to tonight's tenants meeting but said they will be at the next one. Once a few more of us are signed up, they'll come around the building to raise awareness; I joined, so they are getting involved. I don't know if everyone needs to sign up, but I guess the more that do, the better it will be. I mean, the more money 'Acorn' can make from the cause of Three-Ninety-One Empire Avenue, the more attention they'll give us. We won't raise as much money as cancer, but I'm sure they'll be able to make a few bucks off of our cause."

Robert chuckled and said, "I love your optimism, Brent; it seems we share the same outlook."

Just as Robert spoke, Eric walked in and didn't even knock.

I asked him, "How did you get in?"

He didn't bother to hide it and was grinning away, "I made myself a copy of your key; I figured it would just be easier this way."

I shook my head, looked at Robert, and gave him a 'yup, that's Eric' look.

Eric was excited to see us talking and walked straight to the computer setup to check things out. "Hi Robert, it's good to see you again. Bingham, way to go—you turned everything on! You've been able to record some stuff too, right on."

We sat and talked for a bit as Eric got ready and Robert briefed us on events. Before we left, Eric wired me for sound so he could record the meeting and any conversations I might have. The meeting was at the library just five minutes down the street, and as we walked, Eric jumped out in front and started recording.

I wanted to make sure that Robert was happy assuming the role of our leader, so I had to ask him, "Hey Robert, before we get in there, I just wanted to make sure you are okay about taking the lead and becoming our 'de facto' leader for the cause now that Benjamin is gone."

Robert liked seeing Eric film, and you could tell he played it up a bit when we were rolling; you could see the difference between 'natural Robert' and 'when the camera is rolling Robert.' When the camera was rolling, he stretched out everything he had to say; sometimes, you never knew if he was done speaking or if he was taking a dramatic pause; over time, it would be an inside joke between me and Eric of whether he should cut or keep filming when Robert was speaking. The funny thing was when you were talking to Robert off-camera, he spoke a hundred miles an hour, but on camera, it was quite the opposite.

Robert said, "It's OK, Brent, I don't mind stepping into Benjamin's position. These guys have pissed me off, and I'm not going anywhere. I'll fight until the end; I have nowhere to go. I'm too old to start looking for a place now, and I'm going to wait until they throw my ass out. But I hope you'll help; I hope you will stay to the end, and if you are, I hope you'll fight."

I reassured Robert, "I'm just like you. I've got nowhere to go, and I'm not going anywhere until the wrecking ball makes me."

He smiled at that, and I continued, "I won't be able to afford to live in Toronto anymore; anywhere I go will be out of the city. Maybe if I want to live in a shitty studio apartment in a shitty part of town, I could afford Toronto, but who wants to pay two thousand dollars a month on something like that."

I continued, "Robert, I'm making the documentary; I want to document this whole process. I will investigate and learn as much as I can about this, and I want to expose how things are so out of control and how landlords are taking advantage of tenants. I think you'll be happy to see that I'm willing to fight now more than ever. I've been a little bored with my life lately; this will give me something to do; might as well do this, right?"

I looked and winked at Eric off-camera; in return, he flipped me the middle finger. I smiled and continued, "I'll announce the documentary to the group tonight at the meeting, and I've got forms for everyone to sign. It's a simple one-page release that says we can use your image in the movie. We won't film them if they don't want to do it. And Robert, please don't worry; I'm not here to argue with anyone or screw up our 'case,' if they don't want to do it, no problem, I won't involve them. But I hope I have your support for it. So far, we have gotten great feedback about it. Everyone loves the idea, and everyone says the more eyes on this, the better, right?"

Roberts' reply reassured me: "I support it, but you know the people in the building. Some of them might have a problem with it. I'm sure everything will be fine, but we'll find out soon enough."

I nodded and agreed, "Also, I'll explain 'Acorn' tonight and give everyone the forms. Other than that, that's all I need to say. Unless you want to tell them about 'Acorn,' I have no problem. Either way, I won't talk for long, and don't worry, I'll just sit there until you cue me."

When we arrived at the library, we didn't know where to go. The librarian directed us downstairs to the 'Community Room.' Krystle, Nolan, Bob, and old Brian had already arrived. We started saying hello, and Eric went straight to a chair at the back of the room, with everyone's eyes following him.

I said, "Oh, hey folks, that's Eric."

Eric gave a little wave, and I added, "Uh, he's with me."

Most of the tenants were starting to arrive, and I was at the back of the room with Eric. I saw Robert motioning for me to sit with him at the front of the room, but I didn't want to be upfront and center; I didn't want the tenants looking up to me as one of the leaders or coming to me for advice and information. One of the reasons I loved being an 'extra' was for the very fact that I had no responsibility for anyone else. I was the only one I had to look after, and I was the only one I had to worry about. I didn't want anyone to depend on me, and I didn't want to depend on anyone, either. But at this point, and how things were working out, I had no choice. I got up to sit at the front of the room and sat beside Nolan and Krystle; I looked over at Eric, flipped him the finger, and started to get ready for the meeting.

Robert stood up and said, "It looks like everyone is here except Reggie and Tommy; maybe they're not coming, we'll get started anyways."

I looked at everyone around the table. I knew most of the people by name, and I recognized the others from around the building and neighborhood. We were all from different walks of life, but everyone here was getting screwed by a system none of us knew anything about; we didn't even know who we were fighting against. Looking around, I started to get a little more pissed off.

Robert started by welcoming everyone and saying that there had been no new eviction letters from the landlord and that we were still at the five-hundred-dollar buyout offer. Robert couldn't contain his laughter as he said, "And, oh yeah, that will expire at the end of the month."

Everyone nodded in agreement, and a few started laughing.

Robert continued, "But we have some unexpected news."

People's heads started looking around quizzically at each other, and Bob yelled, "Where's Benjamin? Shouldn't we wait for Benjamin to start the meeting?"

People started agreeing and asking each other where Benjamin was.

Robert raised his hands to stop and calm everyone down and said, "Yes, this is about Benjamin, so please listen up. Unfortunately, Benjamin is moving out."

There were gasps and swearing, and people looked around the room; it looked like something right out of a movie.

Bob was the first to ask, "So what happened to Benjamin? I didn't like him, but we needed him. How much did they offer him? Ten thousand? Twenty thousand?"

Robert continued, "Benjamin said that it came up unexpectedly and at the last minute; his girlfriend is being transferred to Montreal for work, and he's going with her. He wanted me to tell all of you that he's sorry that he can't stay to see this fight through to the end. He wishes he could say more, but he did take the buyout, and with the buyout comes an NDA. Benjamin had to sign a Non-Disclosure Agreement, so he can't talk about any part of the agreement; we will never know how much they paid him to leave and to keep quiet."

I looked at Robert and then around the room at everyone. I wondered what they would say if they found out Benjamin got five thousand dollars. Would that be enough for one of them, some of them, or all of them to leave? Everyone has a price, and I wondered what theirs was. Which then made me wonder, what was mine?

There started to be a lot of talk amongst everyone, and I heard people saying, "Five, ten, Twenty Thousand?"

Robert shushed everyone down and told them to all listen up. He explained, "I don't know how much they offered Benjamin to leave, but I'm sure it's not as high as that; it just happened to be good timing for him. We have no idea how much they offered him, and don't worry, we asked."

He glanced at me and kept talking, "But he wouldn't tell us; he signed an NDA, so we're never going to know how much he got."

Bob, surprisingly, was the most vocal, and he was pretty succinct for a drunk guy; it seems all the action with the building was waking him up, and apparently, he was getting a bit feisty, "Ah, this is bullshit; do you really think Benjamin is moving to Montreal or is he just moving out of here and in with his girlfriend? You don't think he just took the money and ran? Do you think this is all coincidental? How do you know he didn't just sell out?"

I started to like Bob; he didn't hold back.

Robert glanced at me, and I looked at him in agreement; I shrugged the 'I don't have a clue' motion, and he understood immediately. It was true; how do we know what happened? Can we take Benjamin at his word now that there was money to be made? Maybe he didn't get five thousand; maybe that's why he felt comfortable telling us five when it was higher. Either way, it was another reaffirmation that everyone is in it for themselves. I didn't know who or what to believe, and I'll bet he got more than five thousand dollars wherever he went.

Robert raised his hands, saying, "Quiet everyone, quiet, please. There's nothing we can do; he's gone. He gave me all the information and all the work he's done. I'm willing to coordinate everything and be the point man on this, your de facto leader if you will."

Old man Brian yelled out, "Why you? What makes you think that you are our leader? Maybe someone else wants to do it."

Robert's reply was straight to the point, "Well, Benjamin knocked at my door with a bunch of papers and said he was leaving. He felt I would be the best person to handle all this and asked if I wouldn't mind taking on the work he had done up until now."

If you didn't know Robert, you would have thought he was getting mad, but he was just being passionate. "I didn't ask for this. I would rather not do it, but I don't have a choice. If any of you would like to be 'our leader,' please, by all means. Brian, do you want to do it?"

He looked around the room, and it was silent; no one said a thing.

Brian replied with a laugh and said, "OK, I just wanted to make sure."

The room laughed after Brian's comment, and Robert's color started to get a little less red.

He said, "OK folks, listen, we are all in this together; I'm not the leader; I'll just coordinate what's happening and ensure everyone is in the loop. Benjamin has already done a lot of work; he got the meeting place here for us tonight, he has arranged for the community lawyer to represent us all, and he has reached out to some of the politicians already. So, we have to run with what he's done. Tonight, we'll talk about our strategy, the community lawyer, the Acorn Community Group, Politicians, and the Press. First, Krystle and Nolan are working with the lawyer, and I'll let them explain that part."

Krystle stood up right away and introduced themselves, "Hi everyone, I'm Krystle, and this is my husband, Nolan," he stood up and gave a little wave, but it was Krystle who was going to have the floor.

She continued, "Well, we met with Richard Wessler from The City of Toronto Legal Aid Office, who Benjamin had found. He's a community lawyer, and because this is considered a 'low income' or an 'affordable housing' issue, it seems Legal Aid will be able to help and defend us. So far, only half of us have signed up, and before he can do anything on our behalf, we all have to be signed with him so he can legally represent us."

Bob was on her even before I could say anything, and he was direct to the point. "This guy is a 'community aid' lawyer?"

"Yes, Bob," Krystle said, smiling.

"This means he works for the Government?" Bob was on a roll.

Still smiling, Krystle said, "Yes, Bob."

Immediately, he said, "Well, if he works for the Government, how do we know he's any good?"

The smile left Krystle's face, and now I liked Bob even more. It was an honest question and one worth asking, but one Krystle had no way of answering;

after all, Benjamin found the guy, and when it comes down to it, in our situation, we get who we get.

Krystle said, "I don't know, Benjamin found him. He works for Legal Aid East, and he's the lawyer who handles cases in this area, so it's who we are stuck with. He's given me the representation forms and asked everyone to call him to schedule a meeting. He said he would attend the next meeting once everyone signed up. So, does anyone have any questions?"

Of course, Bob had to ask something, "So, this isn't going to cost a thing? He's going to do it Pro-Bono, absolutely free, no strings attached?"

Krystle seemed relieved that that was the only question, and she said, "Yes, Bob, absolutely free."

He replied, "Is that supposed to be a good thing or a bad thing? You know the saying, 'You get what you pay for."

Krystle nodded in some agreement and made it a point to say, "Like I said, Benjamin found this guy, not me. But, short of retaining and paying someone, this is our best option. I work in the social services field; I know some people in the legal aid system, and they say that the lawyers are good, so it's probably our best option. We met with Mr. Wessler, and he seems all right; please talk to him and make up your own mind. You can go on your own if you want, but as everyone is saying, we have a better chance of fighting this together, you know, strength in numbers. Thank you, everyone, and please, try to get in to see him ASAP; we need to be ready."

Robert stood up and thanked both Krystle and Nolan. Nolan didn't say a thing; you could see who was in charge of their relationship. But Nolan was cool. He looked at me and scrunched his face quizzically and comically as if saying, 'And Nolan, for what?' We had a good laugh.

Robert continued, "I want to remind everyone that we are all signing with the lawyer, but everyone is free to do what is right for themselves. If something arises and you make 'arrangements' with the landlord..." He was rubbing his thumbs and fingers together, indicating money as he said 'arrangements.' "Then that is your business; everyone has to do what is best for them. If, at any point, someone leaves, we won't think anything less of you. Best regards, we understand, and don't worry. On that note, I will pass the floor over to Brent, who is looking into a couple of things, Brent."

"Thanks, Robert. Hi everyone, uh, I know some of you, and some of you I don't. Uh, I'm Brent. I live on the third floor in seventeen and I was there when Benjamin told Robert he was leaving. He did a lot of work, and one of the things he was working on was involving the Press and getting some community activism involved. Are any of you familiar with or know of the community group, Acorn?"

I was surprised; four or five hands went up, "OK, good, uh, I went and met with them, and yeah, it seems they are familiar with evictions, or these

'Renovictions.' They have some groups going through this exact thing, and they say there are tons of buildings going through this all over the city. If we get them involved, they'll help us draw public attention to the matter, they'll organize their members for marches and rallies around our building, and as events proceed, they said they'll have a couple of citywide rallies that will happen at high profile places like City Hall or the Landlord and Tenant Board. They'll get posters and flyers printed for our building and send people around the neighborhood knocking on doors to create awareness; basically, they'll create some public attention. Now, the deal with them is they are membership-driven, which means they only assist their members. That's the hook, and in our situation, it's what we need. I have signed up with them, so has Robert, so maybe that's enough to get them involved, but I would still recommend signing up with them as it will give you a voice. They said they would be around the building in the next couple of weeks and will be at our next tenant meeting, so you can sign up when they come around or at the next meeting."

Now, it was time to talk about the documentary. Everyone seemed OK with me so far, so I thought, here goes nothing.

I continued, "Also, when I told a friend from work what I... I mean, what we are going through, it gave him an idea, he wants to film our fight and make a documentary about the affordable housing crisis, about 'Renovictions' and about how the rental market really works. I work in TV/Film, I'm in ACTRA/SAG, and he's in the Directors Guild; he works on the crew side and is an amateur filmmaker. Everyone I have spoken to thinks this is a great idea. First, no one believes that someone could actually do this to us, and it be legal, but more importantly, they say this is something they would watch."

I introduced Eric to everyone, "My friend Eric, who is at the back of the room, will be filming me throughout this... adventure, for lack of a better word." I honestly didn't know how to phrase it. "It will focus on me, but if you want to participate, we'd love to speak with you. The more personal and the more honest this is, the better it will be; we want to hear everyone's story and how this is affecting you because this is total bullshit."

I continued, "So, he will be on me in meetings and stuff, but if you sign the agreement, you can be in it just as much. If not, it's no problem; we won't point the camera at you, or we can blur you out. I'll respect whatever you folks want."

I looked around the room to get a sense of how people might be feeling, and it looked like it was a mixed bag. It was odd because the people I thought would be into it weren't, and the people I thought wouldn't like it, liked it.

The biggest surprise was Sarah. She outright said she didn't want to be involved. She was young, lived alone with a few cats, and always had boyfriends who were never around for long. Right now, the guy she's dating likes to walk around with his shirt off, and before that, there was a parrot guy, a biker guy, and a drug guy, just to name a few. Robert and other tenants were constantly arguing with her, and it was usually about her dumbass boyfriends. The tenants would complain to her about parrot shit and bikes in the hallway or drug deals taking place. Initially, they would try to help her, telling her that these guys didn't care about her and were taking advantage of her. But the problem was, she always defended and stood up for the idiot boyfriends to the point that it pissed most of the tenants off. They gave up trying to help her; no one cared what she had to say, and I was no different.

Sarah stood up and snarled, with both hands on her hips and one hip cocked out to the side, and said, "I have a huge problem with this."

I thought she was going to snap her fingers across her face when she was bitching at me.

"I'm not agreeing with this; this is a private matter. I don't want people to know my story; this is embarrassing. I don't want to be on camera, and on behalf of the group, I don't think you should be doing this."

She didn't snap her fingers, but she raised her hand with one finger to try to add affirmation to her blabbering.

I saw some heads turn and look at her in disbelief; everyone shook their heads. I knew I had to put her in her place because there was no way I was going to let this idiot have any say in what I did.

"Well, thank you for your concern, Sarah; like I said, if you don't want to be in it, that's fine. This is my story, and he'll be following me. I have spoken to a lot of people about this and have received nothing but positive feedback. Benjamin loved it (Benjamin wasn't aware of the documentary) and people I have spoken to at work think it's a great idea, and you know what? It's motivating me even more to fight these greedy pricks. The more people I tell about this, the more stories I hear of it happening all over the city, it's alarming, and it's scaring the shit out of me. As for speaking for the whole group, let's ask them?"

I didn't give her a chance to speak and immediately asked, "Folks, do you agree with Sarah? If you do, I'll do whatever you guys want, I promise. Have you all agreed that she speaks for the group?"

I could see Sarah's dumb look as she tried to process the fact that someone had called her out.

People randomly said, "Nope, not me; she doesn't speak for me."

The best line was from Melissa, "The little hussy doesn't speak for me!"

I was done with this topic, and laughingly, I said, "Thanks, Sarah. We won't shoot you, look at you, or comment about you. Don't worry at all, OK? Great."

I felt bad and wanted to make my intentions known to the group; I had to say, "Hey folks, I'm in this with you. I feel sick about what's happening; I'm nervous as hell, I'm anxious, I'm not sleeping, and I'm not eating. I know it's not easy waiting for that eviction notice to come at any moment. I'm disgusted that we are in this situation; it sucks. It isn't morally right, and it shouldn't be happening, but it is, and from what people are telling me, our best chance to fight this is with publicity; the more eyes on this, the better."

I was honest with everyone, and it was as if I was pleading to myself, "We have to expose the people doing this to us and their greed. I'm here to fight; I want to expose whoever is doing this, expose them to their friends and family, and expose them for the morally broke, greedy pieces of shit 'they' really are, whoever 'they' might be. I don't know what else to do. I don't like bullies, and I don't know how to fight back. This is the only way I can see, so please, let me fight. I won't do anything that hurts us; we will be respectful and professional. Eric is awesome, and I'll send you his YouTube link if you want. And guys, with this documentary, I will learn everything I can about the rental market and 'Renovictions', whatever I come across will benefit the group. Trust me, I won't do anything that will jeopardize us. I'll give you the releases, and if you want your story told, talk to Eric or myself. Thanks, everyone."

Robert stood as I sat down, and he helped my case by saying, "I know some of you may not want it, but everyone says this is a great idea, and people tend to pay attention or take notice when there's a camera and lights around. I have signed the release, a few others have as well, and Brent has already found out some good information about evictions and the system. It will help us in the long run, and hey, it'll give us all the chance to be movie stars." Robert chuckled and snickered, and there were some laughs and comments from around the room.

I handed out the releases and quickly explained them. To my surprise, the old guys signed them immediately and returned them to me. I thought I would have trouble with them, especially since Brian seemed to respect Denise, but surprisingly, most were really into it. They started talking about all the different reality and documentary shows they watched. They mentioned 'Ice Road Truckers,' 'Gold Rush,' and 'Marketplace.'

And Bill, who hadn't said a word, spoke and said, "I really like the movie about the McDonalds, you know, that skinny fella who ate all the McDonalds and filmed all the fat people eating the McDonalds too."

Nolan and Krystle didn't sign right away, which surprised me.

Nolan was about to sign, but Krystle grabbed his hand, and without looking at him, she said, "Well, let's just take our time to look this over before we sign."

He looked at her and then back at me. I could see the look in his eye that said, 'Sorry, man. I have to wait to see what she says.' It was written all over his face.

I smiled and replied, "No worries, take your time. Eric will be filming me mostly, so don't worry. But I hope you guys do it because we need all the help we can get."

Robert ended the night by asking if there were any questions, and there was one.

Brian was straight to the point and asked, "So what do we do now?"

Robert shrugged and said, "Well, we sit tight until we get another letter. We can start working with Acorn, and if anyone knows any reporters or anyone in politics, please make them aware of this and get them involved. If you haven't signed up with the lawyer, Mr. Wessler, please do it as soon as possible; we need everything in place for when the next letter comes because it is coming. Thanks, everyone; we'll keep in touch; keep your eyes open around the building, and everyone, have a good night."

No one hung around to talk; Robert, Krystle, and Nolan were talking, but everyone else had just left. No milling about, no talking, nothing; everyone just left.

After the meeting, I was excited and disappointed. I thought there would have been more mingling, a little 'camaraderie,' or discussion about the future. Instead, everyone just went their own separate way.

Eric had packed everything away and said he was done for the night.

I agreed with him, and I had to say, "You know, I'm surprised at Sarah's reaction, even though she's not that bright; I thought, being younger, she would want to stand up for what's right; I thought she would have been all for the documentary."

Eric nailed it by saying, "That's a millennial for you, whiny, entitled, wants to scream about things that don't mean anything and ignore the things that really mean something. She especially does not want a 'privileged white male,' that's you Bingham, telling her what to do. She'll scream to all bloody hell to fight against whatever side people like you are on, even if it's to her detriment apparently; poor kid doesn't even know what's good for her."

He asked me, "What are your thoughts about her? Do you think she will go the distance in the fight?"

I didn't hesitate, "She's deadweight and will probably give us trouble, but her pets are cute, so they'll look good in the story. Besides, a lot of people would care more about pets getting thrown out than they would care about people being thrown out. She'll be no help except to show the public how unaffordable Toronto is for young people, giving them no chance to accumulate any savings at all. She has actually said that five hundred was a good deal. I've heard from people in the building that a couple of her boyfriends even ripped her off, and one of them stole most of her furniture one time. Normally, I would feel bad for someone like that, but she is so crazy and rude that she might even deserve what she gets. I think she'll make it hard and actually try to fight us. It's amazing how forceful, stupid people can be when they think they're right, but unfortunately, they're too stupid to realize they're wrong; that's Sarah."

Eric agreed, adding, "Yeah, she'd probably sue us if we used her. We can blur her out, and we'll blur out her cats' faces as well, just in case. Actually, we will do that; it'll be hilarious."

We had a good laugh and walked back to the building. Surprisingly, a few people were outside, milling about and talking. Andrew and Bree were there and gave me their signed releases. They said they supported the documentary and would do anything to help. Bob was there with Bo and had his release signed. He even wrote Bo's name on it to include him.

When he handed it to me, he said, "Make sure you get a lot of Bo in this; it ain't fair they're throwing him out too; people should see that as well."

I laughed, "Are you kidding me, Bob? He'll be the star of the show; nobody will care about us being evicted and thrown out on the street, but show them a cute dog like Bo being evicted, and they'll take notice. Their hearts will get warm and fuzzy, and they'll think, how can someone do that to a poor dog? But people getting evicted? They won't think twice about us."

Bob agreed and mumbled, "People suck," as he stepped away to light a smoke.

As soon as Bob walked away, Andrew came back and asked me in a worried tone, "So what's Bob complaining about now?"

I laughed and told him not to worry, "Nothing now; he's just giving us his and Bo's support for the documentary."

Andrew said, "You know we're not going to win, right Brent?"

I sighed, Andrew shared my outlook on big money and the system.

He added, "You know we are going to get pushed out of here one way or another; it's just a question of when."

I agreed but tried to be positive, "Yeah, I hear you, Andrew, but I'm getting excited for a good fight. If you want to get involved with the doc, talk to Eric. I'm sure he would love to have you on board, and it would look good on your resume."

Andrew was a squirrelly, nervous guy. He wore glasses and always played the intellectual 'smart guy' at work. He was always in whitecoats as a doctor, scientist, or lab guy because he was like that in real life, he was smart.

You could tell he wasn't a confrontational kind of guy, and his answer reaffirmed that, "I'm sorry that I don't want to get involved, Brent. I'll be in the documentary when you guys are shooting, but I don't want to be interviewed or singled out."

I said, "no worries."

He was a nervous kind of guy and probably got kicked around by a system or two. But I thought, this is the problem; half the people in the fight don't even want to fight.'

And can I blame them?

Andrew and Bree said good night, and as soon as they walked into the building, they came flying out immediately. Bree had a piece of paper in her hand and was waving it over her head.

She yelled, "It's starting; they're starting tomorrow."

She passed the letter to Robert, and he started reading: "Attention, Dear Tenants of Three-Ninety-One Empire Avenue." He looked up, winked, and snickered as he said, "It doesn't say 'dear'; I added that."

The look on his face was priceless; he adjusted his imaginary jacket and tie, held the letter out in front of himself, and in a formal, almost 'town crier' position, he proceeded to read and declare, "In forty-eight hours we will be commencing renovation work on the building, this will include and not be limited to, individual units, hallways, stairways, common areas, front entrance, garbage areas, laundry room, boiler-room and furnace areas. This will involve representatives from our contractors, engineers, electrical, plumbing, and HVAC providers having access to the building. Because of the nature of the work, there will be intermittent shutdowns of water and electricity, and it may require entrance to your units to access the plumbing or electric. Proper notices will be given. Your patience and understanding are appreciated."

Robert finished by saying, "And it's signed by Brownstone Management on behalf of One-Four-Seven-Zero-Zero-Seven LLC. The end. I added, the end," and he winked.

He held the letter and said, "Well, everyone, it looks like it's starting sooner than we thought. Let's just see what happens, and don't worry. They have to give us proper notice when performing certain repairs and shutdowns. If they are working outside the rules, we've got the phone numbers for City Standards, so everyone, keep your eyes open. If you see something, say something."

Myles Bradley

Chapter 8

The day after our tenants meeting, I was awoken by people going up and down the stairs and Robert's voice asking for their names and what they were doing in the building. I put on some coffee, my robe, and flip-flops and walked out into the hallway. There wasn't anyone around except Robert, standing at the top of the stairwell with a clipboard in his hand, taking notes. He said that there had been a few guys coming and going, and it looks like they're using the empty unit up here to store stuff.

I asked him if he wanted a coffee, and he said no; I told him I'd be back once my coffee was ready. I went back in, sat down, closed my eyes, and thought, 'Now I have to deal with this shit in my home?' I almost dozed off but made a cup of coffee once it was ready and returned to the hallway.

As I walked out of my door some workers were coming up the stairs, and Robert was asking their names and grilling them, "Who do you work for? What do you do?"

They kept going past Robert with their heads down and didn't say a thing, which annoyed him. He tried to get under their skin and asked, "What's the matter? You don't speak English?"

When he said that, the boss came up the stairs. He was a six-foot-two, two hundred fifty-pound Italian contractor who definitely spoke English and apparently didn't like Roberts's questions or his tone.

He looked me up and down quizzically with one raised eyebrow, smirked, and went right into Robert, "I speak English, Sir; those are my workers; they are professional and courteous, and they have been instructed not to communicate with the tenants of the building. It's per the owner's instructions, who has contracted us to do the work; if you have a problem with any of them, please let me know. My name is Lorenzo, and since I speak perfect English, is there something I can help you with?"

Robert didn't back down. He went straight into a tirade about the rules and regulations of working around the building. He stated how proper notices must be given and the times of the day they are allowed to work. He started reading Lorenzo the Riot Act.

Lorenzo smiled; I could tell he was an easy-going kind of guy; he didn't get all frustrated and angry with Robert; he calmly replied, "I understand your concerns, sir, but it's ten thirty in the morning; we are just going up and down the stairs putting some equipment in the empty unit, so there is nothing to worry about or get upset over. And though a couple of my guys might not speak English, they are very polite, professional, and respectful; you won't have a problem with any of them. Now, is there anything else I can help you with?"

Robert wasn't letting up. "Who do you work for? Who is your boss? Do you work with the building's owner? Do you work for Brownstone?"

Lorenzo replied, "Sir, we don't work for Brownstone; they are a separate company. I am the owner of this contracting company, and we've been contracted to do work for the owner of the building, One-Four-Seven-Zero-Zero-Seven LLC."

Robert kept going, but you could tell he was running out of things to bust Lorenzo's balls with. "Well, are you a licensed contractor? Can I see your license?"

Lorenzo smiled, looked at me, then at Robert, and said, "They told us there might be some trouble with tenants in the building, so sure, here's my license."

He passed it to Robert, who recorded the information on his clipboard. He handed Lorenzo back his license and stormed off into his apartment.

Lorenzo looked at me; I shrugged my shoulders, pretending not to care. I smiled and asked, "Would you like a cup of coffee?"

He chuckled and said, "No, thank you, sir." And went about his business.

I went back into my apartment and was finally able to be alone with my coffee. Since I didn't have to work for the next few days, I hadn't planned to be up this early. I had made my appointment with the community lawyer today at two pm, and I thought I could relax, but I guess not. I guess that's how it's going to be until this crap is finished; it's going to be a lot of inconveniences.

I sat in front of the computer. I had my list of questions for the lawyer, but I wanted to know more about this guy. I went online and did my best sleuthing, only I couldn't find much about him; he wasn't making headlines defending any significant or newsworthy cases, and it didn't seem like anything was listed with this guy's name. There were the usual links for Facebook, LinkedIn, his contact page with the City of Toronto website, and… MySpace? I thought, what? A grown man with a MySpace account? That wasn't promising.

I started with his LinkedIn profile to see what he was about; there wasn't much to it. This guy was almost sixty years old, and he only had one job listed in all that time, 'City of Toronto, Legal Aid Lawyer.' wow, this guy has been a government employee ever since he graduated from Law school over twenty-five years ago, that didn't make me feel good at all. Next, I went to his Facebook and looked around, but there wasn't much there either; there were just pictures of him and his cats and a lot of camping pictures. He looked like a nice guy, but there wasn't anything too revealing about what kind of lawyer he was.

I had tried to get Eric to come with me, but he wasn't available. I wasn't too concerned about that, as it was my first meeting with Wessler. I didn't think a lawyer would be too excited about having a camera shoved in his face and probably would never allow filming anyway.

Eric had suggested that I take my phone and record myself in front of the building, stating what I was doing and who I was meeting with, so I had to remember to film a little before and after. When it was time to leave, I grabbed my questions and headed out. I had a general idea where the office was on Queen Street, and the number indicated that it would be a ten—to fifteen-minute walk.

As I got close, I knew right away where the office was; it was located in a community center with a methadone clinic, and as I approached the office, I had to step over some people on the sidewalk out front, which wasn't encouraging, to say the least. It seemed that everywhere you go in Toronto, you see homeless people and drug abuse. Just from walking the streets, you could tell there was not only an affordable housing crisis in this city but also a mental health crisis and a drug crisis, and it seemed nothing was being done about any of it. When I got to the door, I pulled out my phone and recorded myself. I made a little introduction, stated where and who I was meeting with, and said what I hoped to get out of the meeting. I felt a little weird recording myself, and I wished Eric was there to motivate me and give me some encouragement, but there wasn't much to be said.

I tried to enter the building, but the door was locked, and I had to get the receptionist's attention to be buzzed inside. Before she let me in, she had to look me up and down to make sure I wasn't one of the guys from the street looking for their methadone. When I went into the office, it was empty.

I checked in with the receptionist, who asked if I needed a translator for the meeting. I smiled and said, "I don't believe so, as long as the lawyer speaks English, right?"

She laughed and gave me a pile of forms to fill out and read while waiting.

After about twenty minutes of waiting, a skinny bald man came out of a door and started doing some photocopying. I recognized him from his Facebook profile; it was Wessler. As he was using the photocopier, I thought, 'he doesn't even have someone doing his photocopying for him?' When he finished up, he turned around with a stack of papers in his arm and called my name. I stood up, said hello, and followed him to his office. It was a dump; it was small and unorganized. There were papers, books, and newspapers everywhere, and his window looked right out onto the street where all the people waiting for methadone were hanging out. As I went to sit down, he had to move a stack of papers off of a chair for me.

I looked out the window and said, "That's a lovely view you have."

He chuckled, "It isn't great, but it reminds me of why I am here; these are the type of people that need help."

That was an interesting answer, "Well, that's motivating. Have you been doing this a long time?"

He answered vaguely, saying, "Seems like all my life."

I thought that was a weird reply.

He went straight to the point and began to discuss business. "So, I understand you live at Three-Ninety-One Empire Avenue and are having trouble with a new owner. Do you have any questions about the paperwork? Does everything look acceptable?"

I said, "Yes, it all looked pretty straightforward except for one thing. What is this clause stating that you won't negotiate any buyout or settlement amounts on behalf of our client?"

He leaned forward and explained, "When it comes to lease terminations, evictions, etc., sometimes the owners will try to pay off the tenant for them to go away; we aren't here for that. The city of Toronto gets involved in cases like this to save affordable housing, and that's it. When situations like this happen, it reduces the number of affordable housing units available to rent, and that's what we are interested in; saving affordable housing units is our priority. So, when it comes time, if you are going to take a payout, the city is no longer involved; that becomes a private matter between you and the owner.

I had to ask him, "Is the city truly putting its heart into saving affordable housing? I mean, increased rent means higher property values, which means increased property taxes and more money for the city. So really? How interested is the city in actually saving affordable housing?"

He said, "Good point, but see those people out that window. Do you know how much homelessness costs the city? I understand your point about the taxes, but those people out there are a bigger burden on the taxpayers."

He almost sounded like a politician when he answered.

He asked me, "So, what do you want to get out of this case? Are you looking for a payout, or do you want to stay in your unit?"

I said, "Sir, I just ordered a new sofa, and suddenly, some guy comes along and tries to throw me out. I don't think that's fair or legal. All I want to do is stay in my place, pay my rent, and live my life without strife, but this guy isn't letting me."

He looked at some papers and said, "OK then. We're all ready to go. Tell any other tenants that haven't been in yet to sign up as soon as possible. I've been working with Benjamin, who has already signed up some people."

I guess he hadn't heard yet, and I'm surprised Benjamin didn't tell him. I felt awkward that I had to be the one, but I didn't care. "I guess you haven't heard, but Benjamin has taken a buyout; he's moving to Montreal with his girlfriend; at least, that's what he's told us; either way, he's not in the building anymore."

He leaned back in his chair, "He hasn't informed me yet; that's a shame. He was passionate about this; he would have put up a good fight."

He grabbed a folder, took out his pen, and put a big stroke through what I assumed was Benjamin's name. Then he sighed, "I hope there's enough of you left when we get to a hearing."

He explained that his job was to represent the building as a whole and that he could represent us as long as we all had the same common goal: to stay in our apartments. He said that even if someone drops out, like Benjamin, he will keep representing the remaining tenants, fighting for the same initial goal: to stay in the units. He asked if I could agree to that and if I would 'stay the course.'

I reassured him again, "I'm here till the wrecking ball comes. I have cheap, affordable rent in a cool neighborhood, and I don't want to leave just because some rich prick thinks he can throw me out."

He smiled at that and said, "Sounds good, Brent. For now, there's not much to do yet. The first eviction letter was illegal, so you don't have to worry about it, and until they give you a new one, there really isn't a case yet."

I walked out of his office and didn't believe a word this guy said. First off, because he's a lawyer, and every word out of their mouths is usually a lie. Second, he's a lifelong government employee who has only had to show up for work to keep his job; he hasn't had to be accountable to anyone for years and is most likely un-fireable no matter how bad of a lawyer he was. He probably doesn't care about us, but I hope he cares about winning.

When I left the building, I was more determined than when I walked in. I decided to talk to my camera right in front of his window where all the homeless meth head fentanyl addicts were sitting, or should I say lying in the street. I started speaking into the camera, explaining my conversation with him inside. I hoped to feel better and more confident after talking with the lawyer, but I didn't. In the meeting, he reassured me that the City of Toronto was doing everything possible to save affordable housing. But looking at the people sitting, sleeping, and camped out in the street made me think, if this is the result of the city doing everything it can do to help the drug crisis, it doesn't look like it's going to work out too well for affordable housing.

As I was wrapping up on camera, I could see Wessler through his window, and the homeless encampment outside reflected poetically off of it. He was talking on the phone, hunched over with his head in his hand, and when I saw that, I felt like we didn't stand a chance.

After the meeting, I walked back to the building, taking my time; all I could think about was the homeless people and wondering where they were supposed to live. As I walked, I noticed how many there were; it was rampant. I decided to stop at 'Reliable Fish & Chips' for the city's best Jerk Chicken Burrito, which always made me feel good. They were great people at Reliable and a staple of the neighborhood; it was funny; they had the best fish and chips, but I never ordered it. Whenever Joy, the owner, saw me coming, she always asked, 'One jerk or two, Brent,' with a wink.

I would laugh because she knew it was always for two, and her husband, Ben, in the back, would yell out, "Stop jerking the customers, Joy."

Reliable was just down the block from my place, and as I got to my corner, I could see people from the building outside with letters and envelopes in their hands: Bob, Nolan, Krystle, Sarah, and some guy who I was assuming was Sarah's boyfriend because he was shirtless. Bill had also wandered out, as had Brian, Andrew, and Bree, with 'Teacup.' Even Reggie was outside, sitting on the stoop with the letter in hand, trying to breathe.

As I approached, Andrew waved the letter up and down and yelled, "They are trying to buy us out again."

He was angry: "They're on every door; everybody has one. They want to offer us one thousand dollars to leave by the end of the month, and they also said, 'This will be the last settlement offer; there will be no more negotiations after this.' Looks like that's it. It looks like a thousand dollars is all we're going to get."

He looked at the building and started yelling at it, "These pieces of shit are trying to buy people out of their homes."

I looked at Andrew, "Yeah, this is fucked up." I stood on the step and said, "Well, folks, this is probably a good time to remind everyone to sign up with the lawyer; it looks like things aren't slowing down, and we need to be ready."

Andrew looked at me, and I could tell he wouldn't hang around for a fight. I was the opposite, the more bullshit they pulled, the more I wanted to fight, but I guess it wasn't the same for everyone. I wasn't going to take this shit from them, and with the chance of making a movie out of it, I thought, what the hell, I was in this fight one hundred percent.

But not Andrew; he looked at me like this was going to be too much bullshit and said, "I don't know, Brent, I referred you here, and now all this shit is happening, I feel bad, kind of like it's my fault for bringing you in, but I don't know if… I don't know if we're going to stick around."

I was surprised. "Andrew, really? Yeah, you referred me, but don't worry about that at all. I thought you and Bree would stick around."

Then it hit me: they had two separate units, so technically, they didn't live with each other; if they each took the thousand dollars and moved in together, they get two grand instead of one. And I guess pocketing two thousand between them was appealing. In a defeated tone, he sadly said, "I think we're out of here; I don't need this bullshit in my life. You know we're not going to win, right? It's just a matter of time before we have to leave. We might as well take some money and run; why not make some money from it?"

I couldn't argue and had to agree with him, but I replied honestly, "Well, if it makes sense for you and Bree to leave, go for it, but for me, I'm in this until the end. You guys have to do what's best for yourselves, and like we said in the beginning, no hard feelings; everyone has to do what's right for themselves. Now, I'm not advising you or anything, but this is just the beginning. Andrew, you'll get more money if you stick around; this is early in the negotiations, it's just a step in the process to shake people out. I'm telling you, don't go yet, stick around, and you'll get more, I swear."

He just shook his head and looked down at the ground.

I patted him on the back and said, "Don't worry, think about it; if you find a decent place, great, and if you don't, just stay and make them pay you more."

Andrew said, "Well, they said there wouldn't be any more buyouts, so is this it? Will there be more? I don't know. I think we're going to take the money and go."

Andrew was a bag of nerves and didn't want any trouble from the system or anyone; he had been a para-legal in his previous career, so I'm sure he saw some shit in the system, but as for this scenario, he was right, no one knew what would happen. But that was another two down; our numbers were already dwindling, and we hadn't even gotten to the worst of it yet.

Robert arrived back at the building as Andrew was ranting about the letter. Seeing everyone with letters, he rolled his eyes and asked, "Oh, great. So, what does this one say now?"

With a smoke hanging from his mouth, Bob replied, "It's another buyout letter from our lovely new owner. It's the final offer: one thousand dollars in exchange for us to be out by the end of the month and it says no more negotiations after this."

"Well, then." Robert said to everyone, "This is where it gets good. If you haven't signed with the lawyer, I recommend doing it immediately; get in there as soon as possible because it sounds like shit is going to hit the fan."

The commotion settled, and people went to their units while Robert and I stayed outside for a bit.

"Well..." he started to say.

I looked at him and said, "Yup. Well, I guess that might be it for buyouts for now, but I'm sure there'll be more games. We'll have to wait and see what we get next, an eviction letter or bullshit letters about repairs."

Robert agreed and said, "In the meantime, keep reminding everyone to sign up with the lawyer, and I'll put a notice up about our next tenants meeting. Hopefully, the politicians, the lawyer, and Acorn can attend.

I looked at Robert and said, "Andrew and Bree are leaving."

He shook his head, "I'm not surprised; you could tell by that little teacup that they weren't the fighting type. Let's worry about us now. I'll set up another tenants meeting, you get Acorn to attend, and we'll get people talking about this."

I went upstairs, and my letter was stuck on my door; I grabbed it, went in, put everything down, and opened it. Sure enough, it was an offer to leave for one thousand dollars. I walked to the desk and added it to the file. I got my food out and couldn't even enjoy my jerk burrito. Now, these guys were really starting to piss me off.

Just as I started eating, my door swung open, and Eric came flying in. I asked him, "Where the hell have you been?"

He laughed and said, "Don't worry, Bingham. I'm always working. Come downstairs and help me bring some stuff up."

I followed him downstairs. He pulled me in close and said, "Don't let anyone see anything, OK?" He opened the trunk of his car, and there were a couple of hockey bags and a bunch of black garbage bags, each tied up with a loose knot. He slung a hockey bag over his shoulder and grabbed two garbage bags; he told me to do the same and headed up the stairs.

I didn't get a word in with him. I untied a bag and saw a red gas can inside, the kind you use when you run out of gas on the highway. I lifted it, and it was heavy as hell. I grabbed the other one, and it was almost empty. I looked around; I was worried someone might see. I slung the hockey bag over my shoulder, grabbed the garbage bags, and carried them up to my place as fast as I could. Luckily, we didn't pass anyone, and hopefully, nobody saw us.

Once we got up to my place, I closed the door and immediately asked Eric, "What the hell?"

He replied as calmly as if I were asking him what time it was; "It's for the daydream sequence, props. Don't worry about it; it's going to be great."

A little concerned, I said, "OK…maybe we need to have a talk."

He walked into the bedroom and said, "Go downstairs and get the other bags. And oh, don't forget the tiki torches. They're in the backseat; bring them up, too."

I was walking towards the door when I had to stop and process what he said, "Wait, what? Tiki Torches?"

Eric said, "Yeah, grab them, and don't worry; it's going to be great." Famous last words said on a movie set.

The torches were also in hockey bags, so no one could see what they were— thank goodness. It would be hard to explain gasoline and tiki torches to someone.

When I returned upstairs, I asked Eric, "Remind me again, what part of the documentary was this in?"

He chuckled, "This was for the cutaway dream sequence."

"OK, I remember, but I don't remember you talking about a fucking Lua. I honestly didn't think you were serious about that aspect. Anyway, put the stuff in the bedroom; no one will see it in there. But you know we're going to have to have a talk about this production sooner or later."

Eric smiled, "don't worry, so what's going on now?"

I said, "Nothing too exciting. It's just another letter with another buyout offer, this time for one thousand, and it says this will be the last offer."

Eric looked around, laughing. "Ooh, the big bucks, sounds like things are heating up."

I started to tell him about Andrew and Bree, "Andrew and Bree are taking the money; they don't want the fight; they'd rather take some money and run. I think they might be a couple; if they are, that's two thousand bucks if they move in together, so I guess they thought, why not? The letter also said this would be the final buyout; there will be no more negotiations after this, and I think that spooked them."

Eric started to quiz me about the lawyer. He asked me what kind of lawyer he was. Was he like a lawyer from LA Law, Johnnie Cochrane, or Saul Goodman?

After a few questions, Eric said, "You don't like this guy, do you? Do you have any hope in this guy's skills?"

I said, "Well, let's see what we are up against first; so far, it's just been buyout letters, so still really nothing to fight against. We did lose two more people, so there is that. We're losing people, and the real bullshit hasn't even started yet.

There was a knock at my door; it was Robert; I invited him in and asked him what was happening; he was full of energy and pissed off.

He was in fine form and started speaking immediately, "Well, the lawyer has everyone in the building signed up and ready to go. Everyone will be at the next meeting: the politicians, the lawyer, maybe a reporter, and hopefully, 'Acorn' can come too."

Just as he said that, we could hear someone in the hallway. Robert opened the door, and there was a guy with a vest and lanyard putting up a notice stating that the water would be shut off in forty-eight hours; even though this was more than proper notice, it triggered Robert. He chased the guy down the hallway who was putting them up; the poor guy was just a young construction guy hanging notices in a building; he had no idea what was going on and didn't have a clue as to why Robert was going off on him and giving him a hard time.

I yanked the notice off my door, read it for Eric, laughed, and said, "I better get some big ass bottles of water."

Eric kept the camera going, and we talked for a bit; it was good to have him around to vent and talk about this.

He asked, "What are you going to do if they play some games and keep the water off for a while? You should keep your bathtub filled up, bathe in it, and dip into it when you need to make soup."

I said, "Yeah, I'll use my bathwater to cook spaghetti with."

We laughed, and I continued, "But seriously, that's a good point; I'll buy a few big jugs of water, and why not? I'll fill the bathtub to use for dishes, it can't hurt. I have my gym membership; I can shower and shave there before work or after; it's twenty- four hours; it'll be a hassle, but it'll work."

I chuckled, "Dam, this is like 'prepping.' I gotta' get ready in case they mess with me and shut down my necessities."

I wasn't going to put anything by these guys; I was going to be ready for everything.

Chapter 9

Waking up to see gas cans and tiki torches in my bedroom was a little alarming, but it made me laugh. It made me laugh because today was the day they were shutting the water down; imagine the building catching fire and this stuff going up in flames and no water to put it out; wouldn't that be funny! It also made me think I should keep my bedroom door closed. If anyone saw this stuff, I'm sure they would have some questions—I know I would. If anyone saw this stuff, I'm sure they would have some questions; I know I would. I guess I wouldn't have anyone in my bedroom for a while, which wasn't anything new.

As I was putting on the coffee, someone was knocking on my door. I dragged my ass over, and as I looked out of the peephole, I could see Robert pacing back and forth in front of my door like a dog. As soon as I opened it, he blew by me, shoved a letter into my hands as he went straight past me towards the kitchen where he started to pace.

I looked at the letter and asked him, "What's going on?"

"Well, they didn't waste any time. We got it today, taped to everyone's door. We all got the eviction letter today. There it is. It says we have sixty days to get out for renovations, and it says nothing about a buyout. They might as well just tell us the truth, at least be honest, and tell us that you are trying to 'Renovict' us, you slimy bastards."

I opened the letter as Robert was ranting. This one was from a paralegal company called D&D Paralegal, and it was sent on behalf of Brownstone Management and on behalf of 'One-Four-Seven-Zero-Zero L.L.C.' I thought, 'Wow, that's a lot of 'on behalf of's.' It seems like there are a lot of people trying to get their piece of the action of affordable housing.

Even though we knew we were getting an eviction notice and we were all expecting it, it doesn't hit you until you actually see it in writing. That's when you realize you have no idea where you'll be living in sixty days- it hits you like a punch in the gut, and it's scary as hell. I had zoned out a bit, and when I looked back up at Robert, I got a little nervous. He was starting to show some rage while pacing back and forth, and there was something in his eyes that freaked me out. It's as if he left the building and was thinking of another time or place; this triggered him back to something.

He was pacing so fast, getting redder and redder. That white stuff in the corner of his mouth was back. What worried me was that he looked like he was searching for something to smash. I saw his eyes lock on the rack of clean dishes drying by the sink, and as he took a step forward, I saw his arm moving, and I stepped forward, but I was too late. He swung his arm and threw the entire rack on the floor, breaking dishes all over the place. The smashing sound brought him out of it, and we just stood there looking at each other.

I wasn't going to say anything until he said something first; we must have stood there for at least a minute until he spoke.

He looked at the floor, then me, then back at the floor, and said, "Oh man."

Even though it was alarming, I wasn't angry; I was used to 'crazy,' so I asked him, "Do you feel better now?"

He smiled and said, "Yeah, actually, I do."

He got down on his knees and started cleaning and apologizing profusely; he was picking up the cutlery and broken pieces of dishes and wouldn't stop apologizing. He was babbling as he scrambled to pick everything up; it was as if he was having a breakdown. This is when it hit me that landlords like this are causing people a lot of pain and suffering with this process. Everyone in a building like this probably has some personal issues from the past, and as long as they stay in their daily routine, they are fine, but once you take them out of their routine or shake their world even so slightly, look out. Apparently, Robert was one of those people.

From working with and listening to him so far, I found Robert to be an intelligent guy. Yes, he was a little 'squirrely'—he looked like Don Knotts from Three's Company—but he was always very polite and well-spoken. In the past, I had jokingly compared him to the Unabomber since he was so quiet and kept to himself, but now I am wondering if he is more like the Unabomber than I had initially thought.

I had to calm him down and get him some paper towels for a couple of cuts on his hand. I went across the room with caution and said, "Don't worry, Robert. I don't care about the dishes. Just relax, man. We're going to get through this. You have to keep your cool. Remember, you can't let them see you sweat, and where's Eric when you need him? That would have made great 'TV.'

I smiled and winked at him, and he smiled back, apologizing. Once we got everything picked up, he started to relax.

He sat, cleaned his hands with the paper towel, and apologized. "Sorry, I lost my cool. It's just been so stressful. The letter set me off. I'm so sorry, Brent. Please don't worry about this happening again. I'll remain calm."

I told him again, "Don't worry, but next time it happens, just try to break your shit and not mine."

We laughed, but then he got very serious and said, "I'm calling my friend who I asked to do the business search on these guys, and we're going to find out who this son of a bitch is that's doing this to us. If he's going to make me crazy, I'm going to make him crazy; I don't know how, but I will get this guy."

I agreed with him and said, "Don't worry, Robert, 'karma is king,' and he'll get his; we'll make sure of it."

I looked at the letter still in my hands and said, "Well, it's July third, and it says we have to be out by August thirty-first."

As soon as I said that, Robert grabbed the letter out of my hand; he read it out loud again and started swearing, "Son of a bitch, son of a bitch! It's another bullshit letter. These people are either morons or they're up to something. Look here, they say we have sixty days to vacate our unit and that we have to be out by August Thirty-first, but that's less than sixty days' notice. By law, they have to give us sixty days' notice; I was so mad I didn't do the math; it's not sixty days; they wrote sixty days, but those dates are fifty-eight days. I'll send the letter to the lawyer and call him; we'll see what he says. Don't worry; I'll make sure I talk to him today. I'll confirm the meeting space for the next tenants' meeting and try to get the politicians to attend; I'll let you know."

As he said that, my phone rang, and it was the door downstairs. "Delivery for Brent Bingham."

I wasn't thinking straight; I thought it was some bullshit from the owner or Brownstone Management, so I gave them some attitude about delivering stuff without notice.

But they said, "No, sir. We're from Leons'; we have your sofa."

I apologized, buzzed them in, looked at Robert, and said, "Oh, good. My new sofa is here just in time for me to move out."

I didn't know how to feel about receiving the eviction notice and sofa on the same day; I wasn't sure what kind of sign that was. When they got upstairs, I apologized further, got them a couple of bottles of water, and explained that there was some bullshit going on in the building with the new owner. They were very cool about it and sympathized with us; no one was on the owner's side on this, no one.

When they left, I called Eric, who wasn't working either. I told him about the letter and that we'd be doing a lot of stuff today, and he loved it. He asked me to hold on until he got here; he said he'd be here in thirty minutes and just hung up.

I explained to Robert that Eric wanted to film us working and figuring stuff out, and a big smile came across his face; he brushed his hair with his hand and said, "Yes, Mr. DeMille, I'm ready for my close-up." Robert was old-school.

He said he'd go home, try to contact a couple of people, and be back in an hour or so, hopefully with some updates. When the door closed, I turned and looked at the sofa, it was a nice-looking sofa. But the question was, do I unwrap, return, or keep it wrapped for when I have to move? I sat on the plastic wrap and left it until Eric arrived. I decided to shower and get ready so I wouldn't be a total mess when he was filming. As I stepped out of the shower and got ready, all I could think about was that this is what I have to do now: I have to spend my days off learning about and dealing with Toronto housing issues; it's true; you don't care about something until it happens to you.

All we ever heard in the media was about how great property values were doing, how housing prices were soaring, and how the Toronto real estate market was booming. The media, the banks, the city, and all the companies making money off it didn't care if people couldn't pay their rent or were getting evicted illegally throughout the city. They didn't care if there was a 'social class cleansing' taking place; just as long as everything was going up, no one cared about the people being pushed out at the bottom; everyone was blinded by the bubble.

When Eric arrived, he knocked on my door but just let himself in with the key he had made, which made me think that I had to ask him when he was able to do that.

He came in with the camera ready and was surprised by the sofa, "Wow, what's this? A new sofa, Bingham? They tell you they're evicting you, that you have to move out, and you say, 'Screw you, I'm ordering a new sofa!' What were you thinking? It'll be cool to move it when you have to leave. Did you order it out of spite, thinking I'll show them?"

We both were smiling and laughing. I said, "Yeah, you're right. I thought, who the hell do they think they are!"

I got serious, stopped smiling, and asked, "No, but seriously, what do you think I should do with it? Open it? Return it? Or should I leave it wrapped because it's just a matter of time until I move? Should I try to sell it?"

Eric looked up from behind the camera. "Sorry, Bingham. I wish I could tell you, but no one knows; it's all part of the story."

I said, "fuck it, it has been over twenty years since I had a new sofa to sit on; I'm going to enjoy it while I'm here."

I cut the plastic off, sat down, rubbed the cushions, bounced a little, and looked at Eric.

He asked, "So, how is it?

"Not bad," I got up and continued, "Now, let's get to work; I don't want to have to move this fucking thing."

I grabbed the letter, showed it to Eric, and said, "Not only did I receive my beautiful new sofa today, but I also received my official eviction notice." I read it to Eric and then explained Robert's thesis about how the letter was illegal once again.

I explained how they screwed up the dates and said, "Well, we'll see if this buys us more time since it's illegal."

I sat at the computer and told Eric it was time to make some calls.

I told him I had been trying to get in touch with Acorn after going down there and signing up, but it was as if they were ignoring me. I wanted to try to organize and get things moving, but they never answered and didn't even call me back. I told them we had received our 'official' eviction notice and that the entire building had sixty days to get out. To 'sweeten' the deal for a callback, I said that everyone in the building was ready to sign up and that there was also interest from people in the neighborhood who also wanted to sign up. Hopefully, the 'carrot and stick' of new members would get their attention.

I sent an email stating the same thing; I hit send and looked at Eric, "I don't understand how these guys work; I haven't heard a thing from them."

My phone started ringing almost immediately, and Robert knocked on the door at the same time; I let him in and answered the phone; it was Kyle from Acorn calling back.

In a monotone voice, Kyle lazily said, "Hi Brent, it's Kyle calling from Acorn. How are you?"

I was straight to the point with him and wanted him to know I wasn't too impressed with Acorn so far, "Well, Kyle, I'm not too good; we got our eviction letter today. I have been trying to contact you guys and haven't heard anything. Have you forgotten about us over here?"

His professionalism was non-existent, and he replied in a flat, dull voice, "No, we're busy over here. What can I do for you?"

I wanted to jump through the phone and shake the hell out of him, "Well, we're getting thrown out, and when I came to you guys, you told me you could help. You acted very concerned with what's taking place in the city; well, we have received our eviction letter, and we have sixty days before we are homeless, and everyone over here is getting nervous. I'm wondering if you guys want to help us and if you can do anything at all. I haven't heard anything from you."

This guy showed no emotion at all. It was like talking to someone from Amazon customer service about a missing order.

He said, "Okay, Brent. You said you received the 'official' eviction notice, so it is confirmed they are trying to throw you out illegally?"

I wanted to yell at him to get the point across, "Yeah, they made it official today, and we have two months to get out."

Obviously, Kyle didn't have the same concern as I did and casually said, "Okay, we're having an Acorn 'Renoviction' meeting on Saturday. Acorn members from across the city will be there, and you can get a sense of what we're about and what we can do to help you. Are you having a tenant meeting anytime soon?"

I replied, "That's a good question, Kyle," I looked at Robert as I repeated the question, "Are we having a tenant meeting anytime soon?"

Robert shook his head and mouthed, 'Monday at the Library,' and he held up his fingers for seven o'clock.

I told Kyle, "Yes, Monday, seven o'clock, at our local library."

He said, "That's perfect; come to the meeting on Saturday and tell everyone in your building to come too. You'll meet other people and other buildings going through this; there'll be a couple of community organizations there, including someone from the Parkdale Legal Aid Office. After that, me or someone else from the group will come out to your tenants meeting on Monday, and we'll start to coordinate some activism for your building."

I thanked Kyle, said it was reassuring speaking with him, and said I looked forward to working with Acorn. I figured a little pandering couldn't hurt. We exchanged details for the meetings, and I hung up the phone.

I sat at the desk and looked at Eric and Robert, "I don't trust these guys."

Robert loved it when Eric was around with the camera. When Robert returned to my place, he was nicely dressed, his hair was neatly combed, and he hardly looked at me when speaking; he loved the camera.

Robert asked, "Why don't you trust them? What gives you that feeling? They're a non-profit; they do this to fight injustices and to help people who need help, like us."

He was looking at Eric when he asked me.

I shook my head and shrugged, "I don't know. It just seems that there is something off about their sincerity. They're in it just for the money, and that's it. I don't get the feeling they care. Either way, they're in. They'll be at our next tenants meeting."

He was looking at Eric and replied, "Well, that's good news. I wasn't able to speak to any of the politicians, but I left messages. Hopefully, we can get them to pay attention to this."

I wasn't hoping or expecting much from them. In fact, I didn't even know who our local reps were. I hadn't paid attention to politics or politicians for the last twenty years, which made me start to think, maybe that's why I'm in the position and mess I am in now. When I was young, I voted and paid attention to issues, but the older I got, the more I realized most politicians were liars, thieves, and cheats, basically in it for themselves.

I thought of all the people I knew throughout my life, and though a few of them may have cared about politics, the majority, and I mean most, didn't care or pay any attention to what was happening politically at all. This made me wonder what our society would be like if people cared more about politics and less about their favorite sports teams.

I'm an intelligent but uneducated guy; everything I learned was from life experience and paying attention to the world around me. But people I have known who thought they were smart just because they were educated, paid zero attention to politics. Why? I mean, they're supposed to be the smart ones. I avoided politics because I thought it was nothing but theatre, filled with cheaters and liars. So, what was the smart people's excuse for not paying attention to

86

politics? If they were so bright, why weren't they paying attention? And if they were paying attention, why weren't they smart enough to see how corrupt the system really was?

If people and society had more discussions about politics and weren't told over the years that 'talking politics' was rude, would society be in a better position? Why was it beaten into us not to discuss 'Religion or Politics'? Is it because if we did, we would get to the truth? I'm pretty sure we wouldn't be in the shape we are in now, and I'm pretty sure that criminal politicians wouldn't have been able to rob society blind. Toronto is a crumbling shithole, and the politicians don't care; it's like they only care about themselves and are working unchecked because no one wants to talk about it. I mean, the new 'Light Transit Rail' system in Toronto has been under construction for fourteen years, and not one Light Transit Train has traveled on it, and absolutely nothing has been done about it. People need to wake up.

I asked Robert who our local politicians were, and he looked at me and shook his head in disappointment. I guess he had the same epiphany I had, but he had it long ago.

It was as if he had read my mind: "I'm assuming you don't vote, Brent?"

Regret hit me immediately, "you assumed right, Robert."

"Have you ever thought that this is why our society is in the shape it is? Good people like yourself don't care; people like yourself assume the politicians would take care of everything; how is that working out for you now?" He was smiling but serious as he lectured me.

He wasn't trying to be an asshole; he was just trying to open my eyes, and I couldn't argue with him; he was right. He proceeded to educate me, "Our local city Councillor is Pauline Flatch, and our Member of Parliament is Bernie Peters."

I said, "Never heard of them."

Robert laughed, "I didn't think you would have."

I asked him if he had any opinions on either of them.

His reply made me laugh and feel sad at the same time, "Yeah, they're politicians. They're only in it for themselves and can't be trusted. If they do get involved with us, I'm sure it will only be for the press and publicity. They don't care, but they'll pretend to care if they can benefit from us."

Robert's phone rang. I decided to jump on the computer and research these politicians, and I heard Robert say, "Hello, Councillor Flatch. Thank you for calling me back."

Eric jumped up and mouthed, "Speaker, speaker."

Robert hit the speaker button so we could all hear the conversation. Robert explained the situation to her, and she agreed and sympathized with us, but her replies and words seemed insincere and disingenuous. Even though she was trying to be sympathetic, she sounded very patronizing.

As they spoke, I typed her name into the computer and was amazed at how many links came up. From my initial reading, most were negative; it didn't seem like anybody had a good thing to say about her. There were news articles about how she sold out the people over developers for a condominium project, articles about how she rezoned parkland for commercial development, and stories of how she was hardly present at City Hall for votes. And there a couple of stories of how she was caught submitting inflated and bogus expenses, and most interesting of all, which I found on the tenth or eleventh page of the search, was how she was caught accepting 'unreported gifts' from a lobbyist for the 'Outdoor Recreational Structure Association.'

As I was reading the article, Robert finished his conversation with Councillor Flatch, and he hung up the phone; when he was off, I started to read the end of the article aloud, "…though there was an appearance of a 'pay to play' scheme and an exchange of money for favors, Councillor Flatch did admit the transaction took place, but claimed it was just an 'accounting irregularity'. Councillor Flatch claimed that all monies received were within the rules and regulations of the 'Toronto Lobbyist Registrar' and were only accounted for incorrectly."

The article finished by saying, 'There will be no further inquiry from the Registrar."

I looked up at Robert and Eric, shaking my head, "And this is who will be fighting on our side? Oh, we are so fucked…"

I looked back at the computer and typed in Bernie Peters; again, thousands of links came up; these politicians love seeing their names and faces in the news. But the links for Bernie weren't as bad; he was the Member of Parliament for this area and had been so for about fifteen years, and people seemed to like him. The articles weren't bad, but they weren't great; there wasn't anything of substance to this guy; there were no articles about crusades or fights, no articles of him 'clashing' with the opposition; it was just articles of him making appearances, cutting ribbons at local fairs and community events, nothing of true civil importance. He wasn't trying to make a change; it looked like he was just a politician making appearances and kissing babies, and oh, not to forget, probably collecting a two-hundred-thousand-dollar a year salary, a pension, and benefits for life. All for just smiling, waving, and agreeing with everyone.

I looked back up and said to Eric and Robert, "And this Bernie guy? It looks like he doesn't care about anything except how he looks when his picture is taken."

Robert came over and looked over my shoulder. I showed him a couple of articles, and he just shrugged, "Well, it's all we have, hopefully they pay attention and talk about our situation to the press and anyone who will listen.

They might help swing public opinion and get people to pay attention to the situation. So, what else do we need to do?"

He answered his own question and said, "Reporters! We need reporters. We have to contact the press and get this story in the media." Again, though he was talking to me, he was looking at Eric with the camera the whole time.

I typed in the word 'Renoviction' and started searching, trying to find some reporters who may be covering and writing about the topic, but the results were no surprise. As I discovered before, there were no real big stories in the mainstream media; no one was focusing on or talking about it. Sure, there were a few articles about evictions, but no reporter was constantly following or trying to dig into the story of illegal evictions. But then I saw one girl's name on a couple of articles in different small independent publications and news websites; it was Joanna Chow and her byline always read, 'freelance reporter.' She was the only one paying attention to the situation, so I sent her a detailed email explaining our plight. After her, I wrote down the few names of people who had written the odd story on this subject, and we emailed all of them. When I say all of them, I mean only four or five.

Robert's phone rang again, and before he answered, I heard Eric say, "This is starting to look like a 'war room'; I love it."

Robert answered, and it was his friend who was doing the 'search' on the L.L.C. He grabbed a pen and paper and started jotting down notes. Eric asked to put the call on speaker, but Robert smirked and shook his head no, so we only got one side of the conversation.

As Robert took notes, he would occasionally interject and ask questions. There were comments like 'Really?' or 'How about that.' One of the last questions he asked was, "And how do you spell that? Ok, L-i-a-n-g J-i-a-n-g, wow ok. Thanks, that's great info. Thank you for looking into this for me. Yup, okay. I'll talk to you later."

He looked at me and smiled, so I had to ask, "Okay, Robert, I'll bite. What the hell is a Liang Jiang?"

He smiled, had a look of satisfaction on his face, and said, "That, my friends, is the man who is trying to throw us out of our homes, Mr. Liang-Jiang Huong."

"Son of a bitch… way to go, Robert!" I gave him a high five, sat back at the computer, and said okay, "Let's find this S.O.B. online and see what we can learn."

I typed in his name and started with 'images'; tons of pages with what must have been thousands of images popped up. Next, I searched through 'all' on Google, and almost twenty million links came up. I clicked one that said, 'Find people named Liang Jiang Huong,' so I went there first. There were pages upon pages of people with that name.'

"Wow, Robert, I think you found the 'John Smith' of China; there's tons of them. Let me look on Facebook; I hope he's on there. "I laughed when I saw the results, and I had to say, "holy shit, there's like twenty pages of them."

We laughed while looking at all the 'Liang-Jiang Houng' on Facebook, but then it hit me. We should be on Facebook. If we were going to raise awareness and put a spotlight on this issue, we had to be online; we needed social media. I pulled out the whiteboard I had behind my desk, blew the dust off it, propped it up, and wrote 'RENOVICTION' in caps across the top, then I wrote 'Facebook, Instagram, Twitter, and Reddit' underneath it.

Robert said, "Now you're thinking Brent."

Eric added, "Now, it really looks like a war room."

Just then, Roberts' phone rang again, and as soon as he answered, he put it on speaker so we could hear the conversation. It was our Member of Parliament Bernie Peter's office, but it wasn't Bernie himself; it was his assistant. I guess when you are a Member of Parliament, you are too important to make your own phone calls, and to me, that shows tremendous disrespect. The assistant just asked about the situation and what was happening; Robert filled her in and told her about the upcoming tenants' meeting. All she said was that if he was able to, the Honorable Mr. Peters would be in attendance. She thanked Robert and hung up.

I could tell he was angry. He put the phone down, looked over, and said, "Your tax dollars hard at work."

I shook my head and wrote on the whiteboard, 'Tenant Meeting Monday— Attending: Pauline Flatch and MAYBE Bernie Peters, then I added 'Acorn.' Writing Acorn on the board reminded me to ask Eric and Robert if they were going to the meeting with me on Saturday, and both said they wouldn't miss it.

Robert said he would put a notice up in the lobby for everyone, and before I could catch myself, I said, "And if anyone needs a lift, let them know I can drive."

Eric looked at me from behind the camera in disbelief. I looked at him surprised, also, and he said, "How about that? Bingham is opening up a little. Good for you Bingham."

It made me smile, and I satisfactorily said, "Yeah, how about that."

I looked at my phone to check my emails, and lo and behold, Joanna Chow had gotten back to me already. I said, "Hey guys, Joanna Chow already replied; let's see what she has to say."

I read it aloud to them, "Dear Brent, thank you for your email. I am very sorry to hear about what you and your fellow tenants are going through. I have written some stories on this subject, and yes, I am following the affordable housing crisis in Toronto. And as you said, I am the only journalist following this issue. I would love to sit down with you and/or the other tenants of the building

90

and hear your stories. Hopefully, I can follow the situation until the end and until there's a conclusion. Please call me anytime so we can set a time to meet that is mutually convenient. My contact information is below. I look forward to hearing from you; thank you, Brent. Truly, Joanna Chow."

I looked at the guys and said, "I guess no time like the present."

Not only did I want to set up the meeting, but I also had a couple of questions for Joanna about the whole housing situation and, just simply, what the hell is happening in Toronto? I dialed Joanna and put it on speaker for the boys to hear. She answered on the first ring, which impressed me: "Hi Joanna, it's Brent Bingham. Thank you for replying to my email so quickly. I appreciate that."

She didn't sound any older than sixteen, but she was very professional and straight to the point. She started by saying that there is 'an affordable housing crisis' in Toronto, and it's becoming a plague. She told me about a couple of stories she has covered and a few of the publications/websites she has written for, and she flat-out said that she has been trying to get this out into the mainstream media, but no one wants to pick up the story.

I immediately had to ask her why, and I liked her response.

She was straight to the point and said, "Just follow the money and votes, Brent. Losing affordable housing makes the government look bad, but it doesn't pay the bills, so when need be, they'll stand in front of the cameras preaching about saving 'affordable housing' while at the same time accepting money for rezoning and selling the public out. It's politics, and it's sick. Increased property values mean more money for anyone involved except for the renter at the bottom; sorry to lay it out like that, Brent, but that's the situation."

I said, "No problem, I'm an honest guy. I can admit what's going on. It's a transference of wealth from the bottom to the top. Everyone was in on it, and now so am I, but unfortunately, I'm right at the bottom."

She replied, "damn, that's good. Can I quote you?"

I told her about the Acorn meeting on the weekend and our tenants meeting on Monday, and she said she would be at both. I finished the call, added her name to the whiteboard, and got a big thumbs-up from Eric.

I went to the fridge, grabbed a couple of beers, and gave them to the boys. Robert shrugged his shoulders and said, "Why not? I'm sure it's five o'clock somewhere."

I looked at the clock, laughed, and said, "Well, it's four forty-five here."

I raised my drink, and we 'clinked' our bottles together. I said, "We made some progress today. It looks like we're starting to get our ducks in a row."

We sat and chatted for a while, and getting to know Robert was very interesting. He told us how he used to work in accounting for the publishing industry. The accounting firm he worked for was very prestigious back in the day, and he worked with some of the most well-known magazines in the world. He told us that the firm handled companies like Hearst Media and Time Inc.; he even told stories of meeting Bob Guccione and Larry Flynt when they came to town.

I thought to myself, 'damn, Robert has been around and has some crazy experience; I think our new landlord might be underestimating the people he's messing with. After more beers, Robert opened up about why he lived in a building like this. After having a promising, rewarding career, his wife died, and he had a breakdown; after raising his three kids, it was hard to keep up with the rigors of his career and family, and he burned out. Though he may have lived an exciting, extravagant life throughout his career, he was just a 'worker bee.' When global conglomerates gobbled up the print industry in the nineties, there was no room for the little guy, and he was forced to retire. He needed to reduce his expenses, so living in a building like this was all he could afford, and it was all that he needed.

After listening to Robert, I was even more motivated. This is why affordable housing is so important; life happens, people lose their jobs, people get sick, and mental illness prevents people from functioning within society. And where are they supposed to live? They are still part of society; are we just supposed to shove people aside and displace them away from their friends, family, and community because they are poor?

Robert and Eric left after a few hours, and I had a good buzz going. I felt like more drinks and doing more work. I decided to make social media accounts for our cause, but the only problem was that I wasn't a social media kind of guy. I didn't use these apps and I didn't have any of them on my phone. I wasn't one of those people constantly looking at their phones—but I guess I was about to learn and become one of them. It was pretty simple, and I think I got lucky; I was able to create a page on Twitter, Facebook, and Instagram all called 'Renoviction.' When I typed 'Renoviction' in the search field for each, a lot of different pages came up, but they were all called 'Renoviction Hamilton' or 'Acorn Renoviction Group,' a lot of variations of 'Renoviction,' but nobody had claimed the plain and simple name, 'Renoviction.'

I had to think of my first post. All the accounts were linked together, so when I posted to one, it posted to all of them. I wondered if I should wait and ask Eric and Robert what the first post should be, but I decided—no, this is my fight. If this guy wants to throw me out of my place, then I want to make sure he knows who he's up against. I want him to know what I think about him, and I want him to know that I'm going to embarrass him and call him out in public. I'm going to make sure that his friends, his family, and everyone that knows him, knows that this is how he makes a living; being a greedy scumbag prick.

I didn't know what to say, and I wasn't sure if posting this while drunk was a good or bad thing. I started to type, 'I'm getting thrown out...', I stopped typing, deleted what I had just written, and tried to think. I got up, grabbed the vodka in the freezer, and took a shot; that was my way of thinking. I sat at the computer with my head back and eyes closed. I don't know how long I sat there with my mind spinning when it finally came to me. Just be honest and tell the truth. Say what you mean and mean what you say. Don't be rude. Don't be mean. Be funny. Be polite. Tell the truth.

I leaned forward, put my fingers on the keyboard, and started typing.

'Renoviction definition: 'The illegal eviction of a rental tenant on the grounds that renovations are planned.''

'Welcome to Renoviction. A page dedicated to educating and informing people of the ever- rising affordable housing crisis and the plaque of Renovictions. The tenants of Three-Ninety-One Empire Avenue are being illegally evicted by our new anonymous owner/landlord. The goal of the 'Renoviction Page' is not only to raise public awareness about our situation and the affordable housing crisis in the city, but to expose, confront, and show the world how these greedy, speculative landlords make their money.''

I sat back in the chair and looked at what I had written. I was pretty satisfied with myself, but more importantly, I had to see how it looked in the morning when I was sober.

Chapter 10

When I woke up Saturday morning, I was excited about attending the Acorn meeting as it would be our first time getting out with the camera to see how this affected people in the city. The week leading up to the Acorn meeting had been pretty busy. I was on set every day and had been posting eviction and housing stories on Facebook all week. I had sent the links to everyone I could think of, which wasn't a lot of people, but when I asked people at work from set to join and share the page, the sites started to get some traction.

People in my industry included actors, actresses, dancers, models, wannabe influencers, OnlyFans models, and a whole lot of narcissistic personalities who were really on top of their social media 'game.' These people had thousands and thousands of followers; they spent their lives online. Everyone I told our story to was sympathetic and willing to help. People in the arts are always willing to support whatever 'social justice cause' of the week comes along, just as long as it gets them more likes and friends. And who's kidding who - if it gets 'Renoviction,' more likes and followers, who cares? By the end of the week, we had almost one thousand followers, and I was starting to understand the addiction to social media.

I had a couple of hours until we were all to meet in the lobby; I made coffee, sat at the computer, logged on to Facebook, and thought to myself, 'What the hell am I doing logging on to Facebook first thing in the morning?' I felt dirty. I decided to try to find our owner, Liang-Jiang Huong. I typed in his name, and when I hit enter, nineteen pages of that name came up. I could tell there were a lot of bot accounts as well as real accounts, but all of them were in China. This was going to be more complicated than I thought.

The next thing I had to do was look up the 'Toronto Lobbyist Registrar,' which I came across when reading about Pauline Flatch. I typed 'Lobbying in Canada,' and a few interesting pages came up. First, there was the 'Toronto Lobbyist Registrar,' which is the office responsible for bribing politicians at the municipal level. Then there was 'The Office of the Integrity Commissioner of Ontario', which is the office responsible for bribing politicians at the Provincial level. And lastly, 'The Office of the Commissioner of Lobbying Canada,' which is the office responsible for bribing Federal politicians.

There it was, right in front of my face, everything that's wrong with our government and society today; no wonder poor people didn't have a voice in politics; we are living in a 'pay to play' political system. If you have the money, you can sit down with a politician and ask them to change laws so that they're in your or your industry's favor, and if you're poor, you can't. The late great comedian Robin Williams was right when he said, 'Politicians should wear sponsor jackets like NASCAR drivers; that way, we know who owns them.'

I started with the municipal site; I had no idea what I was looking for or how to navigate the website; all I knew was that my old friend, Kerwin, and 'The Alliance of Commercial Housing Rentals' were in there somewhere. I found the search section for lobbyists and lobbying firms, so I started there; I typed in Kerwin Cummings, and lo and behold, there he was. He's been registered to 'influence' government officials for twenty years. He must be doing pretty well if he's been paying off politicians for that long, and he must be pretty connected. It's funny; we use that same term, 'connected,' for gangsters and criminals, like 'don't mess with that guy he's connected.' And I don't think that's a coincidence. What is truly sad is that this guy is considered an upstanding, respected member of society, yet that couldn't be further from the truth.

Next, I typed 'The Alliance of Commercial Housing Rentals.' Their listing indicated they had only been around for four years, which made me think the organization was a creation of Kerwin Cummings. Apparently, if there was an industry to exploit, Kerwin would be involved in it. I checked the other two registered lobbying websites, and sure enough, Kerwin and his 'Alliance' were registered to buy politicians at every level in the country.

I went back to the City of Toronto Registrar's website and searched until I found the 'lobbyist activity' section. This was where they listed all the meetings between politicians and lobbyists, and it also listed how much money was 'contributed' to the politician's office. This was when I realized how fixed and corrupt the system was; it's set up to keep the rich, rich, and the poor, poor. I typed Kerwin's name into the search field and couldn't believe what I saw. He had met with what I'm assuming, was every City Councillor. I didn't know how many City Councillors Toronto had, but it looked like they were all listed, and they all received the same amount of money from Kerwin, three thousand dollars per meeting. I opened another window and googled, 'How many Toronto city Councillors are there?' There are twenty-five; I went back and counted the meetings he had, and yup, twenty-five. 'The Alliance' had spent seventy-five-thousand dollars on city politicians in one year alone, and for every single meeting, it listed the same topic, 'Affordable Housing.' Wow, that's pretty affordable to have a discussion. I couldn't wait to see what he had paid to the provincial and federal politicians in the name of affordable housing.

After learning this, I was curious; I wondered how many 'registered' lobbyists there were. There wasn't a total number of lobbyists listed, so I had to search and add them up manually. After I counted them, I knew why they didn't list a total - it was offensive. I stopped counting at five-hundred-seventy-five, and there were countless more. It was unbelievable, these politicians were having money thrown at them from every angle and from every industry.

I was scared to see what I would learn from the provincial and federal lobbying websites. First, I had to educate myself. I typed into Google, "How many Members of Provincial Parliament does Ontario have, and how many MPs does Canada have?" I was shocked when I learned that Ontario had one hundred twenty-four Members of Provincial Parliament, and Canada had a whopping three hundred thirty-eight Members of Parliament. I immediately had to go to the lobbying websites and see how many lobbyists were registered for these folks.

First, I went to the 'Office of the Integrity Commissioner of Ontario' the website for Provincial lobbyists. I always found it funny to see the words 'integrity' and Government in the same sentence. I found the registered lobbyist section, and after a half hour of adding over three thousand of them, I gave up. Federally, it was even worse; I stopped tallying when I reached six thousand. The scary thing was that that wasn't even all of them; my guess was that there could be upwards of ten thousand slimy, slithering lobbyists registered on that website; that's thousands of bribes a politician could receive.

After learning this shit, I was disappointed but justified that I was right about our political system; it's corrupt and full of criminals, what 'smart' people call politicians. If you don't believe our political system has been hijacked and stolen by financial interests, take five minutes and look into lobbying. You will learn that financial tyrants are running us, and we, the 'people,' don't stand a chance because most of us don't have a clue what our politicians are up to.

Learning all this lobbying shit made me wonder if our building had even the slightest chance of winning. I went back to the City Councillor lobbying website and had to look; I had to see what our city Councillor and M.P. were up to with my friend Kerwin. When I did, it was like a punch in the face and made me feel like a sucker; these politicians that are supposed to be on our side are just putting on a show. It was all just theatre for them. Councillor Flatch has had two meetings with Kerwin in the last two years and has accepted a three-thousand-dollar campaign contribution each year from his 'Alliance.'

Bernie Peters was no better—actually, he was worse. He has met with the 'Alliance' twice in the last two years and accepted four thousand dollars for each meeting. I guess the higher you go in politics, the more money you can take in bribes. After discovering this, I felt sick to my stomach, knowing we didn't stand a chance.

I had gone down the rabbit hole and didn't even notice the time until there was a knock at my door. It was Robert. He asked me if I was okay and said it was time to go. He said that I was already ten minutes late to meet everyone downstairs.

I apologized, "Yeah, sorry, I got distracted with something."

He turned to walk away and said, "Well, hurry up, let's go; we have to go and stick it to the man." He raised his arm and fist over his head as he disappeared down the stairs.

It made me smile to see him do this, but deep down, I felt terrible. I felt that all this fighting and protesting was going to be an exercise in futility.

When I got to the mailboxes, Eric was there with his sound guy, Robert, and Bill, the quiet old guy. They said Nolan and Krystle had just left and would meet us there. Sarah, the dingbat, was coming out of her apartment as we were going out, and Robert asked her if she was coming to the Acorn meeting.

She said she wanted to, but that she was too busy. She asked us to let her know what happened. Her reply was exactly what was wrong with today's society: people were too busy or too stupid to focus on issues directly affecting them.

The old guy Bill, whom I didn't know and had never spoken to before except for the odd 'hello' in passing, asked her, "If I may ask you, young lady, what in this world could be more important than fighting to save your home?"

I liked him immediately.

Smiling proudly, she replied, "I'm going to see the new Fast & Furious and then sushi with my friends."

"Well, okay then, I hope you enjoy," Bill held the door open for her, and as she left, he turned to us and said, "And that, gentlemen, is why the world is going to shit."

Eric wired me up for sound, and we all piled into my car. The meeting wasn't too far away, so it didn't take us that long to get there, but Bill spoke the entire way. Eric had asked him one question, and his answer was pretty damn long-winded.

When we got out of the car, Eric looked at me and joked, "We're going to have to do a lot of editing when Bill speaks."

We laughed and got ready to go inside.

As we walked towards the meeting, I asked Eric what our plan was when we got in there.

He looked at me and said, "Bingham, just be yourself, and let's see what happens. This is real life; there's no script for this."

I looked at Eric, pretty impressed, "Damn, we should be recording you making statements like that."

The meeting was taking place in the basement of a church, and when I heard that, I was a little taken aback; I wasn't too fond of the Catholic Church ever since, well, you know, the whole pedophilia thing. I assumed the church wouldn't do much to help any group unless the collection plate was involved, so I'm guessing these Acorn folks had to pay full price for the room.

I walked inside and headed downstairs, with Eric following. I saw Kyle, and he was talking to a beautiful, dark-haired woman who was either Greek,

Italian, or, most likely, Middle Eastern. She was wearing a pair of jeans and a red 'Acorn Community Member' T-shirt - and she made it look amazing.

I waved to Kyle and headed over to them.

I greeted Kyle and said hello to the beautiful 'Acorn' woman.

Kyle introduced her as 'Laila,' the 'Lead Community Member' for this area, and I thought to myself, of course, Middle Eastern.

I shook her hand and said, "It's very nice to meet you. I'm Brent."

I looked at her T-shirt and said to Kyle, "You didn't tell me there were T shirts."

He smiled and went directly into a sales pitch for the shirts: "Oh, didn't I tell you? Yes, we encourage everyone to wear them, which helps with the organization and raises awareness and funds. It's great if everyone in the building gets one, and we can also set you up with larger quantities that you can sell in your neighborhood to raise awareness; it helps cover the cost of printing flyers and posters for your cause."

I knew I didn't like these guys, and I just realized why. Kyle was smarter than he appeared to let on, and he knew exactly what his job really was. I'm here because I'm thrust into a situation of fighting an illegal eviction, and this guy is here to hustle t-shirts and memberships; not only that, but now he wants me to hustle t-shirts, too.

I just placated him by saying, "Hey, that sounds great. I'll let you know."

I got angry and thought, 'Everyone is looking out for their own angle, whatever the situation is, whether it be 'charities,' 'activists,' and even 'churches,' everywhere you look someone always has their damn hand out to trying to make a buck. It's like everyone is trying to grab the last dollar they'll ever earn; sadly, this is what our society has become.

I put my disillusionment aside and got back to why I was here. I looked at Laila, told her how nice it was to meet her, and explained my whole situation. After stumbling through the story of the building and getting a bit worked up, she grabbed my hand and stopped me.

Smiling, she said, "I understand."

I thanked her for listening and apologized for ranting; I was very curious about what such a beautiful woman was doing here and why she was even fighting with 'Acorn,' but all I could muster to say to her was, "So, what brings you to 'Acorn'?"

She smiled and explained, "When I first came to Canada, I couldn't afford much; my first couple of landlords played games with me, and then one tried to use the excuse of renovations to evict me. I contacted Acorn, and they put me in touch with some smart people who helped me; I'm still with them so that I can help others. They brought so much attention and publicity to my issue that the landlord gave up and agreed to negotiate a new lease, and he let me and the other tenants stay."

Her accent was amazing, and her reply impressed me more than the Acorn T- shirt she was wearing; Laila was making an impression on me. I wasn't sure if I was staring too much, but I was enamored with her. I wanted to say so much, but I kept it short, "Good for you for fighting and standing up."

Her reply was firm, "I lived in Iran. If you don't stand up and fight against bad people, bad things happen to good people. This isn't Iran; this is Canada, but people behave like it is Iran. They do nothing, not because they are scared or afraid, but because they are lazy. No one wants to fight back in this country."

I laughed and said, "Yeah, I hear you, and most will say, 'it is what it is'."

She looked at me angrily and said, "No, it is not, 'it is what it is,' what does this even mean? That you can't change anything? What is that phrase? It's the worst thing I have ever heard, 'it is what it is'? Accept anything and everything that happens to you, no matter what? What is wrong with these people? They want to give up; no wonder the system is so corrupt and crushing them, 'it is what it is."

Damn, I liked Laila, she didn't mince her words. "I one hundred percent agree with you, Laila; please, continue…" she smiled.

I told her about the documentary, and she loved the idea. She said she would announce it at the beginning of the meeting so I could see who would be interested.

She grabbed me by the hand and led me to a seat at the table. I saw Nolan and Krystle sitting and said, "Hey guys, good to see you."

The room was set up with everyone sitting at tables in a big square so everyone could see each other. There were people from all walks of life, old, young, disabled, single, couples, and people new to the country, but the one thing we all had in common was that we all had affordable housing, and our landlords wanted us out.

Laila stood and called the meeting to order. She welcomed everyone to the meeting by introducing the building addresses dealing with evictions and 'Renovictions.' She welcomed three addresses and introduced us as a new building joining the fight. She was so energetic and happy. Laila also introduced other people who were here to support or help us in one way or another; she introduced Joanna Chow, the reporter following 'Renovictions' who wanted to hear our stories, and Mark Richards from the Parkdale Legal Aid Office. Surprisingly, she also introduced me, making me feel awkward.

Laila told them I was going through a Renoviction myself, explained the documentary, and pointed out Eric at the back of the room. She did a great job selling the documentary; everyone was into it and when she was finished explaining the movie. I raised my hand, Laila said, "Yes, Brent,"

I stood and mentioned the social media pages, adding, "We're on Facebook, as 'Renoviction.' I hope everyone can join, follow, and share away. Sorry, that's it, thank you," and I sat back down.

Before my ass hit the chair, everyone pulled their phones out and started typing; after a couple of swipes of the phone, I could see everyone smile when they found the page. Then I could see their single finger clicking 'Join,' which made me smile.

Laila started the meeting by recapping everyone in the room and explaining the situations that were taking place. She was very passionate when she spoke, and she got very emotional when speaking of the injustices the landlords were trying to get away with. She was able to get the room worked up and motivated to fight. Everyone here represented four buildings, including ours, that were going through some sort of illegal eviction, renoviction, or downright fuckery from their landlord. She started with Four- Eighty-Nine Dovercourt Road; the room laughed when they heard the number, and a voice shouted, "Five Years!"

Laila smiled, "Yes, we know, five years," everyone in the room gave a quick little clap. She reviewed some dates and forms they needed to complete and shared results from an engineering firm they were waiting for. She ended by saying, "Hang in there, guys. They aren't getting you out."

She went through the other two buildings, one of which had the landlord go bankrupt and try to sell the whole building to 'family members'. I say 'family members' in quotes because he was obviously trying to evict the entire building illegally.

The next building wasn't doing repairs; the owner of that building wouldn't fix anything until the tenants pushed him to the final 'straw.' Tenants would have to go to the Tenant Board for the most minor and pettiest matters. It was so frustrating to the tenants having to file the paperwork, take time off work, and attend the hearings, but meanwhile, it's nothing for the landlord; they have their rep or paralegal at the Tenant Board for the day seeing case after case. This bullshit clogged the system, and it was totally unfair to the tenant, but the process was perfectly legal; it's the way the system worked, and it's the way they wanted the system to work.

Next, Laila asked me to say some words about our building and situation.

I stood up and smiled at Laila, "Thank you, Laila. I can't believe the stories I've been hearing and what landlords are doing out there. We live at Three-Ninety-One Empire Avenue, it's a little three-story walk-up. Our building was recently sold, and our new owner has sent an eviction letter to everyone claiming, 'that due to renovations, we have to vacate our units,' and he's given us sixty days to get out."

I looked at Mark Richards from the Legal Aid Office and continued, "We're meeting with Richard Wessler from the East End Legal Aid Office on Monday at our tenants' meeting, and that's all we know right now. We won't know much until we speak with the lawyer, and then we'll know what our next step is."

Laila stood back up and impressed me with what she did next; she asked for volunteers to help knock on doors in our neighborhood to help spread the word about our 'Renoviction' situation. But she didn't simply ask; she spoke to everyone as if we were all one; she used phrases and words like 'stand-up,' 'together strong, divided we fall,' 'solidarity,' 'neighbor,' 'community,' 'justice,' and 'right and wrong.' I would have followed Laila into a fire after her speech. About fifteen people, almost half the room, raised their hands to volunteer. I looked back at Eric, and we gave each other a look of surprise.

Laila finished by saying, "We'll plan a neighborhood walkthrough and then a rally. We'll tell everyone about it when we go door knocking, and we can get some flyers made up for the building. Brent, can we set that up together?"

I was surprised at the offer and said, "Uh…" I stood up and looked at Laila, "Uh, yes, I'd love to do that." I sat back down, smiled, and thought, 'I'm going to be working with Laila!'

The meeting wrapped up, and Laila told everyone to mingle and have some coffee and donuts at the back of the room. I grabbed a coffee and made my way to Mark Richards, and Eric was soon to join us.

I introduced myself to Mark and proceeded to fill him in about our situation, which I learned, he was all too familiar with. He said that ninety percent of his time and energy is spent on defending tenants from getting evicted these days, and the landlords have abused the system so badly that there is a backlog with the Tenant Board. He told me there are ways to fight and win, but it is rare. He said the building at four-eighty- nine Dovercourt Road has been going through this for five years because they always find a way around the landlord's bullshit and lies. It had taken a lot of work and a lot of expert technical witnesses to refute and debunk the bullshit the landlord was telling the Tenant Board, but they've won so far.

I said, "It sounds like a lot of work and hassle."

He looked me directly in the eye and said, "Oh, it is, and it's going to take a lot of energy to fight; it's going to take a lot out of you; it's not easy."

I asked him if he knew our lawyer, Richard Wessler, who worked in the East Toronto Office. He said he knew of him but that they had never talked.

I asked him if I could pick his brain for a little bit, and he said no problem. I was honest and asked, "So what is really stopping them from throwing us out, and how does this play out once we're done with the Landlord and Tenant Board? Whether they tell us we gotta stay or gotta go?"

He raised his eyebrows and sighed, "Well, there's not much stopping them. There are fines, but they're minimal. If you're ordered to leave the unit, you might get a buyout. If you refuse to leave and choose to fight this, and the Board rules that you can stay, you win, but you'll still lose."

I looked at him confused and said, "What do you mean we lose? I thought if we win, we win. Are you saying we can't win?"

He nodded yes and explained, "After all that is said and done, after all the reports and arguments, let's say you win, and you get to return to the unit after the repairs or renovations are done. What if there are delays? What if it takes them nine months to do what they originally said would take three weeks? There's no timeframe for how long the work can take, and if they run into 'unforeseen' delays, all they have to do is file an extension at the board, and it could be another six months. They can play the system and keep you out of that unit for as long as they want to. And how long can you do that for? You need a place to live, so eventually, you'll walk away and find a place to live. The hearing, the Tenant Board, will only delay the inevitable, and that is you leaving the unit."

When I walked away, I wished Mark was our lawyer; he knew what was happening. I spoke to half a dozen people, and the stories were all the same: their landlord wanted to evict them so new tenants would pay double, even triple, the amount. The only different thing was their circumstances; some people were on disability or pensions, and many people were on fixed incomes, so they couldn't afford to any more rent even if they wanted to. Some were young families; some were people who had lived in their buildings most of their lives and didn't want to leave their homes and communities.

Laila approached us, and Eric walked away to talk to other people in the building. I complimented Laila on the meeting and her commitment to the cause.

She replied, "Brent, if I'm not doing it, who's going to do it. A lot of these people are vulnerable and don't understand the system. If they get an eviction letter, a lot of people think they have to move. They can't comprehend that their landlord, maybe someone they have known for years, would do something illegal and unscrupulous to them, and they accept it as right."

I agreed with her and added, "We have a couple of those people who just took the old owner's word and thought she would never do them wrong. Meanwhile, she was trying to get them out to earn a few extra bucks on top of the millions she sold the building for. It was disgusting, and still, these guys didn't see that she was doing something wrong to them."

Laila shook her head, reached out, and softly grabbed my arm to make her point. She was upset and said that she couldn't believe how some people behaved. She got a little feisty and then punched her fist into her hand. She was a lovely, passionate woman, but I wouldn't want to see her angry. I was starting to like Laila.

She asked for my phone number, and I almost fainted. It surprised me and lifted my spirits, but then I realized it was to coordinate for the 'march' and 'rally' we would be organizing. Either way, Laila is going to have my phone number.

I said goodbye and noticed Joanna Chow waving me over to where she was speaking with Robert. I went over and just listened as they spoke. Robert was very poignant, knowledgeable, and direct to the point; he was way more intelligent than he looked and smarter than he led people to believe. He made the case for what was wrong with the situation by explaining how real estate investing was different from other asset investing since the investor deals with peoples' lives and homes. He was saying the rules need to be stricter and harsher, and investors and speculators shouldn't be able to buy an undervalued building and throw everyone out to increase their profit. They shouldn't think they are guaranteed to make money just because they bought the building. This kind of investment is a risk like all other investments, but society feels that just because someone made the investment, they should make a profit risk-free.

He wrapped up speaking with her by making a great point; he said, "Where do you think we are going to go? Sure, some of us may find new homes, but some of us might end up on the streets, and if we end up on the streets, all of society pays, whether it's for shelters, food banks, or mental health support. We all pay for that. And why, because one rich investor wanted to make a profit. It's horrible, and it's a plight on society."

Joanna thanked him, and I introduced myself. She said, "Wow, you guys are really serious about this."

I replied, "We have to be."

She asked, "Where will you go if you lose Brent?"

That made me think; I hadn't thought that far ahead; I was only thinking about the fight in front of me. Deep down, I didn't see us winning, but I never actually connected that losing meant moving.

Now that I had thought about it, I had to say, "Well, I'll probably have to move out of the city. I'll have to move away from my community, away from friends and family, away from anything familiar, and further away from my work, which means more time on the road commuting. I'll be away from everything that I have ever known."

I wrapped up with Joanna, who said that she would be at our tenants meeting, so we could talk some more then. I made my way back over to Eric just as he finished speaking with an elderly man who was flailing and swinging his arms as he talked. We gathered Robert, Bill, and the sound guy and headed toward the door. As we left, I looked back and saw Laila watching us leave. I smiled back at her and waved goodbye.

Eric caught it and said, "What was that, Bingham? If you get involved with Laila during this, I'll kiss you. A love story? I couldn't ask for anything better. Oscar material buddy, Oscar!"

I told him to shut up, and we made our way to the car. Bill talked the whole way home. Between Robert, Eric, me, and the sound guy, we must have said no more than five words; it was all Bill.

When we arrived back at the building, we began to say our goodbyes, and Bill continued his diatribe of dribble; he was recapping and talking about the meeting, his thoughts, and his feelings. We all stood there for a minute or two, but enough was enough.

I said, "That's great, Bill; you guys keep chatting and keep us posted."

Eric and I headed up the stairs. I looked back at Robert, who was trapped by Bill and the look on his face said it all. As we walked up the stairs, I told Eric I had done some digging and that we needed to talk about lobbying and the evil lobbyist.

His smile was sinister, "Yeah? It's time to get this lobbyist scumbag?"

I said, "Well, let's talk, and I'll let you decide."

Eric was giddy when he said, "Get the beers, Bingham, and let's get down to business."

We went into the apartment, and Eric started setting up the camera immediately. I grabbed a couple of beers, turned on the computer, and put some music on; I had made a playlist of motivational and protest songs to help me get into fight mode, songs that would encourage me to stand up and fight. I was a big music guy and believe music sets the mood and affects your energy. There was a mix of songs about riots or social movements, revolutions, and peaceful civil disobedience; the first song was *'Street Fighting Man'*, by 'The Rolling Stones,' which seemed appropriate.

I sat on the sofa beside Eric with my laptop; I gave him his beer and started to explain my findings, "OK, I followed the money, and I started researching what was going on with 'lobbying' and this city.

I laid out and explained everything I learned. I explained the different levels of government and how much money they can each receive in 'campaign contributions.' I showed him the 'Registered Lobbyists' section. I told him how many politicians versus how many lobbyists there were, and he was floored. Neither of us could have ever imagined that it was this bad.

I showed him how I found the meetings between my friend Kerwin and the very politicians who are going to sit at the same table as us, look us in the eye, and tell us that they are one hundred percent on our side.

I said, "I found out how much money Flatch and Peters have received from the Alliance and my friend Kerwin. If this wasn't a conflict of interest, I don't know what it is. And this is how the system works?"

Eric loved what I was saying, so I kept going, "I took it a step further. I did a general search on the lobbying sites for 'housing,' 'apartment,' or 'developer' lobbying groups, and I found eleven. Every politician could potentially have eleven different people throwing money at them to support their company's needs regarding affordable housing."

I started shaking my head and getting angry, "Then I went to the meeting section of the lobbying site to see how many of these groups our politicians have met with?" I looked at Eric, shaking my head, and sickly said, "Eleven, they have met with all eleven. I can't believe this. They're raking in so much money, they won't give a shit about us, it's all smoke and mirrors, it's a fucking show."

Eric agreed and said, "Bingham, they don't know that we know this stuff; we're not saying anything about this until we know what to do with it."

I agreed with him, "I'm not saying anything about these politicians and the money to anyone. I want to see how they behave at our meetings and what they say to our faces. I want to see if they put their arms around us and tell us they care and that they want to do all they can to help us while they're stuffing money in their pockets with the other hand."

Eric immediately replied, "Exactly."

I continued, "For the record, our Councillor Flatch has received six thousand dollars, the maximum, from each of the eleven lobby groups representing some facet of commercial housing over the past two years. That's sixty-six thousand dollars for meetings. Now think about this: that is only one industry in the city; imagine roads, garbage collection, contract services, and suppliers; it's no wonder why there are so many lobbyists. These politicians are raking it in and getting rich while they turn a blind eye to the people they are hurting, the very people that vote them in, and the very people they are supposed to be representing and protecting."

I got up and grabbed two more beers. I was so pissed off I kept pacing, "These politicians are abusing their power, plain and simple; it's criminal, its bribes, but it's legal, it's fucking pay to play, and it's how the system works. So, if there's no way we can win, let's expose them all; every cog in this fucked up system, no one is off limits. It's time for the gloves to come off and time to give these bully thugs the exposure they want. They want the spotlight - they're going to get it."

Chapter 11

The weekend flew by, and tonight was our first tenant meeting with the lawyer attending. It had only been two days since the Acorn meeting, and nothing had happened in between. I wasn't working today, so I planned to sit around all day, drinking coffee and relaxing until the meeting. I put the coffee on and sat at the computer. I logged on to Facebook, and I couldn't believe the traction we had gained after our meeting with Acorn on Saturday. The account had skyrocketed with followers; apparently, one of the things Acorn brings to the table is the ability to get attention on social media.

They had accounts set up in most social media apps named AcornToronto, AcornMontreal, AcornVancouver, and basically every city; their accounts impressively had hundreds of thousands of followers. Today, we had over five thousand followers on each site. People were liking the page, sharing it, commenting on it, and even posting their own stories of *Renovictions*, and sharing advice on what to do. There were over one hundred direct messages to the Facebook page alone. I tried to reply to as many as I could, but it was hard. I decided to post an update on our situation and keep the story going in the feed. I tagged reporters and hashtagged every relevant topic I could think of. Damn, here I was—hash tagging and linking—hoping for more followers and likes. I could feel myself getting addicted to this social media shit. Unbelievable.

Eric got to my apartment ten minutes before the meeting. I asked him to relax with the filming on the way there. He agreed, and just wired me for sound before we left. We knocked on Robert's door and made our way to the meeting. It started at seven. We were about half an hour early.

As we were walking along Queen Street, Robert spotted our esteemed Councillor Flatch doing some shopping.

"Hey, that's Pauline Flatch in that clothing store."

We all stepped back and looked in the window like kids looking at a toy store. I had no idea if it was her or not.

I asked Robert if he was sure, and he said, "Yup, that's her; I recognize her from her pictures."

She was the only person in the store, standing at a rack browsing through some sweaters; there wasn't much stuff in the store, which meant it was probably pretty swanky and pretty expensive.

I immediately pulled Eric and Robert out of view; I said, "Eric, get your camera and film her shopping, but don't let her see you."

Eric slung the camera on his shoulder and ran across the street. Robert grabbed the camera case, and we moved out of view.

After a few minutes and after buying one of the sweaters, she came out and headed down the street towards our meeting until she decided to go into the next clothing store.

Eric came back over to us and asked, "What do you want to use it for?"

I had no idea and said as much, "I have no idea; maybe it'll come in handy later."

We were the first ones to arrive at the library. Eric got everything ready, headed toward the back of the room, and said, "OK, I'll see you when we're done."

That was the good thing about Eric: He was everywhere and nowhere at the same time, so you never knew what he was shooting. I had no idea how he did it, but he caught everything on camera.

The room started to fill up, and at about six fifty-eight, both politicians walked in. I didn't see Councillor Flatch holding the shopping bag, but when I looked at her designer pocketbook, I could see it sticking out a little.

Robert greeted them and thanked them for coming. He asked them if they would like to speak, and Bernie replied, "Certainly, I'd love to say a little hello and to tell everyone my concerns. I'm here to learn from you folks, right, Pauline?"

Pauline agreed with him and reaffirmed that they are 'deeply' concerned and want to do everything they can to help. Spoken like true politicians, they sounded like they were reading from a script.

After they sat down, Laila came in, and I went straight to her, "Hi, Laila. Thank you for coming. I'm really glad you could make it. It's so nice to see you again."

She smiled, "Thank you, Brent. It's my pleasure and nice seeing you as well; working together should be fun."

All I could muster up to say was, "Uh, yes, it will be."

She reached out to shake my hand. At first, I used one hand, but then I went in for the 'really caring' two-hand handshake. I shook and held her hand a little too long and maybe too tight, but thankfully, she smiled and joked about it: "Brent, I like holding your hand, but can I have mine back right now? I think we need to start the meeting."

I apologized with a nervous smile, and all that was in my head was, 'She said she likes holding my hand.'

I told her that tonight, I was just another observer trying not to get kicked out of my building and that Robert was running the meeting. I asked her if she would like to speak about Acorn and their involvement with our 'Renoviction,' and she said she'd love to.

It was seven o'clock, and the lawyer hadn't even arrived yet, which I thought was very unprofessional. Robert, being a stickler for the rules, started the meeting at precisely seven o'clock anyway.

He began by welcoming everyone from the building and introduced what he called 'our special guests,' the Esteemed City Councillor Flatch and our Member of Parliament, the Honorable Bernie Peters. He continued, "Both have expressed their interest and are deeply concerned about our situation. Councillor Flatch, would you like to say a few words?"

She stood up and began to speak in that usual condescending political tone, "Thank you, Robert. I'm sorry we all have to be here tonight, and I'm sorry you are in this situation. It's happening far too often in our city, and I am very concerned. I would like to announce that I'll be forming a Sub-Committee on Affordable Housing. I will be setting up a public council meeting next month, and I hope you will all attend and tell your stories. Thank you, I'll turn it over to Bernie."

Bernie stood and didn't say much. I think he was here just to mark the date in his agenda book in case anyone ever asked him, 'What have you done for any of the people, and how have you spent your time in office?' All he said was that he sympathized with our situation, that he is 'gathering' all the facts and starting to 'dig deep' into the affordable housing crisis that is taking place.

That was it—that's all he said before he sat down. It was the most 'politician' answer I had ever heard.

Robert thanked them and introduced Laila. As he did, our lawyer scurried in. His right pant leg was tucked into his sock, he was carrying a bike helmet and wearing a backpack.

I thought to myself, 'Our lawyer is riding a bike? This can't be good.'

Laila began to say that next weekend, she'll have people from Acorn come to our neighborhood to knock on doors to help raise awareness and tell everyone about a rally we'll be having at the end of the month. She asked the room, "How does the last Saturday of the month sound? July twenty-ninth for the Rally?"

Robert looked around, and the room agreed that it was fine. I put my hand up to ask a question.

Laila looked at me, smiled, and said, "Yes, Brent?"

Hearing Laila say, 'Yes, Brent,' and seeing her smile was so nice.

I smiled back and said, "Thank you, Laila. What does the 'door knocking campaign' consist of, and what happens at the Rally or this march that you're talking about?"

She said, "Thank you for asking, Brent. When we go door to door, we send as many Acorn members as we can to your neighborhood; their mission, along with you, the tenants, is to knock on as many doors as they can and canvass both local residences and businesses to raise awareness of what is happening in the neighborhood. Because generally, no one else has a clue that this is even happening other than the people going through it. We get a great response using this tactic because everyone cares about it. People are disgusted that people in their own neighborhoods are being illegally evicted and thrown out of their homes. They're also upset that landlords and greedy developers are pricing out local businesses."

She was very passionate when she spoke, "and the businesses care because these evictions just raise rental rates. They know that when their lease is up, their rent will increase, and they could be the next ones to be evicted. Overall, everyone is very supportive. The Rally is for the same purpose; we aim to raise awareness and get as many eyes on the situation as possible. The rallies are very effective, and they're truly something to see. We invite Acorn members from all over the city, people from the neighborhood, the media, politicians, and as many people as possible to join us at your building. We'll have speakers, and then we'll do a small walkthrough of the neighborhood, and we'll end back at the building. Our members have flags, banners, and picket signs, and if the media comes with cameras and microphones, it gets the attention of passersby and hopefully gets us on the news, it's quite the scene."

Laila finished by saying she had the forms to join Acorn and that everyone could sign up at the end of the meeting. She thanked everyone for listening and added, "The more people we have, the better. Thank you."

Laila sat down, and Robert asked Wessler if he was ready. Wessler stood up, took his spot at the front of the room, and unimpressively said, "Hello."

Almost everyone from the building was here except for the usual absentees, Reggie, Tommy, and Sarah. He looked around the room and said, "Normally, we would have to meet alone, just the tenants and myself, no offense to our esteemed Council Person and our Honorable MP."

I thought, 'There it is again, esteemed and honorable; what is it with these people?'

Wessler continued stumbling along, speaking to everyone, "All of us here are on the same side, so I will speak about the 'case' with everyone here anyway. So far, the owner has only sent a letter from their representatives, and nothing from the Landlord and Tenant Board. The dates are wrong, they haven't given you sufficient notice to evict you on August Thirty-First, and they haven't officially filed anything yet with the Board. Now, do we all still have the same intention? Everyone wants to stay, and none of you want to leave, right?"

Everyone clapped and agreed.

Wessler continued, "Well then, I'll write a letter. In essence, I'll say that we don't accept this as legal notice and intend to remain in the units as per the

Residential Tenancies Act. I'll get it to them by the end of the month, as I intend to drag this out as long as possible."

Wessler continued, "When they receive our letter, they will send their next letter out as soon as they can, and you can be sure they'll give us the proper sixty-day notice; they're not going to screw this up twice. They'll likely file with the Landlord and Tenant Board and make it formal, officially starting the clock. I think we can expect that letter on the first of next month. We'll also file with the Board then, so this will be the 'official' legal beginning. Right now, we wait. We're at least six months away from any ruling, so don't worry; this will take some time; nobody's going anywhere anytime soon. Well, that's where we are. Does anyone have any questions?"

Robert asked, "How many cases have you been involved with using this Renoviction tactic?"

Wessler replied, "I've had dozens of individuals being evicted, but this is the first time defending an entire building."

I raised my arm and asked, "What is the penalty if they just throw us out? What's the punishment for that? I mean, what's actually stopping them from evicting us?"

His answer didn't instill hope, "the fine for illegally evicting a tenant is fifteen thousand dollars."

There were a couple of comments from people, 'I would take that,' and 'That isn't bad.'

I replied, "OK, you said a fine? Who gets that fine? Do I get it? Does the displaced tenant get that fine?"

His answer didn't surprise me one bit, "uh, no. That fine is payable to the city." I smiled and jokingly asked, "Does the city ever collect the fine?"

I wasn't expecting him to answer, and it shocked me that he did: "Not really. It's another step in the process, another round of court appearances, and we're extremely understaffed as it is, so it is tough to follow up."

I shook my head in disbelief; I wasn't expecting an answer, but an answer like that?

Everyone groaned and moaned when we heard that; it wasn't encouraging. I looked at Wessler; I think he even knew how ineffective his existence was in this process.

Brian, the old guy, asked, "How is that fair and even legal? What compensation is there for the actual person getting thrown out?"

Wessler stared at him blankly; he didn't have an answer.

Everyone in the room rumbled with displeasure—well, everyone except the politicians and the lawyer. None of this affected their lives, so why would they care? Wessler asked if there were any more questions, and everyone was quiet.

Robert stood and wrapped up the meeting by saying, "Well, I guess we just sit tight. Mr. Wessler will send the letter, and you'll let us know if there is any reply?"

Wessler answered, "Yes, and if there is any correspondence from the landlord to you guys, please let me know as soon as possible. In the meantime, if there are any issues in the building with the workers, don't hesitate to call 'three-one-one,' the city helpline. They'll put you in touch with the building inspectors for your area to come by and monitor the situation, and if need be, they can serve notices of infractions to the contractors."

Robert added, "Don't worry about that; I have already spoken to the inspectors, and I'll be on top of any infractions or illegal activities that might go on."

After sitting through the meeting, I wasn't confident about Wessler. I wished Mark Richards of the Parkdale office was our representation.

Before the meeting wrapped up, I had to ask Wessler one last question; I raised my hand and said, "I'm sorry, I have another question. I spoke with Mark Richards over at the Parkdale Office. He seems pretty knowledgeable on the subject, but more importantly, he has been going through this a lot in Parkdale. Do you guys ever share information or tactics? Do you guys ever talk?"

Wessler started to reply, and right away, I got the feeling he was offended by this; his body language was saying, 'How dare I question his ability or his authority.'

"We don't get together too often, but when we do, yes, we discuss cases and issues each of us are encountering."

I asked him, "Well, have you discussed this entire building's 'Renoviction' with him?"

He said, "Yes, thank you. We have discussed the issue," and he started putting his papers together and packing his bag.

It was a bullshit answer because Mark Richards said they had never talked. I assumed Wessler said this to shut me up, which gave me the sense that this guy doesn't go out of his way to do anything over and above what's required: a true government employee.

Robert thanked him for coming and asked the room if there were any more questions for our lawyer, and no one had anything to ask.

Robert finished the meeting by saying, "Well folks, I guess that wraps things up; if you have any questions or issues, please don't hesitate to talk to me, Nolan, Krystle, or Brent, and we'll make sure we address any concerns you might have."

Everyone started packing their things up to leave. I went over to ask Eric what he thought of the meeting. He said it was it was all right and that it went pretty smooth.

As he said that, Wessler approached us, looking angry, and asked me, "Who's this?" looking directly at Eric.

I was very polite and said, "Oh, I'm sorry. This is Eric. He's the filmmaker I'm working with, the one making the documentary, trying to help us."

Wessler started lecturing me immediately, "I thought he was with the politicians. Why was he here filming everything without everyone's permission? I don't want to be part of it, and I don't want to appear anywhere on camera." His tone and demeanor were downright hostile; it was as if he was angry and pissed off with me.

I didn't lose my cool, I didn't get angry, and I decided I wouldn't question why he wasn't in favor of this. Instead, I decided to answer calmly and professionally, but it was apparent he didn't like me and probably never would. I couldn't care what this guy thought about me, but I honestly didn't understand where his hostility was coming from.

I looked at Eric, a little confused, and said to Wessler, "Mr. Wessler, don't worry. I have spoken to everyone in the room, and they are all fine with the documentary. Most people have signed the release, and they all think it's a great idea. I have even spoken to the politicians about it, they have also said it was a great idea. But hold on, you said you thought he was here with the politicians? So, it's OK if he was here with the politicians, but because he's here with me, you have a problem with that?" I was getting upset as I sensed some kind of double standard here and I didn't like it.

Eric had walked away and started filming us from across the room; I think he had a feeling I was going to do or say something 'film worthy.'

I was losing my patience with this useless idiot Wessler already, "I'm not sure why you think it's a bad idea, but we are going to proceed and get this movie out there. But I thank you for your concern, Dick."

This angered him and, in a raised voice, said, "Well, you can do it without me. I don't want to be in this at all."

His tone and volume started to piss me off, but I kept my cool and remained courteous. I smiled and politely said, "No problem, we won't use you or film you; also, we can blur your face out or put some kind of graphic on top of your face, maybe a clown face or a crazy face emoji, so no one will recognize or even see you. Don't worry, Mr. Wessler, we'll follow the law just like everyone else is in this process."

I hope he caught my inference, but I'm sure he didn't. At this point, I was getting upset and wondering what this guy's problem was, but I was more confused about why he didn't support us doing the movie and why he didn't want us to raise awareness about the situation.

After Wessler left, Joanna Chow approached us and said hello. I greeted her and said I didn't see her come in. She said she'd been there the entire time and asked about my exchange with the lawyer.

In a sarcastic tone and with a look of disbelief, I answered, "He was showing us his support for our cause. He's upset because my friend Eric and I are making a documentary about 'Renoviction. What's really funny is that a reporter was sitting at the back of the room, and he didn't even notice or care about them, but he has a problem with Eric. He seems like a sharp guy."

I had a good talk with Joanna. She explained that she writes for the Metro, the free subway handout, which is part of the National Post. She said if her story runs in the paper, it will appear in the Metro, and the only way it will be in the National Edition is if the powers that be want it to be.

That didn't sound too promising, and it made me wonder why they would let it appear in the smaller 'Metro' paper if they didn't want it to appear in the national paper.

Before she left, Joanna asked a favor. She said if she had a picture of the group, it would help sell the story and give it a better chance of getting published.

I said to her, "OK, tomorrow I'll send you a picture of a few of us, with their pets and kids, in front of the building. Will that work for you?"

She laughed and said, "Perfect," as she walked away.

Robert and Laila came over to me, and we chatted about the meeting a bit; I asked what had happened to our 'esteemed guests.' Robert laughed and said they had left as soon as the meeting ended and didn't look back. I kept talking with Laila and trying to give Robert the nod to go so I could speak with Laila alone, but he wouldn't get the hint and just kept on talking. Finally, Eric swooped in and led Robert away by getting him to do a walk and talk in front of the camera.

Laila laughed when Robert walked away doing a commentary to the camera.

She said, "That man loves the camera, doesn't he? It's very nice seeing you again, Brent," and she touched my arm as she said it.

All I could think was, 'I like this woman;' I'm not sure what I said in return, but I think I was smiling because she smiled back, too.

She continued, "Kyle is making flyers and handouts for your building, and I'll pick them up for the door knockers. If you want some of them, I can meet you for a coffee this week if you would like to?"

All I could think was, 'IS SHE ASKING ME OUT? IS SHE ASKING ME OUT?' I was screaming it over and over in my head. I don't know how, but calmly, I replied, "I would really like that, Laila. That sounds like fun."

She said she had to run because the babysitter was about to go into overtime. I thanked her for coming to the meeting and told her I was really looking forward to seeing her again and getting those flyers.

Eric and Robert came back over. Eric was still camera-up, and Robert was still talking away. Eric said, "Wow, Bingham, how did that go?"

I started to tell him, and he just cut me off, "Don't worry, I know how it went; I got it all; I shot it all over Roberts's shoulder. Sorry, Robert."

Robert looked at him, confused, and just shrugged.

We were getting ready to leave. Eric was about to take the mic off of me when I told him to hold on. I asked if he minded grabbing one more thing, and of course, he didn't. We left the library and headed home. On the way, we stopped at the clothing store where our 'esteemed' Councillor Flatch bought her sweater.

I said to Eric, "I want to find out how much sweaters cost in that place. It's a swanky little shop, so I don't think it's cheap. Film me from across the street. I'm going to go in to look at the rack where she grabbed the sweater from and see how much they cost. Cool?"

Eric was ready and said, "Right on, go."

I went across the street and went in, and in a store like this, the sales clerk will ask a guy like me, 'Do you need some help, sir?' the minute I step in.

I laughed, "Hi, it's my mother-in-law's birthday, and I was told to come look at some sweaters."

She laughed and let me wander around; she gave me a couple of looks as I said the price of some things out loud and commented to myself. "Wow, there are only eight sweaters on the rack, and they range in price from the 'low-end' of three hundred dollars to five hundred dollars. Damn, our councillor has some good taste."

I thanked the clerk as I left the store and walked across the street to Eric and Robert; all I could do was shake my head in disbelief.

We made our way back to the building and discussed the meeting. The consensus was that we were in trouble, especially since we learned there were no real repercussions for these landlords when they break the law. I asked their opinion of the lawyer and if they had any faith in him.

Eric right away said, "hell no."

Robert took some time to answer, and finally, said, "It doesn't matter if I have faith in him or not; it's who we have. We could have Saul Goodman representing us, and it still wouldn't help; this is a lose-lose situation for us."

We all agreed that we might be able to get a new lawyer if we paid for one, but what would be the point? We might be able to delay this, string it along for a while, and keep kicking the can down the road, but sooner or later, we're going to get to the end of that road, and we'll have to move out.

We arrived at the building, and I asked if they wanted to come in for a beer. Eric was up for it, but Robert wasn't and said he had enough excitement for the night. We started making our way up the stairs, but Eric stopped and said he had to grab something from his car; he told us to go up without him, so me and Robert headed up the stairs. Before we went into our apartments, Robert said he would try to contact more reporters and that he really wanted to kick up a storm. I reminded him about the social media sites, and he said he wasn't on any of them. I laughed and told him neither was I until this shit came up; I told him to make a list of the names of all the people he speaks to, and I'll make sure to add and invite them to Facebook; we'll make sure they see our profiles, and we'll try to get this thing going.

I said goodnight to Robert, went inside, grabbed two beers, and sat on the sofa. Looking down, I stroked the cushion and thought, 'damn, it is a nice sofa.'

Eric came in and was carrying some sort of long copper or brass piping apparatus; attached to it were black rubber hoses, valves, gauges, and a bunch of knobs. He blew by me before I could say a thing, and he put the thing in the bedroom.

I asked, "What the hell was that?"

He smiled and casually said, "It's a 'flame bar.' I got it from a guy at work."

"A flame bar?" I had no clue what he was talking about.

"It's a 'flame bar' used for fire scenes. You put it in front of a window, and it makes the place look like it's on fire. I'll get the propane tank later." He raised his beer and 'clinked' bottles with me.

I shook my head and said, "I don't even want to get into that tonight, but we're going to have to have a talk about this daydream sequence sooner or later. In the meantime, what are we going to do with Kerwin Cummings and his Alliance?"

Eric rubbed his hands together and said, "Ooh, glad you asked."

He pulled a piece of paper out of his pocket, reviewed the notes, and started saying, "We're going to do a hidden camera on him; I'm getting a camera that looks like a pen; it's amazing. You're going to call him, you're going to play it very casual, and you are going to pretend that you just stumbled across his name on the website. Tread lightly; at the end of the conversation, mention his office address and tell him you are down that way all the time, ask him to meet you for lunch, and hopefully, he bites."

We clinked our bottles in agreement.

I said, "That sounds like a plan. Now, let's talk about the dream sequence."

Eric cut me off and said, "Don't worry, it'll be great."

I got up and got some more beers, and we relaxed for a bit. To help forget about the bullshit and to unwind, we watched some Seinfeld; just as we were getting a good buzz going, there was knocking on my door, Eric instinctively grabbed the camera, and I answered it.

116

It was Robert, and he was in fine form. As usual, he flew by me and started pacing at the back of the room. Thankfully, the dishrack was empty, and there wasn't anything within his reach to smash. As he was pacing, he began to talk and stare in the direction he was moving. It was like we weren't even there.

"Well, I talked to my friend who did the business search, and he's found out more. He was waiting for all the information about this 'LLC.' He said he knew that the owner was Liang Jiang Huong and had just received a listing of vehicles and bank accounts registered with the company. This led him to the address of a house that led him to another bank account, which had some different names."

I was confused. "Different names, OK, so what are you saying? This guy owns the building, or doesn't he? Or do other people own it?"

He had that white stuff in the corner of his lips again, and he exclaimed, "Both."

Confused, I said, "What do you mean both? It's a big company?"

Robert replied excitedly, "No, he's a frontman and probably isn't even in Canada; he lists his house as Thirteen-Sixty-Seven Meadow Lane, Richmond Hill, but when you look at the land transfer for Thirteen-Sixty-Seven Meadow Lane, it is owned by these two guys and their bank accounts are in China."

I went to the computer and typed Thirteen-Sixty-Seven Meadow Lane into Google Earth; as I was typing, I looked back at Robert and asked inquisitively, "How did you find this stuff out? This isn't your 'run of the mill' general information you find online in a business search; who do you have looking into this?"

He grinned and said, "You don't want to know; let's just say I called in a favor."

I looked nervously at Eric, wondering who Robert's connection was. Then, the address came up on the screen.

Robert said, "I knew it. Look at this guy's house. There's no way someone living there is buying a building like ours; there's no way he could afford it. But this guy's money comes from other people, and the money comes from the accounts in China. The owner of our building isn't Canadian at all; he's Chinese and lives in China!"

I wasn't too informed about the whole global economic situation. I didn't care or pay attention to real estate or the stock market as I didn't think it affected my day- to-day life, but I just made the sad realization that it does.

I looked at Robert in disbelief, "You're telling me I'm getting thrown out of my building by someone who doesn't even live in Canada?"

Robert went back to pacing and replied, "Well, it's looking that way."

I looked at Eric, and he knew this time I was pissed off and angry.

I repeated, "You're telling me that I'm getting thrown out of my building by someone who doesn't even live in Canada?"

I was floored. I never imagined such a thing could be possible. I couldn't believe Canada had gotten this bad; now I was angry. I looked at the guys and asked, "How is this even possible? Is this really Canada? Have we really given our country away to anyone, anywhere in the world?"

We all looked at each other in silence and disbelief.

Chapter 12

It had been a few days since our tenants' meeting and a few days since Laila said she would call me about our Rally and flyers. I was anxious to hear from her, but I didn't want to bug her. I'm pretty sure she gets hit on by every guy she meets. Today was the day I was supposed to call my friend Kerwin at the Alliance, and Eric was coming down to record it. As I waited for Eric to arrive, my phone buzzed; it was Joanna Chow; she was texting to tell me that her article would be in the *'Metro'* tomorrow morning and said there was no word about appearing in *'The National.'* Either way, it was good news. I was looking forward to seeing our story in any news publication.

I texted her back, and I heard a commotion outside my window from the street below. I looked down, and saw a van parked up against our building, with some guys unloading some equipment. We have a huge sidewalk in front of our building, and there was more than enough room for the van to be parked against the building and for people to feel safe and comfortable as they walked by. From what I saw, none of the people walking by seemed to have a problem with it. But the one person who did was Robert, and he was out there in less than a minute.

I grabbed my coffee and went downstairs in my robe and slippers to see what was going on. I strolled up to Robert and Lorenzo, sipped my coffee, and leaned against the wall.

Lorenzo was trying to tell Robert that he'd only be there for ten minutes, but Robert didn't care. Technically, Robert was right; there wasn't any parking allowed on the sidewalk, as it was a fire route, but it really wasn't upsetting or affecting anyone.

Red as a beet, Robert said, "Oh, you're not going to follow the rules, are you?" and stormed off and went inside. He didn't even wait for Lorenzo to answer.

I looked at Lorenzo, and I could tell by the look on his face he wasn't in the mood for another angry tenant, and he wasn't going to take any shit right now. But that wasn't my style; I wanted to play the good cop to Robert's bad cop.

I smiled, raised my mug, and said, "Welcome to Three-Ninety-One Empire Avenue. I hope you enjoy your stay. Coffee?"

He laughed and leaned on his van, saying no thank you. We introduced ourselves and talked for a bit, and even though I was in my bathrobe, Lorenzo saw that I wasn't angry and figured he could have a rational conversation with me.

He chuckled, shook his head, and asked, "Why is that man so angry with us? You know, I was warned about this building before we started; I was told the tenants might be 'trouble,' I was told there was a lot of mental illness and drug abuse in the building, and to ignore the tenants at all costs."

I wasn't surprised that the owner would say something like that. It's a tactic that has been used forever, primarily by politicians. Accuse your opponent of what you are doing, lie, repeat the lie, and keep lying, and people will believe you. Guilty people always use disinformation to cloud people's perceptions, and they are the first ones to point a finger at others, and it's exactly what our new owner was doing.

I laughed and said, "Well, there's mental illness in the building but nothing to be scared of, and as for drugs, sure, there's pot, but there's probably more Lipitor and blood pressure medication in here than anything. Did the owner say any other reason why we would be trouble?"

"No, that's all he said." Lorenzo paused, looked at me with some judgment, and said, "I'm going to be honest with you, Brent. I've never talked to the owner directly; I only talked to an intermediary; a guy named Louie."

I replied, "I haven't heard of a Louie, and I'm going to be honest with you as well, Lorenzo; since you were honest with me, I'll tell you what's really going on around here."

Lorenzo nodded in thanks, and I told him everything. I told him about the letters, the buyouts, and how the owner was trying to evict us and throw everyone out of the building illegally. He wasn't surprised and said that explains a lot of things. He also said he's never received a check from the LLC directly; all the payments have been e-transfers and sometimes cash.

I said, "That seems a little suspect. And as for the gentleman that is so angry with you, he did a search on your bosses, and he found out that the people who own this building, who really own the LLC, live in China; they're not even Canadian, it's why we are pissed off. It's not you, it's us."

I thanked Lorenzo for the talk, and I started to make my way back inside.

He said, "Yes, it was beneficial. Let's make sure we keep each other up to date, thank you."

I think I had a friend in Lorenzo; we understood each other. Now that he knew what the owner was capable of, I think he realized he was most likely going to get screwed over by this guy; he realized I wasn't the enemy and that his boss just might be. Lorenzo was a nice guy, yes, he was just doing his job, but he was on the wrong side of this; he was working for the bad guy.

I went up to my apartment, and I was pissed off. I sat at the computer and went to the 'The Alliance' website. I figured this 'Alliance' was just another lobby group made up to rob the political system under the guise of 'affordable housing.' I opened another window and logged into Facebook. I found Kerwin and looked at his picture; he looked like a politician; looking at his eyes through his two-inch thick glasses, I saw the eyes of a liar.

As I sat staring at Kerwin's picture, Eric came in and asked, "What's with the van in front of the building? Because it's getting a ticket right now."

I replied, "That's the worker's truck; Robert probably called and got the ticket guys on them."

Eric looked at the computer and saw Kerwin Cummings's picture. He said, "Ooh, you're psyching yourself up staring at the enemy? Bingham is getting in the zone; I like it."

He grabbed his phone and said he had the perfect song. I started laughing when I heard the first four beats. He had put on Rocky's theme song, 'Eye of The Tiger.'

I was nervous about calling; I had no idea how Kerwin would be with me after all these years. All I remember is that we had a good relationship, but here we were twenty-five years later, on the opposite sides of a crisis, one of us on top and the other on the bottom, one guy with everything and the other with nothing to lose. He didn't know it yet, but we were going to get to know each other again, and I don't think he was going to like me now. I dialed his number and put the call on speaker. I nervously leaned forward with my elbows on my knees till he answered, and when he did, I stood up and started pacing.

He answered, "Kerwin Cummings, may I help you?"

Smiling, I almost yelled, "Kerwin Cummings, Brent Bingham, Red Knights Baseball, how the hell are you?"

I was smiling because even though we were on opposite sides, it's always nice hearing a voice from the past. Seeing or hearing someone from my old days always makes me think of better times.

"Brent Bingham! I'm great, how are you doing? How's your Dad?" I could hear Kerwin smiling on the other end as well.

Everyone loved my Dad. "I'm good, he's good. You know you can always find him up at the park, any given night."

Kerwin was an old neighborhood guy. He said he saw my Dad last year at the park, stopped and had a hot dog, and watched a game for a bit. So, unfortunately, because of my Dad and our history, I did have to treat Kerwin with some sort of respect. But he was the bad guy; I said, "Kerwin, I'm going through a little bit of a 'housing' thing, and I stumbled across your name on the website for 'The Alliance of Commercial Housing Rentals."

I was playing stupid with him, so I asked, "Can I ask you what this Landlord and Tenant Board stuff is all about? Seems like you're familiar with this kind of thing."

He went into a well-polished answer, talking about old housing, outdated property values, rising costs, and rental laws. Everything he said, of course, was on the side of the landlord; he sounded like a true politician.

I wasn't liking adult Kerwin. I mentioned that I was looking at the website and said, "I see your office is on King Street. I work down that way all the time; we should 'do lunch.' Are you around on Thursday?"

He immediately agreed, "I look forward to it, Bingham; it'll be fun."

"Sounds great, Kerwin; see you then." I hung up the phone, looked at Eric, and said, "That was easy."

The next day, Joanna Chow's article came out. Luckily, the 'Metro' was also online, so I could look at it when I woke up. If the print version was the same as the online version, we were on the front page. I had sent Joanna a picture of the group in front of the building including Bob with Bo, Robert, Brian, Bill, Krystle, Nolan, Melissa with her two kids, Sarah with her cats, and myself. We were standing on the steps of the building, and of course, we put the pets and kids up front and center.

The headline read, 'Evictions for Profit'. It talked about the owners' dirty tactics and how this affects the lives of the people involved and the community they live in. She used our building as a springboard to talk about the affordable housing crisis; it was a good article.

I was quoted as saying, 'If the landlords would follow the rules, there wouldn't be these kinds of problems, but when you break the rules, you should be held accountable. It's people's homes and lives you are playing with, not stocks and bonds."

Robert was quoted extensively. He mainly spoke about the rental market and the state of housing in Toronto. He said that owners, speculators, landlords, and even politicians themselves were responsible for the crisis, which is now becoming a plague on our society. Robert didn't hold back.

The article also mentioned our Rally taking place on July twenty-ninth at our building to protest our 'Renoviction' and to help raise awareness about the housing crisis. I was happy and sad to see myself in the paper. I was sad that I was getting thrown out of my apartment because I was poor, but I was happy to bring some attention to the matter.

I posted the article on Facebook and typed, *This is our story, folks. Please stay tuned and come to the Rally on Saturday, July twenty-ninth, at two p.m. Three-Ninety-One Empire Avenue. Come out and support us, speak with reporters, media, and local politicians, tell your stories, and help raise awareness about the growing plague of 'Renovictions'.*

I couldn't believe I was hash-tagging and linking people and starting to like Facebook. I also couldn't believe we had almost ten thousand followers. People at work were telling me that that was an awesome following to have in such a short time; I had no clue. I wasn't a big fan of social media, but this 'Renoviction' thing was getting some traction and attention.

I wasn't looking forward to the meeting with Kerwin, but Thursday arrived in a hurry. When Eric showed up at my place, he wired me with the camera and microphone. I was impressed by the camera; it looked just like a pen. He looked at me dead seriously and said, "Don't ask how much this thing costs Bingham, and don't fuck it up because I have to return it for a refund as soon as we're done."

As we drove down, he asked me what I'll be saying to Kerwin; I said, "I don't know, I'm going to keep it friendly, but I do have to call him out on some of his bullshit, all the while I have to try to keep smiling and remembering that we were once friends. I don't want to get angry with him; I'll just be a smiling smart-ass."

When we arrived at the restaurant, Eric switched me on. He had to throw me out of the car as I was nervous and hesitant to go inside; I finally got out and went in. We were meeting at a place called 'The Porterhouse,' a little steakhouse near his office, and as I walked in, I realized that this lunch would cost me more than I make in a week. I figured the place was frequented by people in his political circles, and as I looked around, the décor reaffirmed that. It was wall-to-wall portraits and pictures of nothing but politicians; every inch of wall space was covered by a portrait or picture of politicians from Canada and all over the world.

Kerwin was already there and stood up when he saw me coming. We hugged hello, sat down, and said things like, 'Look at us, who would have thought we'd make it this far?' and 'Can you imagine, ha-ha-ha'—the usual things old people say to their friends from the past.

We caught up in some of the gossip we had heard about people we went to school with. He said, "Did you hear about Kim's new special?"

I replied, "Yeah, good for her, she deserves the success. Did you hear about Jason's sentence?"

He replied, "Yeah," in a sad way.

I laughed, "Everyone has their stories, and there are always two sides, a winner and a loser, which brings me to my situation, Kerwin.

The waiter came, and we had to order first. We each got the chicken Caesar salad, as it was a little early in the day for a steak.

I began to tell my story to Kerwin. After hearing it, he said, "I understand, Brent. And yes, illegal stuff like this is happening all the time. There are a lot of bad actors in this industry, and no pun intended about the bad actor comment."

I laughed and said, "Thanks, Kerwin."

He continued, "My members don't behave like that, Brent. We have a code of conduct, laws, and regulations, and we encourage our members to abide by them."

I laughed and said, "But Kerwin, your job is to buy politicians to change laws in favor of your members. Come on, you lobbied for the auto insurance industry. I don't know what laws you changed in that industry, but all I know is that everyone complains about how expensive and useless their car insurance is. Did you have something to do with that?"

Kerwin smiled and proudly put up 'jazz hands' as if to say, 'guilty.' And he actually said, 'Guilty.'

I continued, "What about 'The Loan Shop'? Buddy, that's predatory payday lending; everyone loves those guys, don't they, Kerwin? What laws did you change for them? Service fees that never end? Are you the reason I see ads everywhere now for this bloody industry and loan stores everywhere I go? In some neighborhoods, all you see are boarded-up stores, payday loan stores, and Popeye Chicken locations. Do you have something to do with that? I mean the payday loan stores, not the Popeyes."

He raised his hands again, shaking them in the air, and with a sick smile, he said, 'Guilty.'

I was smiling and trying to make Kerwin feel like shit, but he was proud of what he's done.

He looked at me and said, "It's a hell of an industry, Brent."

I sighed and said, "I'll give it to you that you're making a shit ton of money, I'll give you that, but you're not a good person. You're exactly what's wrong with the system. You buy politicians, plain and simple."

He laughed and replied, "What you call buying, we call 'Lobbying.' I didn't create it, Brent; it's legal, and it's the system, so don't hate me because I figured it out. Come on, don't be naïve Bingham."

I shook my head defeatedly, "Yeah, but Kerwin, your work hurts people; it costs them money; what you do for a living causes suffering, and now what you do can cause people to be homeless? That's a pretty shitty way to make money. You sleep alright at night?"

He chuckled and said, "Brent, it's a shitty way to make a TON of money, and yes, I sleep great at night; politics is a great game. Eat Up, Enjoy."

I wasn't hungry anymore. I pushed the plate away and said, "Kerwin, I'm up against a landlord who is trying to throw me out."

He smiled and said, "I know, Brent. I read the Metro yesterday. If something is said about the rental markets in the media, I know about it immediately; it's my job. I'm sorry to hear that, so what is happening? And, you know, I can't say anything about this…"

He continued, "You know Brownstone is one of our members. Come on, Brent. I know you're not stupid; it's what led you to me, but Brownstone is one of mine, so I can't say a thing."

I smiled because we understood each other; I asked, "How can you represent scumbags like this, Kerwin? I mean, there's a guy in my building that has been there for forty years, a couple of people for twenty-five, guys on disability, people on pensions, fixed incomes, a single mom with kids, and starving artists, for god's sake." I laughed and put my arms up to indicate myself.

I continued, "These guys have nowhere to go; they can't afford anything in the city; one guy might end up homeless; one guy is a vet, for god's sake."

Kerwin just kept eating, and I said, "Come on, Kerwin. You were better than that. What you do affects people's lives. Car insurance rates, predatory lending, this stuff costs people money. Now, you represent commercial landlords, and there's a housing crisis? When you break it down, I don't think many people would respect what you do for a living, Kerwin."

He tried to change the subject, asking, "So, have you seen anyone from 'back in the day' lately? Any other juicy updates?"

I said, "Yeah, there's one update, remember ahh…ahhh…" I stopped as if I was trying to remember someone's name, snapping my fingers, and I said, "Yeah, remember Kerwin Cummings? Well, he turned out to be a huge dick."

Kerwin laughed, "Brent, don't worry, I won't be involved in this matter. How one of our idiot members behaves is on them, but they are our member. I can call them, remind them to keep it civil, and remind them that everyone in our membership works within the law."

I didn't mince my words. I said, "You mean you are going to call them and warn them about me?"

He looked up and said, "Yeah, basically."

I had to say to him, "Kerwin, we go way back, but you are on the wrong side of this. You're the bad guy. You're part of the problem with the rental market and the world, and you're probably part of the reason why I'm getting thrown out."

I had to get a little information from him before I left; this couldn't just be me bitching about the situation. "OK, Kerwin, Brownstone is your 'member.' Do you work with my owner at all? Does he pay you, or should I say, is he a member of yours?"

Kerwin smiled, "OK, Brent, I'll play. I know your owner, and yes, he is a member, but I don't work directly with him; I work with his representative and Brownstone."

Now I was curious, "OK, so if you work with Brownstone and the owner, what came first, Brownstone or the owner?"

Kerwin, being the prick he was, smiled and said, "Brent, I get approached by many different interests, and my job is to introduce people. If someone has investment money and wants to enter the market, I can help them. If their investment requires 'certain changes' to the building, I can introduce them to one of our companies that specializes in that sort of thing."

I looked at him and said, "You mean companies specializing in illegal evictions and 'Renovictions,' don't you? When you say 'companies,' how many companies do you have doing this? I know you gave over ten thousand dollars to our two politicians over two years. How much money is going through your hands?"

Kerwin had no shame for what he was doing, and I realized he didn't care what damage he caused. "Kerwin, you're just the middleman, you're a fucking bagman for a legal mafia. Did you know the owner throwing me out isn't even in Canada? He's not even a Canadian citizen. The guy evicting me is in China. Did you know that? And if you did, you knowingly have Chinese Nationalists in your association? That's fucked up, Kerwin, even for me."

Kerwin smiled, "Well, I knew he was Chinese, and I knew the check cleared, so there wasn't a problem."

He laughed and added, "I hope you're not recording this; I could be in trouble with that comment."

Kerwin was comfortable and relaxed with me; he probably thought I was just dumb stoner Brent from high school, so it was time to take advantage of that and get his release on camera.

I was laughing with him. I looked him straight in the eye and said, "Yeah, Kerwin, I am recording this. Can I use it?"

There was silence as we stared at each other for at least fifteen seconds, which seemed like an hour. He started to look worried, and then he started laughing again.

We were both laughing, and he said, "Sure."

Now I was laughing for real, I sucked him right in. At least if the buyout doesn't work, I can always blackmail him.

"I would say I should get this on film Kerwin, I don't think people would believe what a 'sellout' piece of shit you became, but since I'm filming, I won't need to convince them, they'll see it for themselves."

He started to say, "Everything we do is done within the rules, Brent."

I laughed, "Kerwin, you're taking money from foreign investors and giving it to our politicians, and in return, you're asking them to keep the housing laws lax so that those foreign investors can evict people and charge exorbitant rents. You're unbelievable."

He was relatively calm and eating his lunch without a care in the world. "Brent, you are getting too wrapped up in this. The only thing I can say is to start looking for a place to live, think about a buyout, and realize that you aren't going to win in this situation. Sooner or later, they'll get you out."

He winked and smiled at me; in between bites, he said, "We always do."

"Well, Kerwin, it was nice seeing you again, but get ready because I'm fighting this, and now you're involved. I'm going to expose you and everyone involved for being the evil, greedy pricks you are, and apparently, it isn't going to be that hard at all. Kerwin, you are truly an 'enemy of the people.' You know, during a revolution, when the people figure out what's really going on, when people figure out that financial tyrants and criminals have hijacked their political systems, you're one of the first ones that they'll hang in the town square. Give it a shake, buddy."

Nothing was going to get through to Kerwin, so I wanted to guilt him a little and have some fun, "You know my Dad isn't going to be happy hearing about this."

I stood up and finished by saying, "I'm not paying for this either. Charge it back to Brownstone; call it public relations for Three-Ninety-One Empire Avenue."

He laughed and said, "Of course, I would never pay for this myself. Say hi to your Dad for me when you see him."

I looked back, said I would tell him, and flipped him the finger as I walked out.

Eric was waiting around the corner for me and could tell I was upset when I got in the car. All I could do was rant, "Son of a bitch, lying, cheating, thieving politicians and lobbyists, screwing the people just to make sure they get paid. It's horrible, Eric, it's so fucking rigged; the whole system is a setup, it's set up so people think they have a chance of justice, but it's just an illusion. It's like a carnival game; everyone knows they're rigged, but when we see them, we think we have a fighting chance at winning, so we keep handing over our money to play, but deep down, we know we don't have a chance. The fix is in, and money rules all. If you have the money, you can make the rules."

Eric looked at me and asked, "Is it that bad?"

Dazed, I looked out the window and said, "Yeah, it's that bad."

Eric made me laugh with what he said next, "This is the moment in the documentary when we cut away to your dream sequence; it's your 'Falling Down' moment."

'Falling Down' is a reference to a Michael Douglas movie about a man pushed over the edge with the daily bullshit of society; if you haven't seen it, I highly recommend it.

Eric dropped me off at home and I was feeling pretty down. Having to see my rich high school friend because I'm poor and getting thrown out of my apartment made me feel shitty. It was embarrassing. But I realized that if I kept my mouth shut to protect my pride or just so I could tell people, "Everything's great," when they asked how I was or If I didn't talk about this shitty situation, a lot of people wouldn't hear about this story. This isn't something someone would brag about or even talk about in public; this is something most people would try to hide and be embarrassed about, and most people wouldn't want anyone to know about it. But like I said, I wasn't like most people; I didn't care if people knew I was poor, and I certainly didn't care what other people thought of me.

Chapter 13

A couple of days had passed, and nothing was going on. Lorenzo and his crew weren't around the building, which I thought was odd. I hadn't heard from Laila, and I was getting a little anxious to hear from her. I didn't want to bug her, but I wanted to see her again. I thought, 'What the hell, I'll use the flyers and the rally as the excuse to talk to her.'

I sent her a text, and to my surprise, she replied immediately. She said that she had just gotten all the flyers and posters from Kyle, and they were great. I was nervous about asking her to meet, but I didn't have to. She asked to get together first, and I was ecstatic. She said she was available Wednesday or Thursday, and I said either day would be great. I was pretty sure I wouldn't be working one of those days, and if I was called, I would actually turn down the booking; that's how much I wanted to see her.

I got booked for Tuesday and Wednesday, so we decided to meet on Thursday. It's funny—there wasn't much happening, but those two days felt like a week. We were going to meet at Beanzies so I could get the flyers and discuss the 'doorknocking' campaign and rally. That was the plan, but I wanted to talk to her about so much more and ask her everything about herself.

When I woke up on Thursday, the first thing I thought about was what I would wear. This surprised me because I didn't care how I looked unless I was working. At work, I usually played 'the suit guy'—a doctor, lawyer, detective, or slimeball politician type. I wore expensive suits, always had to be clean-shaven, and never had a hair out of place. So when I wasn't working, I wouldn't shave, I'd wear sweatpants and ball caps, and I wouldn't care about my appearance at all. But today, I was meeting Laila, and even though I might be homeless soon, I didn't want to look like it.

I made a great breakfast, had coffee, and lounged around, relaxing. I didn't do any research or social media posting because I didn't want to stress about anything. This situation was constantly in my head. I would always be thinking about some aspect or different angle, and it was getting exhausting. Today, I wanted to be stress-free. It was bad enough that I was nervous to spend time with Laila.

After coffee, I headed to the gym to relieve some of my stress, and I was glad I did. After working out, I sat in the massage chairs for ten minutes and walked out of the gym feeling amazing. I got home a few minutes before meeting her, so I threw my bag inside and headed down to 'Beanzies.'

When I arrived, Sally started making my coffee; I had to stop her and tell her that I was expecting someone to join me.

"Oh?" she said, "not drinking alone for a change."

I smiled and said, "Yeah, imagine that."

Laila walked in. She was wearing jeans and a sweater, and she looked amazing, but she would look good in anything. I greeted her and asked what she wanted to drink; she said coffee would be fine. Sally gave me a surprised look, smiled, and winked at me. I ordered two coffees and two apple fritters, which Laila objected to, saying that she didn't like donuts. I asked her if she liked apples, which she said she did, so I reassured her that she would like these. We went and sat at the booth by the front window.

I was nervous, but she put me at ease immediately. I had to tell her how nice she looked, and I hope I didn't come across as creepy: "You look beautiful, Laila. It's so nice to see you again. I hope you found the place, okay?"

She smiled and said, "Yes, no problem. Thank you, Brent. It's very nice to see you as well."

I liked her saying, Brent. Right away, she started talking about the signs and flyers; I thought there'd be more small talk, but it was straight to business.

She said Kyle did a great job on the flyers, and she was right; he did. The flyers were eye-catching, with red and black coloring that said, 'No Renoviction for Three-Ninety-One Empire Avenue,' the fonts were sharp, and the contradicting colors really caught your attention. He also made a little handout that could be put on message and community boards. It had a couple of bullet points about our buildings' pending 'Renoviction' and included information about the rally. I was impressed with what Kyle had done; Laila also impressed me with how passionate she was about this stuff. People with a passion for social issues have always amazed me. Nowadays, you rarely see someone caring about an issue or problem that is outside of their world or their wallet. And, if they weren't getting paid for it, they wouldn't get involved or wouldn't care.

Sally came over with the coffees and fritters, and I could tell Laila was unsure of what she was looking at.

She asked, "What am I looking at? This doesn't look like a fritter."

I laughed, "These guys make old-fashioned apple fritters. This is how fritters were supposed to be before they were bastardized. Originally, the fritter was a lightly battered, quickly deep-fried thick apple ring with cinnamon, but like everything else in this world, it got wrecked. Apples are expensive, and dough is cheap, so over time, fritters evolved into the lumps and clumps of dough with the specks of apple that you see today. These guys do it old-school."

Laila took her fork and poked it around on her plate, which made me laugh. She had a piece on the end of the fork and said, "Yes, things seem a little better when they're old-school. Do you like old-fashioned things, Brent?"

I had to think about it; I replied, "I never really thought about it before, but I think I do. Our 'Renoviction' is a symptom of progress. We live in an old building, yeah it might be a bit run down, but it's a beautiful building, it was built

130

in the fifties and is an example of early 'modern architecture,' and it's solid as a rock, sure it's not great, but it's got character. Eventually, it will be torn down and replaced with what? Steel and glass? Where's the character in that?"

Laila took a bite and smiled as soon as she tasted it: "This is delicious. It's nothing like a donut store fritter. I like old-fashioned fritters. Thank you, old-fashioned man."

I laughed at that. I never thought of myself as 'old-fashioned,' but it was nice coming from Laila.

We returned to the rental market conversation and 'Renoviction.' I expressed to her that I assume people are going to lose in situations like this, but Laila saw it from the other side; she saw it from the side of 'there is a chance to change things' and 'that it only takes one person to make a change.'

I had to ask her straight up, "Laila, why do you do this?"

"Do what?" She said, smiling, looking down and around at something she might have done; it was cute as hell.

I said, "this…" I picked up the flyers, looked her straight in the eye, and asked, "Why are you helping with our building? Why get involved when you can spend time on yourself? Like the other night, you said you had to get back to your babysitter, but there you were, out at a meeting helping others, helping us. Please, I'm not judging; I mean, your determination is very, very admirable."

She smiled, "Thank you, Brent, that's very nice, I think? And yes, I do care about this issue, maybe too much, but Acorn really helped me when I was going through this same thing a few years ago. I wasn't with my husband anymore; I was new in the country and didn't know the rules or laws. I was living in a building where the landlord tried so many times to get me out, and Acorn helped me; they put me in touch with like-minded people, and it's people helping people."

I listened to everything she said, but the only thing I heard was, 'I wasn't with my husband anymore,' her story moved me.

She continued, "I'm not sure if you remember, but I'm from Iran, and if good people don't stand up to bad people, bad things happen; I know because I've seen it; it's better to stand up. Shortly after I came to Canada, I split with my husband. I was in a couple of bad apartments, and I couldn't believe how corrupt and heartless some of these landlords were. I didn't know the rules, I didn't know what they were and weren't allowed to do; I assumed they would be doing the right thing, the proper thing, but they never were, none of them. Everyone tried to take advantage of me and make money; it wasn't until I was with Acorn that I learned the rules. You know, Brent, I never imagined the level of corruption in Canada could be what it is in Iran, but it's worse here; the only difference is here in Canada, the corruption is built right into the system; corruption is written right into the rules and laws of this land."

I loved every word she was saying.

She was passionate when she spoke, "Here in Canada, I've learned the most corrupt people wear the nicest clothes, they wear suits and ties, and they hold prominent public positions, but they are more corrupt than the criminals where I come from. I don't think it's fair, and that's why I like to help. Besides, it gets me out of the house, and if I'm lucky, I get to meet nice people like yourself."

She reached across the table to grab the flyers but ended up grabbing my hand instead. I just stared at her.

I couldn't hold back my words: "I like you, Laila. You're a very strong woman with conviction, and you don't see a lot of that these days."

She smiled and said, "Thank you, Brentley; you are a nice man, too."

I had to add, "And you are very beautiful, Laila. I'm glad you are here in Canada; we're much better off having you. And it's just Brent; it isn't short for anything."

She giggled, "I know it is, but I like saying Brentley for some reason. Now, stay focused, Brentley; let's get back to business. The posters are for the local businesses to put up in their windows to raise awareness; you'll find that they are usually more than happy to help. And the handouts and flyers are for anyone that will take one."

We finished the coffee and talked for about an hour. We both agreed that it would be fun working together and that getting to know each other would be nice, and that was good enough for me. As we were getting ready to leave, Laila asked if I wanted to see what to say when talking to businesses about the window sign.

I looked over at Sally, who was bored behind the counter, looking and swiping at her phone. I said, "That would be cool, Laila. Thanks."

This was going to be good to watch. Sally knew all about this. She'd heard it from Robert, from me, and from everyone in the building. She knew we wanted to put something in her window, but I wanted to watch Laila.

We walked to the front, and Laila went into the 'pitch.' She was very good, made some excellent points, and was very convincing.

When Laila finished, Sally said, "So this is the flyer you want to put in the window, Brent?"

Laila looked at me surprised and slapped my shoulder for making her go through all that.

Sally laughed and said, "No dear, don't worry. You were so sweet I didn't want to interrupt you; you did such a good job."

We walked out on the street. She wanted to say goodbye, but I asked if I could walk her to her car; she was hesitant initially but said yes. She was just around the corner, so there wasn't much time, I told her I'd like to see her again and maybe not about 'Renoviction' stuff. She laughed and said that we would talk in a day or so about the door knocking. We stopped, and she motioned to a car and said this was her. To my surprise, she was driving a top-of-the-line Mercedes, which caught me off guard. We said our goodbyes and promised to speak to each other in a couple of days. As I walked away, all I could think was, 'What the hell is she doing driving a Mercedes? And it's going to be a long two days waiting to call her.'

I went back to the building, and as I walked in, I wondered if I should put up a flyer. At first, I thought no, but then I thought, what the hell, why not. I put one up by the mailboxes and one in the window facing the street. I might as well start advertising it now; everyone will know about it sooner or later. When I got upstairs, I called Eric and told him I got the flyers from Laila, so we were, 'a go' for talking to local businesses and raising awareness.

He was happy to hear that, but then he got all serious and started to make me nervous. "Bingham, you didn't meet Laila without me, did you? How could you? Did you film it, at least? Come on, Bingham, you're better than that."

I laughed, and thankfully, he laughed, too. I mentioned I would be talking to Laila in a couple of days about the door knocking campaign, so we agreed we would go out filming and knocking when she had the Acorn volunteers out there as well.

After a couple of days, and I mean two, I texted Laila, and again, to my surprise, she replied right away. She had the door knockers all lined up and ready to go for Saturday, but to my disappointment, she said she wouldn't be able to attend.

This threw me off as I hoped that the door-knocking campaign was when I would see her again. The second she said she wasn't coming I told her I was disappointed, and without really thinking or worrying about the repercussions, I asked her when we could get together again. She laughed, thanked me, and said she was also disappointed; I used that as my 'in' and didn't waste any time. I asked her if she'd like to have a coffee next week and review what's taken place, and to my surprise, she said yes.

When Saturday came, Eric was at my place first thing in the morning, and he arrived with a surprise: he actually brought the coffee with him.

I laughed, grabbed the flyers, my staple gun, and we headed out. As we got downstairs, Eric ran ahead and started filming. I looked around and wondered where to start. I said to Eric, "We'll start at Reliable Fish and Chips. They love me in there, and we can start with a jerk burrito."

When we got to Reliable, Joy and her husband were at the counter talking, and they looked stressed out. I approached Joy, who was shaking a letter angrily at her husband.

I said, "Hi guys, how's it going?"

Joy didn't hold back; right away, she told me what was going on, "Again, another increase, they're raising our rent again; every year, they won't let us sign a lease longer than a year, and every year they increase it, we can't afford it anymore. They're trying to push us out again, hoping a 'Popeyes Chicken', an 'A&W', or a bloody check cashing store will move in; they can jack up the rent because they know these corporations will pay; they're killing small businesses, and the government is helping them with their bullshit laws."

I looked at Joy surprised and said, "Joy, I didn't think that language was in your vocabulary."

She shook her head, and you could tell she looked very defeated. I figured I should order four burritos to show my support for them. I ordered one for me and Eric to eat now and one for each of us when we were done canvassing the neighborhood.

After I ordered, I brought up our 'Renoviction' issue. Considering what they had just learned, she was right into it and was more than willing to put our flyer up in the window. Eric asked her if she wanted to talk about it on camera, and she said she was okay with it.

Speaking with Joy was very enlightening and disheartening. Joy and her husband immigrated from the Philippines ten years ago and opened 'Reliable Fish & Chips' when they arrived. She told me how they had already had two different locations before ending up where they are now on Queen Street, where they have been a neighborhood fixture for the last five years. She said that this would probably be the last straw; with this increase, there was no way they could survive without raising their prices, but raising prices means less business. Their choices are to shut down or risk staying open, paying higher rent, charging higher prices, and hopefully, their customers will still come. This meant they would be taking a huge gamble that might bankrupt them; it was a sad situation for honest, hard-working people to be in.

After listening to her, I realized that this was a bigger problem than I thought; it wasn't only affecting individuals renting but also hurting small business owners. Queen Street was already littered with empty stores, and it was because landlords were asking for rent that was way too high; the landlords just had dollar signs in their eyes. And because of tax credit incentives from the City, owners would rather let their units sit empty for months, hoping a corporation will come and rent it for the big payday, rather than rent it out to an entrepreneur or small business. Toronto was being run by idiots and greed.

As we walked, we went into some stores and not others; we didn't bother trying to speak to any corporate stores; not only would they not care, but the poor managers working there had no say at all in what happened in their stores. Some stores only had hourly workers, but some were independently owned, and the owners were more than happy to put the flyer in the window. All of them were sympathetic and wanted to hear all they could about the situation because they knew they could be next.

By the time we were finished, we didn't have any flyers left, and as we walked, we were pretty impressed with ourselves - looking down the street, you could see the flyers everywhere. They were on the phone poles, in the store windows, and even stapled to park benches, we outdid ourselves.

As we finished and returned to the building, a flatbed truck with a ten-yard dumpster pulled up. A worker jumped out of the truck and started directing it up against the building; as the truck began reversing, it also started beeping.

I looked at Eric and said, "Robert isn't going to like this; I give it one minute before he is down here."

It didn't even take him that long; he was downstairs in thirty seconds. He came straight to us and asked what was going on.

I shrugged and said, "I have no idea. They pulled up, and now this guy is parking a dumpster here." As Robert was getting ready to tear into the workers from the truck, which I thought would be a bad idea, Lorenzo thankfully arrived on the scene.

Robert went straight at him. "You can't park this dumpster here. This is a sidewalk. I'm calling the City; this won't stand."

Lorenzo smiled, raised his hand, and unrolled the plans tucked under his arm. They were drawings of the sidewalk and the building with a dumpster right in front of it. Attached to the drawings was a City Permit for the dumpster.

As he showed it to Robert, he calmly and politely explained that he had obtained a special permit to park it here while some demolition took place. Since there was limited parking and the road was so small, this was the only option, and they were allowed an exemption for two weeks.

There wasn't much Robert could say; Lorenzo had done everything within the law. As he wrapped up the plans, the truck dropped the dumpster with an incredible bang, and Robert stormed off and up the stairs.

Lorenzo laughed and looked at me. I liked Lorenzo, he was just trying to do his job and didn't want any bullshit, but he was forced to be knee-deep in it.

He looked at the dumpster, shook his head, and said, "It's going to start getting busy and very messy around here tomorrow. We're gutting the basement and the empty units. I'm hiring some extra guys to help rip it apart since we only have the dumpster for two weeks. We'll do our best to keep it clean, but it's going to be hard, and it's going to get ugly."

He looked at the building and said, referring to Robert, "That gentleman is going to lose his mind."

Right away, I thought about the rally we were supposed to have on the twenty- ninth, so I had to ask him, "You said two weeks; when is this thing gone?"

Lorenzo looked at the permit and then at the flyer in the window. He said, "It will be gone on the thirtieth. This might get interesting."

I thanked Lorenzo for the heads up and asked him if he wanted a beer, as it was a little late for coffee. He laughed, said "no thanks," and we went our separate ways.

The following day Lorenzo didn't disappoint; he was there first thing in the morning with his crew, ready to rip the shit out of the building. But before they began, they tried to protect the place by taping cardboard to the walls and covering the floors in plastic as thin as saran wrap. Anyone worth their salt could tell that this was a half-ass job; it was as if it was done only for show, which it probably was.

After a few days, the stairs and walls were covered in dust, the cardboard and plastic were mostly ripped to shit and coming untaped. The basement had been completely gutted, and all the walls that separated the rooms were gone. It was an empty, wide-open space that looked like a demolition zone. The windows to the street were now exposed, so anyone walking by could look in. The condition of the basement was an invitation for an infestation, and I don't mean from insects. If any of the junkies looked in, they would think that it was an excellent place to break into, get high, and squat for a while.

As time went on, I started to see more of Lorenzo around the building; his crew was very good at ripping the shit out of everything and hauling it out, even though their equipment and safety standards left something to be desired. He seemed to be a nice guy; he always had a smile, and his workers seemed to like working for him. But Robert was starting to get under his skin; so far, Robert had called the building inspector on him three times and the parking ticket guys six times. Lorenzo wasn't too impressed with that.

It was the end of the day, and Lorenzo was wrapping up. I asked him if he wanted a beer, and to my surprise, this time, he said yes. I told him to hold on while I ran upstairs and grabbed a couple. He told me to meet him in unit two-zero-three; we could have a beer there and talk about the unit.

We met there and toasted to Three-Ninety-One-Empire Avenue. I asked him how the work was going, and a serious look came over his face.

He sat on a windowsill and said, "Well, Brent, the work is OK, but I'm starting to see a problem with the money; payments have slowed down. The owner is saying I'm not working fast enough; look around, Brent; look how fast we gutted this place; no one could have done it faster. We do good work, Brent, but this guy isn't paying for good work, so we have to cut some corners; he likes to play games, but I have to pay my guys, and he delays the payments to me. I'm already starting to go into the hole with this job."

I shouldn't have felt sorry for Lorenzo, but I did. Here's a guy just taking a contract trying to fix up a building, make some money and move on, but instead he'll probably get screwed too.

I said, "You know Lorenzo, I gotta be honest with you; I'm not supposed to like you or feel bad for you; you work for my enemy. But I do feel bad. You seem like a nice guy, but I don't think you realized who you were doing business with. And yeah, you're probably going to be taken advantage of; not only is this guy going to illegally evict us, but it looks like he might screw you too."

Lorenzo sipped his beer and said, "Yeah, looks that way."

I had to lighten the mood a little; I joked with Lorenzo and asked him, "What happened to the plastic and cardboard you put down to protect everything? It's ripped and looks like shit. Is that the kind of work you do?"

He looked at me, a little shocked, but when he saw me smiling, he knew I was messing with him.

I continued, "I mean, it's all torn to shit, and the hallways and stairwells look like a war zone; how are they supposed to rent this place for four times the price."

He laughed and replied, "Well, like I said, he gets' what he pays for, but also..."

He looked me dead in the eye and said, "Louie, the guy that pays me, said that they didn't care about what happened to the building or interior right now, and they wouldn't sign off on any supplies for cleaning or safety. They said to make it look like we're trying to keep it maintained or clean and just to focus on the empty units. They want us to finish the demolition as soon as possible, but they don't seem to be in a hurry to get anything renovated."

We talked for a little while about where he was from in Italy, about Western Society, and the differences in our cultures. He said things were too complicated here, including business, banking, government rules, and regulations. He chugged the rest of his beer and said he had to run.

I thanked him for showing me the empty unit, complimented him on his demolition work, and reminded him that the rally was in a few days. I said to him, "When we're having the rally, we're going to have some visitors and cameras in the building that day; you might want to keep your head down."

He thanked me and said it might be good to take that day off, and we went our separate ways.

Chapter 14

When rally day came, the building looked like hell. The basement was ripped to shit, the hallways and floors were covered in plaster and dust, and cleaning wasn't at the top of Lorenzo's list. I didn't mind; it played right into our whole 'slumlord' narrative that we had going. Anyone that would see this mess would undoubtedly know that there was some bullshit going on.

I woke up feeling good. I was a little nervous about the rally, but I was more nervous to see Laila again. I looked at my phone—it was nine a.m., and the rally was supposed to start at two. I put on a pot of coffee and jumped in the shower. Eric said he was coming by early, and knowing Eric, that could be at anytime.

I showered, dressed, and sat at the computer, and as I did, Eric came in. "You made coffee; you read my mind."

I poured him a coffee and said, "Make yourself at home." I was glad to have Eric on my side through this.

I sat on the computer and went to Facebook. I said to Eric, "We're up to ten thousand followers; we're getting some people in the U.S. now and a couple of international people."

I started writing a reminder post about today's big 'rally.' I wasn't sure what to write or what would happen, so I posted a picture of our poster and wrote: *RENOVICTION RALLY - Join Us at Three-Ninety-One Empire Avenue today for our 'Renoviction Rally.' If you have been evicted or 'Renovicted' or know someone that has, come on out. If you are concerned with the affordable housing crisis in the City, come on down and tell your story and hear others speak."*

As soon as I hit enter, there were a few likes and a comment. I said to Eric, "Look—someone replied already, saying he was just given an eviction notice today at his building, and he'll be attending today. This shit is out of control."

We sat around, drank coffee, surfed the web, and watched Seinfeld before the rally started. There was a knock on the door. I got up, and it was Robert. He entered the usual way, but this time, he went straight to the window.

He said, "Look out the window. The Global News truck is parked outside—and look, the CBC is pulling up."

Eric asked, "Wow, Robert, who did you call?"

He looked out the window and said, "Everyone."

I went to the window and looked out. There were a couple of news trucks, and a small crowd was starting to gather. I patted Robert on the back and complimented him, "Good job, Robert. We're off to a good start."

We headed downstairs at twelve-thirty, and people were starting to gather. There were people from Acorn in red shirts, some people I recognized from work, and a lot of people just milling around. Eric's sound guy with the boom mic, City Pulse News, and a couple of other reporters also showed up. I looked around, and soon, the street was full of people; I was really impressed and surprised with the turnout—really surprised.

Eric was beside me, and I began to wonder, "Hey, do you think anyone from the other side is here watching? Do you think Brownstone would come down to see what's happening?"

Eric started filming all around and agreed, "I would if I were them."

We looked across the street, and people were watching, but how would you know who they were? A couple of people had their phones up, which was not surprising. A few people were standing and having coffee. One of them had a huge mustache, and Eric joked that he didn't see anything suspicious—unless someone was hiding in that guy's mustache. Eric had a great wit and was quick. We looked at each other and started laughing.

People at the rally started to overflow the sidewalk into the street; our building had a great setup for this kind of thing. People speaking could stand on the steps of the building and talk over the crowd on the sidewalk a few steps below, and when they spoke, their voices carried over everybody's heads. Only Councillor Flatch came out to the rally, and Bernie Peters stayed away; he seemed to be keeping his distance from our situation, trying not to take a stand. After all, he was taking money from the other side. But the councillor showed up; I guess she has less shame and wants it from both sides; she wants the money from their side and the publicity from our side. She took her place on the steps with Robert, Bill, Krystle, Nolan, and Sarah with her cats, Melissa with her kids, and Bob and Bo; it made for a great picture. Mark Richards from the Parkdale Office was also here, but our lawyer wasn't, which I thought was strange; why wouldn't this guy want to attend this event with his clients, raising awareness and support? We all thought it was weird that he wasn't here, and Robert was very insulted that he wasn't.

But at least Mark, from the Parkdale Office, was here; he didn't mind speaking about the subject. The Acorn people had brought some picket signs that said things like, 'Say No to Renoviction' and 'No To Illegal Evictions.' They had a couple of sandwich board signs with, 'No to Renoviction for Three-Ninety-One Empire Avenue,' and some people had big Acorn flags; it was quite the site. I was impressed at the effort that went into helping us. It looks like they really put some effort into it, or maybe some of their member's kids made the signs as art projects; I still wasn't sure who was doing the work or paying for this.

As soon as I saw Laila, I went over to say hello.

She was talking to some of the members, and when I tapped her on the arm from behind, she swung around and, with her big, beautiful smile, said, "Hello, Brentley."

It melted me.

She hugged me and said, "It's so good to see you again; today's the big day."

"It's good to see you as well, Laila; thank you for being here; you look amazing."

And she really did.

She was very excited. She lived for this kind of thing. She liked sticking up for people who couldn't defend themselves; she wouldn't be bullied, and I liked that. I walked her up the steps, and we took our places for the start of the rally.

I said to Laila, "Robert will be doing most of the talking; Kyle said he doesn't do public speaking?"

Laila shook her head and said, "Yes, it's only the members from the community, never Kyle."

I smiled at her, "That's fine. I'd rather listen to you anyway. You are an amazing speaker, Laila. I could listen to you all day long."

She smiled, slapped me on the shoulder, and told me to pay attention; I smiled ear to ear.

It was almost two o'clock, and Kyle approached Robert with a bullhorn and asked him if he'd like to start the rally. Robert's eyes lit up when he saw it. He looked around; there were cameras, reporters, a crowd, and now a bullhorn. He was looking forward to this, and rightfully so. He thanked Kyle, grabbed the bullhorn, looked at me with a twisted little smile and a look in his eye as if he was going to do something crazy.

He stepped up in front of everyone on the steps and began talking to the crowd. He was straight to the point, poignant as usual, and there wasn't any of that white stuff in the corner of his mouth. He thanked everyone for coming, talked about housing costs, and compared the rental market to the 'Wild West' because of the weak laws and regulations with non-existent fines and penalties.

He continued, "The Landlord and Tenant Board doesn't work for the people; it works for the owners and landlords."

The crowd applauded, and people yelled in agreement with him. To end off, he blurted out the Facebook page and told everyone to sign up, tell their stories, and help other people who might be going through this. He was quite the salesman. The crowd gave Robert a round of applause, and he put his fist over his head as a salute. Robert was enjoying the moment. Next, he introduced Mark Richards from the Parkdale Legal Aid Office and passed the bullhorn to him.

Mark was harsher than Robert. Mark had been fighting landlords for years, so he knew what they were capable of, and he didn't mince his words. "Landlords have been getting away with far too much for far too long. They're criminals. The laws must change, and we need harsher penalties if we are going to change anything."

He was very good at explaining the situation and talking about how the rules are being abused and that the landlords have no repercussions; the crowd cheered his words, and then he passed the bullhorn to Councillor Flatch.

Like every politician says, 'Never let a good crisis go to waste,' and Flatch was no exception. Our eviction was nothing but a 'crisis' for her to exploit. She used our rally to introduce her creation of a 'sub-committee' that will focus on affordable housing. She called it 'The Toronto City Council Sub-Committee on the Evaluation and Sustainability of Affordable Housing.'

Wow, that was a mouthful. I had no idea what it actually was, and I don't think anyone did; it's probably just some government B.S. to make it look like they're doing something, a 'trying to get to the root cause of the issues' kind of thing.

She continued, "I will get to the root cause of the affordable housing crisis, and I will come up with the solution! I am proud to stand and walk with the tenants of Three-Ninety-One Empire Avenue and their neighbors. I am proud to help fight against illegal evictions and the illegal practice of Renovictions; help us fight Renoviction."

Everyone cheered when she said that. It was nice to have a politician yelling about our cause, even though I knew she was selling us out as she spoke.

Laila took the bullhorn next. After a passionate and moving speech about corruption, Canada, and greed, she rallied the crowd and cameras to begin walking. She yelled, "We will walk along Queen Street and come back to the building. 'Acorn People,' hold your signs and flags high, wave them proudly, and make sure everyone sees them."

When we headed out and started around the block, there were a couple hundred people following us. Acorn had a few of their own flags, and there were a couple of Canadian Flags being waved; combine the flags with the picket signs, the cameras, and the crowd, it was quite the visual, and it drew a lot of attention. At one point, so many people were gathered on the sidewalk that the crowd started to overflow onto the road, making traffic slow down; people were honking and yelling in support.

There was only one guy who was pissed off with what we were doing. The guy was in a hurry and didn't care about what was going on; he yelled out his window, "No one cares, stop wasting everyone's time," he flipped us the finger and yelled, "Get a job," as he drove off.

The march didn't take long; it only took about twenty minutes; the crowd walked two blocks and headed back to the building. Roger was using the bullhorn to incite the crowd and led them with chants. As we walked, a lot of people on the street asked what was going on and had questions, and when anyone did hear or learned about the housing situation and 'Renovictions,' they were pretty outraged about it; a lot of people didn't know that kind of stuff was happening, they had no idea, and why would they, it wasn't affecting them.

The rally served its purpose. It raised awareness throughout the neighborhood and caught the attention of the traffic, everyone on the street, and everyone in all the stores. The TV cameras got their shots, and the politician got her face and soundbite on TV.

We arrived back at the building, and by now, the police had arrived. I looked at Eric and said, "Looks like it's about to get good."

They got out of their cars and were asking people what was happening as they approached us.

I said to them, "Thanks for coming, officers; it's a good thing that you are here. We need your help. Our owner is trying to throw us out illegally. He's trying to break the law. Can you please arrest him?"

Though I said it comically and politely, the officer replied as if I was serious. He didn't even understand that I was joking. The other cop understood and stood back as the bright one spoke, "We're not here for that, sir. That's a civil matter between you and your landlord; that's a Landlord and Tenant Board matter. You'll have to take that up civilly. We can't help you."

I replied, "What? Really? The police aren't able to help? Come on?"

He didn't like my reply and started to get serious: "We're here because we got a report of protesters blocking the street and impeding traffic. What's with the crowd? Do you have a permit?"

I looked at him and said, "For what?"

He said, "for the crowd."

I replied to the officer, "It isn't my crowd."

He looked around, confused, and asked, "Well, whose is it?"

I shrugged and said, "I don't know; maybe you should ask them."

The cop looked around again and asked me, "Ask who?"

I saw Eric smirking behind the camera as Councillor Flatch came out of the crowd to speak with the officers. They spoke briefly, and the officers said they would stick around to ensure there weren't any problems and to assist with traffic.

There were two reporters, and they wanted to speak with Robert and myself, so we took turns between them. I was speaking to the reporter from CBC News, who asked, "Why are you out here, Brent?"

I tried to summarize the situation. I was honest and to the point. I said, "I know this is an investment property, but kicking people out isn't allowed. You can't buy an undervalued building with tenants and kick them out to minimize the risk and maximize your return on investment. Being a landlord is different from other investments."

I waved my arm at the crowd as I spoke, "Look how many people came out today to protest for one little building; this is happening all over the City; it's happening everywhere and way too much. The Landlord and Tenant Board needs an overhaul, the fines are outdated, the laws are lax, and evicting tenants is just another cost of doing business for landlords; we're just another line on the balance sheet that says, 'cost to evict' and then they move on to the next. The system isn't set up to help the little guy in this fight."

The reporter thanked me for the time, and to shamelessly promote ourselves, I mentioned the Renoviction Facebook page. She said she was okay with it and repeated it in her tagline when she signed off.

I saw Joanna Chow approach, and she congratulated me on the rally. She couldn't believe the turnout, and I agreed with her. She said she'd been talking to a lot of people and hearing too many stories of this taking place all over the city.

I looked at her and said, "Joanna, I had no idea what I was getting into when I started this, but the things I'm learning about and the stories I'm hearing are terrible; these people are downright criminals. Now, are you ready for the scoop of the day?"

She said, "Ooh, I'm always ready."

I smiled, "we found the owner of our building."

I got my notebook out and continued, "The company is owned by a Liang Jiang Huong, who we really can't pin down; that name is like 'John Smith' or 'Mohammad Abdul,' there are thousands of them. But that name is on the business registration, along with two others whose names I can't even pronounce; we found them, and all of them live in China. We found a house and two cars registered to the business, and two bank accounts from China, all owned by all three of these guys, two of whom are definitely in China. So, in essence, our building is owned by foreign money, and the people trying to evict us aren't even Canadian Citizens and don't even live in Canada."

She couldn't believe it. I gave her my notebook and let her copy the names so she could look them up.

As she copied my notes, she asked, "Are you sure, Brent? Are you sure this is true? It's shitty, but it's a great angle to the story,"

I begrudgingly said, "Yeah, it is, and yeah, it's true." She thanked me for holding on to that little tidbit for her. As she said that, Laila came over and stood right beside me. She locked her arm into mine and pulled me in tight. It was energizing.

Joanna said she had some good stuff and great pictures, so hopefully, her follow-up story will appear in the Metro next week. She said her goodbyes, and off she went.

Everyone from our building was standing around, and there was a moment of awkwardness.

I looked at the group and then at Laila and I knew who I'd rather be with. I asked her if she would like to get a bite, and she said she would love to.

She looked at everyone else and asked the group, "Who wants to get a bite?" They replied with big smiles and said, "We'd love to."

Robert exclaimed, "To the Duke!"

'The Duke' was Toronto's best little dive bar with a fantastic five-star kitchen. It wasn't fancy—you probably couldn't get farther from fancy than 'The Duke,' but it served good, cheap, quality food.

We started to walk off in that direction, and Laila slid her arm into mine. She reached over with her other hand and put it on my arm. She leaned in, talked softly, and said, "Brentley, I'm a Muslim woman, and we should have an escort or chaperone on our first few dates. It's not proper without one." She made a devilish smile when she said that.

I looked at her and smiled, "date? Ok, by me."

When we arrived at the Duke, some people from the rally were already there; Councillor Flatch was getting an order to go; one of the reporters and her cameraman were sitting at a table, and beside them was a group of red shirts from Acorn. We sat at a big table, the boys ordered beers, and out of respect for Laila, I just had a Coke. As we waited for the drinks, I looked around.

I said to the table, "You know it's a shame; this is exactly what the landlord is killing. Places like 'The Duke', sure it's a dive bar, and yeah, it's not fancy, but it attracts all walks of life. 'The Duke' doesn't care who you are. At 'The Duke', we're all the same, come as you are. But the people moving into the neighborhood don't think like that; they hate 'The Duke'; they say it's an eyesore that attracts the wrong kind of 'element' and should be torn down. That's the problem with this gentrification crap."

Everyone agreed. The drinks arrived, and we cheered ourselves and patted each other on the back for a good day and a job well done. Melissa and Krystle started exchanging pictures they had taken throughout the day and insisted that I put some up on the 'Renoviction' site; I said, "Of course, I'd be happy too."

I was learning that Nolan and Krystle were cool people. We never hung out or even really spoke to each other in the building, and it wasn't until this situation that I got to know them. They lived in the building because they were looking to save money to buy a house, but property values were rising faster than they could save. They wanted to stay in the building for another couple of years until they had a down payment for a house, but this 'Renoviction' was throwing a wrench in their plans.

We were all eating and coming down from the day's highs and thrills when Krystle said, "OK, now what do we do?"

I looked over at Robert and Eric and wondered that, too, "I said, yeah, guys, what do we do now?"

We were all clueless and unsure of where to go from here.

I said to everyone, "I told Joanna who our owners were; I told her about the 'China Connection,' and she said she was going to include it in the next article, but she also said, 'That is, if there is a next article.'

Robert added, "The reporters at the Rally said they would be running the stories tonight on the ten o'clock news."

I invited everyone to my place if they wanted to watch, but everyone had to get home; only Robert, Eric, and I had no lives and nothing to do. When we left the Duke, we were all a little bit closer. We started to walk back to the apartment, and I walked with Laila.

I told her I had fun today and that I enjoyed watching her do this kind of stuff. I asked if she wanted to come up to watch the news, I smiled and added, "You'll be with everyone; there'll be people around; you won't be alone with me."

She said she'd like to, but she had to get back to her son, who would be home soon. The guys went back to the building, and I walked Laila to her car. We said our goodbyes, and she leaned into me to give me a hug. When she did, I snuck a kiss on her cheek before she could get out of the way.

She smiled, laughed, and gave me a little slap; I apologized and said I had to.

She laughed and said, "Thank you, Brentley. You are a nice man. I will see you again soon."

I walked away feeling great; I wasn't even thinking about being homeless in a few months. Laila made all those thoughts disappear.

Back at the building, I went upstairs, and they were at Robert's place. I went to my place and grabbed some beers, went into Roberts, and joked, "Good thing you're in here; I don't even have cable. We couldn't have watched the news at my place if we wanted to."

Robert told us to relax, and turned on the TV. He lived in a pretty small studio apartment, and when I looked around, I wondered what he was paying for the place.

I had to ask him, "OK, Robert, I gotta ask you, how much are you paying for rent?"

Robert smiled, and, as if he were getting away with something, he said, "Four hundred and fifty a month."

Eric nearly spat out his beer.

"Wow!" I was shocked; I didn't think rent that cheap was possible in Toronto, "Good for you, Robert; I'd be fighting tooth and nail, too. How is that even possible? I didn't think anyone would be paying rent that cheap!"

He laughed, "It was three hundred when I moved in. Some years, Denise raised the rent, and some years, she didn't. When the law came out in the eighties that landlords could only raise a small percentage, I knew I would never leave; the rent was just too good."

I said, "damn Robert, no wonder you don't care about work and are out golfing all the time."

Then I got serious and said, "Robert, with you gone, this unit is easily worth an extra twelve thousand dollars a year to our greedy owner; he could easily get fourteen or fifteen hundred bucks a month for this place. The funny thing is, nothing would have physically changed with the unit; one day, you are paying four hundred and fifty, and the next day, they say it's worth fourteen hundred, and why? What changed? Just because there's a new owner and he wants to maximize his ROI? That is supposed to justify it; that makes what's happening, OK? Just because a rich investor should be guaranteed to make a profit?"

I was getting angry, and Robert agreed.

He got very serious, "That's why I know a buyout of five thousand is nothing; that's why I want a buyout of at least twenty thousand dollars."

Hearing that made me realize that I hadn't even considered my price; what number would I agree to leave for?

I didn't want to move again; I was only thinking about staying here, "Well, I don't know what I would take. I guess twenty sounds good, but I'd rather just like to stay."

"Well, so would I, but come on, Brent, the chances of that are slim to none." He had a somber tone when he said that.

I shook my head, went to my place, and grabbed some more beers. When I returned to the room, the CBC news was on, and Eric and Roberts's eyes were glued to the T.V. We flipped back and forth between CBC and City T.V. to see who had it first. CBC came back from a commercial, and there was a wide shot of the protest taking place at our building. The reporter talked about illegal evictions, 'Renovictions', and affordable housing. She interviewed Robert, and they went on a walkthrough of the building. The plastic and tape on the floor and drywall-covered cardboard on the walls were quite the visuals and made the building look horrible, made it look like a war zone.

When that story ended, Robert flipped over to City Pulse to wait and see what they did. I said to Robert that he looked great and that it was a great idea to do a walkthrough of the building with the reporter; the building looked like utter hell.

I said, "You did a great job putting down the landlord, but you did it in a polite, political way; you were perfect."

We were all happy with the CBC story. We were talking for a bit when Robert pointed to the TV, and City TV was showing our segment. It was our building, with all of us standing on the steps. It was a nice shot, and we all looked surprisingly good— not too sad. The reporter began by talking about the Toronto Housing situation. She discussed the increase in evictions and the fight to save affordable housing. There was a quick shot and a five-second sound bite with Robert and me.

After watching the City T.V. piece, I felt that their coverage of the event was more focused on Councillor Flatch and her Sub-Committee; it seemed we were just the springboard or a segway to promote Flatch and her bullshit. I had heard of 'grandstanding' in the past but never really witnessed it, but here I am standing with a politician using us to promote and push her new 'sub-committee'; in my mind, this was the epitome of grandstanding.

After the news, we sat around having a few beers; our phones were constantly buzzing with messages from people who saw the news. People were saying it was a great piece and praising us for our commitment to the fight.

I even received a text from my Dad, which was surprising. Communication wasn't his strong point, so I was surprised when he sent me a text: 'Sorry you are going through this. I saw you on CBC. Good story. I'm proud of you for fighting back.' I read it aloud to Eric and Robert and joked that I almost had a tear in my eye.

Eric, always with a zinger, said, "How about that Bingham, all those years of trying to impress your Dad working hard trying to be successful, and he didn't say shit to you. Who knew all you had to do was be a failure and get evicted to have him say that he was proud of you."

I looked at him in bewilderment and laughed, "You're an ass, but you're right." We all had a good chuckle about the irony of his statement.

I grabbed my phone and went to Facebook; I said, "Holy shit, guys, we have sixteen thousand followers now; this thing has a life of its own. Eric, I think we have something here."

Robert got excited and jumped up towards his table; he got his notes out and said, "Let's do it. Let's post the owner's name. Let's tell everyone that this is foreign money, foreign citizens evicting Canadian Citizens. You know, when you do hear it like that, you can't help but be a little offended."

Eric said, "You're going to get haters; people are going to call you out for being racist. You can't go after Chinese people or anyone for that matter."

I answered Eric, "I'm not going after anyone; I'm just telling everyone what's happening to me; everything is public knowledge. I don't care if it's Chinese, Japanese, Scottish, Irish, or people from fucking Mars doing this to me; what I do care about is that Canadians living here in Canada can't afford to own a home because of people who don't even live in this country that want to make money off of us. I do care that Canadians are getting thrown out of their homes by people not even in this country, so I don't think I'm being too crazy or

148

overboard about this at all. Wherever and whoever they are, it isn't right. We have laws and regulations set up to protect our society, and these people, foreign speculators, and investors ignore them. Do you think they care about the rules and laws of our society? Do you think they care about us, or do they just care about making money?"

We kept drinking and were sitting around when I received a text from Joanna Chow. It read, 'Great news! Your story is running tomorrow on the front page of Metro, and there was talk of The National.'

I replied right away, 'That's great to hear. Thank you. Did you see the story on the CBC?'

She replied, 'Yes, and the phone call about tomorrow's Metro came five minutes after it aired.' I laughed and typed back, 'Congratulations, and thank you for your help, Joanna.'

I was a little drunk and pissed off, so I decided to write a post; what could go wrong? I went to Facebook, and I was going to tell everyone about our owners, the foreign money, and the foreign ownership.

I started to type, and after a few words, I had to delete everything; I thought to myself, Joanna is publishing this tomorrow; I shouldn't say anything yet; she'd be pissed. Losing Joanna's support would hurt our coverage; she's the only one who has been following our story, and she's the only one who has said she wants to see this through until the end.

Instead, I decided to post about the rally. I thanked everyone for coming out, supporting our fight, and helping raise awareness about the illegal evictions in the city. I posted a few pictures different people had sent me; and they looked great; the streets were filled, people were holding signs, marching together, and everyone looked happy. In some of the pictures, you could tell people were singing or chanting in unison, waving their hands up in the air, and it looked like a great community event, which it was.

Robert had said the CBC news report was now online. He sent me the link, and I posted it along with the pictures; I thanked the CBC reporter for the great coverage and tagged her and everyone I could think of.

I started receiving other texts from friends and people at work who saw the news. Most were sympathetic, and some congratulated me on my courage to fight and bring attention to this issue. I texted back, 'Thank you.' I didn't know how to respond. 'Thank you' was all I could think of, and I wasn't sure if it was an appropriate reply. It was almost midnight; Robert threw us out, and we said our goodbyes.

Eric followed me into my place. I asked him if he wanted another beer, and he said, "Sure, Bingham. We've been drinking since the afternoon, so I gotta' crash here, I might as well have another. Don't worry; we'll film something in the morning. It'll be great."

I grabbed a couple of beers and sat on the sofa. I asked him when he was planning to shoot the daydream scene and if he was actually going to use fire.

"Bingham, the tiki torches, the flame bar, it's all props. Just like this world, nothing is real; everything's controlled. We'll film in here and up on the roof; no one can see us up there unless we're at the edge. And don't worry, it's not as bad as you think."

I said, "OK, I have gas cans, flares, fireworks, a propane flame bar, and tiki torches in my bedroom. You're right; it's not as bad as I think."

Eric looked down, rubbed the sofa, and said, "You know, this is a cool sofa."

I woke up early and dragged my hurting body and pounding head to the kitchen. Eric was sprawled all over the sofa, and all he was wearing was his boxers.

I put on coffee, sat at the desk, and looked at him almost naked on the sofa, "Come on, man, I gave you blankets. Why aren't you using them? Put some pants on, my poor sofa. Now I'm going to have to burn the damn thing."

We were both a little foggy from the night before, so we sat and sipped coffee for a bit before either of us came back into reality and spoke.

After a few minutes, I asked, "Well, what happens next?"

Eric said, "Now you and I get to work trying to get some answers. We're going to go see some people. We're going to see your owner. We'll go to that address we have for him, wait until someone comes or goes, and confront them. Then we'll go see Kerwin again; this time, we'll try to get an interview."

I was looking forward to this. The more I learned about Renoviction, the madder I got. These owners were using downright dirty tactics, and their only motivation was greed. Throwing people out of their homes just for more profit disgusted me. The more I learned, the more I wanted to expose them and show how rampant the problem truly was.

After the coffee kicked in, I remembered Joanna Chows' story should be online. I went to Metro online, and we were on the front cover. There was a picture of us with the crowd, and it was a good picture; it looked like quite the 'protest' event.

I started to read the story and the byline out loud, "By Joanna Chow as reported in 'The National'. Holy shit, 'The National!'"

I went to the online edition to see if we were there. I guess Robert had his door open as usual and must have heard us talking and freaking out about the article.

He knocked, I let him in, and he had 'The National' in his hand. He blew by me and headed straight to Eric and the camera. He had already been out and gotten a few copies of the paper. He held it up, and there we were on the front cover, the picture of all of us from Three-Ninety-One Empire Avenue, with the Councillor and the crowd in front of us.

150

The headline read: 'Canada's Affordable Housing Crisis, Turning into a Plague.'

I said to the guys I was surprised to see it in the National paper.

But Robert, being the smart one, laid it out for me. He said, "Brent, there's an election coming up, so it's time for these politicians to start spreading the message that they care about the people. They'll tell us that they're looking into the situation and that they deeply care, and at the same time, they'll tell the owners and landlords not to worry about a thing. It is all theater, political theater."

Something else had pissed Robert off; he pointed to the article and said, "Look, after it talks about the foreign ownership, there's a quote by Trudeau saying that 'foreign ownership needs to be looked at and changes need to be made to help protect housing for the Canadian People."

He had a file folder in the other hand and pulled a copy of an old article from the folder. He shook the paper in the air and slammed it down on the desk. A few years back, Trudeau changed foreign investment laws to favor international investments. Robert started reading the article and said, "Here it is, Trudeau saying, 'Canada needs to open up our real estate investment market to the global economy to help allow Canadians to compete on a global level.'"

Robert went into a rant about the article, "How the hell is this helping us compete globally? We're getting screwed globally and this is our government's fault. First, they changed the laws that broke the system, and now they want to be the heroes to fix it. They'll never fix it; they'll just say they want to; they'll lie their faces off to get themselves voted in, and then they won't do a damn thing."

He was fuming, pacing back and forth, and I was glad I didn't have dishes drying on the counter. I reminded him that it was a productive article and at least it drew attention to us. Then I reminded him we were going to come across a lot of bullshit in this process.

I sat at the computer, looked up at Robert, and said, "Trust me, Robert, the best is yet to come." I typed 'Federal Lobbying Canada' into Google, and the 'Office of the Commissioner of Lobbying Canada' appeared on the screen. I said to the guys, "I didn't search federally last time; I only looked up the city and the provincial lobbying groups. Let me see what our boy Kerwin has been doing at the Federal Level."

Robert looked at Eric and me and said, "Kerwin?"

I started telling Robert everything I had learned about Kerwin, his Alliance, and his bags of money from the landlords to the politicians. I told him about Kerwin's history, 'The Alliance,' how many meetings he's had with our politicians, and how much money they have received from him.

His reaction surprised me. I thought he would go ballistic and smash something, but he didn't. He stood in place, hands on hips, eyes looking to the ground, and started laughing. You couldn't blame him; the situation was a joke.

I had typed Trudeau in the search bar, and pages upon pages came up—hundreds and hundreds of pages—all of his meetings and appointments. I typed 'Alliance,' and sure enough, Kerwin met with Federal Housing Minister Stephen Clarke four times. When I looked at the money, Kerwin and the Alliance kindly donated twenty-thousand dollars to the Housing Minister's campaign. I couldn't believe how much money Kerwin was throwing around and how much money went from industries to politicians through lobbying.

I couldn't believe it was legal; I really couldn't; in other countries, lobbying is called bribery. But here? It's part of the system. Everything they ever taught me about government, about laws, and democracy, even that fucking cartoon with the Bill dancing around, talking about how a bill becomes a law, I was never taught this part of the system. Nobody ever explained to me what a 'pay to play' political system was or that lobbyists pay off politicians so they'll vote in their industry's favor against the people. Nobody ever explained to me how our system was so corrupt.

Robert finally sat down, and surprisingly, the anger came back to him when he sat, "I'm going to give these politicians a piece of my mind; I'm going to tell everyone how corrupt and full of shit these people really are; I'm going to…"

I stood up and had to calm him down; I said, "Whoa, whoa, Robert, we need to hold our cards close right now; we can't call them out on it yet; we need them on our side until we go the distance, we need them until we don't. And when we know we don't need them anymore, then 'have at 'em,' but you make sure you do it on camera. I wouldn't want to miss that."

I winked and smiled at him, "I want to get these guys as much as you do, Robert. Don't worry; we'll get them."

Chapter 15

It was the Monday after the rally and the first of the month. We were all expecting a new 'Eviction Letter' with the correct dates on it, and we weren't disappointed. I woke up, and before making my coffee, I opened my door to see Lorenzo standing in the hallway, who looked at me in my robe and chuckled. I looked down, and sure enough, there was an envelope on the floor with my name on it. This time, it wasn't a regular envelope with a single letter; it was a big manila envelope about two inches thick, and it was from our friends, 'D&D Paralegals.'

I picked it up, looked at Lorenzo, and said, "Oh, look, a present from your boss. This one is from his paralegals. It looks like he's stepping up his game."

Lorenzo shook his head and asked, "How was your rally? Did the reporters like the state of the building?"

I asked, "Did you see us on the news?"

As I said that, a couple of his workers came up the stairs with brooms and garbage cans and started cleaning.

He said, "Yes, I especially liked the walk-through of the building; it looked like shit; it was a very poor reflection of the owner."

That's when I realized Lorenzo did us a favor, and I said, "Yeah, it did look like shit. Do I have you to thank for that?"

Lorenzo looked at me and smiled, "I thought I would leave the cleaning until today."

I smiled and thanked him. I picked up the envelope and laughed, "I'm guessing this is our most recent eviction letter, but there seems to be more bullshit with it this time."

I held the envelope as if I was trying to weigh it. I walked into the hallway, wearing just my robe and slippers. I walked to the window and put all the papers on the ledge for Lorenzo to see. "Look, look at this bullshit."

I started with the eviction letter, "Yup, here it is—the eviction letter. It says we have sixty days to vacate the unit for our safety due to repairs on or before October 1st and it looks like they got their math, and dates right this time, October 1st was exactly sixty days."

I explained to Lorenzo how they had screwed up the dates on the previous letters, but I said that everything looked right on this one.

I looked at the stack of papers, "I guess this is what has been filed with the Landlord and Tenant Board; I guess it's official."

I started going through the papers and reading out loud what each one was: "This one is an engineer's report; this stack is from an architect; this bunch is from an electrical company; here are the plumbing diagrams, and this one is from an abatement company."

Lorenzo asked, "What are these reports?"

I replied, "I don't know; they look like reports about everything that needs to be done in the building."

Lorenzo was taken aback and said, "Well, I've never seen these."

He grabbed them from my hand and started looking through them, "I haven't seen any of these."

He pulled out some papers from his clipboard and said, "The only thing the owner has given me is plans for the individual units."

He pulled out the blueprints, laid them on the ledge, and compared them to mine, "These building plans are different, and they're from a completely different architect. I have never heard of the engineer or the abatement company either. This is all news to me, and considering we ripped the basement apart, this would have been nice to know."

I didn't know what the hell was happening, but Lorenzo did, and he was pissed; looking at the plans, all he could say was, "That son of a bitch."

He explained it to me. The owner doesn't plan on paying him, or any of these other guys for that matter. He didn't share the plans, and it happens all the time; you keep the work separate and compartmentalized, so no one knows of the other companies involved until it's too late and the liens are filed, so when he doesn't pay one company, we won't hear or find out about it from the other. If I hadn't seen these papers from you, I would never have seen them; it's classic dirty tactics."

I shook my head in disbelief; I looked at Lorenzo, "So this guy not only wants to throw out the people who live in the building, but he also wants to screw you and all the other companies that do his work as well? This guy is too much."

Lorenzo thanked me, looked at me briefly, and said, "Brent, I think we have something in common."

I said, "Yeah, I think we do, Lorenzo."

He said, "Let me show you something."

He took me downstairs to one of the empty units. He showed me some work that had been going on in the unit, then showed me his plans, and he told me to look at the unit again.

I did and said, "OK, what am I looking for?"

He pointed to a semi-partition wall that had been built and said, "So it looks like a one-bedroom to your eyes and on the plans, right?"

I looked and said, "Yeah, it's a one-bedroom."

He showed me another set of plans and said, "Look closely."

I looked at the second set of plans, and the apartment looked like a two-bedroom unit. Some sort of door structure had been added that would 'create a room.'

I walked into the 'room' and said, "This is a room? If you're lucky, you'd get a twin bed in here, and that would be it. And don't plan on turning around in here either."

He said, "Yes, exactly, they build it like this, so when it is inspected for permits, it's inspected as a one bedroom, but after inspection, they put up a bullshit French door divider, and they call it a room, and now they can advertise it as a two-bedroom apartment. And that adds how much more to the rent? Another thousand dollars on top of what they are making?"

I looked at Lorenzo and shook my head, "Are you serious? These guys break the rules every step of the way; they find a way to cheat every step of the process. This is crazy; this is out of control."

Lorenzo replied, "Yes, it is Brent. Welcome to the Wild West of Canadian real estate."

He let me take a picture of the blueprint and the actual unit on the condition that I wouldn't use it until after they had rented it out as a two-bedroom apartment. He stressed and made me promise not to use it until both of us were long gone from this place. He thanked me for the information, and I thanked him right back for his.

We shook hands and had a good laugh; I had a good relationship with Lorenzo, we both knew we were dealing with a real asshole, and we knew that we weren't each other's enemy. We said we'd speak to each other soon; he went down the stairs, and I returned to my apartment.

I went inside, made my coffee, and sat on the sofa. I spread all the papers out beside me and decided to do some reading; I guess I knew what I was doing for the day.

I started with the eviction letter. It was almost identical to the last one, except for the dates. Everything looked correct on it, but what the hell did I know?

Next, I grabbed the paperwork they filed with the Landlord and Tenant Board; this was about a dozen pages; it was a questionnaire with some 'check the box' and some 'please provide a brief description' type of questions. When asked to describe something in detail, they just wrote one-word answers that were so vague it could cover anything. For example, one of the questions was, 'What are the main reasons that justify the building being empty for repairs?' Their answer, 'safety'. Under the reason for 'termination of the lease agreement,' their answer was 'renovations'—that's it, that's all they wrote.

Also included in the package was an engineer report on the structural integrity of Three Ninety-One Empire Avenue; an 'abatement schedule' from an Environmental Company; an architect's package called 'Revised Drawings of Three Ninety-One Empire Avenue'; electrical plans, plumbing drawings, and fire sprinkler plans. Some of the reports looked to be a hundred pages long, and there must have been seven hundred pages in all.

I called the lawyer, but the secretary said he wasn't available. When I told her my name and that I was calling about Three Ninety-One Empire Avenue, she replied, "Oh dear, OK. Did you get the package from the owner?"

I inhaled deeply and said, "Yeah, I got the package."

She said, "Mr. Wessler is aware of what's going on and will reply shortly. I'll put your name on the 'To Call' list; you're number nine. Hopefully, he will call you back today." She ended with, "Thank you, honey; hang in there," and she hung up.

The moment I put the phone down, it buzzed. I picked it up, and it was Robert. He texted that he had spoken with Wessler and that we were going to have a 'Tenants Meeting' Friday night. He'll be there and will tell us what our options are and what our reply will be. I typed back, 'Sounds good.'

I kept drinking coffee and reading through the papers. Every report led back to the conclusion that the tenant had to be gone to perform the necessary work. I wasn't a smart guy, but when I saw all the reports, a thought popped into my head that these paralegals, 'The Durbanskys,' might be trying to bury our lawyer in paperwork, trying to overwhelm him.

I decided to go online and check out these 'Durbansky' guys. It was a shitty website; it was plain, the colors were bland, and there wasn't much to it. There was a picture of the Durbansky's, and it looked like they were brothers; both were short, round, and tubby. They looked like twins, one with a mustache and one without, and after reading their website, it seemed like this eviction stuff was their bread and butter.

Everything on the website was about landlord-tenant disputes. They claimed to be experts on the 'Residential Tenancies Act' and proficient in the processes of the Landlord and Tenant Board. The website said things like, 'Maximize your rental returns by maximizing tenant turnover.' They offered things like 'New building conversion guidance' and 'How to get the best ROI on your rental real estate investment.'

These guys were scumbags; they made their living evicting tenants. They are hired guns, the mercenaries hired to do the dirty work of landlords evicting the tenants and throwing people out. It made me wonder if the Durbansky's knew they were working for foreign owners with foreign money. I assumed they knew, and they probably didn't care. Based on the package of reports they gave us, it looks like these guys know what they're doing; I wondered what our lawyer, who I'm starting to think might be in over his head, was going to do about the package.

Just as I was thinking about Wessler, my phone rang, and it was him; I took that as a sign, but I wasn't sure if it was good or bad.

We said hello, and he said, "I understand you received the package."

"Yes, outside my door this morning, it looks like they're using everything under the sun to get us out. So, what's the plan? How do you, how do we handle this?"

He said, "First, we have to reply. We'll state our case, inform them that you don't plan to leave in sixty days, and we'll have to go prove why you should be able to stay; we'll discuss that when we are all together."

I replied, "Yeah, OK, Robert mentioned a tenant meeting on Friday?"

He said, "Yes, we'll all talk there and agree on how to proceed."

I said, "Thank you, I'll see you Friday," and hung up.

I sat and took pictures of all the reports. I went online to the Facebook page. I couldn't believe it. I almost dropped the phone. We had twenty-five thousand followers.

I texted Eric and told him to go online and look at the Facebook page. I started to write a post about our most recent eviction notice and the reports we received, and I remembered to keep it honest.

I typed: *We received the most recent eviction letter today, along with half a dozen reports about how unsafe our building is. Look at these reports; at least five hundred pages to read through; it's amazing that our building is still standing according to these. How is the average person supposed to fight against this kind of thing? They're not; the owners, the landlords, and the so-called building management companies know this; the people they are evicting don't have the time or the money to fight back; they are bullies, plain and simple.'*

About an hour later, Eric texted me back, saying, 'It's viral.'

I wrote back, 'What's viral, that rash you have?'

He replied, "Good one, no dumbass the post, it went viral."

He asked if I had been to Facebook since I texted him. I said 'no,' and he told me to look again. I couldn't believe it; there were fifty thousand followers and hundreds of comments. I couldn't count how many direct messages there were, and they just kept coming.

I knew what 'viral' meant, but I didn't realize its implications; now I do, and I see why social media is so addictive; seeing those numbers gave me a rush. I felt good; I felt like I had hit a jackpot on a slot machine in a casino. I kept looking at it and hitting refresh; every time I did, there would be more followers, more likes, and more comments; it was a real dopamine rush. I started trying to reply to everyone and their comments, but there were too many. I went into the DMs, and there must have been a few hundred by now.

I started to read through, and most messages were people telling their stories of getting evicted or all the shitty things their landlords had done; some people were congratulating me for trying to fight back, and some people were asking me for help and advice.

There was no way I was going to give someone legal advice or tell them what to do; hell, I didn't really know what I was doing; all I did was point people in the direction of resources that were available for them online and in the community, like the Legal Aid Clinic. I had some good conversations with these people; I had never met people online before or had 'online' relationships, and to have people open up and tell you details of such a challenging experience that they are going through was very enlightening. I could feel their pain. I got through a lot of the messages, but more and more just kept coming. I looked at the time; four hours had gone by. I couldn't believe it; it felt like twenty minutes.

Reading and returning everyone's emails was tiring, both emotionally and physically. I sat at the computer for hours typing, but hearing and thinking of everyone's story about being evicted was emotionally draining. I was lying on the sofa when Eric and Robert came in, and they were ecstatic.

Eric pulled out his phone and said, "Check this out. It was Drake. Drake retweeted our post about the protest."

I had no idea what he was talking about; my only reply was, "What?"

Eric repeated, "Drake tweeted about our protest! Well, kind of, he didn't tweet about us. He used our protest picture with a link to our page, so we are getting retweeted like crazy, and that's why it's going viral, because Drake tweeted it."

I looked at Robert and Eric, "How the hell did Drake know about our building? Why would he even give a shit?"

Eric laughed and said, "Well, he didn't, and he doesn't. His favorite Jamaican patty shop, Randy's, announced that they had to shut down. Their lease was up, and the landlord wanted three times the rent of what it is now, so they are being pushed out, too. And apparently, Drake really likes 'Randy's,' and he tweeted about it, with our picture saying, 'Sad to see Randy's closing, we should protest for Randy's like these people are protesting to save their home. What is happening to my Four-One-Six?'

Robert looked at me and said, "Who's Drake?"

Eric said he had no idea how he heard about us or why he would retweet us. The only thing he could think of was that Randy's announcement and our protest both happened on the same day. Maybe he saw our picture, and it's just a coincidence. Maybe he used our story because it was relevant and convenient.

When I read the tweet, I had to laugh. I looked at Eric and said, "You're kidding me. This is why we are getting so much attention? Drake's tweet had over one hundred thousand likes. This is what people are more concerned about? They're more concerned about a Jamaican Patty Shop closing down than people being thrown out of their homes? Yeah, that seems about right."

Eric blurted out, "Seventy-thousand, holy shit."

Robert leaned over and asked again, "Who's Drake?"

The next few days were hectic around the building; Lorenzo's crew was starting to bring in fixtures and supplies into the empty units and were beginning to get the units ready to be rebuilt. Robert lost his mind regularly, but Lorenzo handled it well. Sometimes, Robert was right, and Lorenzo would fix whatever was going wrong, but most of the time, Robert was complaining about anything he could. Sometimes, it was even too much for me, but I was glad he was doing it and appreciated that he was looking out for the building.

If I happened to be around when Robert started to go off on Lorenzo or a worker, I would give them both a couple of words of encouragement and go on my way. Robert went off on people a lot, and I wanted to stay the 'good cop.'

When Friday came, I wasn't working, and it was getting close to meeting time. Eric was going to be here any minute, and I was fairly sure Robert would also meet us. I had a shower and was finishing the dishes when they came in.

Eric was great; he asked, "Bingham, how much do you want for the sofa when they throw you out?"

The meeting was in an hour, so we figured we would get some coffee, relax, and slowly wander toward the library. Queen Street was awesome; you didn't need a TV if you lived here on Queen Street. There were street guys that fought over the best spots to beg for change; people with guitars busking for tips; mentally ill people yelling in the streets; preachers on the corners; junkies in the park; people on stoops drinking out of paper bags, and people with dogs and strollers worth the price of a small car would walk and maneuver around it all.

We walked slowly with our coffees, stopping occasionally to sit and talk about the neighborhood and its future. We were all very unsure, but we were sure it didn't include us. Nolan, Krystle, and Sarah came along as we were talking. We said our hellos, and I asked them what they thought the neighborhood's future would be.

They were unsure, but Krystle was as skeptical and angry as we were and said, "Who cares? They don't want us in it, so the hell with it."

We all had a good laugh with that one; it was sad but reassuring to see that the other people were as pissed off and upset with the situation as well; everyone was starting to get mad.

We continued to walk to the library, enjoying the sights and sounds of the neighborhood. There were always the lights and sirens of police cars, ambulances, or fire trucks, as well as the odd yells, hollers, screaming, and fighting of the crazy homeless people.

Robert said, "Come on, guys, who would want to leave this place!"

When we arrived at the library, almost everyone was already there. It was five minutes before the meeting was supposed to start, and the lawyer wasn't even here yet. We sat around chatting, and when seven o'clock came, Robert stood at the front and said he would start things off while we waited for Wessler.

He started by welcoming everyone: "We almost have a full house. Has anyone seen Reggie or Tommy?"

Everyone shook their heads; no one had seen them.

Robert continued, "While we are waiting for our lawyer, we'll just cover what's been happening so far. Brent has some good 'online' attention going with the Facebook and social media pages. We know who our owners are, and we will pay them a visit with the cameras soon. Do any of you have any questions or complaints about what's been happening in the building?"

Bill immediately said, "It's dirty. It looks like a war zone. The stairwell is dirty; the tape, plastic, and cardboard are all coming down, and dust is everywhere."

Robert agreed and said the building's cleaning isn't happening, and it's becoming a hazard. I'll call the inspector tonight after the meeting. Is there anything else?

Brian yelled out, "Yeah, what about our owners?"

Robert passed around the paperwork and explained what he had learned. He finished by saying, "We're not even sure if this Liang Jiang is even in Canada. Brent, Eric, and I are going to pay him a visit with the camera to the house that is listed as his address in Canada. We'll confront him if he even lives there, and we'll see what he has to say.

Brian was mad as hell. He started ranting about the state of Toronto and the country and how greedy politicians had given it away. He stood up and said, "Robert, you get those damn politicians back in here. I want to have another meeting and see what they say about this. I want to see what lies they are going to tell me to my face, those bloody cowards."

Robert agreed that it would be a great idea but then stated the cold, hard fact that they already got their publicity and pictures with us in the paper and said, "I'm not sure if they're going to pay much attention to us now."

Wessler finally walked in about fifteen minutes late. The first thing he did was ask Eric to leave and wait outside; Eric didn't argue and went into the hallway.

As Wessler unpacked and took his jacket off, Brian asked, "Did you say seven or seven-fifteen, Mr. Wessler?"

Wessler just looked at him and smiled as he was getting ready.

Robert looked at Wessler and said, "Whenever you're ready, the floor is yours."

Wessler began, "OK, I see everyone got the papers, and as you can see, they filed the eviction notice with the Landlord and Tenant Board; now the next move is ours. We have two choices but really only have one. First, we can try to negotiate something with them. You would leave the building so they could do the work, and it's agreed you would come back, paying more rent, and who knows how much that will be. But based on their behavior, it doesn't look like they're up for any negotiations. Our next and only option is to oppose the eviction; we'll tell them there's no basis or reason for you to vacate your units, and we'll prove to them that the request to remove you isn't justified."

I politely asked, "Thank you, Mr. Wessler. How do we do that?"

He didn't even look at me when replying, "Well, we take their reports, and we'll refute them."

I looked at Robert and winked, then back at Wessler, "That sounds great, Mr. Wessler. And again, how do we do that?"

He still wouldn't make eye contact with me, and I thought, 'What a pussy', but at least he was answering my questions.

"We get experts to say the opposite of what the reports say." He was looking at me now.

I continued to ask him, "That sounds great. How do we do that?"

He looked at me, and I could see he was starting to get frustrated. "Well, we get people qualified in these areas to refute what they are saying."

I put my arm up like a smart ass, and again I asked, "That sounds great, but again, how do we do that? It sounds expensive."

This guy was useless; he couldn't even answer me about what we would do to fight this.

I had gotten to him, and in a frustrated voice, he replied, "Well, Brent, if you really need to know, we can get people from the City Engineers Office to write a report refuting everything, along with the Electrical, Plumbing, and Environmental Departments."

I was glad he finally answered and said, "Thank you, that's all I was wondering."

He continued, "First, we need to respond and say that this notice is unwarranted, and we will not vacate the premises. We have thirty days to reply and file our dispute with the Tenant Board, and from there, they will schedule a hearing to get a ruling."

Wessler explained, "This is a tremendous amount of documents. When we do get the hearing, and I have no idea how long that could take, I'll ask for an adjournment. We'll tell the adjudicator we need more time to prepare and examine all the reports. With the extension and holidays, we won't be back for another hearing until the new year, so don't worry; we have lots of time."

This wasn't sitting well with me, 'an adjournment?' That was this guy's plan? To go into the hearing and ask for more time? Wessler was already pissed off with me, and I didn't want to piss him off anymore, but I was squirming in my chair, dying to ask him about this 'ingenious' plan of an adjournment.

I looked around the room and wondered if anyone else had a problem with this; no one said anything until Bob asked, "So what if they don't give you an adjournment? What do we do then?"

Wessler said, "We don't have to worry about that. I have never seen them deny an adjournment at a first hearing; they always grant it."

Bob persisted, "And what if they do deny the adjournment?"

Wessler gave the same answer: "They won't; I've never seen it happen."

Now everyone started to get worried; Krystle plainly said, "Well, shouldn't we be ready with our 'defense' anyway, just in case?"

Wessler stood firm; "Don't worry, people. I have worked with the Tenant Board for years and have never seen them deny an adjournment."

Robert didn't like this answer either. He chimed in, "I think we should be ready. I rode the subway for twenty years and never saw someone defecate on the train until I did. Something doesn't happen until it does."

Melissa yelled, "Agreed."

Wessler started packing his things up and finished the meeting by saying, "I'll reply to them in two weeks, and in the meantime, I'll contact everyone from the various departments at the city and get them in the loop about the situation."

He thanked everyone, tucked his pants into his socks, put on his helmet, and left.

Robert took the spot at the front of the room, and I waved for Eric to come back in.

Melissa asked, "Well, now what?"

We were all left looking around at each other without answers; we didn't know what to do.

Melissa continued, "We just go back to our apartment with the dirt, dust, and repairs? We go back to the constant water and power shutoffs and putting up with the owner's bullshit, wrecking our home life and our sense of well-being? We just sit around and wait for the bureaucracy to get to us, and when it does, we're going to ask the system to wait for us? This is our plan?"

Robert asked the room what we thought, and we were all in agreement that we should look for alternative representation. Robert said he would try to schedule another meeting with the politicians, and in the meantime, he'll start looking around for a new lawyer. He suggested we all do the same.

We were all sitting there wondering what to do when I said, "Oh well, I guess that's it for tonight. I think Wessler is a wanker; I don't like him."

Everyone laughed; there was no real formal wrap-up to the meeting; it just faded out. We walked back to the building as a group, and there wasn't much talking. We got home and said good night to each other. Eric went home, and everyone went to their apartments. Now it was time to sit and wait and see what bullshit was going to happen next.

Chapter 16

Time was dragging. I was counting down the days until I would see Laila again. I wasn't even out of bed when the phone rang. It was Eric. He was downstairs and needed me to meet him out front. I put on my slippers and robe, started a pot of coffee, and headed down. Eric was leaning against the car, chewing his nails, and nervously looking up and down the street.

I looked at him and said, "Nice poker face. What did you do, rob a bank? What's going on?"

He laughed and raised his eyebrows. "Good morning, sunshine. I hope you have some coffee ready, and oh yeah, I brought some stuff over."

I looked over his shoulder into the back seat, then back at Eric, who was smiling. Rubbing my eyes, I had to ask him, "Is that a kiddie pool? Why did you bring a kiddie pool to my place? And what's that—more gas cans and a propane tank?"

Eric smiled and said, "Don't worry. You take the kiddie pool up, and I'll carry the tanks; they're heavy."

I looked at Eric and asked, "What do you mean they're heavy? They're props, right? Set dec, empty, right?"

He said, "Well, yeah, they're props, but how am I going to light the tiki torches and the flame bar? Come on, Bingham, think."

Eric laughed and said, "You're just as guilty as me—accessory after the fact. Now hurry up and get this stuff out of my car before it blows up or someone sees it."

I agreed, "Yeah, let's get this dangerous, flammable material out of your car and into my bedroom, where it'll be safe."

We got it in my apartment, and now I was getting worried. I didn't think it was too safe to keep tanks of gas and a propane tank in a six-hundred-square-foot apartment, let alone all the other crap.

I looked at him and said, "No, seriously? Is it safe to store this stuff in my apartment? I don't think I should put it in my bedroom, should I?"

He laughed, "Don't worry. It's safe, and it won't be for that long. We'll shoot it soon—it'll all be gone before you know. Before we do that, we have Councillor Flatch's Sub Committee thing coming up. I'll get some guys to help film it and a sound guy; I think we'll be covered for it."

He started looking at some notes he pulled from his pocket and said, "But before that Sub-Committee BS, I want you to meet with your friend Kerwin. Maybe we can get some ammo for the politicians. We'll try it politely. Let's call him now, see if he wants to meet, and agree to an interview for the documentary."

I had no idea what I was going to say to him, but I knew I had to keep it polite because I wanted to have an interview with him on camera. I thought I better have information in front of me in case we started to have a discussion. I went to the Federal Lobbying Site, and when Kerwin's information came up, I was blown away and shook my head in utter awe. I couldn't even start to count how many meetings this guy has had or how much money he's given to politicians. As I scrolled through the pages, I realized Kerwin is a heavy hitter in politics; it looks like he's met with every Federal, Provincial, and City Politician in Canada.

I was out of my league; I needed to use our relationship from the past to get anything out of him. Eric pointed at me, and I dialed the phone. I looked at him, and he pointed to his face for me to smile. I just stared at him and gave him the finger. I didn't want to talk to Kerwin.

I have to give it to Kerwin. He answered his own phone, and within a couple of rings, he said, "Kerwin Cummings, may I help you?"

I put on my biggest smile and said, "Kerwin, it's Brent Bingham. How are you?"

Kerwin answered as if our first meeting had never taken place. He was very short and standoffish. "Brent, how are you? It's been a long time. How have you been?"

The way he said, 'Long time,' I couldn't tell if he was being sarcastic because our recent lunch date wasn't that long ago or if he was trying to make it sound like we hadn't spoken for years.

Damn, he was good, "Hey Kerwin, you know I work in TV/Film, and being wrapped up in this illegal eviction thing, I was approached by a guy who wanted to make a documentary about the affordable housing crisis and Renovictions. The reason I'm calling you is that I've been doing a lot of research and going down the rabbit hole of the Rental Housing Market, and the funny thing is, your name keeps coming up."

There was silence on the other end, and I waited until Kerwin finally said, "Thank you for being honest with me, Brent. I'm sorry to hear about what you are going through with the eviction. If there's anything I can do to help, please let me know, but honestly, I don't know what I can do to help."

I kept it professional and toned down the conversation as if we didn't really know each other. I said, "Well, I'd like to sit down with you for the documentary, ask you a few questions, and get your opinion on the rental housing market."

It was a very dry discussion. Kerwin held back any hint of a relationship between us, and I was stalling. He politically said, "I don't think 'The Alliance' would like to participate. We wouldn't be interested in something like that, but thank you."

I laughed and said, "But Kerwin, you are the Alliance; who's we?"

He replied with a little chuckle, "Thank you, Brent, but I don't think we'd like to be part of it."

I thought it was time to ask him as a friend, "Come on, Kerwin. That's not the old 'Red Knights' spirit. We go way back, and I need help. Please help me understand this stuff. Explain how you justify representing an entire industry that is causing a huge social issue. You're creating a lot of the factors that are responsible for this."

I couldn't hold back; it just came out of me, honestly.

And that was all it took. He said, "Sorry I can't help you, Brent, but thank you for calling. Say hi to your Dad for me, and have a great day."

He hung up before I could say bye. I put down the phone, looked at Eric, and said, "Well, I guess that's someone I won't be talking to at the next reunion."

Eric said, "Yeah, I guess that's a 'no' for speaking to us on camera." He looked at me and asked, "How are your interview skills? I want you to have some conversations with people in the building. I want to get their thoughts and find out where they will go if they are thrown out. I want you to be Joe Rogan, get them to talk, and I want some tears, Bingham."

I looked at him and said, "I better clean up if I'm going to talk to people."

I came out of the room, and Eric was ready to go. I said, "First, we'll go downstairs to Beanzies and grab a coffee, then we'll come back to the building and loiter around for a bit; we're bound to run into someone. We went downstairs, and it was a nice day; I made Eric get the coffee and told him I would hang out at the front of the building and wait.

As I was waiting, Laila texted. I put my phone away and was grinning ear to ear when Eric came back with the coffee.

He asked me what I was smiling about and said, "You either found a quarter on the ground, or you got booked on a show for five days."

I said, still smiling, "Neither; Laila just texted."

We sat on the stoop for about twenty minutes before Nolan walked up with some groceries; Krystle wasn't around, so we might have a chance to hear what he really thought. I asked him if we could talk to him on camera about what was happening, and he agreed. Eric started recording, and we just started chatting; I wasn't going to interview him; we were just two guys sitting on a stoop, shooting the shit. While talking, I could tell he was frustrated; he was hesitant at first, but once he started speaking, I could tell he wanted to vent.

He said they were in this building for two reasons. First, it's cheap rent so they could save some money for a house, and the other reason was Krystle's mother, who lives nearby. She had been in a car accident a few years back and was prescribed Red oxycontin, and, well, it's the usual story, she's a fucking mess now, and Krystle has ended up being her caregiver. Of course, she wants to stay in the neighborhood to help her. Me, I want to get as far away from this bullshit as I can; honestly, getting thrown out of here and moving far away would be a relief. But then, what happens to her Mom? Now, she'll become a burden on the system; she'll need social workers, home visits, and God forbid if she dies because Krystle wasn't around to help. If we're thrown out, we can find a place. Yeah, it will cost us more, and we'll have to move far away, but either way, we lose. Krystle has been worried sick; living like this sucks, and having this shit hanging over your head eats away at you."

All I could do was agree with him.

He had opened up, and as he walked away, he added, "And yeah, please don't mention this to Krystle; you can use it; we'll be far and gone by then, but just don't say anything to her."

Eric put the camera down, looked at me, and said, "What kind of world do we live in that some rich asshole can just buy people out of their homes, and the government is complacent. Look at the fallout; it will affect Krystle's mom, who doesn't even live in the building. Now she's going to be a burden to the system, and for what, for one guy to make a profit; wow, this is an education for me; our society is fucked."

Once again, all I could do was agree.

After speaking with Nolan, Bill came along. I asked him if we could talk on camera. After a twenty-minute rant about the 'honesty' of film and the 'importance of truth,' he agreed.

I liked Bill, but he was very long-winded and liked to talk. He had some very insightful thoughts about our situation, economics, and society in general, but it took him so long to express himself that it's no wonder no one paid any attention to him.

We spoke to him for about an hour. His story was different from Nolan's and Krystle's but was going to end the same way; both would have to leave their homes. The difference was that Nolan and Krystle could still work and start over somewhere else, but Bill couldn't. He was seventy, and it was too late for him to start over.

After we spoke to Bill, I told Eric I didn't want to talk to anyone else; it was just too depressing. We went back to my place. Eric could tell I was getting a little upset and angry, so we just sat around watching episodes of Seinfeld and laughing. It was hard to relax and have a good time lately; when something comes and disrupts your homelife like this, it consumes you, and it's all you can think about; you might have little moments when you forget about it, but within seconds you are right back to wondering what's going to happen and wondering where you might be in a year. It was nice to have Eric to joke and laugh with; he helped me forget about the issue.

We only had a couple of things planned for the documentary, Councillor Flatch's bullshit Sub-Committee Hearing and paying a visit to the address we had for our owner and the LLC. Other than that, the only thing on my mind was Laila. I couldn't stop thinking about her and was trying to think of what excuse I could use to see her. After thinking for a bit, I thought I would invite her to confront our owner; I'm sure she would get a kick out of that.

I texted her and asked what she was doing on Thursday and if she would like to have coffee and do a 'little something' for the documentary. I was surprised she texted back immediately and said she'd love to. I replied that we could meet at Beanzies for coffee first and then meet up with Eric and Robert to do the documentary stuff.

Einstein was right; everything is relative, and waiting for Thursday felt like forever. And when it did, I was excited, not about going to confront our owner, but for seeing Laila; she was consuming my thoughts, which was genuinely nice as she took my mind off of the bullshit of being evicted.

I arrived at Beanzies before her and took the booth at the front window. Sally held up a cup, and I replied, "Thanks, Sally, but I'm waiting for someone."

She smiled and said, "Who? The pretty little protest lady? Oh, that's nice, she's a sweety."

"Thank you, Sally. Now go over there. Don't embarrass me in front of her; be nice." I winked and smiled; she laughed and went about her business.

I could see Laila walk by the window, and when we saw each other, she gave me a big wave. She stepped around the corner and came in. The bell on the door rang as it did with every customer, but there was something in the way it sounded when Laila stepped through. I stood up when she came in, and she gave me a big hug before we sat down.

She sat and looked out the window, saying, "I love this view—almost the whole street. I could people-watch from here all day long."

I looked at her in amazement, "I couldn't agree with you more. What would you like to drink?"

She said, "Coffee would be nice, and one of those fritters would be great."

I liked that; it was nice and easy. Sally brought the coffees over; she already had them ready as she was listening to everything we were saying. She passed them over, winked, and said, "I'll have the fritters over when they're done."

We just sat looking out the window and talking about the different things we saw. We talked about her life in Iran, and she explained about marrying her husband, who was her senior, but she never did say how much older he was. She explained how it was hard for her to break free and get a divorce once she was here because it was such a small community, and he controlled everything. But things have worked out; he takes care of their son and sees him every two weeks, so it's getting better.

Just as Laila was wrapping up, Sally came over with the fritters. She put them down, smiled, and thankfully, she didn't say a word and just skipped away from the table.

Laila laughed and said, "You're a little spoiled here, aren't you, Brentley?"

I laughed, "Yup, Sally takes care of me; she should. I'm in here almost every day, and I tip."

From behind the counter, we could hear Sally chime in, "Yeah, but he doesn't tip that well."

Laila had a good laugh at that one.

After another hour of talking and eating fritters, we decided it was time to head back to the building.

As we waited downstairs on the street, Laila noticed that many of the stores still had our 'Say No To Renoviction' signs in their windows. Laila complimented me on how many we were able to put up.

I said to her, "Sadly, it was easy. Everyone sympathized with us and thought what was going on was wrong.

I looked over at Laila, who was staring at me, and she said, "You're very passionate when you want to be, aren't you, Brently?"

I squeezed her hand and said, "Yes, I can be. I don't like people picking on weak people; gotta' stand up for those who can't sometimes, right?"

She squeezed my hand and said, "Yes, Brently, sometimes you do."

Bob and Bo walked up as we sat and waited on the stoop, and I introduced them. Not surprisingly, Bo was all over Laila, and shockingly, she was able to tell him what to do. Bo went to jump up on her; she held up her hand and said, "Bo no, sit…. Bo sit," wouldn't you know it, Bo sat down and stared at her motionless.

Bob and I were shocked and started laughing. Bob passed the leash to her and said, "Well, he's yours now; I've never seen him listen to someone like that before."

Laila smiled and said, "You just have to show him who the boss is, and then they will listen."

She looked at me when she said that and gave me a cute, mean look, and I started laughing.

Bob asked what we were up to, and I told him we were going to try to find the owner.

He said, "No shit? Good for you; what are you going to do when you see him?"

I really didn't know and answered as such, "Well, I don't know. I haven't thought that far ahead. We have to go and sit in the car outside his house and have a good old-fashioned stake out."

Laila asked, "How long is this going to take?"

I said, "I don't know. We're going to wait for him. If he doesn't come around, maybe we can knock, but I don't think so. I think we have to wait until we see them."

Laila looked at me, apologized, and said she couldn't go. She didn't realize it would take so long and that she had to be home for dinner with her son.

I walked her to her car just down the street and said our goodbyes. When I walked back to the apartment, I was on cloud nine. It's funny. Here I was in a fight to save my place, feeling all sad and mad about it, but all I could think about was Laila. She put a smile on my face ear to ear. I walked back to the apartment, where Eric and Robert were waiting outside, and they saw the smile on my face.

Eric, as usual, had the great line, "Oh-oh, Bingham is smiling; I don't see any quarters on the ground; he must have spoken to Laila."

I laughed, "I just saw Laila, and she's awesome; she was going to come with us, but since we didn't know how long we were going to be, she had to get home for dinner with her son. Which makes me wonder, how long do you think this will take?"

Eric laughed, "I have no idea; I hardly know what we are doing anyway. We should get there close to dinner time, so maybe we'll catch him coming home. We'll hang out in the car until we see him. Anyone got any better ideas?"

He looked around, and none of us had anything to say, "Bingham, have you thought of what you are going to say?"

"Yeah, I'm going to ask him, why is he such an asshole? Do you think he will talk or just run away from us?"

Eric laughed, "What would you do if you were in the business of evicting people, and you saw people coming toward you at your house with a camera and microphone?"

I wasn't confident that he would speak with us, so I said, "Yeah, I guess he'll run away, but I hope he says something."

Erics' sound guy arrived, and we all loaded in the car to head up to the owners' house. We got to his house around four p.m. and parked a few houses down the street. We had a full view of his door and driveway, so if anyone was going to come in or out, we would see them.

I shut off the car and said, "OK, now what?"

Eric said, "And now, we wait. Anyone want snacks?"

I looked at the bag and at Eric, "You brought stinky, smelly Nacho Doritos for four guys stuck in a car for hours? I don't think this is going to work out well for us."

He opened the bag, and by some grace of God, a car pulled up in the driveway. Thankfully, he put the chips away and got the camera ready, and we sat and waited. Nothing was happening; no one was getting out of the car.

After a couple of seconds of the car sitting there, a man got out. He was at least six feet tall, tanned, and looked as Asian as me. Before I could ask, 'What are we going to do?' Eric and the sound guy jumped out of the car and were followed by Robert, so I guess we were doing this. I jumped out and caught up with them. We crossed the street, and when we got to the driveway, the man noticed we were coming towards him.

The guy saw me, then looked at Eric with the camera and the sound guy with the boom. You could see a look of confusion on his face as he said, "Can I help you guys with something?"

I held up my hands in a peaceful gesture and said, "Hi, uh, I'm hoping you can."

Confused, he looked at us and said, "OK?" He didn't say anything about the camera or mic, so we just kept filming.

I said, "I'm sorry, I don't mean to bother you, but we're looking for a man named Liang Jiang Huong, and we have this as his address. I'm sorry to be bugging you, but do you know him?"

He looked at us awkwardly and paused before he replied, "I know his name but have never met him. Is there a reason you're looking for him?"

We didn't know who this guy was or if he was somehow involved in it, so I wasn't going to give him too much info, but I wanted to figure out what was going on with this address.

I apologized for the inconvenience; I introduced myself along with the guys and said, "He's the new owner of our apartment building. We're having an issue and wanted to talk to Mr. Huong about it."

I'm pretty sure he knew immediately that something more than 'just an issue' was going on. I'm not sure, but it may have been the camera and boom mic that tipped him off.

He said, "Well, he's one of the names we get mail for downstairs; supposedly, he lives downstairs," using air quotes when he said, 'lives downstairs.'

We all looked at each other, and I asked, "Supposedly?"

He started walking to the side of the house and motioned for us to follow: "Yeah, we get his mail. Here, come have a look."

We followed him to his side door, and he showed us the two mail slots beside it. He opened one and said, "Look, I put a bin down. The mail comes, sits for a while, and then the management company comes and picks it up once a month, but he doesn't live here. The basement has always been empty; we've never seen anyone."

I replied, "Let me guess, is the management company Brownstone?"

He looked at me quizzically and said, "Yeah, I'm Arman, by the way, and you guys are?"

I said, "I'm sorry, I'm Brent. This is Eric and Robert, and this is our sound guy. We live at Three-Ninety-One Empire Avenue, and like I said, we're just looking for our owner. Pardon me for asking. It might be weird, but do you rent here? Can I ask who owns the house?"

He looked confused, and before answering, I asked, "Is it One-Four-Seven- Zero-Zero-Seven LLC?"

He looked at me uneasily and said, "Yeah, it is. OK, what's going on here?"

I explained the whole situation about our building to him, how we tracked it to the LLC, then to this address, and then found out it was Chinese-owned.

I said to him, "Liang Jiang isn't a renter; he's your owner."

I showed him the paperwork for who owns One-Four-Seven-Zero-Zero-Seven LLC and how the cars and accounts lead back to names in China.

You could see he was trying to figure this all out when he said, "So, the renter in my basement is the owner, and along with guys from China? Son of a bitch."

He shook his head and started to explain, "I rent the place from 'Brownstone, and that's the only people I have ever dealt with about the house; when I started renting, they told me to write the checks out to the numbered LLC company and if I ever had any questions or issues with the house, to just call them. Damn, so they work for people in China?"

I shook my head yes and let it sink in with Arman. He was talking, or should I say thinking out loud, trying to piece it together, "The person that owns my house isn't even in this country? My money goes to China? I had no idea, no idea at all. I mean, I know I have to rent from someone, and when I did, I assumed I was dealing with someone in the same country as me. All I dealt with was Brownstone. In the beginning, I was curious, and when I asked them who the owner was, all they told me was that it was a local investor. Local? Local to where?"

I looked at Arman and laid it out for him, "That's the thing, Arman. They weren't lying, it is owned by the LLC, which is based in Toronto, in your basement, in fact. So technically, and as far as anyone knows, it is 'local' money and definitely not foreign ownership, which it actually fucking is, and it's their way of hiding it. Sorry Arman, I didn't mean to swear."

He said, "Under the circumstances, it's OK."

After the entire conversation, Arman asked, "What's with the camera?"

I laughed, "You weren't wondering about it earlier?"

He laughed and said no, "I thought I might have won something, but then I was too wrapped up in our conversation, and I forgot about it."

I explained the documentary and asked if it was OK to use it in the film; he agreed immediately and thought it was a great idea. Before we left, we thanked Arman for his time and his honesty; he commented that he wanted to find a new place to live.

We went back to the car and piled in, and it still smelled like 'ass' Doritos.

We started driving back to the apartment, and no one said anything for the first couple of minutes until I had to ask, "Well, what do we do about the owners now?"

Robert summed it up nicely, "The trail to the owners is done; we've found out who they are, they're foreign, and they're hiding behind Brownstone and the Durbanskys. We can't do a damn thing to them; all we can do is keep shining a light on the fact that they aren't even in Canada and keep reminding everyone that we are being evicted by people who live in China. They'll be mysterious entities; they will be the 'they' that everyone is always referring to; we'll make them bigger than 'they' are, and we'll make them sound like 'they' could be anyone's landlord. Hopefully, that keeps it in the spotlight and keeps people pissed off; in the meantime, we keep doing what we are doing. Now, we put the spotlight on Brownstone, Kerwin Cummings, and the politicians. It's all we can do."

We agreed, and I asked, "So where do you think this little weasel Liang Jiang is? Do you think he is actually here in Canada, or do you think he is in China?"

Robert shook his head and said, "The way this country has left itself open for fraud and criminality, everything connecting this guy to Canada is probably only on paper." Robert didn't sound too confident.

I added, "He might have been born here too, but lives there. For years, women from different countries worldwide would fly to Canada only to have their babies here, and once the baby is born here, they go back home, but the baby is now a Canadian citizen for life. When I was growing up, my Lebanese buddy would always have different pregnant women from Lebanon staying with his family. He said they were all 'family' just visiting, but it was, in fact, a little side 'anchor baby business' they had of providing accommodation to pregnant Lebanese women so their little foreign babies would be born as Canadian citizens.

Robert shook his head and replied, "What a country."

When we got home, Eric split, and we all went our separate ways. I just went back to my apartment to relax. I sat by the computer without turning it on and reflected for a moment. I was glad we went and tried to find Liang Jiang. In hindsight, I really enjoyed it.

I turned on the computer and decided to do some more research on the rental and housing situation in Toronto.

I sat and stared at the screen, wondering what to look for; I sat and thought for a couple of minutes, 'I typed condo rental Toronto' and a shit ton of links came up; the first ones were ads for condo rental companies, I wondered what is a condo rental company? I clicked a random link and was directed to 'Condos Toronto – Your Premier Condo Listing and Rental Site.' After surfing around their website, I felt even worse about the rental and housing markets. These condo rental companies allowed individual owners of condos to list their units so that people could rent them out as 'apartments.'

The prices for condos were astronomical; people wanted three, even four thousand dollars a month for a studio or a one-bedroom; the greed out there was spectacular. I checked out a few of these companies websites, and there was no shortage of condos for rent in Toronto, which made me wonder if all these condos are sitting empty for rent, and they say there is a housing shortage; who owns all these empty condos?

There were pages upon pages of links for 'condo rentals'; I came across some articles, so I started going through a few. Every article was praising and saying how strong the economy was, and praising themselves for the condition of the market, convincing everyone that this market would last forever, never mentioning a bubble. I searched for an hour, finding much of the same, until I came across an article titled, 'Toronto Housing – What is Backing It and Who Are The Real Owners?' The article was written by Danielle Smith and appeared in 'The National' over four years ago.

I hadn't come across her name before when researching this, nor had I seen this article. I looked and I was on the hundredth and eighty-first page of the Google search. This article was buried online, and after reading it, I knew why, it was an honest observation of the real estate market and what was taking place.

She was very insightful about the affordable housing problem, explaining how money laundering and mortgage fraud are a big part of the Canadian Housing Market. She then explained that Canada avoided the bubble bursting after the 2008 housing crash by simply making the bubble even bigger. Canada adopted and implemented some of the same US real estate and mortgage practices that crashed the US economy; Canada didn't fix anything; they just kicked the can down the road a little further. Canada had increased subprime mortgages, and mortgage fraud had become rampant. In the article, she also mentioned foreign ownership and the political decisions that will keep this housing and rental market skyrocketing, effectively wiping out all affordable housing for Canadian citizens, their children, and their children's children.

The article talked about the condominium market in Toronto, and she pointed out an advertisement that appeared in Chinese media for the 'Chinese

Foreign Investment Council.' It was an ad for investing in the Canadian Housing market. She translated the advertisement, which compared Chinese banking interest rates to keeping your money in the Canadian real estate market.

Because of our housing bubble, the ROI in our market was ten times greater than keeping their money in a bank. It was convincing Chinese investors to buy our Canadian homes like a commodity, and when I read this, I was furious. Danielle discovered that there were floors upon floors of empty condos all over Canada owned by foreign entities. These investors would make money on the condos, not even renting them out; they didn't care because at the rate property values were increasing, all they had to do was sit and hold. It was a win-win situation for the investor but a losing situation for Canadians who needed a place to live.

She also pointed out that the short-term rental industry was starting to boom with Airbnb, putting further strain on the housing inventory. Now, people didn't want to rent units for long-term use anymore; they only want to rent them for short-term rentals because they make more money doing that, and that greed reduces the housing supply in Toronto even further. I immediately reposted the article on the FB page and tagged everyone I could think of.

After reading that article, it made me wonder about something; I went to the federal lobbying website, typed in 'Chinese Foreign Investment Council', and I couldn't count how many entries came up. I started clicking through their lobbying records and discovered they met and donated to every politician in power. I looked at the meetings between them and the politicians, and whose name kept coming up, Stephen Clarke, Housing Minister, the very person who is supposed to be looking out and protecting Canadians by ensuring the Canadian housing market is fair and equitable for CANADIANS!

Well, surprise, surprise! I leaned back from my computer and couldn't believe it; everyone has their hand out lining their pockets, and they don't care what it does to the people they are supposed to be representing and protecting. Our government is broken and corrupt; it's a pay-to-play system, and the people in power are criminals; politicians like Councillor Flatch and Peters are only in it for themselves. Sure, they'll say they are on your side, but these people are 'on the take' more than any dirty cop in the vice squad; these politicians are dirty.

For curiosity, I typed Bernie Peters, Pauline Flatch and the Chinese Foreign Investment Council into the lobbying sites. The results came up, and I wasn't surprised. I actually would have been surprised if there weren't any meetings between them, but of course, there were. Our MP and City Councillor have had meetings with and have taken, or should I say, 'received' five thousand dollars in contributions from the Chinese Foreign Investment Council. No wonder Bernie wanted to stand back; he knows who pays his bills. Flatch, I guess, doesn't have any shame. The more I read and learned about this system, the more

174

I realized what a joke it was and that all this was, in fact, real-life theatre; it was all a charade.

As I finished making my notes about the Lobbying and the money, I got an email from Councillor Flatch announcing the date for her 'Toronto City Council Sub- Committee on the Evaluation and Sustainability of Affordable Housing.' These politicians were useless; they couldn't even come up with a normal name, and they had to make everything more complicated than it was. It stated that Councillor Tom Tomford and herself would head the committee. Also attending will be city councillors who want to address and help with the affordable housing crisis.

The email asked you to RSVP if you wanted to speak to the committee for three minutes to explain your housing situation and discuss possible solutions for rental housing. I checked both boxes; 'Yes, I will be attending,' and 'Yes, I would like to speak.' After I hit send, I had to call Laila.

I dialed her number, and she answered after the first ring: "Hello, Brently. It's nice to hear from you."

Her voice made me smile, and now I was glad I called. "It's nice to hear your voice, Laila. I have to be honest with you, I didn't know whether to text or call. I know how no one phones each other anymore; I hope you don't mind; I hope you're not too busy?"

She laughed, "No, Brently. It's a nice relief to hear human voices. It's old-fashioned, and it's refreshing."

I smiled in relief, so I jumped right into it: "Anyway, the reason I'm calling is that I would like to ask you if you'd like to go out again. I wanted to ask if you would like to go to Councillor Flatch's Sub-Committee with me and maybe have dinner before or after? It's next Thursday at seven p.m. at city hall. I figure there will be lots of people and chaperones around. Eric, Robert, and I'm sure others will be going as well."

I spoke honestly: "I'm not sure, Laila, is asking you to go to a local political meeting at city hall romantic, or am I pathetic?"

She laughed, "From an outsider looking in, it might seem pathetic, Brently, but looking from here, it is far from that. It's a noble cause, so yes, I will go with you, and we'll have a great time."

My smile grew ear to ear, and I'm sure she heard it in my voice. I said, "Laila, I'm so glad I called. I like hearing your voice, and I'm really looking forward to seeing you again."

I hung up the phone and thought, 'damn, it was going to take forever for next Thursday to get here.

Chapter 17

We were waiting on a letter or some kind of response from the Landlord and Tenant Board, The Durbanskys, or our lawyer. Other than that, it was pretty quiet around the building, which was nice. It was nice to have a little break from the bullshit, but I had a feeling it wasn't going to last long.

I was awakened by a knock on my door. I looked out the peephole, and Robert was pacing back and forth. I looked back at the kitchen, and there wasn't anything lying around for him to break, so I let him in.

He went straight past me, started his usual pacing, and he was pissed off. "I spoke to Wessler; he was expecting to receive a hearing date at the Tenant Board, but instead, he got a date for an emergency meeting. The Durbanskys are saying the renovations are so extreme that there's no time for a hearing and that our safety is at risk. They claim any further delays financially punishes the owner and they asked for an 'emergency meeting'. What is this bullshit? Wessler says it will take at least six months for this to go through, and yet here we are?"

I tried to settle Robert down, "Calm down Robert, it's probably just a step in the process, part of the bullshit; let's just wait and see what Wessler says."

As soon as I said Wessler's name, Robert's phone rang.

I could only hear Robert's end of the conversation, and it didn't last long, "Hello, Mr. Wessler… yes, OK…yes, when? I'll tell them… OK…Yes, I'll set up a meeting for Monday… OK…yup, I'll let you know."

He hung up the phone, looked at me, and said, "Well, the owner already has a date for an 'emergency' meeting at the Landlord and Tenant Board.

As Robert started to leave, he turned to me and said, "I'll book the meeting room for Monday. I'll let you know if I can get it."

I shut the door, went to the desk, and sat with my head down. This was quicker than I thought it was going to happen. I turned on the computer and put on some music. I put my playlist on shuffle, and the first tune that came up was "*Fight the Power*" by Public Enemy. That changed my mood, putting me in a good mood to fight.

I went to the Facebook page. I hadn't posted anything lately because nothing was happening, but now it seemed like I should be posting everything. I wanted to post everything that was happening, but I had to respect people's privacy. I thought for a moment, and then a word popped into my head, 'Redacted.' Governments and criminal corporations use that glorious word when faced with Freedom of Information Requests. Whenever people request documents from the government or, let's say, from corrupt pharma companies, the documents that these companies would send back would be all blacked out, or 'Redacted,' to protect privacy or some kind of 'trade secret' bullshit.

Why can't I redact? I can post letters and hide personal or detailed information; why not? I can make a game of it and have some fun. I grabbed the first eviction letter and a black marker and crossed out most of the information. I made a joke of it; I blocked out everything except for the words 'sold', 'lease terminated,' and 'get out.' It looked funny with all the solid black lines 'redacting' the majority of the information.

I did it with the other letters and blocked out most of the personal info. I thought it was funny, and I didn't know how else to fight back or how to piss these guys off; I figured, why not? I might as well try to have some fun. I posted the letters without commenting and with no idea what the reaction would be.

As I left Facebook, I wondered what to research next. As I was sitting there, I received an email from City Councillor Flatch's office stating that I would be allowed to speak at her 'Sub-Committee Hearing.' That's good, but now I was wondering what I would say. Things were heating up, and it looked like the next couple of weeks were going to be busy, which meant there were lots of excuses to see Laila, as well.

Monday came fast; I had been booked on night shoots straight through, so I didn't see many people around the building, but I did hear Lorenzo and his crew starting to build out the empty units below me. When Monday's tenant meeting came, I wasn't in the best of moods. I met Eric at the library a half hour before the meeting, he wired me up, and we sat and bitched to each other for a while. I couldn't believe how fast things were moving, and he couldn't believe they could get a meeting, which got me wondering, 'Yeah, how were they able to get a meeting so fast?'

We were outside the library when everyone started trickling in. We went inside, and I reminded Eric to stay outside of the room when Wessler was here; he reassured me not to worry and that he wouldn't go anywhere near our 'precious genius' lawyer. We had a laugh, and I went inside and sat down. It was five minutes before the meeting was supposed to start, and almost everyone had arrived; as usual, Reggie, Brian, Tommy, and Sarah weren't here, and everyone said they probably weren't coming. Reggie because he was too tired, Brian and Tommy because they were too old, and Sarah because, sadly, she was too stupid; even Bill said as much as we were waiting for Wessler.

At seven p.m., Wessler still hadn't arrived, but Robert started the meeting anyway. He walked to the door, gave a look out of the room and up the stairs, and began to say, "OK, before Wessler arrives, I looked into alternative representation. I looked into both, paralegals and lawyers. And based on what I told them, they said it would cost a minimum of four to five thousand dollars, and that's without any delays or continuances. Their outlook on our case wasn't so positive either; they all said we didn't stand a chance and would have to be out sooner or later. So, would anyone like to go and hire someone? Pay out of pocket, or stick with who we have?"

The room mumbled collectively, and everyone agreed that sticking with Wessler was our only option.

Robert said, "Well, he's our guy, so don't be shy, don't hesitate to ask any questions, and speak your mind with him, we know Bob does."

The room laughed, and as we did, Wessler walked in, and everyone went quiet.

As soon as he walked in, Robert introduced him, and Wessler began immediately, "Well, I understand everyone received their notice about the upcoming emergency meeting regarding the pending 'devastating' repairs."

He emphasized 'devasting' and said it with a smile, trying to lighten the moment, but this guy couldn't read a room for the life of him because we weren't in the mood to be 'lightened up.'

Krystle went at him right away, "You never mentioned an emergency meeting; what the hell is an emergency meeting for, and what are they basing this on? Are they allowed to do this?"

Wessler put his hands up in defense and said, "It's just part of the process. You can request this type of meeting if there are dire circumstances, but in our case, there doesn't seem to be any; they're just using any excuse they can. We just received the package of all the repairs to be done, so we need some time to review them; these are extensive reports, and it takes time to find professionals and experts to read and figure them out. So again, please don't worry; nothing is going to happen yet."

Bill, who didn't speak too much, spoke first, "That's what you said last time, but here we are with a meeting coming up. So, what do all these reports mean? They don't mean much to me; they look like a bunch of drawings; what are we supposed to do with them?"

Wessler said, "Don't worry Bill, I know what to do with them."

He tried to exude confidence, but it didn't work for him. "I've put a call into the city's building inspectors, and I've called the engineering, plumbing, and electrical departments; we'll have them look over the documents, and they'll tell us what they mean and whether, in fact, we have to leave."

Bob said immediately, "So, we're depending on more government employees to save our asses?"

Wessler didn't read this right and replied, "That's right, Bob, you have all the city departments at your disposal, and they'll be doing everything they can to help you."

Bob coughed, and I swear he added a muffled 'oh shit' as he did. He looked around the room along with the others, who weren't looking pleased.

Robert raised his arm, and Wessler called on him, "These other departments, is this part of their job? Aren't they busy doing their own jobs? Why will they pay attention to us?"

Wessler replied, "Well, Robert, you're right. They are busy, and no, they don't do this kind of thing for the general public, but city departments share services. We'll ask them to help, and under the circumstances, I'm sure they will."

As Wessler was talking, he began packing up.

I thought, 'That's all he's going to say, and he's going to bail out of here?' I needed more information; even though he didn't like me, he still had to help me.

I had to ask, "So what happens at this emergency meeting? Do these reports need to be looked at by 'experts'? Are you going to read them? This doesn't seem like enough time to go through them, and do we all have to be at this 'Emergency Meeting'?"

He was courteous and looked at me when replying, "This is too soon; there's no chance we can reply. I will skim the reports, but I'm not an expert, so it won't help. We will ask for a continuance, which will buy us more time, and they're just delaying this even further. I don't know why they would try this so soon; it seems like a waste of time."

Bob replied with perfect comedic timing, "So again, we're saying our defense is 'we need more time?' How many times are we going to play this card?"

Bob made me proud just by stating the facts and wondering when we were going to get an actual defense. He continued, "What about us? Do we need to go to this bullshit meeting?"

Looking directly at me, Wessler said, "The tenants don't need to attend. I speak for everyone, so you don't need to be there."

Wessler had packed everything up. He swung his foot up on the table, tucked his pantleg into his sock, put on his helmet, and asked, "Well, is there anything else?"

We got the hint that he wanted out of here, but I wasn't finished, "Well, what about the tenants? You said they don't need to be there, but can we be there?"

Wessler looked at me, and I knew he was pissed. I knew he wouldn't want me there, and I was pretty sure of that, but I don't think he would lie.

He looked at me, knowing damn well I would be there if I was allowed, "yes, Brent, tenants can attend. It will be boring, probably very quick, and it's more of a formality than anything, but yes, you may attend."

He grabbed his backpack and swung it over his egg-shaped helmeted head; everything about this guy did not bode well with me.

He said, "Good night," and was on his way.

We all sat there and looked around. Robert stood at the front and said, "Well, I guess that's it. I guess there's nothing else to do."

People weren't too happy and upset that Wessler didn't say more.

Robert said, "Well, you heard him. We don't have to be there, but it's our right. I don't know about you, but I'll be there, and I'm pretty sure Brent will be too."

I looked at him and shook my head in agreement.

Robert wrapped it up and thanked everyone for coming. I didn't feel like hanging around and talking about this shit anymore. I went straight over to Eric, grabbed him, and we headed out.

We got outside, and I looked at Eric, "This is bullshit. Emergency meeting, my ass. What are they trying to pull? Are they going to get us out this quick? And do you think I will let this guy, Wessler, go and represent us and not be there? No way, I gotta see what is going on at this Landlord and Tenant Board; if they're going to kick me out, I at least want to see the guy that will decide my fate. I could see Wessler attending the meeting, and then suddenly, we're all homeless."

We started walking, and I kept ranting. When we got back to the building, I looked at Eric, and he was smiling ear to ear, so I had to ask him, "What are you smiling about now?"

The smile left his face, "Bingham, you got passion, man; this bullshit needs people like you and Robert to fight it, whether you like it or not."

I raised my eyebrows, looked at him, and rolled my eyes, "Are you coming to the 'Emergency Meeting'? Coming to see what the fuck is going on in this city?"

He laughed, "Seeing Bingham in a courtroom setting? Oh, I wouldn't miss that for the world."

We said our goodbyes, Eric left, and I went upstairs. I felt like listening to some music, and since I was talking about money and greed, I might as well put on 'Money' by Pink Floyd and The Flying Lizards, two great 'money' songs. As I listened, the more I wanted to post stuff. Apparently, I was becoming a keyboard warrior. I searched for all the eviction/Renoviction stories I could, and there was no shortage. One article caught my attention; it was talking about 'the rent-seeking mentality.'

I had heard the term before but wasn't exactly sure what it meant. I decided to 'google' it, and when I did, it explained everything wrong in our society today. I had to paste the definition to our Facebook page; it read: *'Rent-seeking is a concept in economics that states that an individual or entity seeks to increase their own wealth without creating any benefits or wealth to society. Rent-seeking activities aim to obtain financial gains and benefits by manipulating (lobbying) the distribution of economic resources.'*

There it was in writing, that this behavior only benefits the owners and not society. The problem is that 'they' have convinced people to accept the crazy rise in housing prices. By increasing the value of homes, they have given people the idea that their wealth is in their homes and not in their labor. Up until the nineteen seventies, wages were people's wealth. People with full-time jobs were able to buy a house and a car, send a kid to school, and take vacations. But since the seventies, the cost of goods and everything else has gone up, yet wages haven't, and no one questions it; no one stands up and asks, 'Why has everything gone up, except for the wages?'

People happily accept the myth that their home is now their wealth; they live with the hope that they can sell it and make incredible money off the next guy. They think, 'it doesn't matter if I don't earn as much money at my job; my home will make my money for me,' unfortunately, that's not the purpose of a home. And that way of thinking is called 'the greater fool theory.' You're hoping a 'greater fool' than yourself will come along and buy it from you for more.

Next, they figure, 'I can get cheap money at the bank, so let's get a bigger home, or even better yet, let's buy a rental home; there'll always be someone to rent to. I can't lose money on real estate.' Thinking that real estate can never go down and can only go up is like the 'hot hand fallacy' in basketball. These were terrible ways of thinking, and people lived by them; it's as if they stood back and said, 'Well, it is what it is.'

I went over to the sofa and lay down. It was the first time I had laid down on it, and not surprising; it was pretty comfortable. I shut my eyes and listened to the music. Pink Floyd kept playing, and now it was 'Pigs,' a song about the power structure. Oligarchs, and greed, which was very appropriate. I dazed off and fell asleep; the sofa was so nice I fell asleep immediately, slept through the night, and I didn't wake up until morning.

I woke up with nothing going on for the day, which was nice. I looked at my phone, and Eric had already been texting me; thank goodness he wasn't pressing me to do anything today. He was texting to confirm that the only events we had coming up were the emergency meeting; and Councillor Flatch's bullshit 'Sub-Committee.' I texted him back, saying, 'That's about right; let's hope it's quiet until then.'

As soon as I said that, Lorenzo's crew started their workday in the units below, hammering and sawing; even though there wasn't much happening, something was always going on. I put the coffee on and cleaned up a bit. I put on my slippers and robe, and once the coffee was made, I took one down to Lorenzo. I had a bagful of cream and sugars, compliments of Beanzies; I grabbed a few of each, put them in my robe pockets, and headed down to the second floor.

As I walked downstairs, I saw Lorenzo standing in the hallway, looking into the unit they were working on. He turned and smiled at me, and as I approached, I handed him the coffee and told him I wasn't going to let him say no this time. He took the coffee, I pulled out the creams and sugars, and he took a couple of them.

I looked at him, smiled and winked, and said, "Compliments of Beanzies."

He raised his mug, thanked me, and said, "Look in there, Brent. Look at the quality of supplies. This guy won't pay for a thing; everything is the cheapest of the cheap. I do good work, Brent. I usually do custom homes, but it's been slow, and this seemed like a pretty simple job at the beginning, but it is turning into a nightmare."

He brought me in and showed me what they were doing, "All we're doing is lipstick cosmetic fixes, this drywall is shit, the floorboards are shit, and this will only last a couple of years at the most; it's all shit. I recommended to Louie what needed to be done, but he would have none of it. We're doing just enough to get it up to code, and we're cutting a lot of corners. It's all shit, Brent, I take no pride in this work, I'm sorry."

I raised my mug and said, "Well, at least you're being honest. It does look good, though. I guess it's like a set at work: It might look good, but don't touch or lean on anything because you might go right through it."

Lorenzo laughed as he sipped the coffee and replied, "Not as bad as that, but close. This is good coffee, Brent."

I asked him, "What have you heard about the building? Do you know we have an emergency meeting at the Tenant Board to throw us out because the 'renovations' are a safety concern for us, the tenants?"

Lorenzo leaned back, sighed, and said, "I have no idea about that; as I said before, you have seen more plans than me; all I have are the individual unit plans, that's it. He paid me for the demolition, but now I have put more money out for this stuff, and I hope I don't have any trouble with that. I've sent him the invoice, and I guess we'll see what happens," he pointed to the supplies lying around, "this is an expensive bill; I'll let you know what happens. As for the other plans, like I said, he's keeping them separate from us on purpose."

I drank my coffee and talked with Lorenzo for a while. He was a good guy. We talked about Italy, where he was from, and the real estate situation in Canada. He couldn't believe what was happening in this country and said he didn't realize how corrupt Canada was.

I laughed and said, "Yeah, I've been hearing a lot of that lately."

It was about two in the afternoon the day before our 'Emergency Meeting' was scheduled. I was lying on the sofa in my robe relaxing when Robert knocked on my door. I didn't even bother looking in the peephole. I opened the door, and as I did, he blew by me and headed to his pacing spot. I noticed an envelope taped to my door. I yanked it off and saw that he had already opened his; all I could think was, 'What now?'

Robert started immediately but wasn't angry; he was more confused than anything, "Well, we don't have to go to the emergency meeting anymore."

I sat back on the sofa and put my head back. "What the hell do you mean we don't have to go? I'm not leaving it for Wessler to go alone. What's going on?"

"We don't have to go because it's not taking place." He was waving the letter in the air as he spoke.

"OK, Robert, so what the hell is going on? Is it canceled or what?" I was thoroughly confused.

"Well, sort of and not really. The adjudicator didn't want to hear anything about this case until a full hearing; he said that based on the reports that have been filed and the amount of information to be read through, an 'Emergency Meeting' wouldn't suffice. He canceled it, and now we have our 'full hearing' in a month, and based on what Wessler said, with the adjournment, we'll have a few months after that," he flicked the letter as he finished speaking.

I understood what he was saying, but I was still confused about how this all came to be, and I said as much, "That's great, Robert, but what was all this bullshit about? How did this decision come to be? We're supposed to have a meeting, but now we're not? Somehow, I don't think this is in our best interest; I don't think the Tenant Board would do something if it were in our favor, especially if we didn't ask for it; it seems like there is some bullshit going on behind the scenes. And now we've got a hearing date? Guess I better start looking for a place to live."

Robert laughed, "Don't worry too much about it, Brent; it doesn't look like anything good or bad will come from this; it looks like it's a wash. Relax. It's one less thing we have to worry about. Now, all we have to worry about is the upcoming 'Sub- Committee Hearing.' I've been working on my speech. I'm not sure how deep into feudalism I want to go, but I think it's pretty good so far."

He stood up straight, adjusted his imaginary suit jacket and tie, and started quoting some classic movie lines. "You want the truth? You can't handle the truth…I'm out of order, you're out of order, this whole Sub-Committee is out of order." He laughed as he said them, and asked me, "Have you figured out what you will say yet?"

"I'm not sure; I don't know whether to go along with the game or to call the politicians out on their bullshit; I guess it depends on what kind of mood I'm in. I have a couple of statements to make, and I have a couple of questions to ask; I'll see what their bullshit answers are, and I guess that will steer me in the direction I'm going. I think I'll be able to keep my cool, but you might want to speak before me."

We had a week until the Sub-Committee, and I wasn't sure what I was going to say. I didn't know whether to play the nice guy or confront these politicians about the lobbying and kickback situation. I mean, how long was I going to play the nice guy with them and hold back what I knew about their bullshit? I wondered how much longer we needed the politicians for, and for what? I went online to check out the Facebook page, and thanks to Drake, as people in my business say, 'my social media game was killing it.' We already had over one-hundred-twenty-five-thousand followers, and it was growing every day. I looked at the last postings I did of the redacted paperwork, and people loved them; they thought they were hilarious. People were commenting and posting their own redacted letters and pictures; they posted redacted eviction notices, redacted notices of termination, and even redacted breakup letters; it was pretty funny, and it was good seeing people having a sense of humor about this bullshit.

Sitting at the computer, I received another email from Councillor Flatch. I opened it, and it was a reminder about the Sub-Committee; included in the email was a link to the City Council YouTube channel. Apparently, the Sub-Committee hearing will be on YouTube for anyone to watch. I knew what my next post was going to be. I would invite everyone from Facebook to the hearing, and if they couldn't physically attend, at least they could watch from home.

I posted the invitation, and it immediately started getting likes, reposted, and shared. People were commenting and the majority of comments weren't positive. They were saying things like, 'the city is full of shit' and 'this won't do a thing to help'; 'Councillor Flatch doesn't care about affordable housing, she cares about who is paying her,' and there were lots of comments with words I don't care to repeat, not many people liked our politicians, and rightfully so.

As I scrolled through the comments, Eric texted me; I replied to him right away and told him the Facebook page was hilarious. He replied to me that he's reading it now and laughing his ass off too. He was excited that the Sub-Committee was going to be on YouTube, and he said that we needed to promote the hell out of that meeting. We need to post it online constantly, we need to get as many people physically there as we can, and as many people as we can watching online. This will be great promotion; you can talk about documentary.

I texted him back, saying that I won't mention the documentary since this is about us getting thrown out, and I'm not distracting from that issue at all. His reply surprised me. He said he understood and that I was right to keep the focus on getting thrown out. He even apologized for bringing it up.

What he said next didn't surprise me, and I thought it was perfect, "Well, is it time to talk about the Lobbying? Is it time to expose Flatch and whatever other politicians are there about how much money they have received from landlords? Call them out on their charade of trying to help us, since we have a YouTube audience?"

I replied, "Let's get 'em."

He replied with two thumbs-up emojis and said he would come by later to discuss the emergency meeting and plan what we would do for that.

I replied, "Actually, no, the meeting has been canceled; they said it was too early to make any kind of decision."

His answer was how I felt, too; he said, "What is that bullshit?"

I replied, "Exactly."

We agreed that nothing much would happen until the 'Sub-Committee,' so we didn't need to get together beforehand. He said to let him know immediately if anything happened.

I figured I'd better get ready for this Sub-Committee Hearing bullshit. I left Facebook and went to the lobbying websites; I thought I better know and have the proof of what I'm talking about. I looked up and printed the lobbying records for Councillor Flatch and MP Bernie Peters; even though Bernie wouldn't be at the meeting, I wanted proof that no one was in our corner on any level. I printed the entire lobbying history of both Flatch and Peters and holy shit! These people are getting money thrown at them from every direction for anything and everything you can imagine. They were getting money from associations, unions, and foundations; it was endless, and these people were making fortunes.

Not only did I print the records for our two politicians, but I also printed the Housing Ministers' lobbying history, and if I thought 'my' politicians were killing it, this guy was getting ten times what they were, it was offensive. I printed the 'Alliances' entire lobbying history as well, and halfway through, I ran out of paper and had to fill the tray; I had to fill the tray three times. I couldn't believe how much money was changing hands in the background behind closed doors, away from the general public, and away from the basic premise of democracy. I looked at the stack of paper and couldn't believe how much there was. It was almost a whole ream of paper, and this was only the lobbying records for three politicians and one lobbying group; I couldn't imagine how much money was flowing from lobbyists to politicians.

Chapter 18

When I got up in the morning, I felt great; I had a good sleep for a change. I put some coffee on and texted Laila. I wanted to make sure we could get together for the Sub-Committee on Thursday night. As I read Facebook, Laila texted back and said she was looking forward to it.

I posted the invitation and YouTube link for the Sub-Committee daily on Facebook, and it was getting some good traction. People were talking about the hearing and our duly elected representatives, but they weren't talking nicely about them. I started to read the comments, and I saw that some of them were pretty mean and nasty. I thought about taking them down or blocking the people posting them, but I thought to myself, screw that. I didn't create this situation; these politicians did; they made the decisions and passed the laws that pissed off and hurt the people, not me. It's time they faced the music; Karma always catches up, and maybe it's time it caught up with them.

When the Sub-Committee day came, I was psyched, not because of the committee, but because I would be seeing Laila. We had been texting and talking through the week, as she was busy with her son, who was playing hockey; she joked that she grew up in a place with no snow and couldn't believe she had a son who loves skating on ice. I asked her how his Mom's skating skills were, and she said they were non-existent, and the way she talked, she was very nervous and scared to try. She even went into a cute little rant about the whole idea of skating. She couldn't understand how anyone could stand on two little thin blades. That made me laugh, and I told her that if she let me teach her, I'd have her skating circles around her son in no time. She doubted that I would be able to teach her but agreed to go skating nonetheless; either way, I had set up another date with Laila. I wasn't even thinking about getting thrown out anymore; all I could think about was her.

I was standing on the sidewalk in front of the building when Eric showed up for the committee. He said he was coming with a 'crew' to film this thing, and he didn't disappoint. He showed up with a camera guy, his sound guy, and Bones. I didn't know the camera guy, but I knew the sound guy and I knew Bones from work. Bones was six-foot-four, two hundred fifty pounds, bald, and muscular. At work, he only played a uniformed cop, SWAT, soldier, bouncer, or a criminal badass. He always portrayed someone you didn't want to mess with—even though he was one of the nicest guys you could know. I jumped in the car, greeted everyone, and we headed out.

It took us about an hour to get to City Hall. Usually, it would take twenty minutes, but because the city is so broken, it takes you at least an hour to get anywhere that you are going; everywhere you went there was road construction or private condominiums being built. I joked to Eric that the same politicians working on the affordable housing crisis must be the same ones working on the roads because, like the roads crumbling and eroding away, so was affordable housing in the city. As we drove, we noticed portions of roads closed for no particular reason. We drove past crews of workers with two guys working while six guys stood around, and we noticed roads where work had just been completed and was already crumbling or falling apart.

After bitching and complaining about the traffic, there was a minute of silence; then I had to say, "Look at these construction road signs. Do you notice all the different construction and engineering company names at every construction site? Now I'm wondering how many lobbyists are tied to this industry."

Eric replied, "Yeah, there's probably some really shady shit going on with this industry too. I guess that's the next movie, we'll call it 'Toronto, You're Fucked."

We parked at the City Hall parking garage; we were familiar with the place because we parked there a lot for work. It was an entertaining place, and even though it was City Hall, there would always be someone shooting up, smoking crack, or living in the stairwells leading up to the City Square. What made it sad or comical, I'm not sure which, was that those stairwells were used by the same Politicians, District Attorneys, Cops, and City employees who were supposed to be fighting and fixing those very same problems. But in those stairwells, they just stepped over the people they were supposed to be helping. All you need to do is look at the actions of the people in power over their hollow words, and then you will realize that they don't care about the people. All you had to do was take a few minutes and look.

As we made our way up the stairs, I asked Eric what Bones was doing here. I looked up at Bones and apologized to him, "No offense, Bones, and thank you for coming to show support; I know what the sound and camera guy are for, but what are you doing here?"

He looked down at me, put his hand on my shoulder, and said, "Brent, Eric wanted me here to lend a hand and just make sure you're OK."

I said, "security?" and laughed.

We couldn't believe what we saw as we opened the door from the stairwell to the Square. There must have been a thousand people milling about at the TORONTO City sign. There were picket signs, flags, and people trying to get scattered chants going through the crowd. It was kind of a mess.

I asked Bones, "Hey Bones, you see a bunch of red shirts anywhere in the crowd?"

It took him two seconds, and he said, "Yeah, they're all right in front of the Toronto sign by the first letter 'T,' follow me." He started to move through the crowd, and when people noticed him trying to pass, they gladly let him by.

I looked back at Eric and gave him the thumbs up; he smiled and said, "Crowd control."

We made it to the red shirts, and I saw Laila standing on the barrier in front of the City Sign, talking to the crowd. I couldn't believe how good she looked. She was talking to her Acorn group, and when she saw me, she smiled and waved me over. I grabbed Bones and headed towards her. She jumped down and gave me a big hug that I didn't want to end.

I looked at her and said, "You're so beautiful when you are protesting; you make the women at my work look ugly."

She just laughed and pulled me up on the ledge with her. As we stood up in front of the crowd, I was overwhelmed. I couldn't believe how many people were here. People were waving flags and picket signs, chanting, and walking around. I looked, and I didn't see any news people or reporters. Either it was too early for them to show up, or they didn't want to cover it.

Laila talked to the crowd about tonight's event. She reminded everyone why we were here and gave the people the talking points to use when speaking to the politicians. To be honest, she was doing a great job. She thanked everyone for listening and coming down to City Hall, and there was a round of applause for her.

Laila finished with the crowd, and we headed inside. The hearing was supposed to start at seven, but because it was a city-run event, it was running late and didn't start until seven forty-five. They severely underestimated the public interest in the hearing, and the event was a mess; everyone had to go through security and check their bags, so it took forever to get everyone in. They hassled Eric and his crew about the cameras and equipment, and even though everyone had phones, they still weren't going to let them in. They were pulled aside by security, and I was nervous. I thought they were going to get thrown out, but thank goodness Eric had the foresight to apply for a press permit before the event, and once he flashed that, they let him through.

As we walked in, Eric asked, "So, are you ready, Bingham? You know what you're going to say?"

I was nervous. I didn't realize the council hearing room was so big, and it was filling up fast. I looked at Eric, and all I could say was, "Yeah."

He quipped back, "Ladies and gentlemen, a man of a thousand words, Brent Bingham."

I found the other tenants from our building and sat with them. Eric went to sit in the 'press' section, and Laila went over and joined the Acorn people. When I looked at her, I noticed the room looked like outside; the different groups or buildings had all gone and sat in their own groups. There were all the redshirts together, groups with all the same picket signs, and a couple of other groups were wearing their own t-shirts too; you could see a small group with blue shirts that said, 'Toronto Federation of Tenants', there were green shirts for the 'Toronto Tenants Association'; and the Tenants Equal Rights Association were wearing pink shirts, it looked like a scene out of 'The Warriors' with all the gangs sitting around segregated in their different groups and colors.

I had never been to City Hall before. I've been in the City Square before for parties and events over the years, but I had never gone 'into' City Hall for anything, and I was surprised how big the Council Hearing room was. There was an elevated long head table at the front of the room, and then in front of that table, there were five half- crescent rows of seating facing the general public; the first couple of rows had nice individual desks with very nice chairs, a microphone, and a vase for water at each of them.

After the rows of desks were a few rows of tables with nice chairs and a microphone every few feet, and after those were a couple more rows of just tables and kind of nice chairs. After the spacious rows of seating, two desks faced the head table, with a microphone and water jug at each. After that, it was regular seating; that's where the plebes and peasants sat, rows of cheap plastic chairs placed so close together they were almost touching, and that's where most of us in the public gallery were sitting, packed in.

I looked over at Eric and his 'crew' sitting in the press section that was to the left of the crescent rows of tables. There were about forty chairs in that section, and it was empty except for Eric, his three guys, and Joanna Chow. He looked over at me and saw the cramped seating we were all in, so he leaned back, stretched out his legs, and put them up on an empty chair. He looked pretty comfortable and was laughing; he shook his head, motioned to the empty seating, and put his hands up in question.

I returned the same look to him as if to say, 'What the hell?'

Just then, Councillor Flatch came in from a door behind the head table and was accompanied by a gentleman in a suit; they waved at everyone in the gallery past the empty rows and took their seats at the head table. They shuffled some papers, and you could hear a PA switch on and come to life. Of course, one of them had a hot mic, and we could hear everything they were saying. They were complaining about the prices in the cafeteria and saying how the city should be subsidizing the cost of food for the councillors. Then they started to say they had to change the format of the meeting because of time.

Someone from the audience yelled, "Pay for your own damn food. So what's the change with the meeting?"

Councillor Flatch looked around in surprise, unsure of how we heard her, and then she shot a mean glance over to the AV guy.

She tapped her mic like an idiot and said, "Oh, I guess you can hear me. Welcome, everyone, and thank you for coming to 'The Toronto City Council Sub- Committee on the Evaluation and Sustainability of Affordable and Rental Housing.' She couldn't even remember the name of her own Sub-Committee; she had to read it from a card.

"I'm City Councillor Flatch, and this is Councillor Tom Tomford. We aim to get to the root of the affordable housing problem in Toronto."

Someone from the crowd yelled, "YOU MEAN, AFFORDABLE HOUSING CRISIS!"

She corrected herself and played to the crowd, "Yes, you're right. We want to find out what is causing this crisis. Our goal is to listen to you, the people, investigate what's going on, and initiate sustainable, affordable housing rules and regulations."

The crowd cheered and clapped a little. They still thought that the people sitting above them at the front of the room actually cared about them. I wonder if they'll feel the same way after tonight.

Councillor Flatch continued, "We apologize for the confusion and delay in getting in today. We underestimated how many people would attend, so we have to limit our time. Normally, we give everyone three minutes to talk, but unfortunately, we must limit it to two minutes. I think that should still be enough time. Speaking of how many people are interested in this hearing, we are broadcasting on the City of Toronto's YouTube channel, and I believe we are breaking viewership records. "She glanced over at the guy sitting at the control board.

He replied, "Twenty-five thousand viewers."

Councillor Flatch asked, "And how many people usually tune in to hearings like this?"

He chuckled when he said, "Two, maybe three hundred."

Councillor Flatch adjusted her scarf and took credit for the interest, "I'm glad I initiated this hearing; I feel this subject needs attention, and the more people I can get talking about this, the better."

I looked over at the 'press gallery', and Eric was trying to get my attention; he was motioning for me to read my texts. Everyone had their phones on silent, so I hadn't noticed he sent me four texts in the last two minutes; when I read them, I laughed and went to Facebook. Eric was streaming the hearing live on Facebook, and we had twenty-four thousand people watching through our page. I had to shake my head in disbelief; just like a politician, she thought it was herself who was drawing the crowd.

I blocked out what Councillor Flatch was saying and started reading the comments people were leaving on Facebook. Not many people were happy. In fact, the more I read, the more I noticed that all the posts were comical and downright angry. People were even ripping on Tom Tomford's name, asking what kind of parent would name their kid Tom with the last name Tomford.

That made me laugh, but then it made me wonder, 'How much money has Mr. Tomford received from Kerwin and his Alliance.' I left Facebook, went to the lobbying site, and typed his name. Sure enough, he's had as many meetings and has taken as much money as Flatch. I guess he doesn't mind playing and pandering to both sides as well. I looked up from my phone to the both of them at the front of the room and thought, 'I hate politicians.'

When I clued back in, I heard Flatch say, "On that note, let's get started, and please remember, two minutes each. We will try to get to everyone, but if we don't, I apologize in advance. Our first speaker is Adina P, from twenty-two Maynard Ave."

Adina took a minute to get to the mic, and you could see everyone getting a little impatient and upset, realizing how long this night would take. Adina told her story, and it was sad like all the others I have heard. Her landlord was playing games, trying to raise the rent and get the tenants out of the building; she started getting emotional and was almost going to cry. They had a warning light on the desk, and it lit up fifteen seconds before the time was up, and when her time was up, a buzzer went off. It startled Adina, and even though she was mid-sentence, they cut her off and silenced the mic; you could see the anger on her face when she stood up.

Councillor Flatch called the next two speakers up. She instructed everyone that if they were called, they should make their way up to the front and have a seat at the 'on deck' desk. People gave her a small clap, and she called the names of the next two speakers to the front.

One after the other, it was just sad story after sad story. At the onset of this hearing, I was unsure of what the actual point was of this event; from what I could see, it was just a bitch-fest. No one had any solutions, but everyone wanted to bitch about their landlord, there were one or two good speakers who had a couple of ideas and solutions, but the rest of the people were whiners. There were even a couple of crazy guys who slipped through the cracks and were able to speak; they started yelling and swearing at the politicians, and one of them even damned them to hell.

There was about forty-five minutes left in the hearing and she still hadn't called on our building, I was getting nervous that I wouldn't get to speak. So far, there was nothing of substance in this hearing, just a lot of complaining. I really couldn't see anything coming from this at all. I looked over at Eric, shaking my head; I could tell we were both thinking this was going to be a big waste of time. I pretended to fall asleep, and as I did that, Flatch called mine and Robert's name. It surprised me, and I jumped up pretty quickly; I looked at Eric nervously, who was laughing at me as I made my way to the front with Robert behind me.

Councillor Flatch introduced Robert and said, "You have two minutes."

Robert started in excellent form, "Thank you, Councillor Flatch. Toronto is broken…"

He delivered another eloquent and heartwarming speech. Everything he said made sense and was down to earth. He discussed property taxes, rental laws, the Landlord and Tenant Board, rental prices, and ownership. He finished by talking about the Toronto he used to love, and he even received some applause from the crowd.

His buzzer went off, he said his thanks and stood up. I stood up and patted him on the back. Robert returned to his seat, and I moved to the 'speaking desk.' I pulled out the stack of lobbying reports and dropped them with a loud thud on the desk. As I sat down, I looked at Eric, who surprisingly gave me the thumbs up instead of the finger for a change.

I sat at the desk; Councillor Flatch said it was nice to see me again and welcomed me to the committee. She introduced me as Brent B, from Empire Avenue, and said the floor was mine.

I said, "Thank you, Councillor Flatch, thank you for fighting for affordable housing; you are a real champion of the people."

Then I paused. I knew her ego would make her respond, "Thank you, Brent. It's a very concerning subject for me."

I said, "I'm sure it is. Have you had any meetings with Housing Minister Stephen Clarke? It seems like he'd be the guy to talk to about 'Affordable' Housing."

She cleared her throat. "Unfortunately, we haven't been able to meet or discuss the issue. It's hard to coordinate meetings, I just can't go to Parliament and walk into his office, Brent."

I asked her, "Why not? Take some of that lobbying money you have received and buy yourself a meeting. Never mind, we'll get back to that in a second. OK, so you haven't met with the one Federal politician that could supposedly help with affordable housing, not even the Federal Housing Minister."

She looked around and tried to avoid the subject: "Brent, I don't think you want to spend your time talking with me."

I chuckled and said, "Actually, I think I do. My story is like everyone else's; I'm getting thrown out for greed and profit. I'm stuck in the Landlord and Tenant Board, so why not use this time to talk to you."

I was smiling when I said that, but the politicians weren't; you could see they weren't impressed.

"May I ask the Esteemed Councillors why there is so much empty seating here this evening? There are a lot of empty seats, considering people weren't allowed in tonight. Why can't they sit here?"

Councillor Flatch removed her glasses at this point. "Mr. B, you're wasting your time. Those seats are reserved for fellow Councillors who sit in on hearings."

I immediately asked, "So where are they? Why aren't they here listening to our stories, learning the facts? Don't they care about Affordable Housing? Obviously, they don't. Or do they support the developers and landlords? You have a couple hundred people outside, and you won't let them in? They care about the facts, and they want to listen and learn. Isn't this room supposed to be for the people? Look at the press section, which is almost empty. Why can't people sit over there?"

I looked at Eric, who flashed the one-minute signal to me, so I had to hurry.

Councillor Flatch started to answer, but I asked my next question, "Are the esteemed Councillors familiar with 'The Alliance of Commercial Housing Rentals?'"

They both shifted in their seats like a ferret was burrowing up their asses, "Not off hand, Brent, now please…"

Not paying attention to them because I knew they would only lie, I continued, "They're the political lobbyists that represent the commercial landlords. Both of you have had meetings with the Alliance. Have you received any money from them?"

"Mr. B! This is inappropriate. We meet with many people and deal with many different issues, I can't remember everyone we talk to. I'd have to check my records."

As Flatch spoke, you could see the ferret was burrowing deeper and deeper in. I picked up the papers and said, "Don't worry, I have your records."

I turned to the crowd and continued to speak directly to them, "Both of these politicians have met with 'The Alliance of Commercial Rental Housing Providers' once a year, and both have received three thousand dollars for each meeting. They're taking money from the very people that we are fighting against, so whose side are they really on?"

I turned back to Flatch and Tomford and looked them straight in the eye, "Well, which is it? Whose side are you on, the people in this room tonight or the landlords who are buying you off?"

The crowd was starting to rumble; there were scattered yells from the crowd saying, 'Criminals,' 'you corrupt SOB,' and people asking, 'What's going on here?'

Tom Tomford finally spoke and said, "We'd have to check our records; we're not aware of any of this."

When he said that, I decided I was done with politicians. They were using us; they knew it, and I knew it. They brought us publicity and helped put a spotlight on our situation, but they're liars. I hated politics and politicians, and now I remember why. They were nothing but self-serving hypocrites, living off the hard work of the people. I was done with these two.

I turned and looked at the crowd. "I have their records right here. You can find these online at the lobbying websites. It's all public information, even though they don't want you to know that. These people lied right to our faces; the system is fixed, and these politicians are bought and paid for."

Eric gave me the thirty-second signal, so I sped it up: "The owners of our building are Chinese citizens. They live in China, and they don't even live in Canada. They have paid money to 'The Alliance of Commercial Housing Rentals,' who, in turn, has given it to these politicians under the guise of 'Campaign Contributions.' Not only that, but they have also received money from the Chinese Foreign Investment Council."

I was sure to use big air quotes when I said, 'Campaign Contributions.' I held up the stack of papers again, "I have the evidence right here. These politicians have taken money from a foreign entity to help evict Canadian Citizens." I continued speaking, looking directly at the squirming politicians, "You might feel better that the money came from a Lobbyist, but that money you receive comes from China to help evict Canadian citizens; you should be ashamed of yourselves, and in my opinion, you should all be in jail."

The buzzer went, and Flatch snapped at me, "Mr. Bingham, that is enough from you!"

She cut off my mic, grabbed her gavel, and started banging it on the table. She used my last name when she yelled, which she wasn't supposed to do, so I know I must have gotten to her.

I packed up the papers and said, with a big booming voice, "Thank you, Councillors. I appreciate your attention to the matter."

I turned to go back to my seat, and the room was quiet; there was some scattered applause, some people were criticizing me, calling me a liar, and some people were asking where to get this information.

I held up my phone, waved it around, and yelled, "Facebook, 'Renoviction.' I'll post all the links tonight. Go and learn about Lobbying; learn what these politicians are really doing."

I saw two police officers approaching me, so I returned to my chair and stopped talking. They approached, and as soon as they got close, they asked me to leave. Now, I didn't care if I got thrown out or not, this hearing was boring as hell, and normally, I would just leave, but if they were going to throw me out, Eric would eat that shit up.

They stood above me and said, "Sir, please, we're asking you to leave." I looked up and asked, "What for?"

"Sir, we need you to leave; please don't make us ask again." As they said that, they stepped towards me.

I repeated, "What for? I spoke during my allotted time, I didn't swear, I didn't threaten anyone, I spoke my mind, and that's all I did. Just because they don't like what I said doesn't mean they can throw me out. That's insane. Where are we living? This is literally the 'Town Square;' what the hell did I do?"

They went to grab me, and I stepped back; they weren't messing around. One of the cops loudly said, "Sir, there's no need to swear. Please leave before we make you leave and trespass you, Sir, please…"

I replied, "I didn't swear, but to show you I'm not any trouble, I'll leave."

I looked at the cops, shaking my head in disappointment, and continued, "You know they're throwing me out because they didn't like what I was saying, and that's it. I didn't do anything wrong; they just wanted to shut me up. You know, everywhere else in the world, lobbying is called bribery. In your 'cop world,' when people take money for favors, you call that bribery, but in their world, it's called 'lobbying.' Right now, you guys are working for the bad guys."

They went to grab my arms, and I repeated, "I'm going, I'm going."

As I was escorted out, the room started applauding, and I wasn't sure if they were applauding for me or for the fact that I was getting thrown out.

I left the hearing room, and once in the hall, I went to sit down on a bench outside the council room. As I did, the cops crossed their arms, shook their heads, and one of them said, "Nope, all the way out."

I stood back up, "come on, guys, seriously?"

They motioned to the exit, and I was escorted all the way to the front door, with Eric ten feet behind us. As we got outside, we stopped and turned around to look back at the cops; we high-fived each other, which made them look at each other, confused.

Eric was excited and said, "That was awesome, Bingham; they were speechless in there; look at the cops; morons don't even know they're just stormtroopers for the rich."

I wasn't as happy as Eric, this hearing opened my eyes to how our system and politicians actually work. We may think that the government and politicians are looking out for and protecting us, but they're not, and if you question them, you're thrown out of the conversation. At first, I thought it was comical, but the more I thought about the situation, the more I realized our system was broken.

The more I thought of what just happened, the more pissed off I got; I looked at Eric and pointed back at the building, "What the fuck was that? They're in there saying, 'We are here to help you; we're concerned for what's happening to the city. Meanwhile, they're stuffing their pockets full of cash. The part that really pisses me off is that the general public in there still believes them; they actually think those people are here to help them. They're sitting at the front of that room, wasting everyone's time, giving the people the false hope that there could be change. They're so full of shit, and when you call them out, they just shut you down."

I couldn't believe how mad I was getting; I wasn't getting mad because I was getting thrown out. I was angry because this proved that the whole system was a farce. I kept pacing and ranting to Eric, "I didn't swear in there, I didn't get violent, and I didn't insult the politicians. I just asked questions and stated facts.

They responded with lies; they were the ones who should be thrown out, not me. How many needles did we see in the stairwell coming up here tonight? And look at all the cops up here. I've seen six different officers so far walking around here doing fuck all. Throwing me out? Please..."

I stopped pacing. "This is where people are supposed to come for help, the City Square. Where are people supposed to go for help? There's nothing left for them anymore. Everything is set up against us. Unless you can pay, you ain't going to play. That's it."

As I said that, people started coming out of·City Hall. I smiled at Eric and said, "It looks like the meeting got out early."

He took off to do his thing, and I just sat to watch everyone walk out. As people walked by, you could hear them complaining about the hearing, the politicians, and the city; a few even stopped to thank me and ask what the name of the Facebook page was. There wasn't a smiling face coming out of that building; no one looked happy. Some people even shot me looks that made me wonder if they thought I was the bad guy for calling out these politicians. I started looking straight into and reading the eyes of the people coming out, and yeah, some people were shooting me daggers with their eyes.

It's amazing when you question authority around people who would never dare question authority. They think you are the bad one. They think, 'How dare you not listen to the 'Dr' in the white coat or the 'officer' in a uniform.' People believe the authority figure has their best interests at heart, which is sad.

The energy after the hearing was definitely not the same as before. People were moving slowly and looking defeated, and I couldn't help but think I was a little responsible for that. People went into this meeting thinking the system would help them, thinking it worked one way, but they came out realizing that it works another way.

Learning the truth about something you thought you knew can mentally rattle you and shatter your belief system. If you have believed you understood how something works all your life, but then you learn that what you thought you knew, what you thought to believe to be true, and what they told you to be true all your life, wasn't. It can rock your world.

It took a while for the rest of my building to come out. I saw them coming towards me, and I could see Robert and Bob laughing and some of them even clapping as they approached.

Bob lit a cigarette, patted me on the back, and shook his head in disbelief. He said, "You got some balls, Brent. I'll give you that."

I looked at them and asked, "But you guys get it, right? You get that they're not here to help, right? That it's all just lip service, and they can't do a thing for us. You see, this is all pointless, right?"

Everyone nodded their heads up in down in agreement; I continued, "So you guys aren't pissed, you're OK with what happened; you know it was the truth; it's all true."

Bob patted me again, "Don't worry, Brent. I didn't have much faith in the politicians from the beginning. They're all liars, and you just proved that. You did the right thing."

As he said that, Sarah came storming out and as usual, she was the last one to the grown-up conversation. She was furious and coming straight for me. I smiled on the inside and thought, 'This is going to be good. This poor kid is going to think the politicians are the good guys. Let's see if she is smart enough to know they're not.'

"What's your problem, Brent?" She didn't disappoint; she was yelling like a child.

I thought I'd play with her a little. I looked around quizzically and asked her, "What do you mean?"

"Don't be a smart ass; you wrecked it; you wrecked it for the rest of us." She was on the verge of having a tantrum.

I pulled out a cigar; these little millennials hate tobacco smoke; vaping and pot smoke are fine, but you are a monster for cigarettes and cigars, so I figured there was no better time to light up. I lit the cigar and saw the look on her face as she went over the edge.

I was laughing on the inside when I asked, "How did I wreck it Sarah?"

She started screaming, "They stopped the meeting. Once they threw you out, they said they had technical difficulties, they said that the YouTube link had crashed, and after that, people started asking questions about the money and the fucking lobbyists, Brent! So many people were yelling questions; Councillor Flatch said they had to stop the hearing due to technical difficulties, and they walked out. People are furious."

I took a big drag on the cigar and let it linger; when all the smoke was gone, I started laughing. I looked around, trying to get eyes on Eric, and when I did, I yelled to him, "Hey man, we crashed the YouTube link!"

When people passing by heard me say that, they cheered, and Eric gave me a big thumbs-up. The cheer was contagious and went through the crowd. For whatever reason, the whole crowd started cheering and clapping.

I looked at Sarah and laughed, "They don't look too furious to me. Did your Councillors answer the questions people were asking Sarah?"

She wouldn't reply, so I kept asking, "Why couldn't they stay to answer the questions, Sarah? What was the technical problem between them and the audience? They don't care about us, Sarah. They won't answer the questions, and they won't admit they take money from the very people trying to kick us out. Do you understand this yet, Sarah?"

I thought her head was going to explode. You could see she was trying to process everything and come back with something to say, but I was right; she was wrong, and I was almost getting through to her.

But there was nothing, her cognitive dissonance ruled her. She yelled, "Well, you can't smoke here. You can't smoke this close to the entrance. Put that out or leave before I get the police."

I thought to myself, 'This poor moron,' oh well, what I said next wasn't my fault, "Listen, little girl, I'm about thirty feet away from the entrance, and that's ten more feet than the law says. Now, get lost!"

She stood there speechless for a few seconds trying to think of something to say; all she could muster up was, "Fuck you, Brent."

Then she scurried away, which made everyone from the building laugh. Even though she pissed me off and was wrong, I felt bad for her; it's people like her that this system preys upon. They prey upon the ignorant and naïve who think that the system will actually be there to help and defend them.

As Sarah stomped away like a child, Laila and the red shirts came out. She looked at Sarah storming off and asked me, "One of your fans?"

I replied, "Surprisingly, no. It's one of our tenants who doesn't understand what's happening."

Laila looked at me. "She seems like a nice girl. Brent, I knew the system was corrupt, but I didn't know how corrupt. You mean to tell me that those two people at the front of the room take money from the very same landlords responsible for throwing people out?"

I looked at her, and I sadly nodded yes.

She stepped in, took my hand, and we hugged. I wasn't trying to get a hug; it just happened; we held each other, knowing we were facing a corrupt system. When I hugged her, it was reassuring; holding Laila reminded me that there was still 'good' in this world and that there were reasons to fight against evil; the hug was solace for both of us. I held her tight and gave her a good squeeze before I let go; still holding my one hand, she stepped back and went to grab the other one when she noticed the cigar.

As soon as she saw it, she let go of my hand, and in a sexy, stern voice, she asked, "What? What is this? Smoke?"

I looked at it and then at her, and I smiled, "Yeah, it's a cigar."

Well, I don't like it; it smells like a dog. "Would you please put it out for me?"

I smiled, threw the cigar on the ground, stepped on it, looked her right in the eye, and said, "Of course, I will."

Chapter 19

After the Sub-Committee bullshit, I was expecting to see something in the news about it, but there wasn't. Even though it was the center of my world for a couple of days and I thought it was an issue the whole city would care about, no one did. People were talking about it on the Facebook page, but that was it. They were commenting on the lobbying sites and sharing them on their pages, saying they had no idea that was how politics worked.

Robert had contacted all the reporters who came to our rally. He contacted everyone he could, but no one came out to cover the Sub-Committee except Joanna Chow. Even though Joanna wrote about the hearing, no one picked up her story. Thinking about the Sub-Committee Hearing and the Facebook page made me wonder about the state of our media. About one thousand people were at City Hall—and not one mention of it was made in any of the city's media.

I have seen news articles and TV reports of groups as small as ten people protesting at City Hall, and for no one to cover or write about this event seemed strange. After all, they were calling it an '*Affordable Housing Crisis.*' You would think that would get headlines. But they don't want headlines. They don't want to draw attention to an Affordable Housing Crisis, as that takes away from the narrative that housing is nothing but golden in Toronto. Going through this process was an education on so many levels: lobbying, corruption, real estate, media, society— and not to mention, greed.

The next few weeks were very uneventful. It was strange; after the rally, there was a flurry of work around the building; when I asked Lorenzo about it, he said that the owner wanted things sped up for some reason. Then, a couple of weeks later, Lorenzo stopped showing up. It was surprising that the work had just stopped. Units that had almost been renovated were still sitting empty, and the demolished units were just sitting there, demolished.

I had previously exchanged phone numbers with Lorenzo, and after I hadn't seen him for a couple of weeks, I decided to text him to ask what was happening. Ten minutes after I texted him, my phone rang, and it was him.

When I answered, I joked, "I'll have to fire you for not showing up."

He laughed and said, "That's fine—this has been the worst job I've ever taken."

He said the owner wasn't paying him, claiming 'breach of contract.' Lorenzo said he had started legal proceedings and that the 'intermediate' was no longer communicating with him, so he had no choice but to take them to court.

After speaking with Lorenzo, I was amazed. This new owner was a real piece of work - his business plan was basically, 'screw everyone I do business with.' This guy, not even in this country, disregards the laws and does whatever he pleases. And why wouldn't he? He doesn't even live in this country, so what consequences would he ever face? But what is genuinely infuriating and demotivating is that no one was on our side; if you stand back from the situation and look at what's really taking place, it's scary.

We have foreign interests giving money, probably even laundering money, to a middleman, who then gives it to our politicians, who in return, change the laws against us and in favor of the foreign entity that is paying them. This level of corruption and bullshit was way beyond me. There was nothing I could do to fix this; all I could do was shine a light on it and realize that this was bigger than our little building at Three-Ninety-One Empire Avenue.

Things had slowed down on the documentary side as well; Eric got booked on a location shoot out of town for three weeks, so he hadn't been around, which was a little unsettling as I was basically still sleeping in an arsonist's supply closet. Since our situation hadn't changed, there wasn't much to shoot or do. We had our hearing coming up soon at the Tenant Board, and that's all we were waiting for; it's all we had left. There weren't any updates from Wessler, and the tenants were going about their daily business; after all, what else could we do? It was sad how fast things sizzled down. It's as if everyone, like Acorn, the reporters, and politicians, got what they needed from us and just moved on. Acorn got new memberships and sold some T-shirts; the politicians got their names and faces into the news supporting the people; and the reporters got their bylines. So here we were, just the building standing together to fight this. But once the owner got their checkbook out, I knew I would be standing alone to fight; it was just a matter of time.

The only thing happening was me and Laila. I was able to spend some time with her away from the Renoviction bullshit. She wanted to learn how to skate so she could surprise her son, so we were able to spend time together doing that. There is nothing better than cold and ice to bring two people together. Being with her opened my eyes; she had such a different perspective on life. She had witnessed some horrific acts in her homeland, and she truly believed that a lot of evil deeds perpetrated in the name of politics or religion were only done for two things: money and power. She was correct; she was right about a lot of stuff. But the one thing I didn't think she was right about was that we had a chance to win our case and stay in our building.

It's weird how life works; when I was faced with this 'Renoviction,' I wasn't too optimistic about anything. Getting screwed by the system was just par for the course for me; it's what happens. I wasn't expecting anything good coming from this. But surprisingly, a couple of good things did - the documentary, and best of all, I met Laila.

I'm always amazed at how time flies but can also lag. It seemed that when we were presented with the first eviction letter, this would take forever, but here we were, a few days away from our hearing at the Landlord and Tenant Board. No one was too sure or had a clue of what would happen or how long we could delay the inevitable with an adjournment. As we got closer to the date, people around the building were on edge; everyone's nerves were getting to them, and there were even a couple of arguments in the building. People were starting to crack, and you could tell the pressure was getting to everyone; thank goodness we would have some closure soon.

As the day approached, I started getting nervous as well. I hadn't heard much from Eric; Wessler was incommunicado; Robert was pretty quiet, and there weren't any letters or communication from the owner. It was eerily calm up until a couple of days before our hearing, and all of a sudden, everything came alive again; Eric was back from his shoot; the work started back up in the building, and we even received another letter from our friends the Durbansky paralegals.

Robert knocked on my door, and when I let him in, he flew by me as usual, waving a letter that he obviously wanted to discuss. I looked at him, he was pissed off, and he was already pacing in his favorite spot. I looked at my door, and sure enough, a letter was taped to it. I yanked it off and threw it on the desk. I didn't need to open it as I was sure Robert was going to give me the full details.

He didn't hold back, "Well, who knows if we're going to get our hearing now?"

I wasn't expecting that, as it's all we had left. I asked him, "What the hell do you mean?"

I picked up the letter, ripped it open, and read it as Robert ranted, "They're trying to break us. They've offered us more money; they don't want us in that hearing as a group. These guys could pay us fifty thousand dollars each to get us out, and they'd still make money off this place."

I scanned the letter to find the amount they were offering, and to my surprise, it was forty-five hundred dollars. That's a tempting but pretty random amount, so I figured I'd read the letter, and when I was done, I wish I hadn't. These weasels wrote a page and a half detailing how and why this amount was decided on, and they didn't hold back any bullshit when they were writing it. They provided a detailed cost analysis of why this was a 'more than gracious offer,' they provided dollar amounts and percentages, quoted cost of living and moving expenses, and a whole lot of other bullshit that made them look like they were actually being generous with us. They referenced case studies and articles about the gentrification of neighborhoods, how it is good for society, and how everyone benefits from it. Then, they started saying that we were trying to hold back progress, which is detrimental to society.

I crumpled the letter into a ball and threw it across the room; I couldn't believe the gall these guys had. They were actually able to 'spin' this situation to make it as if we were the bad guys. After reading the letter, I even felt like I was the bad guy for not taking the money. I hadn't heard anything Robert had been ranting about, but when I looked at him, he was still going.

I asked him, "How many do you think will take this?"

Robert replied, "I think a couple of people will take this for sure, and if Reggie does the math and realizes that this will get him two-hundred-twenty-five pizzas, he'll be out the door and on his way to Domino's."

I broke out laughing, "damn Robert, that's cold. Cold but true."

He made his way towards the door. "I'll write a notice for an emergency tenant meeting tomorrow. We'll have it here in the stairwell. We have to wait to see who shows up and who doesn't. I guess we'll know that way.

As he reached for the door, someone knocked. Robert jumped back and asked, "What the hell is that?"

I looked at him and laughed, "It's the door, Robert. But I have no idea who it is because you're the only one that comes by, and Eric, well, he lets himself in."

I opened the door, and it was Reggie, the minute I saw him, I was pissed off because I knew exactly why he was here, "Hey Reggie, what's up?"

"Hey Brent, oh, hey Robert, I'm glad you're here too." He held up the letter and shook his head, and in a bad-acting voice, he said, "Can you guys believe this? I can't believe we're going to be thrown out. What are we going to do? Why do you think they're offering us more money when they said there wouldn't be anymore? Let's take this, right? Like, this is a good amount of money, right?"

Neither of us answered him; after a few seconds of silence, Reggie asked, "Do you think they'll offer more?"

Right on cue.

Usually, I would want to be honest, I would want to tell the truth, and I would honestly try to help or enlighten someone who maybe didn't see the bigger picture. But this guy had never knocked on my door; he had never given me the time of day, and now, because he wants something, he has the nerve to come into my place, start a bullshit conversation, and lie right to my face about what his intentions are. The only thing worse than a liar is a stupid, bad liar, and Reggie was the epitome of both. His showing up at my door confirmed what I had said would happen. When they brought out the checkbook, people would run to the lifeboats.

But we needed him at the hearing, so I looked at him and said, "Yeah, they'll offer us more."

Immediately, he said, "Really? How much more?"

I didn't want to deal with this guy or his greed. I said, "Hey, Reggie, we're just on our way out. Robert's putting up a notice for an impromptu meeting in the stairwell tomorrow. We can talk about it then. But hey, thanks for coming by."

He turned around and waddled out.

I looked at Robert as he left and asked him, "So what do you think?"

Robert was a sharp guy; he said, "As much as I think he'd take this offer, I think he smells there could be more; he'll stick around for the hearing."

I was tired of thinking about it so I decided to get a coffee and trip around the neighborhood to enjoy what I might not be able to do again. As I headed out, I passed a couple of workers in the stairwell. I didn't recognize any of them, and they had a different 'air' about them. They didn't say hi or even nod their head, and I could feel the resentment coming from them when passing in the stairway. When I got downstairs, a young guy was standing on the stoop; he was wearing a hard hat, had a lanyard around his neck, and was holding a clipboard - trying to look like something of an authority.

I glanced at the lanyard and noticed a different company's name on it, so I knew something was up. I asked him, "Hey man, what's up? Is Lorenzo coming by today?"

He didn't reply or even acknowledge my presence. OK, maybe he didn't hear me, so I politely said again, "Excuse me. Uh, I'm sorry, is Lorenzo…"

He turned, looked me up and down, then turned his back to me and flat-out ignored me.

I thought, 'OK, you want to play like that?'

I stood on the stoop right beside the guy and dialed Lorenzo; when he answered, I didn't hesitate, "Hey Lorenzo, yeah, you were right. They got a new set of suckers in here to finish the work."

As I said that, the guy lowered the clipboard and had no choice but to pay attention because now it was in his interests to do so. And since he could only hear my side of the conversation, I knew I had to have some fun.

I continued, "Yeah, some bullshit name that makes sound bigger than they are…Yeah, that's them, Allied Contracting Services…yeah, how'd you know?" I was pretending Lorenzo was saying those things when, in actuality, he was just cursing on the other end, but it sucked in Mr. Hardhat even further.

Lorenzo then told me to say, Louie, the intermediate contact's name, out loud.

I looked at Mr. Hardhat and spoke to Lorenzo, "I guess Louie is trying to save a couple of bucks with these guys."

When I said that, I knew I had this guy's full attention because he lowered his clipboard and turned toward me. He started to ask me something, and I put my finger up to stop him. I pretended I was focused on and enthralled with what Lorenzo was saying when, in fact, he was still just cursing on the other end.

I said goodbye to Lorenzo and hung up.

Mr. Hardhat asked, "Excuse me, can I ask you something?"

I put my finger up again. I stood silent beside him, glanced around the street, ignored him, and headed down the steps; as I hit the sidewalk, I heard, "Excuse me, sir?"

I looked back at him with a look of, 'You're kidding me, right?'

He asked, "Can I ask you something, sir?"

Laughing, I said, "No, I don't think so."

I gave him a wink and went on my way. Sometimes, you have to know when less is more.

When I returned to the building after a couple of hours, I could see I had gotten to the guy with the hard hat; he was out front of the building, pacing on the sidewalk, talking on the phone frantically. I sat on the stoop and watched him for a bit to have a good laugh, and I wasn't disappointed. I couldn't hear much, but every once in a while, I could hear the words, 'money,' 'extended,' and finally, 'I'm fucked if this doesn't work out.'

Hearing that pissed me off more; here was another guy, just trying to make a living, who was going to learn about the global economy that we were all supposedly benefitting from. I had seen enough, I just wanted to go upstairs and relax for a bit.

I stood up, winked at Mr. Hardhat, and said, "Good luck, kid."

I 'loafed' around the apartment for the rest of the day. This whole process was tiring and put me off being sociable. I didn't even want to go to the tenant meeting tomorrow, and as soon as the thought popped into my head, Eric texted asking me what was going on; he asked if anything was happening before the hearing or if we would meet on Friday. I wasn't sure what to say; I felt I was going into a depression. I just wanted to bury my head under the pillows and never come out. I texted him back and told him what had just happened; he said he'd be here first thing in the morning and said we had a lot to review. Usually, I would have been excited, but I wasn't. I was fed up and emotionally drained. I was done; I didn't want to look at Facebook, I didn't want to read any more case studies or articles about housing, and I definitely didn't want to go to the tenant meeting and listen to people who had no conviction and were willing to sell out for a few thousand dollars.

I decided, 'screw it,' I'm not going to that meeting, Robert was there, and he could handle it. If I had to listen to idiots like Sarah and Reggie anymore, I thought I'd snap; it was probably better that I didn't go.

I let a couple of hours pass, then texted Eric that I got booked for tomorrow and couldn't attend the meeting. That was the thing about our business: when the phone rings with a work opportunity, you take it, and everyone in the business understands that. It wasn't more than ten seconds after hitting send that Eric was calling me. He was pissed I took the booking, but understood, he told me not to worry and that he'd be there and wouldn't miss it for the world.

I laid around watching TV for the rest of the night; I was wondering what I was going to do tomorrow; I would have to get away from the building for a while and lay low, so I didn't get sucked into going to the meeting. As I zoned out watching a movie, I fell asleep on the sofa. I didn't remember falling asleep, but I remember thinking at some point that I should get up and go to bed, but then I thought I might as well sleep on the sofa; I might not have it for much longer.

When I woke up, I felt pretty good, but the minute I started to think about the tenant meeting and hearing, my head felt like shit. The constant fear of not knowing my fate was tiring and demoralizing and it was no way for anyone to live. I must have aged five years in this process. The toll this takes on people is staggering, not only mentally but physically. I am now actually physically tired from dealing with this shit and I wondered how long it would take before I got physically sick from this as well.

I stayed in the building most of the day and only went out in the morning to grab some groceries, and that was it. I logged onto Facebook to make one simple post, and there were hundreds of new postings and tons of DM's; I couldn't deal with any of it; at this point, I could hardly handle my shit.

I sat tucked away in the safety of my place for the day. I watched some movies and made some food, and towards the end of the day, I was starting to feel a little better. Sitting around all day made me realize that if I wanted to have the safety of this place any longer, I would have to fight for it.

I was starting to come out of my funk when there was a knock on the door. I was going to ignore it, but then I heard Eric say, "Bingham, are you in there? I know you're in there. Stop touching yourself. I'm coming in."

I couldn't stop him since he had a key and I didn't want to, so I replied, "Yeah, I'm home."

The door opened, and he poked his head in with the eyes closed, "Can I look, or will I go blind?"

"It's safe; come on in," I pulled my blankets and pillow off the sofa and threw them in the bedroom. I motioned to the arsonist supplies and said, "When are you getting this shit out of here?"

He laughed and sat on the sofa, "Soon, buddy, soon. Don't worry, we're shooting it next week, and everything is ready to go. Can I ask you something?"

He looked at me and said, "You didn't have a booking today, did you?"

I looked at him, and he knew I wasn't feeling good. "No, man, I didn't. Please don't be mad at me. I couldn't do it. I couldn't listen to people ask, 'Will there be more? Will there be more?' So, how was the meeting?"

With a straight face, he said, "It was productive. Everyone was asking, will there be more?"

We both started laughing, and he added, "It's funny because it's true. But in all seriousness, they were asking how much more. But that was a good thing because it didn't take Robert much to convince them that there would be more; it looks like everyone is going turn it down. I even think Reggie is going to stick around for the hearing. Have you been on Facebook lately?"

I grabbed my phone and said, "I was going to make a post reminding everyone that our hearing is tomorrow. I was going to invite everyone to come and see if we could get a crowd. Somehow, I don't think we will. You're coming, though, right?"

He kicked off his shoes, plunked his ass on the sofa, and said, "That's why I'm here now. I'm crashing here and going with you tomorrow morning. This is way better than any movie or TV show I've ever worked on; I'm not missing the final episode of this for anything."

That said, we put on a movie and laughed the night away until we crashed.

Chapter 20

Our hearing day had arrived, and I couldn't believe it got here so fast. I woke up at about six a.m. as it was kind of hard to sleep; I didn't want to wake Eric, so I stayed in bed for a bit and logged on to Facebook. I was amazed at how popular the page had become, almost two hundred and fifty thousand followers, and it had a life of its own; thank you, Drake and 'Randy's'. People were posting and linking, inviting others to join, and talking back and forth amongst themselves. I looked at the DMs, and it was surprising and alarming how many people wanted to tell their stories or were looking for help. As much as I wanted to tell people to fight like hell, I couldn't. I didn't know their stories and circumstances, and the last thing I wanted to do was give someone life advice; I mean, look at mine.

All I could do was send them links to resources that might help. Even though I knew it wouldn't do anything, I wasn't going to be the one to tell them. After all, most people still believe we live in an honest society where the government and people in charge actually care about the people they're ruling over. I heard Eric come to life in the living room, so I got up and went out.

The first thing he said was, "Where's the room service, Bingham? I'm not leaving a good review about this place."

After we got ready and had coffee, it was eight a.m. and time to head out. The hearing was supposed to start 'first thing' at ten a.m. sharp. The bloody tenant board doesn't even open until ten a.m., but I guess missing half of the morning is what Government employees call 'first thing.'

We grabbed Robert and headed out. We got to the Landlord and Tenant Board a little after nine; the doors weren't open and wouldn't open until nine-thirty. We grabbed a coffee and hung around the entrance, waiting. People started arriving, and you could tell who was part of the system and who wasn't. Some people were greeted with a smile and buzzed in by security as soon as they walked to the door, and others were pointed to the sign that said the building opens at nine-thirty, or they were simply ignored.

When the security guard opened the door, we started to file in. As we walked in, he gave a speech about polite behavior and respecting others. I guess they've had some problems; I couldn't imagine why.

As Eric walked in, the security guard stopped him and said, "Sorry, sir, but there's no recording allowed inside."

Eric looked at me and said, "Go on in. I'm going to film around out here, and I'll catch up with you."

We went inside and found our way to the waiting area. Our building address was listed halfway down the docket, and the instructions said, 'Please be seated until the adjudicator calls your matter.'

I looked at Robert, "How do you like that? We're told to be here first thing so we can be told to hurry up and wait. Where the hell is Wessler anyway?"

Robert looked around, shaking his head, "probably trying to find a parking spot for his bicycle," and with that, we sat and waited.

It wasn't until ten fifteen when Wessler came in with one pant leg stuck in his sock; Robert looked at me and pretended he was riding a bike, looking around like a fool; that was our lawyer.

While we were waiting for our hearing, Robert pointed out the Durbansky Paralegals; he noticed their name was all over the docket for many of the cases happening today, and he asked one of them as they went from room to room if they were the Durbanskys. It was funny; the paralegals representing our owner weren't sitting around waiting; they were in and out of 'hearing rooms' all morning, tending to other cases. It seemed their workday wasn't wasted or ruined; this was their workday, and they had a nice little 'Eviction Factory' going on in here. Only the tenants' day was ruined; only the tenants weren't getting paid, and only the tenants' paychecks were getting docked. We had to be here and not at our jobs; this seemed fair.

After sitting around for an hour, we were finally called to 'Hearing Room Four.' The adjudicator came into the room and stood at the front. Sarah, Bill, and a couple of others stood up as if someone had said, 'Please rise,' but no one had said it. Our lawyer and the paralegals didn't even stand up.

I looked at Sarah and thought, 'Poor girl, conditioned and conformed to do everything authority says she should'. She caught me looking at her, and the look on my face must have told her I thought she was a moron. When she sat down, she looked as if she was proud to show the adjudicator that she holds him in high regard and respects his position. There was nothing to respect about this guy; he was placed in this job by his rich commercial developer friends who needed the Tenant Board to rule for landlords and not tenants, plain and simple.

The adjudicator introduced himself, "I'm Desmond Higgins, Adjudicator for the Landlord and Tenant Board. I have been assigned to hear the dispute between the tenants of Three-Ninety-One Empire Avenue and One-Four-Seven-Zero-Zero-Seven LLC."

He greeted our lawyer and then the paralegal team of 'Durbansky and Durbansky.' He spoke to them in such an informal, casual way that you could tell they were very familiar with each other. Lastly, he welcomed Rita from Brownstone.

He began by summarizing the Landlord and Tenant Board's purpose: "Our intention is to resolve disputes between landlords and tenants that cannot be resolved. My job is to ensure that everyone is acting and conforming within the rules and laws of The Residential Tenancies Act."

He continued, "Before we commence hearings, we try to get both sides to come to an agreement. The Tenant Board employs an impartial third party, an unbiased mediator, to hear out both sides of the conflict to try to negotiate an acceptable deal for both parties. So, before we begin, I will ask both parties to sit with the mediator to see if anything can be worked out."

Confused and feigning innocence, I raised my hand. The adjudicator called on me. I stood up and began, "I'm sorry, sir. I don't know if I'm allowed to speak or ask questions?"

He smiled and said, "You and your representative are both allowed to speak, within reason, of course, because, well, there are a lot of you, but yes, you are allowed to speak."

I thanked him and said, "I'm familiar with mediation, sir; both sides working for a mutually beneficial agreement, but my owner has shown nothing but bad intentions and dirty tactics from the beginning. He's lied and tried to break the law to get me out of this building. There has been no goodwill, and I don't see mediation as a viable option based on their behavior. If the only point of mediation is for them to buy me out, there's no point. If they want to discuss an option of me staying in my place, I'd be more than happy to talk in mediation, but if the purpose of mediation is to give them a chance to buy their way out of this situation, I honestly don't see it being a productive use of time."

I looked over at the paralegal, and he stood to answer, "Thank you, Mr. Higgins. At this time, we stand by our position that the building must be vacant, and yes, we are more than happy to try to discuss a mutually acceptable agreement based on that."

I replied, "There you go. There is no point; they only want to buy their way out of this."

The adjudicator didn't care what was happening or what was being said right in front of him; he had his process, and he was sticking to it.

"Nonetheless," he said, "I want you to sit down and try to work out an agreement."

There was no other way. The system wouldn't listen to me.

We were told to wait in the hallway until the mediator was available, and as we walked out of the room, I could feel the eyes on me. The looks from some of the tenants said everything. Most of them were happy, but some weren't.

Bob slapped me on the back and said, "Go get 'em buddy."

Robert smiled and gave me the thumbs up, but most were glaring at me.

Sarah decided once again to be the group's representative and try to put me in my place. "Brent, you show him respect; he's the judge, and you should respect the law."

I started laughing and desperately wanted Sarah to understand. "Sarah, we are the only ones following the law; these guys are trying to bend or break it. And the guy at the front of the room, the 'judge'? He doesn't care about us at all. He just wants this resolved and wants us to go away. Everyone in that room just wants us to go away. Plain and simple."

She waved her arms and said, "Brent, the cameras aren't here; you don't have to act up."

I said, "Sarah, this is THE EXACT TIME WHEN WE HAVE TO ACT UP. This is our last chance. Today, right now, you better wake up because this is your last chance to stand up and try to save your home."

As I finished lecturing Sarah, the door from the hearing room opened, and the two Durbanskys, accompanied by Rita, walked out. As she passed, I caught her eye, and in a very friendly manner, I smiled and asked, "Excuse me, you're Rita from Brownstone?"

She slowed down and hesitantly said, "Yes."

I stuck out my hand and introduced myself, "I'm Brent Bingham. You've sent me some letters about some stuff."

She stopped, shook my hand, looked to the ground, and said, "Oh, hello, Brent. It's nice to meet you."

Still in a very friendly tone and smiling, I said, "It's nice meeting you as well. Can I introduce you to the rest of the people you are trying to evict and throw out onto the street?"

She stood there, frozen for a few seconds, and I said, "I'll introduce you to the gang. Rita, meet the gang. Gang, look, it's Rita from Brownstone who's throwing us out."

It took her a few seconds to realize I wasn't being as pleasant as I sounded, and when she realized it, she could only stare at the floor and mumble, "It was nice meeting you all." And then she scurried away.

I felt a couple of pats on my back, and I was proud that I had introduced myself to her and got in her face. I wanted her to realize that her job was a shitty way to make a living. I understand that she was just the 'property manager,' I know she didn't own the company and wasn't the one making company policy. She was just a minion doing her job. But whatever her excuse, you couldn't argue that it's a shitty way to earn a living, and I wanted her to feel that. I think she realized it as she slinked away down the hall.

Sarah told me to relax as we waited and said, "And when we get into the room for mediation, give it a chance."

Reggie added, "Yeah, let's hear what they have to offer us now."

As soon as I heard that from Reggie, I knew we were only as strong as our weakest link. If they dangled a slice of pizza in front of Reggie's face, he would crumble, sell out in a second, and be gone.

We had to stand in the hall for about fifteen minutes until the 'mediator' was ready. Finally, the door opened to Mediation Room number five. I was surprised that there were five of these rooms, and it made me wonder how many people are employed negotiating people out of their homes. We made our way into the room, and since no one wanted to sit near me, I ended up at the front of the table, across from the paralegals and the mediator.

She introduced herself as Michelle Taylor, Mediator for Toronto City Services. With a smile, she explained that she is an impartial third party employed by the City of Toronto. She explained that her job is to help facilitate mutually acceptable agreements and to help keep the system moving. You could tell she had said this a million times before, and this was just another day at the office for her.

She started to talk in a 'matter-of-fact' way and said, "I had the chance to review the file, and upon first review, it appears there is validity that in the interest of the tenants' own safety, the building should be empty in order to complete the repairs."

Everyone sat silent except Brian, who blurted out, "And is there any validity to us staying in the building?"

He waited. Michelle sat there silently, and there was no reply.

He said, "Yeah, that's what I thought."

I'm glad Brian asked cause if I had asked, everyone would have shit on me for being difficult.

Michelle continued, "I've spoken to Mr. Durbansky, and he has said his client is open to offering additional financial compensation for the tenants willing to vacate their units."

I looked at the Durbansky's and wanted to start pressing their buttons. With a smile, I said "OK, so which of you is the senior Durbansky? Who's the boss? Do I talk to you, or do I talk to the mustache?"

They both laughed and put their pens down. I think they knew I was going to make their day enjoyable, and their smiles showed me they would enjoy this.

Michelle interrupted and immediately defended the Durbanskys as if they were all on the same side, "Mr. Bingham, please show some professionalism and respect to this process; we are all here to do a job."

That fired me up, and I replied, "No, we are all not here to do a job. You, the Durbanskys, the adjudicator, the court reporter, security guards. You are all here to 'do a job.' We're here because it's your job to evict us. We're here trying to save our homes; that's what we're doing here. We're not here doing 'a job', so please correct your statement of 'we're all here to do a job, because that, in fact, is wrong. Let me ask the Durbanskys."

I looked at them with a smile but a serious expression: "Gentlemen, is there any room for compromise on letting us stay in the building, even vacating during repairs and paying more rent like you guys want?"

The Durbansky with the mustache looked me dead in the eye and said, "Absolutely not."

I said, "OK, thank you. As long as I'm clear on what's happening here, thank you for the honesty."

Michelle asked the room, "Would anyone like to come in on their own to discuss compensation for leaving the building."

Of course, Reggie's arm shot up in the air first; he replied as soon as Michelle said, 'Would anyone...'

"Yes, I would like to hear what you have to offer." He tried to play it nonchalantly, like taking a buyout was the furthest thing from his mind, "I might as well hear what you have to offer." He was pathetic.

As he said that, he looked around the room as if sitting down with them was just an informative procedure and that he would never accept a deal. It was sad to watch. There's nothing more pathetic than watching a stupid person think he's getting away with something. All you can do is smile and agree with them.

Michelle smiled at Reggie and said, "That's great; who else would like to discuss alternatives before the hearing?"

Almost everyone wanted to hear what was being offered, but a couple of the older guys weren't interested.

Michelle made it around the table to me, and I said, "Yes, I would like to discuss compensation and see if we can negotiate a deal."

Michelle was angry immediately. "Listen, Brent, we are not going to bring you in and have you waste the Durbanskys' and my time. This is a serious process."

I began to get a little upset, so it was time to mess with Michelle; I asked her, "I'm sorry, so I'm clear; are you saying I don't have a right to see what's being offered by these gentlemen? You're not letting them offer me what they are offering everyone else? OK. So that's what I'm telling the adjudicator when I go back into that room? That I wasn't allowed to negotiate because YOU felt I was difficult?" I looked at mustache Durbansky and winked when I finished.

They looked at each other, both with smiles and a little laugh.

The mustache Durbansky, agreed that I had a right to negotiate and said, "Of course, we want to talk with you, Mr. Bingham."

I turned and said to Michelle, "Can you please note that the Durbanskys are willing to negotiate with me, as opposed to the 'impartial' mediators' recommendation of not to negotiate with me? Thank you. Also, who do you work for? You work for the City of Toronto, right? You don't work for these two gentlemen, you're not their negotiating partner, you're not here to make their day easier, you have a job to do, you are supposed to be impartial, so please, start being impartial."

Michelle stood and said to the room, "Looks like everyone else is coming in to discuss real options. "

She was staring directly at me when she said, 'Real options.'

The other Durbansky said, "We'll start with Reggie in about five minutes. If you could all please go back into the hall, we'll come get you when we're ready. Thank you, everyone."

Back in the hallway, we all stood silent for a few moments. I think everyone knew it was time to take the money and run.

People started whispering, "How much do you think it will be?"

Nolan and Krystle approached me and said, "Brent, this is the end of the line for us; we're going to be leaving."

I was a little surprised, but they were just being honest about it. We all knew that we would have to crumble sooner or later, and the time was upon us. I looked at them and said, "Guys, everyone has to do what's right for themselves; no judgment for what people have to do and no hard feelings at all, but please, just make sure you make them pay; don't take their first offer and make them pay."

They smiled and thanked me. Whatever people decide, there will be no hard feelings. We had gone as far in this process as most people could tolerate; playing chicken with your home is a tough game to play; it isn't for the weak, and I knew many of these people weren't ready to go the distance. They weren't ready to go to the mat with this son of a bitch owner. A couple of them might be, but the old guys weren't; they needed security. Their lives couldn't be up in the air for a year; that'd be too hard on them, it'd be hard on anyone.

We went back to the hallway to wait. Reggie, completely out of breath, asked me, "What are they doing in there? How come I couldn't have stayed?"

I couldn't resist, "I think they're ordering a pizza or something for us; they're getting a slice ready for you."

He looked towards the door with the hopes of pizza being in there, and I walked away. The door opened, and they called Reggie. He struggled to get out of the chair he was sitting in and waddled his way down the hall to the mediation room. As the door opened, I could see everyone in the room with big smiles and extended arms, and they started shaking hands.

Robert approached me and asked, "Well, what do you think?"

I immediately replied, "Oh yeah, he's gone in a second. They'll pull out the checkbook, and he's gone. A lot of these people will take the money, and I can't blame them at this stage; I think this is it; I think this is the end of the line."

Reggie was in there for thirty minutes before he came out smiling. As he walked by us, he stopped and said, "Sorry."

I said, "Don't be; we all have to do what's best for ourselves."

Bob leaned over, looked Reggie in the eye, and, in a voice everyone could hear, said, "Yeah, but you're the first one to crack."

Reggie, with his head down, waddled away from us. Bob said, "Well, that's one down." He stood beside me, looked over the room, and said, "Who's next, I wonder?"

The door opened, and one of the Durbansky's said, "Melissa, you're next."

She made her way to the room and stopped at the door. She turned back, smiled at Robert, and then went in.

Robert leaned over and said, "Melissa is moving back in with her parents for a little bit. She's going to take the money and save for a little while, so she'll be OK. She's got the kids; she can't mess around. I just hope she's in there making them pay."

Melissa was in there for thirty-five minutes, and at one point, we all thought we could hear her crying. We assumed she was playing it up and using everything she could. When she came out, she had a tissue in her hand, was dabbing her eye, and was sniffling. As she passed me and Robert, she gave us a wink and kept going.

One of the Durbanskys, I still had no idea which was which, stuck his head out of the door and yelled out that Bill would be next. They didn't even have the courtesy to come out into the hallway now; it was getting busy, and they had a flow going, a little factory line of buying everyone off and kicking them out of their home.

Bob walked over to me with his arms crossed. He said, "They're picking us off one by one like they're shooting fish in a barrel."

The door opened, and they called for Bill. He didn't hear them and sat there, legs crossed, rubbing his face and looking at the ceiling.

Robert caught his attention and said, "Bill, it's your turn. Get up."

It took Bill a few seconds to get up, and he slowly made his way to the door. As he walked in, he started explaining to one of the Durbanskys the origins of the word 'adjudicator.'

We heard, "Oh, I didn't know that." As the door closed.

I looked at my watch and said, "We have a half hour until lunch, and I'm sure Bill will be in there until then, which will be a good delay for us. We can go for lunch and take some time to regroup and think things through."

Sure enough, Bill was in there for thirty minutes. The Durbanskys came out. One shook his head, the other rubbed his eyes, and Bill just strolled by them. Mustache Durbansky said it was time for lunch and that we would break until one p.m.

I looked at Robert and then the paralegals. I caught their eyes, looked around, and jokingly said, "Where's Michelle? I guess that doesn't matter, does it? You guys kind of run this place anyway, don't you?"

They smiled and, trying to get the better of me, said, "Enjoy lunch, folks. When we return, we will start with you, Mr. Bingham. Please be back promptly."

I smiled, "Of course, I wouldn't miss a second of this, and don't worry, I'll be back on time…promptly."

I told the Durbansky's to enjoy their lunch and asked them, "How's the burger place next door?"

They smiled, shook their heads, and walked away.

We started to make our way out of the building when Robert looked at Bill, "So Bill, what did they offer you,"

Bill went on a ramble about the roots of Rome, Plato, the days of the Senate, and bribes. Even Robert had had enough of Bill; his patience was gone.

He said point blank, "Bill, be quiet; how much did they offer you?" Bill waited till we were outside and said, "Ten thousand."

I thought, 'It's starting to sound like real money; no wonder people are leaving.' I had to ask Bill, "Well, what did you tell them?"

After a long dramatic pause, Bill said, "I said no thank you, and you young gentleman should think about how you are making a living. Then I asked them if they slept OK at night."

Robert laughed and said, "Of course you did, Bill; way to stand strong."

Bill added, "They can just kiss my ass."

And on those last words, we went to lunch.

Chapter 21

We went outside, and Eric was there to greet us, "So, how did it go? What's happening?"

I told him everything that happened, "It's a Renoviction factory in there. They all know each other, the lawyers, the adjudicators, the mediator; every day, they all work together. They are all here for the system and not the tenant; it's fixed."

I told him I didn't feel like eating, so we went to a nearby coffee shop. Everyone that was left from the group went except Bill and Tommy; they just wanted to sit on a bench outside. When we got to the coffee shop, we saw Rita waiting in line. No one said anything to her, but I wasn't going to hold back; I wasn't going to be rude or intimidating; I would just be polite and 'jokey.' She glanced over her shoulder, saw us, and turned away."

I immediately waved and said, "Hey, Rita, Rita! What's good here?"

The guy in line between us looked at me.

I apologized and said, "I'm sorry. It's OK, I know her. She's trying to illegally evict me and throw all of us out of our homes; sorry to bug you."

The guy looked at me with a quizzical, funny look, and I said, "No, seriously, just around the corner, at the Landlord and Tenant Board, this is our whole building; she's trying to evict all of us illegally."

I looked towards Rita and asked, "What do you recommend, Rita? But keep it cheap. You know, I might be homeless after today."

I looked at the guy in front of me. His expression turned from comical to serious, and he turned to look at Rita. He didn't say anything and looked at her. As soon as he did that, she put her order on the counter and walked out.

I mockingly said, "Bye, Rita."

Sarah started getting angry with me. "Brent, stop being so mean. Behave yourself. She's just doing her job."

I looked at Sarah, smiled, and laughed. I wasn't going to say anything else, but when we sat down, Sarah kept giving me shit about my behavior until I couldn't hold back any longer.

I replied to Sarah by speaking to the group, "Folks, this is it. We are at the end of the line. Sarah is criticizing me for what I'm doing and for my behavior. Does anyone else have a problem with my attitude or actions?"

Robert and Bob encouraged me, and Bob said, "As rough around the edges as Brent is, he has this building's best interests at heart. I trust him. Go get 'em, Brent."

"Thanks, guys. Now, Sarah, with all due respect, we're past being nice. They are buying us off one by one in there and making the building weaker and weaker. At the end of this mediation, only two or three of us will be left in the building, and I know one of them won't be you. So, you do what you have to, and I'll do what I have to, but in the meantime, don't tell me what to do, and please, shut up."

A couple of people clapped, so I knew there was some agreement with me.

I looked at Robert and asked, "What do you think?"

Robert stood up, started pacing, and said, "Well, at this rate, it might be hard to get in front of the adjudicator again; if these guys push and stretch out the mediations, this might get pushed and rescheduled, and who knows when that would be."

I sat looking at Robert and said, "Are you kidding me? Our plan is to run out the clock? Not only is our lawyer going for an adjournment, which seems like it isn't going to happen, but now we're going to keep passing the puck around, hoping time runs out too? That's encouraging."

Robert started to get pissed off and started turning a different shade of red.

I said, "Robert, I'm just kidding; I'm just trying to make light of a fucked-up situation."

Robert asked the group for ideas.

Krystle said, "Why don't we just go in there and fire Wessler? We'll tell the adjudicator there's been a problem with our lawyer, and we need to get a new one."

Then Sarah piped up, "Yeah, where is he? Why isn't he helping us get more money? Why isn't he in there with us?"

I said to Sarah and the whole group, "He can't help you negotiate your way out of the building. He's here to help us stay in our units; that's the reason we retained him. If I'm not mistaken, the group's goal was to stay in the building, but I guess you'd rather be bought out."

I asked the group again, "So, what's our plan? What do we do, guys?"

We all just looked around at each other, and no one had anything to say; we were at a loss for words; the end of the road was here, and there wasn't a game plan; there wasn't any more time to huddle and regroup. We didn't even know where our lawyer was. As soon as we said yes to mediation, he was gone. He knew he wouldn't be needed unless there were holdouts, which he probably assumed there wouldn't be.

People finished their coffees and then started to hang out and smoke outside. I told Nolan and Krystle what they offered Bill, and they said that might be their price; they knew we were in a losing position, and they didn't want to go through the bullshit of a long fight with the owner.

I told them I understood. I looked at the clock and said, "I'm going to head back; I'll see you guys there."

I headed back, and Eric came with me. He asked me what's happened so far, and I tried to explain without getting angry, "The adjudicator said we had to sit down with them and a mediator to try to mediate resolving the situation. I tried to 'object,' but the adjudicator told us we were going for mediation whether we wanted to or not. Everyone in there is a part of the system, and it's keeping all of them employed."

Just then, I saw the Durbanskys coming and pointed them out to Eric.

He immediately ran over to them to get some close-up confrontational footage. He went 'indie' journalist immediately, asking, "Is this all your firm does, evictions and work at the Landlord and Tenant Board? Do you guys do anything else? What other slumlords do you work for? Do you pay the Alliance of Commercial Housing Rentals? How much do you pay them?"

The mustache Durbansky looked and glared at Eric when he mentioned the Alliance.

Eric looked at him, "Hey, mustache man, I recognize you. You were at our rally at the building, watching us from across the street. I remember your mustache; you've been watching us all along, haven't you?"

Mustache Durbansky glared at him and took off when he asked that.

Eric asked one last question before they reached the door: "How much money do you guys give to the Alliance?"

The Durbansky, without the mustache, turned as he opened the door, gave Eric the finger, and went inside. As they walked down the hallway, the non-mustached Durbansky kept turning and waving back for Eric to leave, he was pretty pissed off, and Eric was laughing the whole time.

Eric put the camera back up on me, and I summed up the situation, "This could be it. I will try to hang on as long as I can, but after mediation, I don't know who will be remaining. They'll buy four or five people out, no problem. If they want me out, they might offer a bigger buyout. Right now, it's at ten thousand dollars; that's what they offered Bill, but I don't want to leave for less than twenty-five. If they offer twenty-five, I might take it."

From behind the camera, Eric said, "Bingham, no one would blame you for taking the money; if it's the right thing to do."

I shook my head, looked down, and replied, "It's defeat; if I take the money, they win. If they offer me twenty twenty-five thousand to leave, that's real money to me; I can make a change with that. But twenty thousand dollars to the owner is just another entry on the balance sheet, 'Brent Bingham Eviction Payment' Twenty thousand."

I was almost in tears knowing we were close to the end, "I'm going to do everything I can to fight and resist this guy. I'm not going to take anything less than twenty thousand dollars. I don't want to be a sell-out, Eric. I want to fight the 'good fight.' I want to be there until the wrecking ball forces me out. I want to be the guy that turns down the money, the guy that tells them to go fuck themselves, and the guy that sticks it out till the eleventh hour and wins the battle. I want to stay in the building, and I want to help these people keep their homes, no matter what it costs me."

Eric agreed, adding, "Yeah, but can Bingham live off principles and morals? You'll end up with nowhere to live. Is that the smartest move? No, it's not, so you might have to take the money and run."

We were both silent for a bit, looking up and down the street. I watched the people walking by this building and wondered if they knew the bullshit and the pain that was going on inside. Everyone was back from the coffee shop and proceeded inside; I hung back and leaned against the wall.

I said to Eric, "I'm going back in. We'll probably be done when we come out. If I walk up to you and the camera and start speaking, I didn't bite, I stuck to my guns, stood strong, and rejected their offer. But if I come out, look at you in silence, and just walk away, it means I sold out, and I am on my way to get very drunk."

Eric only said one thing, "Go get 'em, Bingham."

I opened the door and went in. When I walked through those doors back into the building, a sudden rage came over me, and I got very angry, I'm not sure why, but all of a sudden, I was pissed off. I didn't know whether to go back to the hearing room or the mediation room, so I went to the hearing room and sat around for a few minutes. No one was coming, so I went to the hallway and saw Rita by the Mediation room with everyone else.

I approached her and asked, "How was your lunch?"

With a sour look, she asked, "You think this is a joke, Brent?"

I was angry, and I wasn't going to hold back on her. "You're the only joke in here, Rita. You probably think you're a good person, don't you? You probably buy your kids Christmas and birthday presents and take them to the movies. You probably try to behave like a moral, decent person, and maybe you even go to church and pray to God. But then you come to do this for a living, illegally evicting people and throwing people out on the street. You're the joke, Rita; your life is the joke. I'd hate to live like you."

I chuckled, "You want to see a joke? Wait till I post about you on our Facebook site; you know we have a couple hundred thousand followers, Rita? That's no joke. I'm going to make you part of the story, and I'm going to put your face all over this and tag the shit out of you. It's going to be easy putting a target on you, Rita. I'm sure people will want to reach out to you and talk about 'Renovictions' and evictions. And don't worry Rita; I'm sure they'll see it from your point of view."

I smiled and said, "Let's get this done. You guys said I was next up, so let's go."

Rita looked up and said, "There's been a slight change of plan. Sarah, you will be going in next, so everyone, please have a seat, and we'll be with you as soon as we can. Sarah, we'll call on you shortly."

We all sat down, and Sarah looked pleased as punch to be going in next; she looked at me, smirked, and said, "I guess they know who they can work with and who they can't. See Brent, it pays to be nice."

I looked at Robert, who overheard it and was shaking his head in disbelief.

I looked back at her and said, "You're right, Sarah. I should be more cooperative and start working with the people who are trying to throw us out."

Sarah was only in there for ten minutes; there was no way she was in there negotiating or haggling at all; they said a number, and like the dumbass she was, she took it; she probably took the first offer. Judging by how long it took, they already had the contract ready; she just needed to sign. They knew a mile away that they were going to pay this little girl as little as they had to. Poor girl, her stubbornness and stupidity cost her, but she came out walking proud, with her head held high. As she walked by us, she gave me a little giggle; I looked back at her, thinking, poor thing, she has no clue she probably could have gotten double what they offered her, but oh well, I guess it's every person for themselves.

Next, they called Brian into the room. He looked back and said this wouldn't take too long.

I wanted him to drag out the meeting as long as he could, so I said, "No, Brian, remember, take your time, and honestly try to negotiate for a number you think is right,"

Brian came out thirty minutes later. He sat back down on the bench with us and didn't say a word. I looked down at his hands, and he held up ten fingers. At least we knew what they were offering, and it was offensive that they didn't even 'up the offer' for Brian, who had been in the building for thirty years—such immoral people.

Next up was Robert; he walked by as he headed in and said, "This should be interesting."

They held the door open for him, and he disappeared into the room. When he went in, it made me wonder what I was going to say when I was in there. I hadn't thought about it yet, and since I was going in 'not to win,' I hadn't thought about my strategy.

The Durbanskys and the Mediator are all part of a system that churns people like me out of their homes daily. Picture the Tenant Board as a giant meat grinder. The poor existing renters fall in the top, and as the landlords, lawyers, mediators, and adjudicators turn the grinder of evictions, and new higher-paying renters are churned out the bottom for higher profits.

After thirty minutes, Robert came out and sat back down with us; even though our negotiations were supposed to be 'confidential' in the room, we didn't care. Robert walked towards me, and his fingers were at his side, indicating thirteen thousand. When I saw that, I realized they were starting to offer some real money, and they wanted us out of there. After Robert, it was Nolan and Krystle, and we knew they would be taking the deal; thirteen thousand would be enough for them to leave.

We sat in that hallway for most of the day; there wasn't much to look at. As I was looking around, I noticed little plaques by each door. I got up and started to stroll around. I walked by the first door with a little placard on it, and it was inscribed, *'This hearing room is generously donated to the Landlord and Tenant Board by Amelian Canada. 'We are proud to provide responsible, equitable housing to the community.'*

The funny thing is Amelian Canada is one of the worst slumlords in the country. As I walked the halls, the more plaques I saw; they were everywhere; they were on the walls of every room, on the artwork, and even in the bathrooms, and everything was a donation. I recognized some of the names on the plaques, 'Amelian,' 'Novastar,' 'CadREIT,' and 'Bluewin'; these were some of the worst landlords in Canada, and most of the other plaques were the names of developers and law firms. I guess the price of making money in the 'rental housing market' starts with donating to the Landlord and Tenant Board. The more I walked and looked around, the more I wondered if there was a donation by the Durbanskys somewhere in this place.

When I returned to the mediation room, Nolan and Krystle were still inside; Brian and Tommy were asleep; Bill was looking up at the ceiling; Robert was pacing; and Bob was playing with a cigarette. Looking at us as a group, we were a real motley crew, but that didn't mean it was OK to evict us. The door opened, Nolan and Krystle came out and they didn't look happy; Krystle was so mad she was beet red. I went to speak with them as they were leaving, and Nolan gave a slight shake of his head with a strange look in his eye and signaled behind him. I looked back, and the Durbanskys were standing at the door, staring at them as they left.

I texted Eric immediately and told him to ask Nolan what had happened. Once Nolan and Krystle were out of sight, the Durbanskys called Bob into the room. I looked over at Bob. He stood up, straightened his ballcap, mockingly adjusted his pants, looked at me, and said, "Don't go anywhere; this won't take long."

He walked into the room, and as soon as the door closed, it flew back open. Bob walked back to his seat on the bench and sat down, stretched out his legs, put a cigarette in his mouth, pulled his hat down over his eyes, and crossed his arms.

I looked back at the door; one of the Durbansky's was standing with his hands on his hips, all pissed off, shaking his head, and the other one with the mustache was smiling and laughing.

I asked Bob, "What the hell did you say in there?"

Bob, who is now a champion in my book, said, "I walked in, told them to go fuck themselves, and I walked out."

All I could do was laugh.

They called Brian's name next. Bill had to elbow him to wake him up. When Brian came to, he looked around and asked Bill, "What the hell are you doing?"

Bill motioned towards the door, Brian looked over, and the mustache Durbansky waved him in. Brian got up and slowly made his way to the room. Once the door closed, I grabbed my phone and called Eric; he picked up almost immediately and put Nolan on, who was pissed off and started ranting right away. I told him to slow down, take your time, and just tell me what happened; I had to wait for him to catch his breath.

Once he was breathing normally, he started off by saying, "Krystle is pissed. They wouldn't budge, they started with the four-thousand-five hundred bullshit, and then they would only raise the offer in increments of five hundred. We got to ten thousand, and that's as high as they would go; they wouldn't go any higher. We didn't want to take it, so we refused it and said we weren't going to leave. Then they started to threaten us, telling us that we would have to leave temporarily for some of the repairs, and hopefully, there wouldn't be any delays with the work. They started to say things like, well, there could be delays; if it's the plumbing that needs repair, it might need to be ripped out through the whole building, who knows how long something like that could take, it could take months. Are you ready to live somewhere for two, three, six, or twelve months? That is, if your unit is still there, it might be remodeled to a three- bedroom unit, and unit Sixteen may not even be unit Sixteen anymore; who knows what will happen. He kept going on like that, and Krystle caved."

I could hear Krystle curse in the background, and I swear I heard Nolan flinch as she hit him, then he corrected himself, "I mean, we caved; it was bullshit; they were doing everything they could to avoid giving us another dime, they wouldn't budge, they wouldn't go higher than ten thousand. We couldn't take it anymore, Brent; it was too much, and we just wanted out; tell Robert we're sorry; this bullshit was just too much for us."

I said, "Don't apologize, you did what was right, you did what you had to, don't feel bad at all, you got ten grand out of them, come on, that's a win, now you can go and buy a house and forget about this bullshit. You did good, don't worry."

"Brent, I trust you. Don't say a thing to anyone, please; the Durbanskys were adamant; I'm not supposed to talk to anyone; they were very insistent."

I said, "Don't worry. Brian is in there now saying no, and then it's Tommy and then me. I'm going in that room just to hear their number and to bust their balls. I'm going in to have some fun, so don't worry, I won't jeopardize anything. I'll see you guys back at the apartment after this, and by the way, I'll be going to the liquor store on the way home. I'll be getting absolutely hammered tonight, please feel free to join me."

Nolan laughed and said, "Yeah, I'm going there now. I'll be way ahead of you. See you soon."

I hung up and sat on the bench. Robert looked at me, and I mouthed the word 'ten.' He looked back at me quizzically, and I looked back, also wondering. We were curious about why they went to thirteen with Robert and only ten for the others; now, I was left wondering what they would be offering me when I went in. The door opened, and Brian walked out. I looked at my watch, and he had been in there for twenty minutes; I guess that was as long as he needed to say no.

I looked down the hall at the Durbansky's, and the mustached one called for Tommy.

Tommy looked down the hall and said, "Nope."

The Durbansky didn't seem pleased, "But Mr. Tommy, everyone has to come in."

Tommy didn't hold back, "I don't have to do anything, young man. I'm not mediating, so go fuck yourself and your brother or whoever the hell he is."

All I could think was, 'Damn, Tommy coming alive in the ninth!'

Apparently, that was enough for them; they just moved on to me and said with a sigh, "Well, Mr. Bingham, it looks like it's your turn."

As I started to walk towards the room, the guys wished me luck. I looked at the Durbanskys, who were having a little chuckle. Behind them, I could see Michelle and Rita sitting in their chairs at the table, Rita had her head down, and Michelle had a pissed off sour look on her face. She looked at the door, and when our eyes met, I could see the disdain she had for me, and that's when I knew I was going to have some fun with this.

As I approached the Durbansky's, I extended my hand in good faith. With a smile, I said, "Well, gentlemen, I hope we can keep it professional. I hope we can have some progressive talks, we're all gentlemen, right?"

They laughed, shook my hand, and said, "I don't think we'll have a problem, Mr. Bingham."

I walked in ahead of them. Rita said hello, but Michelle didn't even acknowledge me. I pulled up a chair and said, "Hi, Rita."

I cleared my throat and said, "Michelle."

There was not even a reply or an acknowledgment, and I thought she was supposed to be the impartial one. As the Durbanskys sat down, I asked them where they went for lunch. The mustache one laughed and said, "The Porterhouse."

I replied, "Ooh nice, pretty pricey; I guess representing slumlords pays pretty well."

Then Michelle interrupted us, "Mr. Bingham, please keep it professional, we are here to have a friendly conversation. We're here for one reason: to come to an agreement regarding your residency at Three-Ninety-One Empire Avenue."

I smiled and interrupted her, "When you say we're here to come to an agreement regarding my residency, do you mean we are here to negotiate how I might be able to stay in my place?"

She looked at me, and her smile was so fake I could tell I was already starting to piss her off, "Mr. Bingham, I think it's clear that it's not possible for you to stay in the unit."

Now I was pissed, time to play stupid with her. "I beg your pardon; I can't stay in the unit. Did I miss the hearing?"

I looked at the Durbanskys, "Hey, Durbanskys, did we have a hearing? Did I miss the hearing?"

They shook their heads and replied, "No, you didn't, Mr. Bingham. You didn't miss anything."

Michelle interjected, "Mr. Bingham, what I meant was, we are here to see if we can reach an agreement; the Durbanskys are here to negotiate on the basis of you leaving the building; that is the position they are taking. If we cannot work out an arrangement based on that, then there will be a hearing, and yes, it will be decided by the adjudicator, but for now, we're here. Would you like to propose what you think would be a fair offer?"

She lobbed it over to me, so it was time to have some fun. I know everyone in this room was looking at me like I was an ignorant idiot, so I figured it was time to play the part. I knew the one thing that would piss them off and force their hand was just to run the clock out; if I just blabbered on and filibustered, eventually they would get pissed off and tell me what they wanted to offer. Negotiating is like sex; you never want to be first.

I looked at the Durbansky's and Michelle. I scrunched my eyebrows, looked into the air, and acted stupid and unsure of what was happening. I started to say, "Well, Michelle, I hadn't really thought about it. I don't know how to put a price on relocating, market rates, and what things cost…"

I kept going on and on and on about nothing in particular; I talked about the cost of parking; I talked about driving versus taking the bus. By the time I got to talking about the difference in the price of coffee in different neighborhoods, the non- mustached Durbansky was so pissed off he cracked.

He leaned forward, looked at his partner, and said, "Ten thousand dollars, ten thousand is what we'll offer you. It's yours, tax-free. Ten thousand dollars today, right now, that you can walk out of this room with. Imagine that."

I played into him a little and started shaking my head up and down, and I said, "Ten thousand dollars? That's tempting. How did you come up with that, like, how do I know this is fair?"

The mustache man leaned in and tried to rope me in: "Mr. Bingham, this offer is more than most people are offered. In the scheme of things, this is very generous. We base it on a few factors, the rent you are paying now, the rent increase you might be facing, and how long you have been in the unit. We take into consideration additional costs you might incur and hopefully we try to put some spending money in your pocket as well.

I smiled, "OK, sounds kind of fair."

I thought I'd have some fun with Michelle for a little bit. I wanted to see what she thought of the ten-thousand-dollar offer. I turned and looked at her with the look of 'well?' She raised her eyebrows, smirked, and gave a couple of approving subtle nods.

Holy shit, I couldn't believe it; the 'impartial' party was encouraging me to take the deal, she may not be saying anything, but the body language, the look on her face, and the nodding were definitely indications that she was trying to influence me. This whole process stunk.

I looked at Rita, who had just been sitting there silently, not saying a word.

I smiled and said, "Rita, you have just been sitting there in silence this entire time. Why am I talking to these people when you're the one with the calculator and checkbook in front of you? You're the one tallying up everyone's exit fees, and you're the one in charge of the checkbook."

She put her pen down, removed her glasses, and looked at me. Now was my chance to have an honest conversation with her.

I looked her directly in the eyes, "Rita, you guys never came to me to talk about this; there was never any goodwill on your side; please don't think I'm a difficult guy; you left no option. Had you come to me and honestly said, 'We want to renovate, and we want to raise your rent,' this could have gone a different way; I would have agreed to pay more rent. But not once, not once, did you attempt to communicate with me, so here we are. Let's be honest, Rita. The only real question is, 'How much money did Liang Jiang give you to spend on us? What's the amount he's given you to buy off the building and clear it out? And, let me guess, how much of a bonus do you get for keeping it low? Come on, Rita, we're all adults here. Let's be honest, how much can you make personally from evicting and undercutting us?"

Michelle tried to interrupt me, "Mr. Bingham, we…"

I interrupted her, "Michelle, the grown-ups are speaking now. I'm speaking with Rita, and we are negotiating, which is exactly what we are here to do, so please do not interrupt us again. Thank you."

I didn't even wait for her to respond. I turned back to Rita, "I'm sorry for the interruption, Rita. So where were we? That's right. How much did Liang-Jiang give you to spend on us?"

Mustache man interrupted and said, "Well, Mr. Bingham, ten thousand dollars. Do we have a deal?"

I shot back immediately, "Fifty Thousand."

The non-mustache Durbansky leaned back in frustration, rubbing his eyes. He threw his pen up in the air, and it bounced on his notepad.

Michelle turned red and started in on me immediately. "This is exactly why we didn't want to bring you in, Mr. Bingham; we only wanted to have serious discussions."

Confused, I said, "What do you mean we? You keep saying 'we,' you aren't acting too impartially, Michelle. Are you afraid of offending your work partners sitting beside you? Are you afraid you might not get the same Christmas present from these guys or that the next envelope might be a little light?"

The mustache Durbansky calmly asked, "Well, Mr. Bingham, in the spirit of productive negotiations, let me ask you, how did you come to the figure of fifty thousand dollars."

I smiled and said, "Thank you for hearing me out. Well, now that I thought about it, I have been able to calculate what moving would cost me. When I moved into Three-Ninety-One Empire Avenue, I planned to live in a building that was a little run down, maybe not in the best neighborhood but had cheap rent. When I made comparisons, this place was four to five hundred dollars a month cheaper than anything comparable, saving me six thousand dollars a year. If I was going to look at a comparable place now; it's probably seven to eight hundred dollars more a month, so that would be an expense of an extra eight thousand four hundred dollars a year. So, if you add it up, what I'd be losing in savings and paying out in extra rent over the next four years is approximately thirty thousand dollars. Then I factored in moving costs, additional transit/commuting time, and expenses that I estimated to be about ten thousand dollars, and that would bring us to around forty thousand dollars."

The Durbanskys looked at each other confused, and the mustache Durbansky asked, "OK, that's forty, so why fifty?"

I said with a completely straight face, "The other ten? That's for you guys being monumental dickheads and putting me through all this bullshit."

When Michelle replied, her voice was angry; there was almost a growl to it; she was pissed that I was messing with her this entire time.

She said, "When you came in here, you didn't know how much moving would cost. Now you're telling me you thought of all this just now?"

I looked at her and winked. I turned to Rita and said, "I'll tell you what, Rita, I'll waive the ten-thousand-dollar dickhead penalty in good faith. I'll agree to forty. What do you say, done deal? I'll walk out that door, and you'll never have to think about Brent Bingham again. Imagine that, forty thousand dollars, and I'm gone. Tell me, Rita, what do I need to do today to get you into this deal?" I smiled a used car salesman grin, winked, and shot her the finger guns.

She closed her book on the table, and said, "It's too high. Come down, and maybe we can talk."

I was surprised she even replied, but her reply piqued my interest, so I said, "Thirty-five."

Surprisingly, she replied again, this time saying fifteen. Interesting, she was starting to budge, and honestly, if she offered thirty thousand, I'd be gone in a second.

I said, "Rita, I'm sorry, but I can't accept that. It's just not economically feasible at this point in time."

Surprisingly, she came back with a counteroffer. She said, "Brent, I can offer you seventeen thousand dollars. That's the highest I can go; I can't go a penny more."

I looked at the mustache Durbansky and then at Michelle, and both had surprised looks on their faces.

The mustache Durbansky looked at me and said, "I know you think I'm lying, but you are being offered one of the best offers I've ever seen in this room."

I sat there in silence, and Michelle, who I figured was the weakest person in the room, cracked first and said, "Is that acceptable? Do we have a deal? Is that how much you want?"

I looked back at Rita, apologized to her for not being able to accept the offer, and said in Michelle's direction, "No, this will not suffice; I think we should see what the 'Adjudicator' has to say about it. Thank you, Durbansky's, good luck in there. Rita, thank you for negotiating with me, but the offer is too low. Respectively, I have to decline. And folks, the next thing I say is directed at Michelle, not you Rita or you guys either."

I looked at Michelle and said, "And you, you should be ashamed of yourself, do your fucking job; you're a sell-out, selling out the people you're supposed to be helping; you're disgusting."

Michelle started to scream, "MR. BINGHAM. THIS MEETING IS OVER!"

I chuckled, looked across the table, and said to Michelle, "I know it is. That's why I said it."

I stood up and walked out of the room.

Chapter 22

When I walked out of that mediation room, I thought I would feel good, but I didn't—I felt terrible. I knew I didn't stand a chance, but being in that room, the realization hit me hard. There was no chance of beating these guys; they would win no matter what. I walked to the bench and sat down. I put my head into my hands and felt defeated.

The door opened, and they all came out: the Durbanskys, Rita, and Michelle; they walked out smiling and laughing; they didn't even turn their heads or bat an eye in our direction when they walked by us, which made me feel even worse. But what really hurt was that the system supported this, and the system supported them. In society's eyes, they were the respectable ones - they were the ones looked upon as 'productive members of society.' Yet they weren't doing any good for society; they were the exact opposite; they actually hurt society, they ruined lives of many, for the benefit one or two.

As the group of greed walked away, I pictured Kerwin Cummings walking with them. I had a sinking hollow feeling in my stomach, and I was getting scared; I was watching in real-time how people are pushed into the streets and become homeless, and I wanted to throw up.

We were sitting in the hallway, unsure of what to do next. There were six of us left: Robert, Bill, Brian, Bob, Tommy, and myself. This left me wondering if anyone would care about us now. But at least we still had Bo; people would care about him.

We were there for about five minutes when we saw Wessler approaching us. No one said anything to him when he came and stood beside us. He looked at us and said, "Six of you left; that's more than I thought there would be. Everyone else took a deal?"

Bob looked at him and said, "Yup, it's only us and Bo remaining; I guess it's up to you now?"

Wessler sat on the bench and clumsily started digging through his bag. He was awkwardly pulling out papers and file folders. I could tell he was noticeably nervous. I looked at Robert, who looked at me and rolled his eyes. Wessler looked up at us standing around him. It was a pathetic sight. We were looking down on this awkward, unorganized man, and he was responsible for our destiny.

He looked up and asked no one in particular, "So, what did they offer you guys, just so I know what I'm dealing with."

I didn't appreciate that he was asking; a weird feeling came over me when he asked it. I felt I was getting backed into a corner. I started to feel that no one was there to help me, and I started to think that Wessler wasn't there to help me either.

Robert told him, ten thousand and he was surprised. He said he didn't think it would be that much and asked, "You guys turned that down? That wasn't enough for you?"

I thought, 'Wow, even our lawyer thinks we should just leave.'

After a few minutes of Wessler getting his papers together, he looked at his watch and said it was time to go; Robert asked him again, "So Richard, what happens now?"

As he scrambled to get himself together, he said, "Well, now we go in front of the adjudicator, we ask for the adjournment, he'll set a date, and we'll come back then."

Robert looked at me with a scrunched face, and I could see the concern in his eyes as he asked, "And what if we don't get an adjournment? What happens then?"

Wessler said, "Don't worry, we'll get the adjournment."

I thought Robert was going to punch him in the face when he said that.

Robert asked again, "Well then, just to make me feel better, let's say we don't get it; what's going to happen?"

Robert turned to me and shook his head in frustration.

Wessler looked at his watch and then at us, "The adjudicator will hear both sides. He'll listen to our arguments for not leaving and theirs for why you should. They'll pull out the reports, and we'll have to refute them..."

I looked around, put my hands up in a questioning manner, and said, "And who do we have to refute them? How are we going to fight? How are we going to prove our point?"

Wessler said, "That's where I come in." And he headed down the hall. Robert and I had to laugh, it was all we could do.

We entered the hearing room, Rita and the Durbanskys were already there but no adjudicator.

Wessler took a seat at the table, and we all sat in the row behind him. The Durbanskys had piles and piles of papers in front of them, and our guy had a notepad and a file folder. We were definitely outmatched. As we waited, the room was dead silent; all you could hear was the hum of the lights and Bob's congested breathing. No one felt like talking on either side.

We were there for about fifteen minutes before the adjudicator came in; he sat at his table and pulled out some papers; he was there for about a minute before he even said anything; I looked at the time, and I started getting really pissed off. It was almost two fifteen, we were supposed to start at two, and we only had until three pm, and this guy was dragging his ass. If we start now, that'll give us less than an hour to decide the fate of our lives; yeah, this system cares about us - what a sham.

He didn't even look up at us and said, "I have read the application; I will be honest; it looks fairly straightforward. I'm ready to rule on this if both parties would like to skip statements and proceed to the ruling."

Robert and I looked at each other in bewilderment. Here we were, thinking that today's appearance would be a request to adjourn, but here we are, and this guy is ready to make a ruling, which I'm guessing won't be in our favor.

I looked at Wessler, and he stood up. "Uh, Mr. Higgins, I'd like to request an adjournment. As you can see, the number of reports and engineering plans we received at our office is overwhelming. Based on that, we're requesting more time to review them, to have our experts look at them, and determine the validity of their request to remove the tenants from the building. Thank you," and he sat down.

I whispered to Robert, "Are you fucking kidding me?"

I couldn't believe that was all he had to say; that was our 'day in court' two fucking lines; the adjudicator says he's ready to rule, and our guy asks to adjourn to a later date? I didn't want to believe it, but what they say about government employees is true: they are useless and unfireable, and their performance reflects that.

This guy had our lives in his hands, and the best he could come with was 'Can I get more time?' It was just as I thought, this guy didn't give a shit and didn't care what happened to us, even the people that the system put in place to help us, the mediator, the adjudicator, and even our lawyer; the lawyer who was provided to us by the system didn't care at all. We were set up to lose from the beginning.

The other Durbansky immediately stood and said, "Mr. Higgins, we have been in communication with the tenants since day one of ownership, which is over six months; we have been sending letters to the tenants constantly, and their counsel has been well aware of all communications since day one of his involvement, which is almost as long. I would like to say that we have never heard anything from Mr. Wessler, no requests, discussions, or anything, so here we are. Any further delay is excessive and punitive to our client; we're ready to make fair offers to everyone, considering the circumstances. If Mr. Wessler could talk to his clients, maybe we can resolve this. An adjournment would financially punish my client; he's owned the building for over six months and can't sustain any further delays or losses. Thank you."

Wessler, who was fumbling with some papers on the desk, stood up. Anyone within a mile could see we were way outgunned. He started to speak, and his voice was shaky. "Mr. Higgins, the correspondence my clients received were eviction letters that didn't comply with the Residential Tenancies Act. They weren't legal and should be irrelevant. We haven't been able to get the reports reviewed by our experts, so we are requesting more time."

Again, the other Durbansky jumped out of his chair and spoke immediately. "Mr. Higgins, with all due respect, Mr. Wessler is just playing games. These are obvious stall tactics to impede my client from moving forward. If there are further delays, we may file a tortious interference lawsuit against the tenants for illegally impeding my clients' business activity."

Are you kidding me? My head was about to explode. This guy had totally flipped the table on us and made our side look like the bad guys. From how he presented the situation, even I believed we were the bad guys for not wanting to leave.

I was squirming in my seat when Robert elbowed me. He leaned over and asked, "What is going on here? We're the bad guys?"

I turned to him in total disbelief. My jaw dropped to the floor, and I couldn't believe what I was hearing.

Wessler was speechless; he had nothing to say in response to the Durbanskys.

I couldn't take it anymore; I stood up and did my best to restrain myself, "Your honor, how can we be labeled the bad guys in this situation? This is crazy. All we need is more time; our 'counsel' is obviously inadequate to handle this. I hope you can see that this is just eviction for profit; look at the people he's throwing out: senior citizens, people with disabilities, and a war vet, for goodness' sake. Tommy has lived in the building for forty years, Brian for thirty, and Robert for twenty. They have nowhere to go; these guys are on fixed incomes; where will they go? Their families, their doctors, their friends, everything they know is in this neighborhood, and you're going to kick us out just so this one guy can make more money? I know my name isn't on any of the walls or art in this building, but that doesn't mean I shouldn't be heard. Are you here to help the people or not?"

Robert tugged my sleeve. I looked around and said, honestly, "Come on, folks. We all know what's going on here. How can you all just sit there and do this? Just because he bought the building and is rich doesn't mean he's guaranteed a good 'Return On Investment.' You guys ignore the laws that are supposed to protect us, the vulnerable. You guys should be ashamed of yourselves."

I sat down and just stared straight ahead.

The adjudicator looked at the Durbanskys, took off his glasses, and asked, "Would you gentlemen be willing to sit down with them again to see if we could work this out once and for all."

Mustache Durbansky said, "Yes, of course, we'd be willing to sit down and try to work with the tenants through this unfortunate situation."

"Gentleman, Mr. Bingham, will you sit down with them one more time?"

I put my arms up in the air, conceding, and said, "Why are you even asking? You're going to make me do it anyway, so why bother? Yeah, sure, let's go boys, let's hurry up and get our asses out of that building."

The adjudicator said, "Gentlemen, I must point out that we are getting short on time. To save time, instead of adjourning to the mediation room, I'll leave, and you can use this room. Mustache Durbansky stood up, unbuttoned his jacket, grabbed one of the spectator chairs, spun it around, put one foot on it, and leaned forward with his elbows on his knees. You could tell he was concerned about us with moves like that.

He started with, "Guys, let's just end this. We know it's an unfortunate situation; no one is winning here. My client bought the building, he's going to put a substantial amount of money into it, he wants to make quality units that will be people's homes, and he's not going to see a profit for years."

I started laughing. I was at the back of the room pacing, not manically, just calmly. I looked at Durbansky and Rita, "Aw, thanks, Mustache Durbansky. Sorry, I don't know your name."

He quickly said, "It's Lou."

I kept pacing and said, "That's OK. In my head, you're Mustache Durbansky; it's easier for me. May I ask why we aren't leaving the room, and aren't we supposed to talk one-on-one?"

He took his foot off the chair and started to walk around. He said, "Well, Mr. Bingham, we've run out of time. We need to progress the situation and bring it to an end, and we all need to move on. Aren't you tired of all this bickering? Don't you want it to go away, Mr. Bingham? We want to be fair to all of you, so if you guys agree, we can do this all at once, all the cards on the table."

I said, "Whatever."

Mustache Durbansky went straight into it, "We'd like to offer you twelve thousand dollars each. Considering how long each of you has lived there, we are willing to let you stay for a couple of extra months to make arrangements for relocation. I want to say this is more than a fair offer. Mr. Wessler, I don't know if you'd like to say anything or talk to your clients, but I'll give you a moment to talk it over."

The Durbanskys and Rita left the room; it was just Wessler and us, the obstacles standing in the way of their profits.

Wessler started speaking, saying, "Gentleman, I don't want to influence or interfere. I'm here to help. If you have any questions or want to ask me anything, please go ahead."

Brian asked him right away, "Is it a good deal?"

I couldn't help but smile and chuckle to myself. I was pretty sure I was about to see Wessler start to interfere and influence us. He grabbed a chair and spun it around so its back was facing us. He straddled the chair and sat down. He crossed his arms and leaned forward on the chairback with a look of concern on his face. I was impressed. It was amazing how, suddenly, everyone was so concerned with our well-being.

"Well, gentleman, I see it as a good deal; it's a fair amount and would probably cover your extra costs for a couple of years. If we go in front of the adjudicator, it looks like he will rule in favor of the owner, so it might be best to at least walk away with some money instead of walking away with whatever he rules."

"What happened to our adjournment? How come we didn't get that?" I'm glad Bob asked because I wouldn't have asked so politely.

Wessler didn't have an answer; his weak ass reply only reinforced my opinion of him; he continued with his bullshit explanation, "I thought we were going to get it, but it seems that the 'Board' is shifting; they seem to be ruling in favor of the owners more and more."

I stopped pacing and said to the group, "It was that first letter and that bullshit emergency meeting; that's what sunk us today."

Wessler disagreed. I stopped him in his place and talked right over him to the group. "It was the first letter; it was never a mistake. It was so they could say what they just said to the adjudicator today, 'that we have been aware of this from day one for over six months, which was more than enough time.' We thought it was a mistake, and you said it was a mistake, but it wasn't; it was our ending. And that 'Emergency Meeting' bullshit? The only reason that was ever scheduled, was to push us through the system. It got them their hearing date months sooner than it would have happened."

I wanted to knock Wessler over with my finger as I pointed angrily at him, "And you told us just to ignore those things; well, guess what? We ignored them, and they sunk us today."

There was silence. We all sat in disbelief, realizing we had lost and never stood a chance from day one.

Wessler asked the group, "So what do you guys think? I don't think you are going to get anything better."

It's funny. Wessler said he couldn't represent us when there were discussions of a buyout, yet here he was, working with them on a buyout. We were all quiet; it seemed Wessler was more eager for the deal than us.

After a minute of silence, Brian asked, "Robert, Brent, what do you guys think?"

I had no idea what to say to him, and thank goodness Robert started speaking first, "I don't know Brian; I really don't know. You have to do what's best for you. We knew we weren't going to be able to stay, so maybe this is the win."

Brian turned and looked at me, "Brent?"

I felt so bad. A seventy-year-old man asking me what the best direction for his life would be, 'take the deal or fight to stay?' Poor Brian hadn't realized how shitty and greedy the world had become.

I was going to be honest; I wasn't going to lie to him, "Brian, I don't know what to tell you, Sir. I know we're going to lose; I know we won't be able to stay; and if we stay the course and keep fighting, I don't know what will happen to us; none of us do. I'm going forward and not taking the deal, but I'm prepared to be thrown out with nothing. I don't know where I'll be living, and I won't have much money, but I can still work. I can couch surf for a couple of years until this is sorted out. I'm in this fight and willing to see it to the end."

I smiled at Brian, winked, and said, "Brian, you're like a hundred and ten years old. Your situation is different. If I could walk away with twelve and be happy, I would take it."

Brian thanked me for being honest and said to Wessler, "I'll take it; I'm done."

Tommy, who was quiet during this whole process, looked up and said, "I'm taking it too; I can't stand this bullshit anymore. All I wanted to do was stay in my home; how can they do this? I just want to stay in my home."

I stood there and looked at the other guys. Their expressions and looks in their eyes conveyed the worry and concern they had for the next decision they were about to make.

I looked at Wessler and saw him looking at his watch; I didn't hesitate and said, "Are we keeping you from something, Dick?"

He looked at me, didn't say a word, and looked away. I'm sure he could see the anger on my face and that I had no respect left for him.

Bill, who had been quiet the whole day, said, "I have to agree with Brian and Tommy. If you guys haven't noticed, I'm old too, too old for this fight. Robert, Brent, and Bob, best of luck to you guys, but I'm with Brian and Tommy. I'm out."

It looked as if Wessler was going to try to negotiate for all of us. But I knew he wasn't going to be speaking for me; if it's every man for himself, I'll be doing what I need to do, and it didn't include Wessler.

He looked at us and said, "Well, gentlemen, what do you think? Mr. Bingham, I assume I know your answer."

Rita and the Durbanskys came back in, saying, "Well, gentleman, can we wrap this up? Do we have a deal?"

Wessler replied, "Well, we have three out of six, three who think it's a fair deal and three that don't."

This was definitely some bullshit, not just because Wessler was talking on behalf of the group for money, but now he's also using words like 'we.' But the fucked- up thing is, the 'we' he is referring to is with our opponents and not with us. It reaffirmed our situation; there was nobody on our side.

The non-mustached Durbansky stood up and ushered Bill, Brian, and Tommy out of the room. Brian objected to leaving; he wanted to stay, but they wouldn't let him. Once they had left the room, the adjudicator came back in. He looked around the room and said, "Looks like we're making some progress. Well, Mr. Wessler, are we going to be able to settle this thing before I'm forced to make a ruling?"

Wessler replied, "I don't think so. My three remaining clients are adamant about staying in their units. They feel an agreement, besides a buyout/eviction scenario, can be reached, and they would like to have the adjudicator hear them out and decide on the facts."

The adjudicator sat down and opened his file. "Well, we can, but I can tell you, based on what I have read, I'm leaning toward ruling in favor of the owner. I suggest you gentlemen listen to Mr. Wessler and follow his advice, and Mr. Durbansky, I suggest you try to convince them a little harder. I don't want to have to make a ruling on this."

I had no idea what he meant by that. Why wouldn't he want to rule on this? He has outright said that he's going to rule in favor of the owner; what bloody difference does it make if he rules or not?

Mustache Durbansky asked Wessler if he wanted to step outside for a moment, 'to have a quick word.' I was amazed; what the hell was this bullshit now? Why are these guys going outside, talking, and 'negotiating' without us? What the hell are they even saying to each other without us there? The amount of bullshit going on was unbearable; the more layers I peeled back at this 'Tenant Board,' the more I saw the real purpose of it. It wasn't for the people; it was for money and public relations.

Its sole purpose was to make it look as if it was a fair system, to give the people the 'illusion' that they had somewhere to go and fight, a place where the 'little' man could be heard, a place where injustices are corrected, where wrongs are righted. Little did we know a place like this didn't exist; the landlord-tenant Board was just a sham and a charade of justice; its sole purpose was to be a Public Relations entity for a corrupt industry and to fool the people that the system cared for them.

Wessler returned to the room and approached us; he bent down and said, "Well, gentleman, they have offered fifteen thousand dollars. As you are aware, I'm not allowed to facilitate or negotiate on your behalf when it comes to money…"

"Yet here you are facilitating and negotiating a financial settlement on our behalf," I said it immediately and in pure sarcasm, shaking my head.

He was overstepping his boundaries, and he didn't care. He looked at me and said, "I'm just trying to speed things along and do what's best for everyone."

I was pissed off but too tired to be passionate, "Yeah, who's everyone, 'the Durbanskys? Rita? The Adjudicator? Liang Jiang Huong? Where are we included in that 'everyone,' Mr. Wessler?"

He just ignored me. "Well, gentlemen?"

Bob looked at Robert and me, ignoring Wessler, and asked us, "Guys, what do you think?"

Robert looked at him, then at the floor, and didn't say a thing. Bob looked at me and asked me, "Well?"

I couldn't lie to him, "Bob, I can't advise you; you have to make your own decision. But Bob, whatever you decide, it's been a lot of fun, and you always have my utmost respect. I think you and 'Bo' should be all right with fifteen thousand, but it's your call, and it would be better to end this with some money in your pocket rather than whatever he's going to rule."

He looked at Wessler and said, "I'm out."

"Me too." I looked over, and Robert was holding his head in his hands. "Me too, Wessler, I'm out. Sorry, Brent. This is the end of the road for me. I can't go any further."

He lifted his head from his hands, looked right at me, and said, "Think about it too, Brent; we're talking real money now. I think we have gone as far as we can; it might be time to walk away."

I couldn't read his expression. He didn't look happy or sad; he was expressionless. He looked like he was done, and I couldn't blame him.

My head was down in my hands, and I could feel everyone looking at me. I could hear Wessler's voice saying something, but it was just noise, like everything else that came out of his mouth.

I don't know how much time passed before I heard him ask again, "Well, Mr. Bingham?"

Again, I don't know how much time passed before I replied. I lifted my head out of my hands, looked at Robert, winked, and said, "Time for you to do some work, Dick. Tell the Durbanskys to go fuck themselves; I ain't leaving."

Bob laughed and started clapping.

"Well, I won't do that, but I'll tell them you declined, Bob and Robert, I'll tell them that you guys accept?"

They both agreed, and as soon as Rita and the Durbanskys returned to the room, they said, "So, gentlemen, are we done?"

Wessler replied as if he were disappointed that I was holding out, "Well, we have two out of three, one holdout."

This time, looking like I was getting under her skin, Rita replied, "Let me guess, Mr. Bingham?"

I looked at her, smiled, and said, "I gotta be me."

She wasn't impressed, which made me laugh, which in turn made her storm out, which made me laugh even more.

Robert and Bob left with the Durbansky's, and I was alone with Wessler.

I had to ask him, "Mr. Wessler, I know you don't like me, but what about everyone else: the senior citizens, Melissa and her kids, Brian, Tommy, Bob, and Bo, for God's sake? You don't care about them? Don't you think this is going to hurt these guys? What about Brian, who needs four doctor appointments just to make it through the week? Or Bob, who's close to drinking himself to death now, what do you think is going to happen when you displace them? Twenty, thirty, even forty years in that neighborhood, their friends, their families, do you think it's going to be easy for them?"

He didn't say a word; he just fidgeted with his papers and kept his head down. After a couple of minutes of silence, Mr. Mustache and the adjudicator came in together. Seeing that made me feel that everyone in this room had conspired to get our building emptied in the cheapest and most efficient manner. At this point, my back was up against the wall, and my corner had all but disappeared.

The adjudicator sat down, started speaking, and didn't even acknowledge me. He began by saying that he was pleased that both sides were able to make such progress, and that mutually beneficial agreements could be reached. But what he said next triggered me; it confirmed that my corner was gone and that I was caged.

The adjudicator didn't even look up and continued, "I am disappointed that we weren't able to resolve the problem one hundred percent. I've been told that the last holdout, Mr. Bingham, is behaving and negotiating in bad faith, and it seems that a reasonable agreement will be impossible to reach with him."

This pissed me off even more, but I wasn't surprised; at this point, I knew and accepted the fact that I was the loser in the room.

Wessler stood, and you would have thought he was on their side with his statement, "That is correct, Sir. I have advised Mr. Bingham, and he refuses to negotiate and isn't acting within reason. I advised him that this offer wouldn't get any better and that he should accept it."

I laughed to myself. I raised my arm like I was in class, waiting to be called on. I was ignored as the adjudicator continued speaking to everyone except me.

I finally blurted out, "Sir, can I talk, am I allowed to speak?"

He ignored me and kept talking. "Well, gentleman, I don't see any way to settle this except to issue a 'default ruling,' but before I do, is there anything you would like to add, Mr. Wessler?"

He stood up, said, "No sir," and sat right back down.

As soon his ass hit the chair, I stood up, "Sir, may I add something? I'm not sure what's going on here, but please, can't we make an arrangement for me to stay? I'm open to paying more rent, and I'm open to leaving and coming back when it's done; why can't we negotiate this? Why aren't the rules being applied? All I want to do is stay in my place. Why is there no one to help me? I followed the rules, I didn't do anything wrong, and I'm being thrown out just because I'm poor; please don't throw me out." I was practically begging at this point; my stomach was filled with butterflies, my knees were weak, and I was getting nervous. I was getting scared as the reality of being homeless was getting closer and closer.

"Mr. Bingham, you had your chance of negotiating independently, but now it's gone. Unfortunately, I have to rule, and as per the rules of the Board, this judgment will be final and binding. As a reminder, all conditions and terms will be recognized and enforced by the Sheriff's department, so don't think you will ignore my ruling like you ignored these proceedings and our processes."

As he said that, the security guard from the front desk came into the room; I turned my head and saw him standing at the door with his arms crossed.

The adjudicator didn't let me say anything else and started his ruling, "Mr. Bingham, can you focus, please? My judgment is in favor of One-Four-Seven-Zero- Zero-Seven LLC; I find renovations to be extreme, and in the best interests of the tenant's safety, the building must be vacated while doing such repairs. I find that Mr. Bingham is acting in bad faith and that there isn't a possibility of an agreement because of that. Therefore, Mr. Bingham will accept the amount of seventeen thousand dollars and will adhere to a strict non-disclosure agreement. I'm adding to the arrangement that Mr. Bingham cease and desist all social media activity regarding this matter, and there will be no more talk of 'Renovictions,' evictions, or any other discussions of this matter. I would also like to remind Mr. Bingham that because of this settlement, this is a mutually accepted agreement to leave the building and is not, in fact, an eviction or a 'Renoviction.' You can never say that you were 'evicted, nor can you say that you were 'Renovicted.' You have been well compensated; therefore, we will consider this matter closed. Do you understand everything I have said, Mr. Bingham?"

In a defeatist tone, I asked the adjudicator, "Sir, how can you do this? How can you force me into this, and how can you tell me what I can and can't say? I don't want the money; you can keep it. I want to tell everyone what a corrupt system you have going on here. I want to tell everyone about the affordable housing crisis and how you guys are actually helping to create it. I don't care; I'm going to keep screaming from the rooftops; I'm going to stay online and be more vigilant than ever against all of you guys."

The adjudicator didn't appreciate what I was saying and started losing his cool. "Mr. Bingham, you agreed to enter this procedure knowing my ruling would be final. We're an arbitrator, and our rulings are final and binding. This is all agreed upon between you, the Board, and your representation. Mr. Wessler, maybe remind your client of how things work."

As he said that, Wessler slid a piece of paper in front of me with my signature that was part of the package I signed when retaining him.

I read it and said, "Yes, Sir, I understand, but at the time, I wasn't aware of how corrupt this Board actually is. I didn't realize that all you are is a spin doctor agency; you're Public Relations for a corrupt, crooked industry, plain and simple. You're here to silence anyone and everyone that is getting screwed by their landlords so it doesn't make it to the press; no wonder we never hear anything about this issue in the papers or media; you buy everyone off, forcibly silencing them. Well, I won't be quiet; I'm going to keep telling everyone what's really going on here; you can't shut me up."

He didn't hesitate to respond and started threatening me immediately on behalf of my foreign landlord owner, "Mr. Bingham, if you say anything or continue online, you will be opening yourself up to a lawsuit. The Durbanskys will commence civil hearings and will sue you for your settlement, for anything you might have, and for anything you might ever have or ever earn. If you think you're poor now, wait until they get through with you. You'll be wishing you took the money and shut up. Now, I suggest you stop talking."

I was speechless and filled with bewilderment; all I could do was stare blankly at him. They had their own rule of law here, and it was whatever the guy at the front of the room thought it should be. I don't know what happened next or how long I was in there, but when I 'came to,' I was sitting on the bench in the hallway, and I was alone. I looked around, and there was no one, no lawyer, no reporters, no politicians, and no fellow tenants, just me and the silence of the hallway.

I looked up and saw Mustache Durbansky walking towards me with an envelope in his hand. For a second, I swear I saw Kerwin Cummings, Rita, Michelle, the politicians, and all the other tenants walking with him. I looked at the envelope and back at Mustache Durbansky; everyone else was gone.

He passed me the envelope and said, "Mr. Bingham, you took this fight as far as you could; you should be proud. This time, I'm being honest with you; this is the largest payout we have ever given. This is real money, and you can do something with it. Consider yourself lucky."

I looked at the envelope in my hand, and my heart sank. In a calm, matter-of- fact way, I said, "Lucky? I just got forcibly kicked out of my place. I was evicted by someone who isn't even a citizen of this country. Lucky? Lucky that I've been displaced by a rich landowner and his henchman lawyers?"

I took a step towards him, and he saw the look on my face.

He took a few steps back, tried to keep his composure, and said, "Mr. Bingham, it's just business. If I wasn't doing it, someone else would be."

I said with sympathy, "That's the excuse of a coward. You are a pathetic excuse of a man trying to justify the pain and suffering you spread. 'Somebody' doesn't have to do this; you choose to do this, and you try to excuse it away because you are a spineless, coward."

He picked up his briefcase and scurried down the hallway like the rat he was. And there I was, alone in the hallway, alone with a check in my hand for seventeen thousand dollars that I didn't even want.

I was sitting on the bench in the hall, staring at the check, when a voice came over the PA saying, 'The Landlord and Tenant Board is now closed; please exit at the front of the building.' I got up and started walking; there wasn't anyone around; it was just me. As I was walking to the door, the check felt like a bag of dog crap in my hand, and I was carrying it as such. As I walked towards the exit, I couldn't believe the system just threw me out. Yes, I had seventeen thousand dollars, but I didn't have anywhere to live.

As I reached the front doors, I could see Robert and Eric sitting outside, waiting for me. I didn't want to go out; I was embarrassed, I felt like a failure, and I didn't know how I would look them in the eye. I walked out the door, holding the check to my side and looking off in the distance; I was trying to look anywhere except in their eyes. As I got closer, I looked at them and had to look away; they looked at me like I had just struck out in the ninth inning of a tied game with two outs and bases loaded.

When I got to them, all I could do was look down at the ground; I was almost in tears and was having trouble breathing, "I tried guys, I tried."

Eric had the camera rolling, so that's all I could say. I started to walk away and kept walking because I didn't know what else to do. The subway was around the corner, so I turned left and kept going. Eric and Robert caught up, and we walked to the subway in silence.

It wasn't until we were on the streetcar that anyone said a word. Robert was the first to speak, "Well, Brent, considering everything, I think we did pretty good in the end. I know it's not what we wanted, but we knew we wouldn't be able to stay in the building; we knew that from the beginning. We knew a buyout was our best-case scenario, and we got it."

He could see from the look on my face that I wasn't impressed. His words didn't make me feel any better, and the money definitely didn't make me feel better; it was making me feel worse. I had the check in my pocket, and it was heavy; it felt like I was carrying an anvil.

He continued, "Brent, we walked away with the most money. We held out until the end; you should be proud. Do you think anyone else on this streetcar has a fifteen- thousand-dollar check in their pocket?"

I looked down the length of the streetcar and said, "There isn't anyone else on the streetcar." I laughed, looked at the two of them, and added, "And my check is for seventeen."

I looked at Robert when I said that, and I could see the wheels turning in his head; he looked at me with that goofy smile and said, "You got more out of them? Good for you, Brent. You hung in until the very end. You didn't have any farther to go, and you risked walking away with nothing. You rolled the dice, and you won. Good for you."

I could tell he was proud and happy for me that I got more, but I looked at him sadly and said, "Robert, we didn't win a thing; the only person to win today was our owner. Guys, I'm going to get off before our building. I'm getting a jerk burrito and hitting the liquor store. You're more than welcome to join me."

They both agreed that a good burrito and stiff drink were in order.

When we got to 'Reliable,' I wasn't feeling any better. When Joy saw me, she asked, "Well, how'd it go? How was your hearing?"

She knew the hearing was today because everyone in my life and the neighborhood knew it was today.

When she asked me, I didn't know how to answer. My first instinct was to say, 'They won,' but I couldn't because, according to them, no one did. The only thing I could say was, "We came to an agreement."

Shaking my head with disbelief, I said, "That's all I can say? We came to an agreement? Sorry, Joy. I don't know what I can and can't say."

I looked at Eric, "I don't know what to say? I have to watch what I say? You know me, Eric, how long is that going to last?"

"Bingham," Eric said laughing, "you'll break that NDA before Joy brings you your Jerk Burrito."

I looked at him because I knew I was in trouble. We left Reliable and headed to the Liquor Store; I headed towards the Vodka section and grabbed the big bottle; I wasn't fucking around.

Eric looked at me and the bottle and said, "You ain't fucking around, are you, Bingham?"

I laughed and said, "Sometimes you can read my mind."

Eric grabbed some beers, and when we got to the checkout, Robert was already there. I had to laugh at his choice, "Malibu Rum, really? We say it's time for a stiff drink, and you get suntan lotion and rum. We better get you some mini umbrellas for your drinks."

Robert laughed it off, and we headed to the building.

When we got there, no one was around; we went straight up to my apartment and started drinking, we put the tunes on, and it was weird; Robert was in celebration mode, but I couldn't get there; I was pissed off.

Eric wanted to film, and I didn't want him to, but he said, "Brent, this is when I want to see your raw emotion. I'm going to film you and highlight the fact that you aren't able to speak anymore. I want to highlight how the system is able to stifle and silence good people who are restricted with an NDA."

I looked at him and thought, 'Did he just call me a sellout?'

A couple of hours went by, and people from the building started trickling in and we were all feeling pretty good. Everyone was playing DJ, so there was quite a mixture of tunes; Robert always went with happy hippie tunes from the classic rock era, and I played a lot of Bob Marley and old Rap. And Eric, well, he was having some fun with me; he was playing the angry protest songs from my mix; every few songs, I found myself getting worked up and angry; even though I was trying to relax and enjoy myself, I always came back to feeling pissed off.

I didn't figure out what he was doing until I heard 'We're Not Going to Take It' by Twisted Sister. I was singing along, stopped, and said, "Dam, I wish we were still fighting this guy."

That's when I noticed Eric behind the camera grinning away, loving every second of it. I looked at him and laughed, "You son of …, you love seeing Old Bingham worked up, don't you?"

I had left the door open, and even though the room was only twelve feet by twelve feet, I hadn't noticed it filling up; Robert, Nolan, and Krystle had wandered in. Bob and Brian stopped by, even Sarah and Reggie. I was a little unsure of having them here, but I thought, what the hell, this is over anyway.

Everyone was having a good time drinking and smoking and enjoying the music, that was until Reggie opened his pie-hole and started talking like he was a crusader. He was treating this like a victory; he thought he had made out so well that he ordered pizza for the whole building; well, he said it was for the building, but we were pretty sure he was looking forward to most of it himself. He was saying how we're all Social Justice Warriors; we're the 'Robinhoods' of our time; it wasn't just sad that he was thinking this; it was sadder that he wasn't even getting the references right.

With a slice of pizza in each hand, he stood up, which was an accomplishment in itself, and he asked for the music to be shut down and for everyone's attention. As soon as he started to speak, I knew it was going to be some bull shit, and he didn't disappoint. He raised his slice of pizza like a glass and toasted the room, congratulating us all on our victory. The more he spoke, the more I realized what an idiot he was, but what he said next made me realize the sad state of people today and it set me off.

He said, "Hey since this is all over and we know we won, let's tell each other how much we got so we can add up how much we made this guy pay us! Whooo, we're the kings of the world!"

I thought, 'holy shit, this guy is a moron.'

I'm glad everyone in the room thought this was a bad idea, and thank goodness Krystle spoke up and said something, but as she was speaking, I had a feeling this night wasn't going to end in comradery and happiness.

Krystle said, "Guys, we shouldn't talk about the settlements. We all have an NDA in place, so now we are bound to keep quiet, so let's respect that. And Reggie, I don't know why you're so happy. You were first to go. The real winners were probably Robert and Brent. They stuck it out till the end and probably made out much better than us."

When she said that, everyone's head turned, and they looked at Robert and me. Robert loved it and was proud; I wasn't.

Reggie started saying, "What? You guys got more money? That's not fair."

Yup, again, right on cue.

That was the spark that lit my powder keg. This guy had no clue, and I was done being nice, "Well, you know I can't say what I got or discuss terms, so I won't, but I don't see anything stopping us from having a conversation about greed and stupidity, which some of you folks in this room seem to know something about."

I was halfway through my vodka and feeling good, but they switched my mood with the talk of money, and when Reggie thought this wasn't fair, I had to say something.

"You know, in the beginning, I thought all of you were very sincere about trying to stay here, and after what's taken place, now I know who was and who was only interested in a payday. And I have to tell you, if you folks were just about money and going for a big payday, you were all pretty stupid in how you handled this. Benjamin was right all along; all we had to do was stay united. The minute they were able to reduce our numbers was the minute they knew they would win, and Reggie, you were the first to crack. I knew from the beginning you would crumble, and so did they. Look at you, making a toast with a slice of pizza like you won; they won, you dumbass."

Reggie's only reply was, "Well, how much did you get?"

This fired me up even more; I looked at him and laughed, "I was the last guy standing, so a lot more than you. Reggie, they knew they had you even before they got you in that room. You were so blinded by money and greed that you couldn't see the bigger picture. Remember when I said they were ordering pizza for you in that room, Reggie?"

He replied without a clue, "Yeah, there wasn't any pizza in there."

I chuckled, "Yeah? There was no pizza? Look in your fucking hand. Now, please, take your pizza and get out of my apartment; in fact, the party is over folks; sorry everyone, that's it for me tonight; I'm done."

Reggie picked up all the pizza boxes and started waddling out behind everyone. Robert was hanging back to stay, but the only one I could tolerate tonight was Eric; I knew he wouldn't give me any bullshit.

I looked at Robert and said, "Hey man, I appreciate everything you've done. Anything I just said was about them and not you. You were awesome through this. But I gotta crash; it's been too much for me. I'll see you tomorrow."

Robert headed out and was still trying to convince me that we had won as he left. I shut the door, and when I turned around, Eric was already passed out on the sofa. I walked to the desk, and before I turned off the light, I looked at the check. I stared at it for a moment and shook my head. There was no joy or happiness looking at it; it was a reminder of my failure. I threw a blanket over Eric, turned the light off and went to my room.

Chapter 23

I had only been crashed for a few hours when I was woken up by Eric scrambling around, grabbing his gear, and telling me to wake up. I got up, and my head was like a rock; I could hear people in the stairwell, but it wasn't regular footsteps; it sounded like jackboots stomping up and down the stairs. I could hear static and beeps of radios with voices talking on the other end, and there was tons of clanging and banging like they were trying to bring something up the stairs that wasn't built to go up stairs.

Eric bolted out the door, and as I rubbed my eyes and tried to wake up, I could see red and blue lights flashing from the window. I got up to look, and the street was packed, three cop cars, two firetrucks, and an ambulance, 'oh shit, what now,' was all my brain could muster.

As I put on a shirt, a female police officer stood in my doorway. I plopped on the sofa and apologized to her, "Sorry, officer. I'm drunk and hungover all at once. What can I do for you?"

"Sir, there's been a death in the building. The fire department has found traces of carbon monoxide, so we are asking everyone to temporarily exit while they do their job and test the building for your safety."

I gathered my stuff, and as I headed out, she asked if I could leave the door open.

I looked at her, laughed, and said, "No."

I closed the door and locked it behind me. I walked down the stairs, and as I went by the second floor, I could see the paramedics trying to get a gurney through Tommy's door. When I got outside, everyone was already there; Melissa and Sarah were crying, Nolan was consoling Krystle, and I looked over at Bob sitting on the curb with Bo, who was already, or still, drinking from our night before. The old guys were staring out in disbelief, and Robert was starting to rant about what had happened; he was angry and wasn't holding back; he was so red I thought he was going to break himself.

Bill was closest to me, so I asked him, "Bill, what happened?"

Bill, usually a man of a thousand words, only said, "Tommy's dead."

As we were all standing around, one of the police officers approached us. He introduced himself and told us not to worry. He said the fire department ran their tests, and there was no trace of carbon monoxide, so the building was fine to re-enter once they got Tommy out.

Krystle blurted out, "Then what the hell happened? What happened to Tommy?"

The officer began to say, "Tommy passed away; it appears that there wasn't any foul play. It looks like he took a lot of his medication, all of it, actually."

He said he needed to ask us a couple of questions, but his tone was flat and monotone as if he were a robot just asking the standard questions they always ask.

He took out his notepad, looked at us, and asked, "Is there any trouble going on in the building, any disputes or issues?"

We turned and looked at each other, a little surprised that he was asking about it but even more surprised that he knew about it.

Robert replied, "Yes, there's been a dispute between the tenants and the owner. He was trying to evict us illegally, but it was all settled today. Can I ask, uh, how did you know that?"

The officer wrote in his notepad as he talked, "So, this has been an ongoing dispute. How long has this been going on?"

Robert said, "It's been about four months, and like I said, it was resolved today."

The officer looked down at a piece of paper in his hand and then at us, "Normally, I wouldn't show you this, but under the circumstances, it seems relevant. Before Tommy died, he dialed Nine-One-One. The only thing he said was that someone was trying to steal his home, and then he hung up."

He handed the note to Robert, who read it out loud, "This is my home; I won't go anywhere; I can't go anywhere. This is my home."

Robert was crying and finished, "Signed Tommy."

He kicked a garbage can into the street and screamed, "this fucking guy, look what he did, look at what they did to Tommy, they killed him; this would never have happened if that son of a bitch didn't come into our lives. He killed Tommy."

The officer, even after hearing Robert yell 'they killed him' and 'he killed him,' didn't care. He looked at us, gave us his condolences, and asked Robert for the letter back, saying it was evidence.

I said to the cop, "Aren't you curious what he meant when he said, 'they killed him, he killed him?"

He asked if we were family, and we just stood there. He didn't say anything in return, took the letter, and walked away.

I said sarcastically, "Thank you for your help, officer. Don't worry, nothing to see here."

I shook my head and looked at Robert, "No one gives a shit about this, Robert, no one."

After about an hour and after seeing the gurney come out with Tommy in a body bag strapped to it, we proceeded to go back into the building. We walked up the stairs and noticed they left the door to Tommy's place open.

I asked, "Have any of you folks ever been in Tommy's apartment?" Everyone said no. We pushed the door open and couldn't believe what we saw; it made me laugh and say, "holy shit, anyone know what time it is?"

Everyone was in awe. I didn't know what the others were thinking, but I was amazed. Tommy's apartment was filled with alarm clocks, clock radios, wall clocks, and timers, and they were everywhere. They were stacked on top of each other, on top of the fridge, on top of the nineteen-seventies TV that he still watched. Clocks and electric power bars to run them were everywhere. There were alarm clocks from the floor to the ceiling on the wall beside Tommy's chair; it was a wall of clocks, and every one of them had the same time, six-forty-seven.

The numbers 'six' and 'forty-seven,' in different shapes, colors, and sizes, were glowing brightly everywhere in the room. It was crazy, but what was crazier was that they were all keeping the exact correct time—they were all in sync. There must have been at least two hundred of them, probably more. The glowing lights gave the room a weird reddish-green glow, and all you could hear was ticking.

I asked them, "Guys, Tommy was a shut-in, right?"

Robert answered, "Yes, everything is either delivered or a family member brings him stuff; he'd be out on the stoop maybe once a month, that's it."

I looked around and said, "Could you imagine sitting in here twenty-four hours a day, seven days a week, looking at clocks, and they're all the correct time? Poor Tommy."

Robert said, "Guys, if any of you feel this bad or are getting sad, please reach out and tell someone. Tell me, call the hotlines. My door is always open. Ask Brent. It's literally open all the time. Come in anytime. I'm serious."

I thanked Robert for that and said, "You as well, don't hesitate to knock. Hey, did you know Tommy's last name?"

Robert said yeah, "It's Raymond,"

I said, "That's the only name on the buzzer at the door downstairs in the original printing."

Robert said, "Yup, not anymore, I guess."

Eric said, "Well, that sobered me up; that's enough for me tonight."

He went home, and we all went back to our apartments. I looked at my bedroom and then at the computer; I decided to sit at the computer since there was no way I would sleep. I couldn't believe it, poor Tommy. I understood how he felt. I've been down in life, I've been faced with things I thought I'd never overcome, and we've all had those dark thoughts. But his apartment was all he had; he didn't know anywhere else; the thought of moving somewhere else scared him too much; it scared him to death.

I went to Facebook and went to the 'Renoviction' page. We had over three hundred thousand followers, and the number was growing every day. I scrolled through some of the latest posts and comments, and the stories weren't stopping; every day, someone told a story about a new address where the landlord was trying to evict people. I scrolled through story after story all about the same thing, greedy landlords trying to evict tenants; I was getting really pissed off; I mean, in my opinion, they killed Tommy. I knew bad things would come from this eviction, but I never really thought or imagined that it could lead to something like this, someone killing themselves over the thought of losing their home; this was out of control.

Before Tommy did this, I was starting to grasp the realities of being evicted, but Tommy taking his own life made me stop and think about what was going on, and I started to get very nervous and scared. I was going to post this on Facebook and tell everyone what happened. I wanted people to see the effects of 'Renovictions' and to show them the real-life impact of illegally evicting people and the toll it's taking on people and society. I wanted to show people that this was more than trying to make a good return on investment; this was peoples' lives, and people are dying because of it.

I started to type, and then I caught myself and thought that I shouldn't tell people about Tommy's death before his family even knew about it. I didn't know if he had a lot of family, but still, they should be told before I post it.

I went to Google and typed in Tommy's name to see what came up; there were tons of Tommy Raymond but nothing that looked like our Tommy. I narrowed it down and typed in 'Tommy Raymond, Toronto,' but still nothing. I looked at the screen and wondered. I typed in 'Raymond Tommy,' and a shitload of links came up. I looked at the images, and sure enough, there was one picture of a young Raymond Tommy, the guy who we called Tommy, wearing an old military uniform. I clicked the picture, which took me to an old archived story from the 'Queen Street Penny Saver,' dated nineteen- seventy-six. It was a story welcoming Tommy, or should I say Raymond, back to the neighborhood after serving a career in the military. Tommy was a highly decorated soldier, including the Victorian Cross, Canada's highest military decoration. And he was awarded that, not once, but twice. The article didn't say what he did to earn them but said that they had only been awarded to ninety-nine people since eighteen-fifty-four, so whatever he did must have been pretty heroic and pretty damn important.

I printed the article and decided to put it up in the lobby so everyone would know about Tommy. I wanted people to know he wasn't always a crazy shut-in guy, a recluse hiding in his apartment. He was a hero, a wartime hero, and this is how the country and society he fought for ended up treating him. It was disgusting, and at that moment, I wanted to kill the owner of the building who had caused this.

I looked at the clock and couldn't believe it—it was eleven a.m. I opened the door and went downstairs to the mailboxes. Someone had already posted a notice about Tommy with his picture, so I taped the article beside it. When I was putting it up, I looked at the notice from Brownstone about putting up notices in the building. I grabbed it and tore it off the wall.

I still wasn't tired, so I decided to get a coffee. I only had my house pants, robe, and slippers on, but I didn't care.

When I walked into Beanzies, Sally laughed when she saw me, handed me my coffee, and asked, "What the hell happened to you?"

I looked at her and started to tell her about the night's events, and it made her cry. She couldn't believe it. She said she didn't know Tommy and maybe saw him on the stoop once or twice, but it still broke her heart. Sally was a good soul.

I went back to the building, but I didn't go in. Instead, I sat on the stoop and watched the people walking by; I was curious if anyone would care. I thought about trying to tell them about it as they walked by; I thought about preaching like a religious man on a soapbox, but no one would care. Being dressed in my robe, house pants, and slippers, I would fit in here, but no one would care. I thought about getting dressed and then doing the yelling, but it still wouldn't make a difference.

I put my hands up in the air, shrugging like it's a hopeless cause, and said to myself, 'screw it, I'm going to have some more drinks.'

Back in my apartment, I had a beer and a couple of shots; I was exhausted, I couldn't focus, and my brain was just filled with negativity; all I could think about was what they did to Tommy. I wanted to write so much on Facebook and start screaming about what happened, but I thought, 'What's the point?' All that would happen is people would write hollow comments, like 'thoughts and prayers' or 'such a shame,' or 'sorry for your loss,' and the page would be filled with 'crocodile tears,' I was sick of the hollowness and shallowness of people.

I'm not sure when I passed out or for how long, but when I woke up, I was hungover and drunk. I was pissed off, upset, and I started crying. I couldn't believe Tommy killed himself; I couldn't believe it came to that. I began to think about what would happen to Bob and Bo, the other old guys like Bill and Brian, and I felt that I had let them all down. I was staring at the check on my desk, and I was disgusted; I couldn't take my eyes off it, and it was pissing me off.

All I could ask myself was, "How am I going to be able to go on with what I did? How can I look people in the eye when I was so vocal and took such a stand? I'm not even allowed to tell people what took place, and I can't even finish the documentary with Eric and get this message out. I didn't want to agree to any of this; I knew the Tenant Board's decision would be final, but I never imagined how bad that decision could be. Sure, laws are written, rules and regulations put in place, but they are put there by the system, and that system was created by the people who profit from it. The system enforces them, and the system decides how they'll be enforced. I felt like such a loser.

At every step in this process, people had their hands out trying to make money from the 'Affordable Housing Crisis.' Well, I guess I had to learn again the hard way that grifters and con men come in all shapes and colors. They hold positions of power and authority and wear suits and ties; they'll smile at you and say they're helping you. They'll shake your hand and use the other to stuff the donations, kickbacks, and dollar bills in their pockets. I looked at the clock, and an hour had passed since I had woken up. I found myself just staring at the check. I felt defeated, I couldn't take it, I felt so bad, I didn't know how I could go on and hold my head high, and I just sat there and cried for another hour.

Chapter 24

As I was crying, I suddenly stopped. It felt surreal. I don't know if it was the alcohol, lack of sleep, or hitting the wall of desperation, but I didn't feel I was in reality. I wiped my tears and looked at the bedroom door. I knew what was behind that door, and I knew it could stop my pain. I thought about the cover of a Rage Against the Machine CD that had a picture of Thich Quang Duc, the Buddhist monk who set himself on fire in protest of the Diem regime. I wondered if something that dramatic would finally get people's attention. I mean, nobody cared about Tommy, who quietly ended his life alone in his apartment. Would another death, but in a dramatic way, finally put light on this 'Renoviction' issue? I thought, screw it. I got up and started hauling out all the props that Eric had planned to use for the shoot, only I wasn't going to use them for a movie.

The check for twenty thousand dollars was an indication of how weak I was. I tried to fight something and was beaten down again, so what was the point? They already had blood on their hands with Tommy; what was a little more? I opened the bags and looked at the supplies. Eric had brought chains, padlocks, flares, a flame bar, a mini blow torch, tiki torches, torch fuel, gas cans, fireworks, metal buckets, a propane tank, and oh yeah, a kiddie pool, which I still didn't have a clue what that was for. I started to fill the tiki torches with the torch fuel; I hooked up the flame bar to the propane tank and put it in front of the window that looked out onto the street. I hauled out the chains and locks and put them by my door.

I had no idea what I was doing. All I knew was that I wanted to burn that check and get people's attention. I didn't care about myself or my well-being anymore. If they were going to ignore the law, ignore common decency, and ignore how to treat their fellow man, well, I guess I would, too.

I got up to go get a coffee. As I left my apartment, Robert came out of his at the same time. He caught a glance inside mine and asked, "What the hell you got going on in there, Brent? Are you OK?"

I looked at him and smiled, "Just shit for the movie Robert."

By the look on his face, I could tell he was a little weirded out by what he saw.

I started to walk down the stairs, and he followed.

He still had questions, "I thought you were done with the documentary? I didn't think you were allowed to do anything now. Are you going to keep making it?"

Before I headed outside, I went downstairs to look at the basement, and Robert followed. I surveyed the basement and went back up the stairs and out the front door; all the while, Robert asked what the hell was going on.

When I got outside, I turned and looked at him and said, "You know, all I wanted to do was fight for the building, right? All I wanted to do was help. You know, I just wanted to make things right and try to help everyone here, right? Robert, do you trust me?"

Confused and worried, he replied, "Yeah, Brent, I know, and yeah, I do, but sometimes things are too big to fight. We tried and walked away with some money. It is what it is, and we did the best we could."

I smiled and said, "Did we? I'm getting a coffee; I'll see you in a couple of hours."

I walked away, leaving him standing in front of the building; as I turned the corner, I glanced back, and he was still there, staring at me.

I went to Beanzies, and Sally was there. She asked if I was alright and gave me my coffee. I thanked her and turned to walk out. I stopped, turned back, looked at her, and asked, "Sally, you think I'm a good guy, right?"

She looked at me quizzically and replied jokingly, "You're not bad. You could be a better tipper, but you're OK."

I smiled and said, "Remember that Sally. And thank you - you're a good person."

I walked out, went back to the building, and sat on the stoop for a bit. I looked around and thought, 'I really enjoyed it here. As crazy as the neighborhood could be, it was a nice place to live.'

I stood up and headed to my apartment. When I got into my place, I put on some music. My first choice was *'Signs,'* my favorite peaceful protest song, and after that, it was The Clash's *'Should I Stay or Should I Go.'* As the music played, I gathered the chains, the locks, some newspaper, tape, and the biggest kitchen knife I had. I put it all in my backpack, and as I left the apartment, I looked back at all the fire gear piled up and thought, 'What the hell, here goes nothing.' I went downstairs, stood in the lobby by the mailboxes, and stared at the fire alarm. Was I really going to do this? I wasn't nervous; I was pretty calm, and I felt that I was in my right frame of mind—well, what I believed was my right frame of mind.

I pulled out my phone and called Eric. It took about ten rings for him to answer, as he was also hungover. He answered and said, "Bingham, what are you bugging me for?"

I needed to get him here as soon as possible; I asked, "How soon can you be here?"

He wasn't that excited about it and said, "What the hell for? We're done, aren't we? I knew Eric was about ten minutes away, so I had a bit of time to think this out, but I had to get him here in time.

I said, "Listen, man, we're not done; it's just the beginning. You won't be disappointed. Grab your gear, get in your car, and call me when you are on your way. OK? And don't stop for anything."

He groaned and said, "What the hell, Bingham, what's going on?"

I said, "You trust me, right? You know when I say you won't be disappointed, you know you won't be disappointed, right?"

I could hear him moving and banging around on the phone, and he said, "Yeah, Bingham, you definitely don't disappoint."

"Well, then get your ass in the car, and call me when you are on your way. It's important to call me when you're on your way, OK? Now hurry up," and I hung up.

I figured intrigue and curiosity would get the better of him and get him over here right away. I went outside to the stoop and waited.

It only took five minutes for him to call back. "OK, Bingham, I'm in the car and on my way; what the hell are you doing."

I walked back in and said to him, "Well, I always said I would entertain you through this, right? So here we go." As I said that, I pulled the fire alarm. It was the 'old-school' type of alarm, an actual bell ringing, and it was loud as hell. I yelled into the phone, "Do you hear that? Now, hurry up."

I put the phone back to my ear and heard Eric yelling, "Bingham, you son of a bitch, what the hell are you doing? Whatever it is, wait till I get there!"

I told him to hurry and hung up. I grabbed my backpack, went outside the building, and just waited.

People started coming out, and as no surprise, people walking by just covered their ears and hustled through. Not one person stopped to ask if there was a fire. Melissa and her kids, Krystle and Nolan, came out. Bill wandered out; Bob stumbled out with Bo leading him, then Robert, and finally, Sarah came out with her new boyfriend of the month. It made us all laugh as he asked her for money to buy coffee, and of course, she complied.

I just smiled and laughed when it happened.

She said, "Mind your business, Brent. What the hell did you do now?" She was going to say something more, but I saw Eric pull up, so I hurried over to his car.

He got out and asked, "Bingham, what the hell?"

I spoke fast and quick. First, I asked, "You trust me, right?"

Smiling, he said, "Well, to an extent."

I wasn't looking at him; I was looking in the direction I could hear the sirens, and I said, "Get your camera out and follow my lead. After the fire department leaves, I will ask the tenants if I can speak with them. When I do that, be on top of the stoop in front of the door, keep rolling, and trust me, it's about to get good."

I walked back over to the building and saw Reggie finally waddling out; most of the building was outside, standing around. I had almost everyone out of the building except for Brian. Two fire trucks pulled up, and there were some of the same guys that were here for Tommy. When they approached the building, they said they were worried they were coming here for the same reason. Krystle expressed concern and told them that Brian was still in there. She told him his apartment number, and they headed in.

Damn, what was I going to do with Brian? It was about twenty minutes before the firemen came out. They had shut off the alarm and reassured Krystle that Brian was fine; as the trucks pulled away, I asked if I could have everyone's attention.

I stood on the stairs, and Eric was behind me; I thanked everyone and told them that, unfortunately, the documentary couldn't proceed because of the NDA, and not surprisingly, not one of them seemed to care.

When I saw their reaction, I laughed on the inside. These people didn't care anymore; they got their money, and that's all they cared about. I took the bag off my back, and as I reached in, fat ass Reggie asked, "Can we go back into the building now or what?"

I looked at him and smiled; I pulled the knife out of my bag, pointed it at him, and yelled, "Well, I care, and you're never going back into this building again, fat ass."

I grabbed Robert, pulled him into a headlock, and yelled at everyone to 'get back' or Robert was going to die. I started backing up the stairs and yelled at Eric to open the door. I threw Robert into the lobby, and he fell to the ground. I pushed Eric inside, who tripped over him, and they were both on the ground. I stepped halfway through the door and smashed the intercom with the butt of the knife before I went inside.

I stepped inside and pointed the knife at Eric and Robert, yelling, "STAY THE FUCK DOWN, DON'T MOVE."

I pulled a chain and a lock out of my bag, chained the front door handles shut, and yelled, "STAY THE FUCK OUT, ANYONE COMES IN, AND ROBERT DIES."

I turned to Eric and Robert and yelled, "GET DOWNSTAIRS NOW."

They got up and scurried downstairs, and I was right behind them. I gave them the newspaper and tape and told them to cover the windows, and I chained the back door so no one could get in. As they were taping up the windows up, which were at street level outside, I could see Nolan and Reggie trying to look inside.

Robert said, "Brent, what the hell are you doing?"

I grabbed the knife I had stuck in my belt and proceeded towards him. I grabbed him by the shirt, and I pointed the knife at his face, and in a dead tone, without emotion, I said, "Don't fight Robert, I've had enough; it's time to make things right, now tape up the windows."

As they got to the last window, the tenants were crouched down looking in, and I could see some passersby had also stopped to look in. I thought, 'Yeah, now people stop to look at what's going on.'

I screamed at everyone, "Stay the fuck out, or Robert and Eric are going to get it; if we can't live here, no one will." I turned to Eric and Robert and screamed for them to get up the stairs.

Robert tried to talk on the way up the stairs, and I told him to shut up and keep walking. As we were coming up the stairs to the lobby, people were gathered on the stoop looking in and tugging on the door; when I saw them, I cut my thumb a little with the knife and made sure to bleed all over it.

Before we got to the top of the stairs, I stopped them; I spun Robert around so he was looking at me. I said, "Robert, I hope you trust me. I'm sorry for this." And I punched him in the gut.

Eric was shocked and yelled, "Bingham, what the hell are you doing?"

I said, let's go; I pushed them up the stairs and told them to keep walking, which Robert could hardly do; he was bent over with the breath knocked out of him, and I put him in a headlock as we passed by the mailboxes.

As we started up the stairs, I heard Sarah scream, "Oh my god, he stabbed him; Robert is bleeding; he's going to kill him!"

We kept going up the stairs, and I thought, 'Thank you, Sarah.'

We got to the top of the stairs and went into my apartment; I ordered Eric to the bedroom, plunked Robert on the sofa, and grabbed one of the metal buckets and one of the gas cans. I put the bucket by the door and poured about an inch of the gas into it, and the stench of gasoline filled the apartment. Robert started begging and pleading, asking why I was doing this. I got the kiddie pool, put it in front of the window by the flame bar, and emptied the full gas can into it. I grabbed a chair and placed it right in the middle of the pool. I went to my cleaning closet, got some zip ties I had lying around, and yanked Robert off the sofa. I sat him on the chair and proceeded to strap his arms and legs to it.

Eric was scared and said, "Calm down, Bingham. What the hell are you doing? Robert's on your side."

I ignored him; I grabbed three buckets, three torches, and a gas can and ordered Eric out of the apartment. He started going down the stairs, and I followed him. We got to the lobby, and Nolan and Krystle were tugging on the door; I yelled at them, "Get the fuck off the stoop."

I looked at the group on the sidewalk; everyone was looking on with concern. Sarah was on the phone, and I was pretty sure I knew who she was talking with. I took one torch and jammed it in the door push bar, and I slid the other torch through, making an 'X'; together, they jammed the door, and I put the two buckets on the floor under the torches. I grabbed the gas can and filled the buckets up until they overflowed. Anyone trying to come in would have to smash the glass, making the torches fall and igniting the gas. I stood at the door and looked out.

Nolan and Krystle begged me to stop, they were yelling, "It's not worth it, it's not worth it, don't do it, Brent."

I looked at them and said, "It's not fair. We didn't have a chance, and they killed Tommy. I don't want to leave, this was all of your homes, this was our lives,"

They were all in shock except for Bob, who was smiling, and cheering me on.

Sarah yelled, "I called Nine-One-One, I called Nine-One-One, you're going to jail Brent!"

I looked at her, smirked, and thought, the useful idiot serves her purpose yet again.

I dragged Eric downstairs, jammed the other torch in the basement back door, put the bucket on the floor, and lit the torch.

Eric tried to calm me down, "Bingham, this is getting out of hand; what the hell are you doing?"

I looked at him and said, "I have no clue, dude. Just get up the stairs."

We walked back up the stairs, and people were pulling on the door. Before I walked away, I pulled out my lighter and lit the torches, saying, "Try coming through that door, and this whole place is going to burn."

I picked up the gas can and screamed at Eric to get up the stairs. As he ran up, I followed him walking up backwards and emptying the can on the stairs. When I did that, everyone jumped off the stoop and stood back on the sidewalk.

I turned and ran upstairs, went into the apartment, and stood in front of Robert.

He was pissed off, yelling, "What the hell is wrong with you? What are you doing, Brent?"

As he said that, I could hear the sirens approaching.

I pulled up a chair and looked out the window beside him. I took a deep breath and tried to explain, "Robert, I wouldn't be able to live with myself with this deal. I gave up, I sold out, and I hate myself for it; I thought you said you trusted me."

He was pissed, "Well, I did, until you did this, you fucking lunatic; now let me go; you don't need to do this."

I patted him on the back and said, "Don't worry."

"Fuck you, Brent," was his reply.

I got the flame bar ready, looked at Eric, and said, "How the hell do you work this thing?"

Eric set the camera down, turned on the gas, set the output, and lit it. I had to admit it looked cool, and from the outside, I'm sure all you could see was flames and Robert sitting behind them.

As I was admiring it, I said, "shit, I forgot about Brian. Stay with me Eric. Robert, don't go anywhere."

Again, he said, "Fuck you, Brent."

We headed downstairs to Brian's apartment, and I knocked.

I could hear Brian's TV, and he yelled, "Who's knocking? I'm watching my stories."

I looked at Eric and mouthed, "his stories?"

Eric just shrugged, I knocked again, and when I did, I could hear voices and banging from outside; I looked at Eric and said, "Oh shit, they're on the fire escape; I've got to hurry."

I knocked again and said, "Hey Brian, it's Brent. I need your help."

The lock clicked, and the door opened. I could tell he wasn't happy. "First the fire department, now you. What do you want?"

I looked at him anxiously while constantly looking down the hall at the fire escape door.

He didn't have a clue about what was happening. Thank goodness he was a little deaf as well, so I said, "Hey Brian, I need your help. I'm trying to make them let us stay in the building. Do you mind helping me out for the movie?"

He looked at me and then at Eric and said, "For the movie, sure. What can I do?"

I smiled and said, "Not much. I need you to come upstairs with me. We're going to hang out and try to get the owner on the phone."

He said, "Sure."

He closed the door and started to follow me to the stairs. I could hear something outside the lobby doors, but I wasn't sure what was happening. All I knew was they'd be in the building soon, so I had to get back into my apartment, where I could contain the chaos.

We got up the stairs and went into the apartment. I was worried Brian would freak out at the sight of the fire bar, gas cans, torches, and, oh yeah, Robert strapped to a chair sitting in a kiddie pool filled with gasoline. But, surprisingly and laughingly, he wasn't that fazed.

He sat on the sofa and said, "Hey Robert, you're helping out with the movie too?"

Me and Eric looked at each other in surprise, and all we could do was smile.

Brian asked if I got channel nine, and I said, "No, but I can put some Seinfeld on for you."

I told Eric we were going back down to check the lobby, and as we headed down the stairs, I asked Eric, "What do you see?"

He said, "Bingham, there are cops, firemen, and ambulances, and I'm not sure, but I think maybe the bomb squad guys are here too, and I'm assuming the guys with the big guns are SWAT."

When he said that, he backed up out of their view, and rightfully so.

I looked at him in disbelief, "Are you kidding me?"

He had the wherewithal to chuckle; he switched the camera off and said, "It's getting serious now, Bingham; what the fuck are you doing?"

I looked at him, scared, confused, and unsure of what I was doing. My reply was, "I don't know, man. I just…I just…"

At that moment, a voice blared over a bullhorn: "Come on out, Brent. Stop this immediately, and no one will get hurt. Let's end this before it gets out of control. We can talk about this."

I looked at Eric; fear had washed over me and taken control. "Go down a couple of steps; let them see you."

Eric replied in his usual fashion, "I'm not going down there, this is your shit, you go down there."

I didn't want Eric to get hurt, so I said, "OK, we'll both go down a couple of steps."

As we inched our way into view, I saw a couple of cops, changed my mind, and backed up the stairs.

Eric was busy looking through the camera, and when he realized I had backed up, he said, "Aw, hell no," and came up out of view, too.

The bullhorn blared again, "Brent, put the fires out before it gets out of control; what do you want."

I froze; Eric asked, "Bingham, what do you want?"

I looked at him and said, "I don't know. This was your plan for the dream sequence. I don't know what I'm doing. What did you have in mind?"

He laughed his usual way, "This wasn't my plan. This is turning into a shitshow, and it's all you; now, what the hell do you want me to say to them."

I was speechless; thankfully, Eric was still able to speak, "Bingham, you gotta tell them something before they shoot you."

That hit home and woke me up. Reality was sinking in, and I came out of it a bit. I said to him, "I don't think I thought this through too well."

He laughed at me and said, "No shit."

I said, "OK, you're going to do the yelling. Tell them not to come in."

Eric yelled, "He says don't come in." then he asked me, "How was that?" I looked at him, "Good job."

Without missing a beat, he said, "Don't worry, Bingham; you're doing great too," rolling his eyes in exaggeration.

I thought, 'God, I love this guy,' and told him so, "I'm glad you're here with me, Eric."

"Yeah, me too," and again, a giant eye roll.

The bullhorn blared again, "We'll have to come in sooner or later. Let's make it sooner before anyone gets hurt, Brent."

I said to Eric, "Tell them not to come in and that there's gas everywhere. I've booby-trapped every fire escape door and the basement door just like this one; if they open any of them, it will knock the torches down. The whole place is soaked in gas. If you touch the doors, this whole place goes up like a tinderbox."

Eric repeated what I said, and I asked him, "What are they doing?"

He looked and said, "It looks like Sarah is talking to them, pointing, and acting out how you poured the gas everywhere.

The bullhorn blared, "OK, Brent, let's talk about this. What do you want? Let us help you. What do you want?"

I told Eric what to say, and he yelled in reply, "He wants to stay in the building, and he wants everyone to be allowed to stay in their homes."

The bullhorn replied, "OK, come out and let us help you do that; we'll make that happen; now, just come out."

This time, I yelled back, "YEAH, I'M SURE I'LL BE FINE WHEN I COME OUT. NOW, DON'T TRY TO COME IN. I DON'T CARE IF THE WHOLE PLACE BURNS."

I tugged on Eric, and we headed back upstairs. Eric said, "That was some tough talk, Bingham, not bad. You had me scared."

I chuckled, "I told you I could act."

Just then, my phone rang, and I had never heard a ring like this. I had the Pearl Jam song Alive as my ringer, but I didn't hear Eddie's voice this time. It was an old-fashioned ring, and it didn't stop; it just kept ringing, one long ring. I looked at the display and got scared. The display didn't show a number; it just read, 'METRO TORONTO POLICE SERVICES' in caps, filling the whole screen.

I mumbled, "How the hell did they know my number?"

Eric laughed and sarcastically said, "I don't know Bingham; they are the cops, after all."

I looked at Eric nervously, who mouthed, 'Speaker,' and I answered, "Uh, hello?"

A stern and rigid voice asked, "Is this Brent Bingham?"

I didn't know what I was going to say, "Uh, yeah."

A stern voice said, "Brent, my name is Sgt Tom Woolhead. I'm with the Toronto Police Hostage Negotiation Division. I'm here to talk with you. Are you willing to talk?"

I was overwhelmed when I heard him say, 'Hostage Negotiation Division.' I replied, "Uh, yeah, sure."

He replied like he was my best friend, "That's good, Brent, because I want to talk. So what's going on in there? Is everyone OK? Can you tell me who's with you, and is anybody hurt?"

I looked around at everyone; Eric was filming, Robert was still swearing at me, squirming in his chair, and Brian was unfazed, watching Seinfeld.

I had to chuckle a little when I replied because Brian was oblivious to what was happening and didn't seem to care: "Uh, yeah, everyone is OK."

He said, "OK, I can hear a little laugh from you, so it sounds like you're calm. Why don't you come out so we can talk? Please stay calm, and we can figure this out. Now, can you tell me what you want so I can help get everyone out of there safely?"

It felt as if they weren't taking me that seriously, so I had to turn it up a notch. I said to him, "I have nothing to lose, and now they've taken away my place to live, they've taken away all these people's homes who have lived here for over twenty, thirty, even forty years, and they killed Tommy. Tommy wouldn't have died if it wasn't for them."

Now, I never played this card in my life, and I never used it as an excuse, but I had to let them know I was serious, so I told him, "I lost my son, Woolhead, and I'm looking forward to the day I get to see him again. I have nothing to lose, and now I don't even have a place to fucking live. Everything has been taken from me, EVERYTHING! So what do you think you can do for me?"

I started to cry a little and began getting emotional; even I could hear the fear and anger in my voice, "I want to stay. I want these people to stay in their homes; I want the system to do what it says it's supposed to, which is to help the people against injustices. I'm sick of the corruption and lies; I'm done talking."

I could tell from his reply that he was getting a little more concerned: "Brent, don't hang up. Stay on the line. Talk to me. I want to know everything."

I said, "Give me ten minutes. I call this number?"

He said, "Don't worry about that. Just open your phone app, and we'll be there."

I said, "OK," and hung up. I wasn't sure what he meant, so I exited my phone app and looked at the main screen.

I tapped the phone app, and as soon as I did, I heard a voice say, "Brent?"

I was surprised that they were right there, and I quickly said, "Nope, just checking. Thanks."

I hung up, looked at Eric, and said, "holy shit, they're right there; I didn't need to dial anything." I was getting scared.

Eric looked at me in surprise, and as I was looking at my phone, I noticed Eric signaling me. I looked at him, and he pointed to his ear and mouthed,

'They're probably listening now,' then he pointed to his eye and mouthed, 'They're probably watching too.'

I freaked out, and in a panic, I opened the freezer and threw our phones in it, and mouthed, 'What the fuck?' to Eric; he shrugged, and his eyes expressed he had no idea.

Robert started screaming and was getting pissed off, he started yelling for help and freaking out, and I thought well, it couldn't hurt, I pulled the phones out of the freezer and rested them on the counter, so they were looking at Robert while I pushed Eric into the bedroom.

I sat on the bed and put my head in my hands, and started to panic, "Oh shit, what the hell did I do? I wasn't thinking. Shit, I'm probably still drunk, what the fuck did I do. What am I going to do? This isn't what I thought it'd be; I was picturing it like a scene in a movie; this ain't no movie. Man, real life sucks."

Eric put the camera down and said, "Well, Bingham, either go big or go home. And since you don't have a home…" he started to laugh.

I looked at him and laughed, "You always know what to say. Dude, you have to act scared. We'll keep the phone cameras from looking at you, but they can hear us, so get scared and make sure they hear it."

I opened the bedroom door and walked out and yelled, "GIMME YOUR PHONE, ERIC, STOP FUCKING AROUND," and I punched him square in the face and knocked him to the floor.

He yelled, "BINGHAM, WHAT THE HELL?" I grabbed his phone and threw it down to him; I screamed, "Call Helen right now. Get her on the phone now!"

I sat beside Brian and said, "Brian, I kind of need you to do something for me. Do you mind if I bind your hands with a zip tie? It won't hurt, and uh, do you mind if I put my sleep mask on you to blindfold you? It'll really help us for the movie."

He said, "Sure if it helps us stay, I've seen this Seinfeld anyway."

I put the sleep mask on him and bound his hands in front of him. I picked up my phone and went to Facebook. I assumed they were probably reading as I typed, but I didn't care.

I started typing, "Nine-One-One. Hostage-taking at Three-Ninety-One Empire Avenue. Fire department, police, SWAT, and bomb squad are all on scene. Reports of fire, explosives, and weapons. Threats of tenant burning the building down due to RENOVICTION."

Eric was getting up off the floor, and I could tell he was pissed; he had his phone in one hand and the camera in the other; he was a pro, he never stopped filming, and he said, "I have Helen on the phone, asshole."

I grabbed his phone, passed him mine, and said, "FACEBOOK LIVE RIGHT NOW."

I had Helen on speaker and started to say to her, "Hey Helen, how's it going? I need you to go to the Facebook Renoviction page. Listen, I have three hostages, there's gas all over the building, and the cops are outside; if I don't get my way, I'm going to burn everything down."

Eric had the phone and camera up and was walking to get a good angle; I screamed at him, "DON'T YOU DARE TRY TO LEAVE ERIC. IF YOU LEAVE THIS APARTMENT, EVERYTHING AND EVERYONE IS GOING TO BURN."

I grabbed one of the flares and cracked it open. The red flame and smoke filled the room. I didn't realize how much smoke there actually was from these things and how bright and hot they burned. I grabbed Eric, went into the bedroom, pulled back the blackout curtain, and opened the window. I pushed Eric in front of the window and held the flare out from behind him. I could hear people scream and gasp on the street below.

I yelled out the window, "DON'T COME IN HERE. THERE'S GAS EVERYWHERE, AND I HAVE HOSTAGES; IT'S ON FACEBOOK LIVE IF YOU WANT TO SEE WHAT'S HAPPENING. IT'S RENOVICTION. FACEBOOK PAGE RENOVICTION,"

Everyone who was holding up their phone filming me stopped and went to the 'zombie' position of looking down and typing into their phones. It was scary how connected people were to social media, but I might as well use it to my advantage.

"THAT'S WHAT'S HAPPENING HERE, WE'RE GETTING EVICTED FOR PROFIT, IT'S RENOVICTION. TOMMY IS DEAD BECAUSE THEY KILLED HIM. AND I'M NOT LEAVING."

I closed my window and the curtain; as soon as I did, I told Eric to show them the hostages. I screamed, "SHOW THEM ERIC, SHOW THEM WHO I HAVE, SHOW ROBERT SITTING IN GAS, I DON'T CARE ANYMORE. THIS WHOLE FUCKING PLACE WILL BURN."

When he turned the cameras on them, I ran to the bathroom and stuck the flare in the toilet; if it burned any longer, I would have killed us all with smoke inhalation.

As he filmed them, the bullhorn blared again, "OK, Brent, calm down. Everything will be OK."

I looked at Eric and spoke to the phone, "Everyone watching, please tell your friends and family, tell them to get down here, tell them to tune into the Renoviction page, and share the hell out of this."

I told Eric, "Keep the phone positioned on Robert and the flames; I'm going to talk to Helen."

I put the phone to my ear, and I could hear Helen pleading with me to stop, so I had to calm her down. I started speaking to calm her down, "Helen, Helen, calm down, calm down."

I knew they had eyes and ears in here with the phones, so I knew I had to watch what I said, but I wanted to calm her down, so I tried to act casually. "Hey, Helen, how's it going?"

She forced a laugh and said, "Oh, I don't know; my friend is barricaded in his apartment holding another friend and two innocent people hostage, threatening to burn down his building while the police are probably ready to shoot him through the window. That's how it's going. Brent, please stop it and come out; you can come live here; I have more than enough space, I have the pool, I have so much room, come on, you'll have a home, just please come out."

I said, "You think they'll try to shoot me? All I want is to stay in my place; I'm not asking too much."

She was getting upset. She was our 'set Mom' when we were at work. Whenever we were stuck long hours on sets together, she would always make sure we ate, stayed hydrated, and did some exercises to keep fit. She had a big heart and cared, and we loved her for it.

I felt like I was disappointing her. "Helen, please relax. Nothing is going to happen as long as they meet my demands. But I want you here. I want you to talk to the cops about me and tell them I'm not crazy."

She tried calming me down. "I'm already on my way, Brent; please just walk out of there before it gets worse. Please come out. Don't do anything crazy, please."

I smiled, and was a little calmer, "You're awesome, Helen. Call everyone you know in the business and get them down here. I want to fill the street, and I want people who might actually be on my side."

After I hung up the phone, I looked out the window, and a crowd was starting to gather. There were so many people that the cops had to start putting up barriers for crowd control, and I smiled when I saw a couple of the Renoviction and Acorn picket signs in the crowd.

I looked at Eric and told him to put the Facebook Live phone on me.

He grabbed the phone and pointed it at me. I looked at him and jokingly asked him, "What's the shot? Full, medium? Follow me."

I went to my desk, grabbed my laptop and the check, and sat beside Brian on the sofa. He was surprisingly quiet and calm; I asked him, "How are you doing, Brian? Are you OK?"

He looked around the room like Stevie Wonder when he replied, "I'm OK, Brent, but the gas smell is starting to bug me. Are you guys using it for the movie or something?"

I gave him a reassuring tap on his leg and said, "Yup, or something."

I looked at the camera and said, "Thank you, everybody, for tuning in. I apologize to anyone this might be affecting or hurting, but I want justice. All I want is for the people who have lived here, some of them for thirty, even forty years, to stay in their homes and their community. But because of the greed, people like this…"

I pointed and motioned for Eric to show Brian and Robert, "…are forced to leave. Last night, one of our tenants, Tommy, an Eighty-Eight-Year-Old decorated war veteran and a recipient of the Victorian Cross, committed suicide. He killed himself because he felt he had nowhere to go. And why? Because of one person's greed. Stay tuned, tell your friends, and share this with everyone you know. In ten minutes, I'll be right back. I'll show you the check I received, and I'll burn it. I want you to know that I am serious. I'll also tell you about the bribery, or should I say the 'lobbying money' that the lying politicians have received in return for selling out affordable housing in Toronto. I'll introduce you to the lobbyist who has helped facilitate their greed and corruption, all at the people's cost. So please share, sit back, and get some popcorn; the show is just getting started; see you in ten minutes."

I flashed the peace sign, gave Eric the cut signal, and Eric killed the feed.

I picked up my phone, hit the phone app, and Sgt. Woolhead was right there, I asked, "Psychic Hotline?"

There was a little laugh on the other end, "It's good to have a sense of humor, Brent, but don't screw around. Are we going to be able to talk this out? Are you coming out?"

I was going to be honest with him, "Well, Woolhead, interesting name by the way, I'm not coming out until we get something accomplished here tonight."

Of course, he was hesitant, and I'm sure they never want to facilitate the demands of a 'crazy' person who's threatening others. His reply was proof, "Well, Brent, it all depends on what you want to do."

I remained calm and collected when I told him what I wanted: "All I want to do is have a simple conversation. First, I want you to get Kerwin Cummings, President of The Alliance of Commercial Housing Rentals, down here. Also, I want our City Councillor Pauline Flatch, our MP Bernie Peters, and a rep from Brownstone Management here as well."

I paused and thought for a moment, "And lastly, I want the owner of the building here too. I want the person responsible for this, here tonight. I want to talk to him. Don't worry, I don't want any of them inside the building; get them down here so we can have an honest conversation. And when they start getting here, I'll start giving you hostages, a one-for-one trade. Except for the Politicians, they're a two-for-one since they are less than decent human beings, and if you get everyone here, I'll let everybody go. I'll put out all the fires I have started in the building and I'll walk out willingly. All I want is a conversation."

His response surprised me: "OK, Brent, I can try to make that happen. So, who's the owner? I need their name."

"Well, Sgt. Woolhead, that's where you'll need your detective skills, but if you get those other people here, it won't be too hard to figure out. I'm going on Facebook live in a few minutes; I suggest you tune in." I hung up, put the phones in the bathroom, and shut the door.

Chapter 25

I walked to the window, where I could see the police command center wagon. I peeked out of the blinds and saw a guy wearing a 'Police Service Hostage Division' windbreaker holding a phone; I assumed it was Sgt Woolhead. I looked at Robert and Brian, and figured it was time to come clean with them. I removed Brian's eye mask and stood where they could both see me.

Robert just looked at me and said, "Fuck you, Brent."

I shook my head, agreed with him, and said, "I know Robert, I'm sorry, I'm sorry. Look, you're in no harm; you never were. You're not sitting in gas; it's just water in the pool. Yeah, the smell of gas is overwhelming in the building, but it's only in a couple of the metal buckets; there's only a little bit in each, and none of them are near any torches or actual flames. I had to put some real gas around for the smell, but all the other gas is just water with some food coloring mixed in to give it the same color and transparency. The flame bar in front of you is used in the movies; it's completely controllable and safe; after we do the next Facebook live, I'll turn it off. Please don't be pissed, Robert; I needed you to act naturally. I'm sorry, buddy."

I looked at Brian and asked him, "Brian, are you OK?"

"Yeah, I'm OK. Do you have any soda?" I don't think he grasped what was happening, but he was being a good sport anyway. I went to the fridge and grabbed him a coke.

I looked at Robert, then to the ground, "Robert, you gotta forgive me. I can't live with myself taking this money and walking away. I have been steamrolled over in life too many times, and if I concede this fight, I'll never be able to live with myself. They've handcuffed and silenced me. I can't finish the documentary with the NDA. And what did I get? Some money? Some money that's only going to help me find a new place and pay my rent for a few months? Then where am I? I'm right back to where I was, struggling to pay my bills and not eating sometimes so that I can make the rent. I can't do it, Robert, I won't. This is the only thing I could think of, and it's the only thing I thought would get people's attention. I gotta do something; I just can't lay down anymore, Robert. I can't, I won't." I had to wipe the tears away when I finished speaking.

His reply made me smile, "Well, you could have told me. I don't care what the hell you do; I got my money, so I'm fine. I can live with it. I'm too old for this shit, Brent, but if you wanted me to help, all you had to do was ask. Now, can you please untie me, and I'll play along."

I looked at him apologetically, smiled, and said, "Not just yet, I have to do the Facebook live first, then we'll take a break, OK?"

"Well, hurry the hell up," and he put his head down.

I went to the bathroom, grabbed the phones, passed them to Eric, and told him to turn on the Facebook feed. I looked at the camera and went to the pile of props in my living room to show everyone I was serious. I picked up a flare and a gas can and went to the window; I looked at Eric and asked him how many were watching. He replied, "holy shit, there's a little more than thirty thousand people now."

Eric played the part well and said, "Come on, Brent, let's just go outside and talk to them. I'm serious, this is getting out of control."

"Shut up, this isn't ending till I get what I want or this place burns and all of us burn; this greedy owner isn't going to win."

I started to address the camera and talked to the people online, "Hi, everybody; thank you for tuning in. Eric, show Robert and Brian, let everyone know they're OK."

I didn't want the camera on me while I peeked through the window — just in case they were going to shoot me. I looked out the window and smiled. The crowd was huge. I could see news trucks up and down the street, people were being interviewed, and there was even a taco truck on the corner. I was happy to see so many people, but my mood changed when I looked at the roof of the building across the street and saw the snipers aimed at me.

I blurted out, "holy shit," and Eric swung the phone back around onto me.

He could see the fear in my eyes and looked at me from behind the camera with concern.

I stood behind the fridge and continued to speak to the camera, "As you can see, I'm willing to do whatever it takes to stay in the building. Now, to prove I'm serious, I'm going to break the NDA that I was forced into."

I grabbed the envelope, held it up, and opened it, "Ladies and Gentlemen, here is the NDA and the check that I received, or should I say, the check that I was forced to accept in exchange for my silence."

I moved to the front of the apartment, took the check out of the envelope, looked at the camera, and said with sadness, "This is what it's all about, ladies and gentlemen, throwing people out of their homes for profits. To show you I'm serious, here's the check, here's my profits."

I held it close to the camera so everyone could see it. "Are you getting this, Eric?"

He shook the camera up and down for yes.

As he did that, an idea popped into my head: I needed to keep these people entertained. I went to the desk, grabbed my Bluetooth speaker, and wedged it in the window facing the street. I figured a little music couldn't hurt, but what would be appropriate? Then it hit me: *'Burning Down the House'* by the Talking Heads would be the perfect song for this. I went to the computer, pulled up my iTunes, and hit play.

I pulled out my lighter, held up the check, and lit it on fire as the music started. I said, "Seventeen thousand dollars is what they wanted to pay me to shut up; well, here's what I think of their bribe."

I burned it on Facebook Live for everyone to see, and as it burned, I could hear the crowd gasp and cheer from outside.

When the check was nothing but ashes, I said, "Now I think you know I'm serious. If I don't see those people down here tonight, the building will be next. If you are watching this and are local, please come on down. It's going to be one hell of a show."

I gave Eric the cut sign, put the phones in the bathroom, and sat on the sofa beside Brian. I rubbed the cushion and said to Eric, "You know, it really is a nice sofa."

I removed Brian's mask, unbound his hands, and he said, "You got seventeen thousand?"

I walked over to Robert and looked at him, "You're not going to hit me, are you, Robert?"

He looked at me and was relatively calm, "Wow, Brent, you burned that check; you're serious, aren't you?"

I said, "Well, I don't think they would have let me keep it at this point," I untied him, sat on the sofa, and started to cry.

I apologized to them, "I'm sorry guys, Tommy's death hit me hard; all I wanted to do was help you guys, I'm tired of getting fucked over by the system, and I didn't know what else to do. But I promise you, I promise you, I won't hurt you guys at all. I just want to expose the bullshit of the system and tell everyone how we got screwed over."

As I said that, my phone started to ring in the bathroom; it was the long ring of the cops, and I ignored it. I was tired, my energy and emotions were drained, my adrenalin must have spiked, and now I was coming down; I just needed to relax for a bit. The phone rang for about a minute, and then it stopped, and when it did, the blare of the bullhorn began.

It was Woolhead. I guess he watched the stream and was asking me to pick up the phone, but I sat there, ignoring him. The guys looked at me and asked what was next.

I sat quietly and replied, "I don't know. We'll see what they do, but I'm not doing anything until Kerwin, Brownstone, and at least one politician is here, so we'll sit tight."

Robert asked me, "Why did you ask for the owner? You know they can't get him here."

I thought a little before I answered, "Well, it would be normal that I would want the owner here, and when they can't get him, at least we can highlight the fact that someone not even in Canada is evicting us. Hopefully, people will be offended by that, but unfortunately, I don't think it will make a difference. At the very least, it will buy me some time to expose the corruptness of the politicians and lobbyists."

The bullhorn blared again, "Brent, pick up the phone; I have a surprise; someone wants to talk to you."

As soon as he said that, the phone started ringing.

I opened the bathroom door, grabbed the phone, and answered it. It was Woolhead. "I thought you said someone wanted to talk to me. I don't think you know what a surprise is, Woolhead."

Woolhead laughed a little and got straight to the point, "I've spoken to the politicians. Flatch is on her way, and Bernie Peters' office is trying to locate him. I've spoken to Brownstone, they're sending a representative, and Kerwin Cummings is on his way. But the owner, we're having trouble contacting him. The phone number just goes to voicemail. Can you help us out with this one, do you have a way of contacting him?"

I laughed, "I'm not doing your job; I've got enough shit going on up here. You're the cops, go do your cop stuff. But I gotta tell you, if they aren't here, that's not going to be good. Now, before I hang up because I think you're wasting my time, what's the surprise?"

There was silence on the other end until a voice said, "Brentley?"

Now I felt terrible. When I started this night, all I could think about was sadness and misery. I had lost all hope of happiness and didn't consider Laila in my thought process.

"Brentley, what are you doing, Brentley?" Laila's voice was soothing. "Please, I didn't think you were this kind of person; please don't hurt anyone."

"Hi Laila, I'm sorry. I didn't think I was either, I'm normally not like this. I don't know what happened, I snapped." I was embarrassed. "It's nice to hear your voice, and please don't worry. Everything is going to work out, but it might take a little longer than I thought for us to go out again, maybe five to ten?"

She laughed a little and said, "Just come out, Brentley. We'll go to Beanzies and grab a coffee."

I sighed and said, "I don't think they're going to let me go to Beanzies anytime soon. Tell Woolhead thanks for letting me hear your voice, Laila. Tell him it put me at ease and made me relax. Take care, Laila, I'm sorry."

I had to hang up; it was hard to do, but I had to give Woolhead the impression that I genuinely thought I might not make it out alive.

After I hung up with Laila, I got really sad, I had finally met a woman I liked, a woman with good values, conviction, and principles, and I screwed it up again. There wasn't a chance in hell we'd ever be able to be together; it was just my luck. My sadness turned into anger, and I was getting frustrated; I wanted to do something but had no idea what to do. Until my demands showed up, I had nothing, but I wasn't going to sit idly by.

I logged back on to Facebook, and over forty thousand people were watching. Apparently, people were paying attention now. I scrolled through my feed and saw that a lot of the news outlets were outside, a couple were broadcasting live, and a lot of them were posting online, attracting more viewers to our page. But how was I going to keep everyone entertained? With today's news cycle of twenty-four hours, people have the attention span of gnats; I know they'll hang around if there's the chance of the building burning down or someone getting shot by the cops, but I didn't want this to end in either of those scenarios. I told Robert and Brian to stand at the back of the room; I didn't want the cops to see they were untied just yet, and I told Eric to go live.

Eric gave me the 'rolling' signal; I looked at the camera, "Ladies and gentlemen, boys and girls, I would like to ask a question, first, to my social media lady Helen, who I hope is watching; I'd like to take a poll online, I'd like to ask, 'Do you believe the politicians when they say they want to save 'affordable housing'? It's a pretty straight- up question; a simple yes or no will do. In the meantime, let's listen to some music, and if you know the words, sing along."

I flashed the peace sign, and Eric cut the feed. I threw the phones in the bathroom and asked the guys in the room, "Do you have any requests?"

Robert nailed it when he said, "*For What It's Worth*, Buffalo Springfield." I smiled, cued it up, and hit play.

After a few seconds of it playing, the phone started ringing again; I just ignored it. It was time to relax and enjoy some music. After I had played that, I thought I'd have some fun, and I put on *The Clash's 'I Fought the Law.'* We could hear people singing in the street. We all looked at each other and smiled. I stood by the window to listen to the voices below. After about two minutes, the phone stopped ringing; I guess Woolhead gave up for now.

After The Clash, it was time for 'Imagine'; I'm sure everyone will know the words for that one. As it was playing, the street was filled with everyone singing along.

Robert peeked out the window and said, "Holy shit Brent, people are holding up their phones out there, it's like a concert!"

I guess Woolhead didn't like what was happening, as the phone started ringing and didn't stop. When 'Imagine' stopped playing, I figured I might as well pick up the phone.

Back to the bathroom for the phones, I answered, "China Delight, we deliver."

Woolhead wasn't impressed. "Not funny, Brent. I need you to turn the music off; I need it calm down here on the street. I have some good news. City Councillor Flatch is here. Now send me out one of the hostages."

"Just Councillor Flatch? I asked you for five people, and I said the Politicians were a 'two for one' deal, remember? Come on, don't change the terms of our deal; that's not cool. I'll give you a hostage when Bernie Peters gets here; tell him he's responsible for a hostage if he doesn't come. And guess what? I doubt that he will even care. You gotta do better than that, Woolhead. One out of five might be good enough for government work, but it ain't going to cut it here… Actually, you gave me the idea for the next song. Do you like The Doors?"

Then I simply asked him, "Why does everyone want to screw me over Woolhead? Why can't people keep their word and stick to the rules? Even you just tried to screw me, we had a deal. I'm sick of the systematic bullshit from everyone, NOW GET ME MY DEMANDS!"

I had to breathe and calm down before speaking again; I thought for a bit and decided to give Woolhead something to do. "Talk to people from my past Woolhead, ask them what I used do for a living, they'll tell you, then you'll know I'm capable of burning this shit down. Now get me my demands and enjoy the music."

I hung up and walked to my computer. I found Five To One by The Doors, and I turned it up as loudly as I could. I wasn't expecting the crowd to react, as it was a very old sixties disobedience song, and Jim Morrison was at his best with his anti- authority anger. After that one, it was time to really get the crowd going, I played Rage Against the Machines', *Killing In the Name Of,*' that would get the crowd going, and I'm sure it would piss Woolhead off. When it came on, I kept it as loud as I could, and I could hear the crowd yelling, 'Fuck you, I won't do what you tell me, Fuck you, I won't do what you tell me...' and some people were even jumping up and down. The phone didn't stop ringing the whole time; I looked at Eric and laughed.

After those songs, I figured I had better settle down a bit. I put on some Bob Marley and let the mood calm down.

Robert asked, "So Brent, what did you use to do for a living? Arsonist or some sort of criminal or something?"

I chuckled, "Worse, I worked at the post office."

I looked at Eric and said, "Let's go live again." I decided to put on a little show and turn my anger up a notch.

I began stacking all the 'fire' supplies in the bedroom and decided to film there. Robert and Brian had grabbed a soda from the fridge and were sitting on the sofa. Brian was happy and content sitting there, and Robert was getting a little antsy.

He got up, came to the bedroom, and said, "Brent, I want to help. I want to 'play up' the hostage role and get into it." He was smiling and looking back and forth at Eric and me.

I looked at Eric, a little unsure of what to do. I shrugged, 'I don't know?'

Robert almost begged, "Come on, Brent, let's give 'em something. I really want help. You know I was up for a good fight with this owner, but I had to take the money. It was too much to say no to. Let me make it up to you and help you sell this."

The look in his eyes was that of someone who knew they could have done more. He knew he took the easy way out. His eyes told me that even though he was happy with the buyout, it would be something that he would ultimately regret. Selling out your principles tends to do that to a man with conviction, and Robert was a man of conviction and morals. We both knew it would have bothered him for years.

I said, "OK, Robert, but after all this is said and done, you have to say you were a hostage. I don't want anyone going to jail except for me; I'm doing this for myself. I have to take a stand and stick to my guns. I want to make a difference. I know I'll never be able to stay here, but maybe you guys can. If I can get some kind of change to the system so others don't have to go through this, or if you guys win, then I might be able to sleep at night. It's a long shot, but it's all I got. More importantly, I want to expose those greedy politicians who sat with us and lied to our faces, saying they cared about us. They looked us right in the eye while they were taking the money, and they lied to us. Robert, they used us, they used us for their gain, and that ain't cool in my book. Payback's a bitch, and I want to expose them for the frauds they are. I'll let you play along, but you promise me, you'll always say you were a hostage."

He was a little taken aback after my tirade, but he shook his head and agreed. With his comical Don Knotts face, he said, "Well, I don't want to go to jail, so don't worry about that."

I looked at Eric and said, "Stop filming. Erase that. They're going to try to confiscate all the footage of this. You can't let them see any of the cooperation with Robert."

After what I said, Eric said, "I didn't think of that, Bingham; what are we going to do? How are we going to get this footage out of here? Everyone will tell them I was filming when you forced me in; what are we going to do when they take all my shit and all the memory cards?"

I hadn't thought about that until just now. With a confused look, I said, "I don't know. I didn't think that far ahead, I had other things going on."

"Come on, Bingham, get it together." Eric was smiling when he said that, and I thought, 'damn, Eric always makes me feel better.'

"What about copying or downloading them to somewhere?" I was out of my element when it came to this recording and movie stuff; I didn't know what was possible.

Eric replied, "Download them to where? The only option is to copy them. The question is, do we have enough cards and enough time? This will take a while."

I said, "Well, giddy up, what are you waiting for?"

Eric got to work, and as he was getting it all ready, he added, "Well, that's all fine and dandy if we get them copied, but how the hell are we going to get them out of here? We'll probably all be questioned and kept in custody until they know for sure that we weren't part of your lunacy."

I thought for a moment and said, "Well, I can think of one thing, but I don't think you're going to like it."

"OK...?" He said it with caution and hesitation.

"Well, many years ago, I went to a wedding in Vegas, and one of the guys wanted to bring some hash down, so he 'smuggled' it the only way he could think of..."

Eric shrugged and said, "Oh man."

I looked at Robert and said, "OK, you want a bigger part? Let's suit up while Eric's copying the files; I don't want this on film either. Robert put his hands together and started rubbing them with anticipation.

I put everything back in the living room. I got all the flares and fireworks and told Eric to take off his vest. He used a fishing vest when filming, as it had pockets and loops everywhere that worked well for holding lenses, lights, and stuff. I figured it would work well holding the flares and fireworks; I thought it might look cool, like a suicide bomber's vest.

I said to Robert, "Ok, I'm going to make you look like a 'jihadist' suicide bomber; I want to strap all these flares and fireworks to you and use you as a shield when I open the blinds. Are you cool with that?"

He excitedly said, "Yeah, that sounds cool."

As I 'strapped' him up with the flares and fireworks, he had this goofy, childlike grin and asked, "How should I act? Should I be angry, upset, crying, or struggling? What's my motivation for this scene?" He said it with a half-smile, so at least I knew he was sort of kidding.

I was so happy Eric was here. As an amateur director, he was used to this kind of BS from actors, so he immediately replied, "Your motivation is not to get set on fire or shot. How's that?"

I looked at Eric and laughed, then at Robert, who was a little shaken by that reply. I patted him on the back, looked at him reassuringly, and said, "Don't worry, Robert, you'll be fine."

I grabbed the sleep mask I had put on Brian, "I also need to put a blindfold on you; I need you to look 'the part,' I need you to be scared and confused, but don't worry. I will stand behind you and yell my demands out the window."

I told Brian I needed to tie his hands up again, but I didn't need to blindfold him. He didn't say a thing, raised his arms, and I bound his hands. Next, I grabbed one of the fireworks, a 'Roman candle,' a pretty simple firework that only shot a few red balls. I told Eric to go live and said, "Let's turn this up a notch."

I moved Robert to the window and reassured him everything would be OK. I pulled up the blinds and opened the window; as soon as I did that, I heard a collective 'gasp' from the crowd. I made sure Robert's body filled the majority of the window; I didn't want them to try to shoot me or shoot tear gas into the room, so I hid behind him. I started screaming, "YOU BETTER START TAKING ME SERIOUSLY; I'M TIRED OF THIS SHIT; GET ME THE MP AND THE OTHERS DOWN HERE NOW OR MORE BLOOD WILL BE ON THEIR HANDS."

Robert joined in the fun and started playing the part, screaming, "I'M SOAKED IN GAS, DON'T SHOOT, DON'T SHOOT, THERE'S GAS AND TORCHES EVERYWHERE. THERE'S GAS POURED EVERYWHERE."

The phone started ringing immediately; I ignored it, and then the bullhorn started blaring as well. Apparently, this scared the hell out of them. Woolhead was telling me to calm down, and he said that the SWAT team was going to take action if I didn't surrender immediately. He asked again for me to let everyone go and come out.

I screamed, "GET MY DEMANDS HERE NOW!" I slammed the window shut and dropped the blinds. I took the blindfold off and smiled at Robert; he was grinning ear to ear. The phone was ringing, and Woolhead was still talking on the bullhorn. Then, all of a sudden, I heard the window in my bedroom smash, and my first thought was that they were coming in. But as I looked into the bedroom, I could see what I could only guess from what I had seen in movies was a teargas canister. Luckily, the apartment wasn't that big, so it was only a few steps and a quick reach to shut the door. I grabbed some towels and put them under the crack of the door, and I quickly taped up anywhere I saw smoke coming from the door's seam.

Eric looked scared; Robert asked what was happening, and Brian just sat there like nothing was happening at all, which made me smile. I looked at the door, admired my work, and thought, 'This shit is getting a little too real.' I grabbed the last torch I had, grabbed one of the buckets, and emptied one of the gas cans into it; I put the bucket in front of the door and wedged the torch by the door.

The phone hadn't stopped ringing, so I picked it up, pretended to cough and gasp, and asked Woolhead, "What the hell, Woolhead?"

He responded, "Because we need to end this, Brent. We need to end this now before it gets out of hand."

I stopped pretending to cough and cry and said, "This building is going to go up in flames pretty soon, Woolhead; I don't give a fuck anymore, screw it. I've got Brian and Robert strapped in front of the windows soaked in gas, and I have a torch against my apartment door. Try shooting something in here again, and you'll kill us all for sure. Is that what you want? Get me my demands, and this all ends; that's all I want, a simple conversation." And I hung up the phone.

I thought I'd really piss Woolhead off and play 'The Talking Heads,' *'Burning Down the House'* again. After about ten seconds of that song playing, I could hear the crowd yelling and singing along, and then the phone started ringing; I just laughed.

When 'The Talking Heads' finished, I thought I would top it off with a good finale that would truly piss him off. I scrolled through my tunes and found 'The Bloodhound Gang,' and I put on the song *Fire Water Burn*. This time, everyone in the crowd was singing, and it filled the street. That made me smile so much that even if nothing came of this, at least I brought people together for a good time.

When the music stopped, I picked up the phone and answered it with my best radio voice, "KRP Radio, what's the phrase that pays?"

"Hilarious, Brent. Can you please stop with the music? It's a little much, and I don't want the crowd fired up like that. Sorry, bad choice of words; I don't want the crowd excited. You owe me the hostages now, Brent; I have most of your demands. Councillor Flatch and Rita are here, and Kerwin is five minutes away. I want you to send the hostages out now."

He was short and to the point. I hadn't thought about how I would get someone out of the building, and I started to worry. I was afraid that they probably already snuck someone in that was just waiting to pounce on me or that they would just shoot me through the window; either way, I had to think. I looked at the pile of props, and there was still the portable blow torch I hadn't used yet; I looked at Brian and the gas can, and it came to me.

I replied, "OK, Woolhead. You kept your word, and I'm a man of my word. But I'm only going to send out Brian for Rita. You still owe me the MP, Kerwin, and the owner. When you get them, I'll give you everyone. You have my word."

There was a pause on the other end; after a few seconds, Woolhead agreed.

I put the phone under the sofa cushion and said to Brian, "Hey Brian, do you want to get out of here? They're asking for you outside."

He stood up, said, "OK," and asked, "Who's asking for me?"

I looked at Eric, and we smirked at each other awkwardly. Then I said, "The guys in the movie want to see you. But before you go, do you mind if I put a little gas on your pants and shoes?"

Without hesitation, Brian replied, "Sure, if it's for the movie. Do you have any more soda?"

I grabbed him another coke, gave him a big hug, and thanked him.

He said, "Thanks, Brent; so are we going to be able to stay now?"

I sighed and said, "We'll have to wait to see how the movie ends, Brian, then we'll know."

I looked at Robert, "Robert, I need your help on this one; I need your help getting Brian out of the building; it might be a little fucked up."

He was into it and asked, "What did you have in mind?"

"Well, I need you to take the torches out of the door and let Brian out; I need you to be my shield." I looked at him apologetically, and I wasn't expecting him to agree.

With a big smile he asked, "Sure, let's do it; how did I do last time?"

I looked at him and laughed, "You did great, Robert, Oscar material."

I grabbed the phone from the sofa, and Woolhead was right there. "OK, Woolhead, I'm sending Brian out. Robert will be with me, so don't try anything. The stairwell is soaked in gas, he's covered in gas, there are buckets of gas everywhere, and I'm carrying a blowtorch; shoot me or try anything, and everyone goes up in flames. Understand?"

He was calm, which made me feel like something was up. "Yes, Brent, I understand. We won't do anything; just let him out. Kerwin is on his way. Why don't you just let Robert and Eric out now?"

I turned on my sarcasm and mocking tone when I replied, "Come on, Woolhead. We had a deal. Why can't anyone stick to the rules? You know this is why we're here, right? When Kerwin gets here, you'll get another hostage, just like we agreed to, jeez…. And I promise you, when the owner gets here, I'll come out, and this will all end, so why aren't you working harder on that?"

That distracted him, and he said, "OK. OK. I'll get him here. Now, just let Brian go."

"OK, Woolhead, we're coming out; get your men away from the door." And I hung up.

I looked at the guys and said, "OK, boys, let's go. Brian, you go first, Robert second, then I'll be right behind you. Everyone ready?'

They all agreed, and we walked out of the apartment. I let them lead and followed a couple of steps behind them. I slowly peeked around every corner and looked down every hallway on the way down; when we got close to the lobby, I turned the torch on high and made the flame as big and blue as I could get it; visually, it was pretty impressive. Robert got to the door, slid the torches out, and slowly opened it; when the door opened, the crowd went wild, and there was a roar of applause, and they were chanting, 'Let them stay, Let them stay,' I was impressed with that one, seems like they understand.

As Brian walked out of the building, the crowd cheered. The guy in the police windbreaker stood a few feet back and said, "Brent, I'm Sgt Woolhead."

I looked around out on the street and said, "It looks like you're having quite the party out here. You got a permit for it?"

He looked around and then back at me and wasn't too impressed. "I enjoyed the music, but can you stop it, please? Now, what can we do to end this?"

It was time to get to business, and I felt that I was getting painted into a corner once again and running out of room. "OK, Woolhead, I'm setting up a Zoom call. I want the politicians, Brownstone, the lobbyist Kerwin, and the owner to be on the call. We can start the call when Kerwin, Rita, and Flatch get here, and once the owner shows up, this will all end, I promise you."

He looked perplexed and thought for a few seconds, then said, "Brent, I have been briefed on what's happened with the building and the tenants. It's not right, but you followed the system. Everyone got a fair hearing, and from what I've heard, some got very generous buyouts, so why do this? Just move on. It is what it is."

When he said that, I got angry and smiled and decided to enlighten him a little bit, I pulled Robert close with one hand and raised the blowtorch, "That's where you're wrong, Woolhead; this system is not 'what it is,' it's corrupt, it's complete bullshit, and there is no resolve for the little guy. Things aren't what they seem, and everyone involved is full of shit. I'll send you the Zoom link, and you can get everyone online. Call me when Kerwin is here."

We stepped back into the building. I told Robert to shut the door. He jammed the torches in, and we went back up the stairs. As we started walking up the stairs, Eric was right there filming. I looked at the camera and said, "OK, let's shine some light on this bullshit corruption."

Chapter 26

When we got back into the apartment, I turned off the blowtorch, and Robert sat on the sofa. He looked down, rubbed the cushion, and said, "This is a nice sofa."

I looked at him, smiled, and laughed, "Robert, do you know how to set up a Zoom call?"

He shook his head and sat at the computer and said, "Since we have everyone's email, we can send them links, and they can probably join in on their phones; we don't need to go through the cops."

Robert started to laugh; his Don Knotts face was beginning to show, he said, "Fuck the police," and he snorted with laughter.

Eric and I looked at each other, a little surprised, and we started to laugh. It relieved the tension.

Robert sent the email for everyone to join, and said it was ready to go. I asked him if he wouldn't mind 'assuming the position' for one last time, and with that goofy grin on his face, he snorted again and said that he would love to.

He sat on the chair, and I bound his hands. He was a real trooper and was starting to get into it. He asked, "Brent, do you mind opening the blinds so everyone can see me? I want a bigger part in the movie. I promise I'll look scared and might even be able to work some tears up for you."

"Robert, you should have been an actor; you missed your calling." I tied his hands up behind him but left the sleep mask off so he could enjoy the show out the window.

I went to the bathroom, grabbed the phones, and went to Facebook. I looked at the poll Helen had set up, and I couldn't believe that people voted.

I gave the phone to Eric and told him to go live; I looked at the camera and smiled.

I welcomed everyone back and started summarizing the situation, "Well, it looks like the police are meeting my demands. Councillor Flatch and Rita from Brownstone are here, and as a man of my word, I gave them one hostage. I still have two hostages, and as I have said, when all my demands are met, I will release everyone. We are now waiting for the lobbyist, MP Peters, and the owner to arrive; once that happens, this will all be over. But in the meantime, let's talk about the poll I posted."

I continued straight to the Facebook camera, "I can't believe the number of people who answered it; over twenty thousand of you took the time to reply, and I thank you very much, but I'm a little disappointed in how many of you have faith in our system. Out of twenty-three thousand, seventy-two percent of you said that you trust the politicians fighting for affordable housing; twenty percent of you said that you don't; and eight percent of you said that you don't trust a word that comes out of any politician's mouth. Well, to the twenty-eight percent of you, you make me proud, and to the other seventy-two percent, pay attention because tonight, I'm going to enlighten all of you of what's really going on with the rental housing market in Toronto and your politicians."

I continued speaking to the camera, "I'm trying to have a Zoom call with our City Councillor and our Member of Parliament who was supposedly helping us. I also want, on the call, the building management company that specializes in evicting and Renovicting people out of their homes, along with the owner of the building. Lastly, I want the lobbyist who represents the Landlords in Canada. For those of you who might not know what a 'Lobbyist' is, he's an enemy of the people; he's the middleman between our politicians and the industries that want to buy them. If he was in the mob, he would be called a bagman, but since he's a 'respected' member of society, we call him a lobbyist."

I kept the 'Facebook live' going while waiting for them to log on and join the call. One by one, they joined the call. First, of course, were the politicians - always eager to get their faces in front of any camera. Next was Rita, and lastly, Kerwin. I looked at the screen and could tell Kerwin and Peters weren't physically here yet and were doing it from their phones in their cars.

I sat in front of the screen and started talking to Woolhead, "Woolhead, I know you're watching; I can tell Kerwin is in his car doing this, and I see Peters isn't here either. I'm keeping my word; you're not getting anyone until they're here, but we can start the call."

I changed my focus and started with Kerwin, "Hey Kerwin, how have you been, buddy? I told you I wouldn't be quiet about this, and if I had my way, you'd be in here with me as well."

He tried to start speaking, and I muted his mic, "Kerwin, you're not going to speak until I have spoken to the politicians, so please wait your turn."

Now it was time for the politicians, "OK, Councillor Flatch and MP Peters, let's talk."

This time, I let them speak. They started begging and pleading for me to let Robert and Eric go, saying that they were my friends and I shouldn't be doing this. Lastly, they started to talk about the buyout I received. They tried telling me that I was the winner in this situation; they tried to explain how I'd be able to move and start fresh with the 'more than fair' payday that I received.

I smiled and said, "I guess you guys didn't see me burn my check, did you? Since you folks brought up the subject of money, let's talk about money; let's talk about the seventeen thousand dollars I received and how it doesn't even come close to what you guys have received in payments from our friend here on the call with us."

They were all muted, but as soon as I said that, I could see their mouths moving and eyes darting back and forth; I didn't even need to hear them, and I could tell they were getting nervous.

I looked at Eric and the camera, "Are you getting all this, Eric? Can everyone that's watching see the screen and the bullshit look on their faces? If you can, can the people on the street give me a cheer?"

As soon as I said that the crowd cheered, they even started clapping, I asked Eric if people online were liking it and he said the hearts were flying across the screen.

I grabbed my 'Politician' file and began, "Ladies and gentlemen, I'm going to explain what I learned through this process. The housing crisis isn't what we think it is. Most people and the media blame immigration. They blame inflation. And while those may be factors, they aren't the real reason. What I learned might really piss you off because it pissed me off. The first thing I learned is that housing is now a commodity; people are trading and speculating on people's homes in Canada like they were betting on 'orange juice futures' or 'Coca-Cola' stock. People overseas are buying Toronto real estate because of our bubble; they make more money owning houses and condos in Canada than they do putting their money in the bank, so why wouldn't they? They don't even need to rent them out to anyone; greed has made it more profitable to let them sit empty than renting them out to people as homes. There are floors and floors of empty condo units in buildings nationwide that sit empty month after month. This bullshit practice not only reduces the supply of homes available to the people living in the city, but it also inflates our housing bubble even further."

As I spoke, I could hear the crowd booing, and when I looked at the Facebook feed, the comments were flying, and not many were nice. I continued, "Another thing I learned is that over forty percent of the rental housing market is part of what they call the 'Secondary Rental Market.' Now, for those of you who don't know what that is, the 'Secondary Rental Market' are units for rent, either short-term or long-term, that are owned by individuals who already own a primary residence and are speculating, trying to make money off of someone else. This secondary rental market includes monthly rentals and 'Airbnb' short-term rentals. Again, not only does this limit the housing supply for people to buy homes, but it also inflates rental prices. These people not only expect someone else to pay their mortgage, but they also expect to make a profit from it. It's this type of greed that is largely responsible for the crisis."

I looked at Eric behind the camera, and he gave me the thumbs up, so I kept going, "This is where many of you might get pissed off. The same politicians who say they are fighting for affordable housing, the same politicians who sat with us crying crocodile tears about our situation, own multiple properties. We were able to learn that Councillor Flatch owns her primary residence along with three additional rental properties, and our dishonorable Bernie Peters owns his primary residence along with four rental properties."

I shook my head in disgust and continued, "There you go, folks, nine homes owned by two people, and you wonder why there's no affordable housing?"

There were boos and yells from outside, which gave me even more motivation; I knew I was in the 'right,' so I continued, "The only way we were able to get this information was through 'Freedom of Information' requests, and we're just lucky that politicians have to disclose their finances. But the sad part is, they sat with us, looked us straight in the eye, and told us all the reasons why this was happening, including how there was a limited housing supply, without ever mentioning how many homes each of them owned."

I sat and looked at the screen and asked them why they didn't mention any of this. They all sat there in silence, not saying a word. Since they were cowards, I thought I'd have some fun.

In all seriousness, I asked them, "If you folks are so concerned with affordable housing, why don't you rent your second or third house or even fourth house to some of us? Let us live there for what it costs you to run it, but with no profit. We'll pay all the expenses and do daily upkeep and maintenance. Come on, put your money where your mouth is. If you are so concerned, why not?"

Again, there was no reply, just 'crickets,' not a word from any of them.

I continued jokingly, "You're like the people who put up the 'I support my neighbors in tents' signs on their lawn, referring to supporting the homeless. Go pitch a tent on their front lawn and see how much they support their neighbors then."

The crowd roared.

"Ladies and Gentlemen, you might be wondering, how does a City Councillor and MP afford multiple houses on a civil servant salary? Now, this is the truly offensive part; the papers I'm holding are the lobbying records of just these two politicians. What are lobbying records, you may ask? These are records of the payments that politicians receive from business interests to change the laws that will screw you and me. The politicians you see on the screen, receive money from the very people who are trying to evict us; let me explain. Do you see the guy with the thick glasses on the screen as well? Come on, Kerwin, wave hello."

He sat there like the bureaucrat he was, so I continued, "Well, that's Kerwin Cummings. He used to work with politicians, and because he worked with them, he turned those relationships into a 'pay to play' political influence industry for himself; he became a lobbyist. He has represented the auto insurance industry, the predatory payday loan industry, and now he represents commercial landlords, through his creation, 'The Alliance of Commercial Housing Rentals'. Now, you might be asking yourself what is the 'Alliance of Commercial Housing

Rentals' because I certainly did. Well, the 'Alliance' is like an 'association'; they are the lobbying group for commercial landlords, slumlords, companies like Brownstone and my owner. They give money to 'The Alliance,' or should I say, to Kerwin, who then takes that money, gives it to politicians, and tells them what laws or regulations need to be changed in favor of his clients. So, these people who sat with us and said they were there to help us were receiving money to do the exact opposite of what they were supposed to."

I rubbed my eyes and shook my head. I needed to know if people were listening. 'Folks, do you understand what I'm saying?"

The crowd exploded with boos, people were yelling swear words, and the energy was growing.

I thanked everyone again and said, "Let's see what they have to say."

I unmuted all of them, and they were all trying to cover their ass, babbling political double talk, trying to justify the payoffs, or should I say, 'campaign contributions.' It was so bad that you couldn't make out anything they were saying, so I muted all of them again.

I started to speak to the pale, worried faces on the screen, "I'm wondering what the people outside and online would think if they knew that you, Councillor Flatch, received six thousand dollars from the Alliance?"

As soon as I said the amount, the crowd got angry; there were mixed yells of, 'Fuck you, Flatch' and 'You suck Flatch,' then they started chanting in unison, 'Bullshit, Bullshit, Bullshit,' when that happened the phone started ringing immediately, I guess I had struck a nerve with Woolhead.

I spoke to the camera and the Zoom call, "Woolhead, unless you have the owner and Kerwin physically here, we have nothing to talk about yet."

The phone stopped ringing.

I looked back at Flatch, "OK, Councillor Flatch, let's hear what you have to say, explain yourself,"

I unmuted her, and she began the usual political rhetoric about the system and how everyone has a voice.

That's when I snapped and cut her off, "DON'T YOU DARE TELL ME EVERYONE HAS A VOICE! The people who pay have a voice; it's a 'pay to play' system, and you're getting rich from it. The developers, speculators, and landlords have a voice; we're your puppets, and your pawns. You used us to get camera time and to garner support for yourself; you sat with us saying you were concerned and wanting to help, yet all the while, it was just grandstanding and angling for votes; you should be ashamed of yourself. And ladies and gentlemen, please don't think she is unique; I have the documents proving the Alliance has paid over four million dollars to politicians on the Municipal, Provincial, and Federal levels."

Flatch tried to speak, and I could see Kerwin squirming in front of the camera.

I said, "Sit tight, Kerwin. I'm getting to you soon."

"OK, let's do Bernie Peters next. I'm not going to call you the honorable Mr. Peters, as there is nothing honorable about you, sir, but I will take it easy on you because you didn't use us to the extent that 'Freeloader Flatch' did. Yes, you did take payments from the Alliance of eight thousand dollars, but you didn't use us. You came to one of our meetings but weren't vocal about the cause; I think it's because you're just a fence sitter. But, sir, you are elected by the people and are supposed to stand up and be the voice for those people; in my opinion, you have failed miserably."

I asked him if he had anything to say about the matter, and he took his usual position, "I hear your concerns, Brent; I will do everything I can to look into the situation and to make sure the laws and rules are fair to everyone involved."

I laughed and muted him. He was a 'walking smile' in a suit, a hollow, opportunistic man just trying to get paid.

After Peters, I turned my sights back on Rita again, I said, "So Rita, how much has your company paid Mr. Cummings and his Alliance? There's public information for the politicians, but I can't find anything on you guys. So, how much does a company like yours pay Kerwin to influence and bribe our elected officials? How do you make those payments, Rita? How often do you make those payments? Do you have him on retainer with a big fat envelope, or do you grease him whenever an issue arises?"

The crowd began to chant, 'Fuck you, Rita, Fuck you, Rita."

I started laughing, muted them again, and turned my attention to Kerwin. I said, "Kerwin, Kerwin, Kerwin, the apple fell far from the tree with you, didn't it? Your Dad was respected, your grandfather was respected, and you, well, you turned out to be a lobbyist. What happened?"

I unmuted him, and there was silence; he surprisingly had nothing to say, so I continued, "How many lives do you think you have ruined, Kerwin? How much blood is on your hands? One of our tenants killed themselves last night, Kerwin. Did you know that? He killed himself because of the shit you do, all in the name of making a profit. I'll tell you what I want and what the point of this evening is. We want to stay; there were only a few of us left at the end, all the old timers and angry little Bingham; you can have all your money back; all we want is to be able to stay. We can talk about paying more rent, which was never an option throughout this process. These guys never gave us a chance to negotiate, so this is how I had to negotiate; this is how I had to get your attention; this was the only remedy I could see in getting anyone to pay attention to this situation."

I held up the blow torch and held it near a bucket, "All we want is the chance to stay; it's all we are asking for. Let us stay, and no one will die today."

The crowd was getting pretty angry at this point and yelling at him in our defense. The phone started ringing, and Woolhead yelled through the bullhorn, "Brent, pick up the phone now. Don't ignore me, Brent. We have a situation, and I need to speak to you now."

I picked up the phone and said, "I'm almost done, Woolhead."

He was angry, and he didn't care if he pissed me off; I could sense that my time was running out.

He said, "Kerwin is here now, Brent; let the hostages go."

Woolhead wasn't going to negotiate any longer. Looking at the zoom screen, I could tell Kerwin was outside. I thought, 'Well, I have to let Robert and Eric go and I have to end this.'

Woolhead continued, "You played me, Brent. You knew we couldn't get the owner here. You know he isn't in Canada, and we had no chance of getting him here. I don't like being played, Brent."

As he said that, Robert started to get excited, "The firemen are approaching the building with a hose, Brent; it looks like they're coming in."

As he finished saying that, they turned on the hose and blew out the lobby vestibule; we could hear glass smashing and the water breaking through everything like a tsunami. I still had the torch by my front door with the bucket, and Robert was sitting in the kiddie pool, so I didn't think they would try to breach the apartment just yet.

Robert continued to play the part, screaming, "Don't come in here. I'm sitting in a pool of gas, and there are torches everywhere."

Eric panned the room and showed Woolhead the situation. With the way they had smashed through the lobby, I didn't have much time, and with so much water, they wouldn't be able to tell that there wasn't any gas down there and that there was no threat of the building going up in flames. But I had to keep them out of the apartment for just a little bit longer.

I went back to the Zoom call and unmuted Kerwin. "OK, Kerwin, how much money do you get from commercial landlords, how much does it take to let you sleep at night?"

He was silent, and I said, "Never mind. I didn't expect an answer."

I went back to Facebook Live, "Ladies and gentlemen, they are unable to meet my final demand; they can't produce our owner. Do you guys want to know why? Let me hear you if you want to know."

The crowd started cheering and erupted with applause.

I looked at the Zoom call, grabbed the blowtorch, and walked to Robert. I turned the blowtorch on high and held it down towards the kiddie pool. Robert played it perfectly. He started screaming and almost even crying. He was so good he nearly fooled me.

Looking at the camera on the computer, I screamed at Kerwin, "Kerwin, you know what I've been through. You know I have nothing to lose; tell me how much you have received from our owner; how much he has given you to evict us? Don't fuck around, or Robert's death is on you. How much foreign money have you received?"

I looked at the Facebook live camera and said, "The cops couldn't get our owner here because he lives in China; he's not even a Canadian Citizen. We're being evicted by someone not even in this country. People from other countries are able to kick Canadian citizens out of their homes for profit, and our government is supporting it. These politicians and lobbyists are making money from foreigners to hurt Canadians. TELL ME RIGHT FUCKING NOW, KERWIN OR ROBERT DIES. HOW MUCH HAS HE PAID YOU?"

I could tell Kerwin was scared. He removed his glasses and leaned into the camera, saying, "OK, Brent, just stop. Stop. Don't hurt anyone." He paused and reluctantly said, "Yes, we receive money from foreign investors."

I was so angry, I had to yell, "THAT'S WHAT YOU CALL THEM FOREIGN INVESTORS? HOW ABOUT FOREIGN AGENTS? WHAT THE FUCK PETERS AND FLATCH? YOU'RE GETTING PAID BY PEOPLE OUTSIDE THE COUNTRY TO HELP EVICT CANADIANS WHO HAVE VOTED YOU IN. WHAT THE HELL IS GOING ON IN THIS COUNTRY?"

I was putting the blowtorch closer and closer to the pool when Woolhead blared the bullhorn begging me to stop: "Brent, please stop. Let's work this out. What can I do to get everyone out safely?"

"You can't do a damn thing, Woolhead; only Rita and Kerwin can fix this. We want to stay, the six people that held out to the end, we want to stay, let them stay, and I won't burn it down or kill anybody. Kerwin, I know you can do the right thing, talk to the owner, and make him let them stay; I know it's in your power. Rita, talk to your master; tell him it's gone too far, and it's time to do the right thing."

I grabbed the last gas can filled with water and poured it all over the floor and the sofa, screaming, "THIS IS YOUR LAST CHANCE."

The crowd was chanting, 'Let them stay, let them stay, let them stay.'

Kerwin left the screen and walked over to Rita. They were now standing together and whispering to each other; Rita finally looked at the camera and said, "OK, Brent, OK, we'll work something out."

That wasn't good enough for me, I knew they would renege on the deal, and I called their bluff, "Bullshit, I know you're just saying that to end this. I want guarantees. Flatch and Peters, will you see this through? Can everyone outside hold these people accountable to their word and don't let them back out of this? Will the people of this city make sure these guys are allowed to stay?"

The crowd chanted louder and louder, 'Let Them Stay, Let Them Stay, Let Them Stay.' Even Woolhead agreed. He said, "Brent, I don't agree with what you are doing, but I understand your frustration."

I could hear the boots stomping outside the door, and I knew it wouldn't be long before they were inside the apartment.

I said to the Facebook camera, "Ladies and Gentlemen, please sit tight, enjoy the musical interlude, and I will be right back."

Eric killed the feed, stuffing the phones in the fridge and I put on the song, 'Gimme Some Truth' by John Lennon to keep the crowd engaged.

I said to him, "OK, man, how are we doing? Is everything copied?" I paused, scrunched my face, smiled quirky, and continued, "It's time to hide the files."

He shook his head yes and said, "Oh man."

He jumped over to the computer and started to organize the cards; he took the last one from the camera and put it in the computer. He rubbed his eyes, and laughingly, he said, "The things I do for the movies."

Once the last card was finished copying, he took them all, stacked them together, and paused. He looked at them and said, "Now what?" He wasn't sure how to proceed, and quite frankly, neither was I. We just stood there staring at each other.

Robert, still tied up to the chair, shook his head, "Unbelievable. Haven't you guys ever seen a prison movie?" I looked at Eric and laughed.

Eric shook his head, "aw hell no." He begrudgingly headed towards the bathroom and muttered, "This better be a fucking Oscar contender."

I went to the computer and contemplated the last song to play. I couldn't think of a fitting last song because we were at the end. I didn't want to get the crowd fired up, but I wanted them to leave smiling. I didn't have much more to say because it was the end of the road; the end was here. As I thought about it, it came to me, and I found the perfect song for the end of this night. I cued it up and thought, might as well go out with a smile.

Eric came out of the bathroom doing walking funny. I asked him how it felt, and in pure Eric fashion, he said, "Surprisingly, not that bad."

I looked at Eric and Robert and asked them, "Well, guys, it looks like the end is here. Are you guys going to be OK?"

Robert said, "Brent, I hope you're able to live with this. In the far chance they actually do let any of us stay, we are indebted. You won't be able to stay; you're going to jail for a long time, but if they let us old-timers stay, we'll never forget this."

I thanked him, walked over, and gave him a hug.

Eric said, "Forget the lovefest, guys. Can we speed this along before I fart out a stack of memory cards?"

I looked at him, shook my head affectionately, and said, "OK, get the camera rolling, and we'll end this. Let me just put a little gas on you guys so you 'smell' the part." I told Eric to get the phones out of the fridge and start rolling on Facebook Live.

I looked at the camera, paused, and said, "Thank you, everyone, for your support. I'm a man of my word, and it's time to end this. I can hear the cops outside my door, so I know they want to come in and end me. Ladies and Gentlemen, please know I didn't want to hurt anyone; I just wanted to show everyone what was going on in this city. All I wanted to do was expose the corruption and the greed of everyone involved in the housing market. Please keep the protest up, be vocal, and write to your politicians. But please, don't stop yelling about the corruption of the lobbying industry and our politicians; please don't forget what you learned here tonight."

I walked to the door, removed the torch, then went back to Robert in the kiddie pool and stood beside him.

I turned on the music, Eric looked at me from behind the camera. Laughing, he said, "Really, Bingham, this is your swan song?"

I started laughing with him. Looking at the camera, I said, "You can come in now guys."

I dipped the torch into the pool and extinguished it; there was a collective 'gasp' and screams from the people out on the street. The door came crashing down, and the guns and tasers were aimed right at me.

I held up my hands with the extinguished torch and said, "It's only water, it's only water."

As Miley Cyrus's *'Wrecking Ball'* filled the air, they fired the tasers at me, and I was done.

When I came to, I was dazed and confused. I was on the ground looking up, and my hands and feet were in shackles. I had trouble focusing my eyes, and as I tried to figure out what was going on, all I could see and hear were the pantlegs and boots of the cops walking around the room.

I heard finger-snapping and a voice saying my name: "Brent, Brent, look up here, Brent, focus, look at me."

I rolled on my side so I could look up. When my eyes focused, I saw Sgt. Woolhead sitting in a chair, looking down at me. My mouth was dry as sandpaper, I was thirsty as hell, and all I could smell was burnt jerky. I tried to speak, but my mouth was so dry all I could muster was, "Water…"

Woolhead chuckled and said, "Like what's in most of the gas cans, Brent? Like what's in all the buckets, like what's in the kiddie pool, Brent?"

He kicked the pool with his foot, and some splashed on the floor beside my head. I was so desperate to quench my thirst that I tried to lap it up like a dog.

"Bet you smell jerky too, don't you, Brent? That's what happens when we shoot fifty thousand volts through you."

He got up and walked around the room, "You did all this, and you had no intention of burning or hurting anyone? You wasted my time and everyone else's time to make a point? Why not take the money and go away? Talk to lawyers, talk to the press."

I could hardly hold my head up to look at him, so I just left it on the floor as I said, "I tried, they were useless, I wasn't planning this; it just happened. When they killed Tommy, I lost it, I snapped, I had no idea what I was doing or what to do."

He pulled out a pack of cigarettes and looked around, "I guess it's all right to smoke in here since everything was bullshit, wasn't it, Brent? Do you want one before we lock you away?"

I kept my head on the floor and replied, "No thanks. And it was worth it. I had to do something; I couldn't do… nothing, it wasn't fair, it wasn't right. I wouldn't have been able to live with myself if I just took the money and ran. I'm sick of the bullshit and corruption. Everyone involved in this system was on the owner's side, a rich, foreign investor. There was no one on our side, no one. Everyone was on the side of the rich guy, even you Woolhead, you may think you are working for the people, but you're working for the rich guy right now."

"Well, Brent, it was, and it wasn't. It was a fucking terrible idea, and they won't have any sympathy for you. They're going to make an example of you and put your ass away for a long, long time to deter anyone else from doing shit like this again. But because you brought so much attention to the lobbying and political aspect, they might just let the old guys stay for good PR. I heard Rita, Kerwin, and Flatch talking; they're trying to cover their asses now on how to avoid looking like the greedy, money- hungry, corrupt scumbags they truly are. They were saying it might be best for everyone if they let the old guys stay. You may not like this, Brent, but you fed the beast; they said they can spin this in their favor and use it to their advantage. They said this was great publicity for Brownstone and 'The Alliance'."

Woolhead picked me up off the ground, and as he walked me out of the apartment, he looked around and asked, "Really, Brent, you were fighting to stay in this place? It's a dump. Why go through all of this?"

I looked him straight in the eye. Without hesitation, I said, "Because it was my home.

The
End

About the Author:

Myles Bradley has been around; whether it was shoved, pushed, or kicked, he always comes up smiling. From being an executive in retail to a Supervisor at the Post Office to a sales executive in a Law Office to working on TV/Movie sets, one thing has remained constant: He has always been around people and has seen the best and worst from all walks of life. Having lived through successes and tragedies, he has gained a perspective unique to himself. After learning about how systems and institutions might not always be what we think they are and that the realities of this world aren't exactly as they have told us, Myles decided that he could no longer remain silent and decided to tell the world what he has learned, through pain, discovery, and acceptance.